C000126270

THE REPUBLIC OF REALITY

ADAM ROWAN

MotherButterfly
Books

www.motherbutterfly.com

For Henry, who was my first reader,
and for Andrea, who liked the sloth.

CONTENTS

The Republic of Reality   vii

1. The Rusty Toaster   1
2. Welcome to Hyleberia   13
3. Corruption   26
4. The Academy   49
5. Divine Repository   73
6. Afflatus Isle   99
7. Guardian Angel   121
8. Golden Cone   147
9. Acting Prime Minister   173
10. The Evil Demon   198
11. Rescue Mission   216
12. Mathias' Plot   241
13. The Library of Divine Laws   264
14. Venus' Moon   287

About the Author   295
If you enjoyed this book …   297

THE REPUBLIC OF
REALITY

CHAPTER 1
THE RUSTY TOASTER

IN THE HOURS BEFORE HIS DEATH, JOSEPH SHIELDS WAS HAVING the most unlucky day of his life.

The morning didn't start particularly well, and that is saying something for him. Over the past month before his untimely demise, Joseph had tripped on a pen and fallen down the stairs, been sent to the hospital twice with food poisoning, and not won a single penny after buying a hundred lottery tickets. His friends joked that he was cursed.

As Joseph was cycling to work, a large black convertible appeared out of nowhere, smacked into him and sent him flying to the curb. He landed with a terrible thud on a patch of grass. A surge of pain enveloped his limbs.

While he slowly got back to his feet, the driver paced towards him with a horrified expression on his face. "Are you OK, mate? I didn't see you there."

Arms and knees badly bruised, Joseph could see stars. His helmet had collided directly with the cracked pavement. It was odd that he'd worn it today, as he almost always forgot.

"No broken bones," he muttered, hardly paying attention to the driver. He limped to his bicycle, amazed it wasn't damaged, tightened his helmet strap and turned to him. "Watch where you're going next time!"

Joseph gulped as he got on and rode away, surprised that he hadn't been more seriously injured. Although he wasn't sure he was entirely fine, he would soon be late for work.

A gangling youth of nineteen, Joseph's flat face was capped with an unruly thatch of light brown hair. With pale skin and a slim build, he was average all around. His most distinctive feature was his eyes, which were different colours due to heterochromia, a rare eye condition: dark silver and bright blue.

Unbeknownst to Joseph, he had very little time left to live. Nevertheless, despite him having absolutely no idea about this, Joseph did have a huge, shocking secret occupying his mind that wouldn't leave him be.

He parked his bike and hobbled into work, the local Southend grocery store, Mace, with a strange feeling gnawing in his stomach that told him his luck was going to get worse. Mace was a tiny but homely shop his mother owned that sold everyday essentials, from newspapers to crisps. Joseph knew every inch of it by heart.

Standing behind the counter, he eyed the clock above and tapped his finger on the cash register. A little girl entered and asked for a 99 Flake, but the ice cream wasn't coming out of the machine's nozzle. He opened the cabinet box full of tangled wires to see if he could fix it, and reached in. At once, an excruciating numbness filled him.

Joseph found himself lying supine on the linoleum floor, the little girl peering over him. Having lost feeling in his body, he leaned over and spotted an exposed wire.

"Do you want me to get my daddy?" the little girl asked as she hugged her teddy bear.

"No thanks, I'm cool," mumbled Joseph, standing up and noticing the hairs on his arms standing up too. He got a cone from the box and pressed the nozzle button, but still, no ice cream was coming out. He sighed. "Nothing I can't shake off. So, would a chocolate bar be alright instead?"

She nodded, and so he sold the little girl a Cadburys. Once she was gone, Joseph took a deep breath and shut down the machine. *Scratch England, I could be the unluckiest man in the world*, he thought, on the verge of laughter. *Oh well. Today can only go up from here, right?*

As he served more customers, Joseph kept looking at the clock and wishing this was as fun as his PlayStation. No more threats to his life transpired during the next few hours, but Joseph's string of misfortune only continued. Seconds after an elderly woman came to buy a coffee, her frail, jittery hands let it slip and fall, and the piping hot coffee spilled over and leaked through his trousers, scalding his legs.

By the end of the morning, having been knocked off his bike, electrocuted and burnt, he was starting to feel distinctly like this day was doomed. When his sister arrived for her afternoon shift, he told her everything that had happened.

"Don't go walking under any ladders for the rest of the day. Or breaking mirrors," Melanie teased, as she put on her Mace uniform and Joseph took his off.

"Thanks, sis. Not sure my luck could get much worse today, honestly," Joseph said, and chuckled sheepishly.

While he stood idly at the side of the till, they caught up, especially regarding Melanie's upcoming wedding, scheduled for December 4th. Melanie was a few years older than Joseph and had fair, curled hair and small ears.

"The venue is booked, at last, so we are starting to think about the guest list. I'm undecided whether to go for a big ceremony or a small one. Michael thinks that we should keep it close family, but I'm not sure. The venue is flexible," Melanie explained.

"I dunno, but don't invite too many people, or there won't be enough cake left for me," Joseph mumbled.

Melanie was always full of beans, and lately, no topic thrilled her more than her wedding. "I'm just so excited for my big day, aren't you? I do wish . . . you know who could

3

come, but . . ." she said as her voice cracked, and she trailed off. "Sorry, I don't mean to be a downer."

"You'll figure it out. Mum and I'll be there, at least," Joseph said, but then he remembered he couldn't actually come due to his terrible secret, which he had not even told Melanie. He looked down at his cheap plastic watch. "Sorry to be abrupt, but I've got to meet a friend now. Thomas."

"Oh, Thomas . . . isn't he at uni now? Anyway, have a think if you want to bring anybody," Melanie said, a note of concern lingering in her voice as she took her place behind the counter.

A customer came up to the till. "Do you have any Marlboro cigarettes?"

"I'd better go. See you, Mel," Joseph said, taking off.

"Let's just hope you don't get stung by bees or anything en route," Melanie quipped, sidling to the cigarette shelf.

Joseph left the store and mounted his bike, not sure whether to be more cautious of being hit by lightning or falling off a cliff as he cycled away.

He locked his bicycle up again after skidding to a halt in front of Western Esplanade. Joseph walked through the flowery seaside Southend park, trying to enjoy the sunny Friday weather. Passing a water fountain surrounded by a bed of roses, he turned the corner and saw Thomas. He was sitting on a rusty iron bench holding the leash of his Dalmatian, Daisy, and wincing at the balmy heat. A cute little dog, her tail was wagging faster than a fan.

"How's things, mate?" Joseph greeted, trying to sound as normal as possible considering the less-than-ideal circumstances. He took a seat next to Thomas on the warm bench, his joints still a bit achy from this morning.

"Not bad. What's up, Joe?" replied Thomas, making room. "Late as usual, I see."

Thomas Howard had a thin, freckly mien, shaggy, rosy hair and cocoa-coloured eyes. Joseph looked at his short-sleeved blue shirt and cropped trousers, and then turned his gaze to his own ragged, hand-me-down t-shirt and torn jeans. He felt like he'd known Thomas his entire life, though they'd met ten years or so ago at Birchwood Junior School.

"Oh, same old, same old," Joseph said, wishing he could be completely honest. "I just came from a shift at Mace. Wasn't too bad until a lady spilled hot coffee on me. And I got electrocuted."

"So, a normal day by your lucky standards." Thomas laughed and craned his neck around the park, swinging his hanging necklace, which had a pendant of the cross. "Do you know when we last came around here? Western Esplanade?"

Didn't mention I got hit by a damn car. My elbows hurt. "Think so. It was that time we went to see the musical at the Essex Concert House. Not long before you went off to uni," he said.

Thomas grinned in nostalgia, and said, "Ah right! The Lion King; I won the tickets. Seems like a lifetime ago. Man, we've grown." He raised an eyebrow, tilting his head. "Well, do you have what you owe me? It must have been a year ago that I loaned it to you. You do take your time."

"Paying back loans is sooo much fun," Joseph said, palms open.

Daisy panting alongside them, he reached for his pocket where his wallet was tucked. But as Joseph's fingers skimmed the well-worn leather, he opened it to find he was scant of anything besides a few coins. He had forgotten to visit an ATM that morning as planned.

"Er," Joseph said awkwardly. "Do you happen to accept invisible cash?"

"Typical Joseph," Thomas muttered, slamming his hand against the bench. "You never remembered your pencil case at school; I should have expected."

"Calm down, calm down. There is an ATM just ten

5

minute's walk from here, by the Subway. We can go now. Or, we could always soak up some heavenly vitamin D first."

"Are you kidding? I need to get out of this heat before I keel over from heatstroke." Thomas stood up, tightening his grip on Daisy's leash and gazing around. "I'm peckish, so maybe we could have a bite to eat too. Let me guess, you've got to dash for another shift?"

"Nah, even cashiers need lunch too." Joseph crossed his arms, feigning a smile. "Fine, let's go to Subway then. Or, anything cheap."

As they walked into town, Daisy trotting happily in front, Joseph caught sight of Southenders setting sail on kayaks, splashing around the shore in trunks, sunbathing and making the most of the weather. *Years since I last went swimming. Would love to go on one of those kayaks. If only I weren't so afraid of sharks.*

Very quickly, Joseph's final hours were ticking away.

Arriving at Subway, they both eyed the ATM fixed on the wall, where there was only a very short queue.

"So, how many millions do I owe you again?" he asked dryly.

"Five hundred pounds, plus one hundred," Thomas said. Joseph shot him a look, which his friend seemed to think was one of annoyance. "I know, I know. . . . I am the mouthpiece of capitalism, Thatcher in the flesh, drooling over green paper. You can tell me if you hate me, Joe."

"Nope, you loaned me the rent money," Joseph said, displaying an outraged expression. "It's only fair. But I mean, I thought it would be five hundred?"

Thomas nodded. "The other one hundred is interest at a rate of twenty percent, as agreed."

Joseph felt his fist coil. "Ah, right. Interest rates these days are exorbitant, aren't they?"

He inputted his card and pin. The hissing of the cash

extractor sounded oddly like a snake as it spit out the money, incidentally emptying his current account.

"That wasn't too hard, was it?" Thomas said with a laugh, slipping the notes into his pocket. "I know the post-Brexit economy can be difficult. Maybe you ought to get a second job."

"I never said it would be, moneybags," he affirmed, rolling his eyes at Thomas' freckled face.

During the meal, as they sat on wooden benches with the thrum of the crowd around them, Joseph and Thomas chatted about their many days together in Birchwood School. Yet soon, he started to notice that Thomas kept intimating that he didn't approve of his current lifestyle. Once they had gorged themselves on most of their sandwiches—cheese and ham for Joseph and vegetarian patty for Thomas—and fed Daisy some crumbs, Thomas looked to be thinking very hard.

Eventually, he asked Joseph, "So . . . are you planning anything much for the future?"

"Winning the lottery would be nice," Joseph said, holding his cards close to his chest. "One thing is I'm thinking of seeing that new film, *Alien Warrior*. My dad and I loved *E.T.*. And getting that new video game, *Star Battle 2*."

"But do you ever see yourself doing something more . . ." Thomas wiped his chin with a napkin, as he looked down at the tablecloth " . . . more, how do I say, meaningful?"

"What the heck!" Joseph exclaimed, wondering grimly what Thomas would say if he knew his secret. "You're saying doing nothing with your life isn't meaningful?"

"Kinda. Let's be honest, between you and me: you are wasting your potential." Thomas shrugged. "That's the harsh result of squandering the years after you graduate school. You're only nineteen now, yes, but in a few years, you won't have a clear career direction. And you need to start saving. You've always been terrible with money."

"That may be," he said, scowling at Thomas' necklace,

"but I have a feeling things are going to turn around once I, er —continue to do nothing for several more years. Come on, where did the fun Thomas I used to know go?"

Thomas placed a hand on his own cheek, voice becoming increasingly monotone. "I'm just looking out for you. No career goals, no car . . . nothing. All you do is play video games and watch films. At the moment, you're a nobody. Plain and simple."

Joseph scoffed, stroking Daisy's black and white coat. "I've never believed in my life needing to have some great purpose, mate."

"The reality is you're getting older, and will be twenty soon. What about the near future?" With a superior expression on his face, Thomas pointed down at his watch. "What do you plan to do when the clock strikes three pm? It's five to. Only a few minutes left."

"Maybe go have a piss. I could be pushing up daisies tomorrow."

"See, you need to make a plan, Joe. Even with small things. It adds up. My dad tells me this all the time. Let me recount a little tale on what grit and concrete goals can get you."

Daisy began chasing her tail under the table, while Thomas rambled on without modesty about his amazing life: how he was doing incredibly well at Essex University; and besides that, how he was planning to infiltrate the stock market, so he could eventually become a billionaire.

"God, you've become so bloody judgemental since you went off to uni," Joseph accused him, sitting on the edge of his seat. "You need to loosen up, go to a party, drink some beers: stuff people our age should do."

Thomas grimaced. "You've taken this the wrong way. All I've been saying is maybe it's time you consider a change. Get out of your mother's store and apply next year for college."

"I guess I could use the invisible cash to pay for a degree."

"Oh, and why is that? Because you spend all your money on lottery tickets and whatever else."

"No, because I don't have a rich Dad like you to pay the bills!" Joseph snapped. "Mine is . . . dead."

An awkward silence spread between them for two minutes after this. It had reached 3 pm, and Daisy was agitating to go sniff a nearby patch of grass. Thomas checked his watch again; he had been gazing around like he urged to leave.

"Well, I've got to get going, or I'll be late for my economics lecture," he announced.

"Fun. I need to go too to buy a toaster," Joseph said. "Mine died last week. I live for jam on hot bread before bed—it's my thing. There's a flea market nearby. I'll see if they have one."

"Sounds good to me," Thomas uttered, visibly uninterested.

Joseph and Thomas binned the sandwich wrappers and walked outside the Subway. As they stood on the pavement, he pensively recalled how they had become best friends at a young age and then never left each other's side, as if they were stuck with glue. At present, the glue seemed to be very weak.

"Nice week. See you," Thomas said goodbye, waving him away.

"*Adios*," Joseph said, and petted Daisy on the back as a farewell, the dog barking in response.

They parted beside a zebra crossing. Joseph had a feeling they wouldn't be seeing each other anytime soon.

He developed a pounding headache as he meandered along a nearby cobbled road, and across an arch bridge. Joseph admired the beams of sunlight flashing through the air, twisting across the leaves and twigs of oak trees onto the discoloured jade waterway below. Having unlocked his bike, it only took him five or so minutes to arrive at the flea market. As he parked the bicycle, his phone beeped and he looked at the text message. It was from his landlord, Susanne: *"Joseph, you're now five months behind in rent. Pay up by the end of the week or I'll have to evict you next month."*

Joseph sighed once more. The police had knocked on his door last night, and left a letter accusing him of being a squatter. He realised now that Susanne most likely had sent them.

Moments later his phone beeped with another text, this time from Thomas: *"I forgot. You owe me another £100 from that time I helped you buy a laptop. Can we meet up again next Wednesday for that?"*

He groaned. The only reason Thomas had money to loan him was that his father was a millionaire stockbroker, who gave him a ridiculous allowance.

As Joseph walked across the street, his terrible prospects and his meagre possibilities ran through his head. What Thomas didn't know was that Joseph's account currently had about £-12,340, money that he had taken out to pay rent and lower mobile phone game and lottery debts, and that the bank was starting to hound him to return, not to mention loan sharks. He had just withdrawn the last sum that he had. In fact, his inbox was full of emails from the lawyers threatening to take him to court.

Nobody else was aware of Joseph's gigantic debt. This was his big, awful secret. It was also, if he didn't want to go to prison, the reason he simply *had* to leave England. Joseph would never be able to pay off the debt, and knew he had been incredibly reckless to incur it, gambling and spending too much. He could only run.

Joseph kicked the curb, a weight on his shoulders that felt like several elephants. If he moved back in with his mother, she certainly wouldn't be pleased. She had been in dire straits attempting to keep Mace afloat lately, so he could not depend on her to help him out. Despite his mother's English roots, nearly all of his extended family was on his father's side and lived in Spain. The only option was to go.

Southend open-air flea market had many stalls offering second-hand goods—clothes, trinkets, jewellery, sweets, furniture and dried fruit . . . but apparently, no toasters. Joseph passed a stall with an impoverished-looking family selling mood rings, and then a T-shirt stand owned by unemployed journalists. *Oh, it's hopeless. Like Thomas said: I'm a nobody. I will leave next week for Spain using up my piggy bank money. Start a new life. I suppose if I am to move, I will still need a toaster. Might as well get it before my flight.*

Several minutes later, and there were still no toasters. Joseph was about to give up, when at last he came to a promising stall. They had hundreds of boxes with cables, TVs, phone cases and other odds and ends. The stall sign read: "Southend Electronics."

"Can I help you, sir?" asked a gruff voice behind him.

"Uh, yeah," Joseph said, turning around. "I'm looking for a very cheap toaster. I'm afraid I don't have much cash."

It was an elderly woman with crumpled skin, a bald head and dark, learned eyes standing next to a plump man of a similar age with a high brow and broken teeth. Joseph presumed they must be married.

"You're in luck then, son. I have a very good second-hand toaster in stock." The lady pedlar chuckled, and pulled out a rusty toaster from the table. "Dirt cheap. You might say a deal to die for! Only one pound."

A shiver ran up Joseph's spine, though he had no idea why.

"Wow, how come it's so cheap if it's so good?" he asked curiously.

"No reason," said the man, as he smiled from ear to ear. "You certainly won't regret this purchase."

"You know what . . . I'll take it," Joseph said, sorting through the very few coins in his wallet.

"Excellent. I'll just get you a bag," said the woman, and gave another throaty laugh.

"Let me just say, that was a very, very wise decision, sir," the man added, his beetle brow furrowing.

The price a steal, in a few minutes he had bought the toaster and was biking home with it. *Thank God that I can have toast now, but I wonder why those pedlars acted so weird*, he pondered as he pedalled past Western Esplanade.

The rest of the day went by faster than a wag of Daisy's tail. Unfortunately, though, this pedlar's offer was the last straw of bad luck that led to Joseph's demise.

In truth, he died that night in his sleep, when a certain second-hand toaster caused a fire and burnt his apartment to a crisp. The blaze had started at 1 am, after Joseph had eaten a tasty slice of jammed toast before bed, and went on to raze his whole flat.

But he would not stay dead for long. The next day, Joseph came to in an unimaginable, faraway land where his new life, in a very unexpected way, was about to start.

CHAPTER 2
WELCOME TO HYLEBERIA

A MAN TURNED ON HIS HEELS, REVEALING A BROAD GRIN, AND warmly exclaimed, "Joseph, you're finally here. I'm Peter. Welcome to Hyleberia. How was your life?"

He was standing by a gilded sundial, a cute sloth stirring in his arms. The bright blue sky hung above the aromatic butterfly garden in which Joseph Shields and Peter both stood, taking in each other's faces for the first time.

"My *life*? It was just fine, thanks, but it would be good if you could . . . uh . . . tell me where we are. I woke up here a few minutes ago, I suppose," Joseph replied, deeply confused.

Peter appeared to be in his mid-forties, and he had the well-sculpted nose and jowl of an impressive man. The tall fellow wore a sharp white suit, contrasting his black hair.

"I will explain everything in a minute," Peter said, gazing at Joseph like an old friend. "By the way, this is my pet sloth, Gabriel."

Joseph met the bright green eyes of the furry creature, who gave him a peculiar look as if recognising him. He surveyed the garden to further get his bearings. Fluffy clouds drifted above, hanging over the ancient-looking pillars around the sundial. An ebbing and flowing river in the distance babbled behind a song of chirping birds.

Although Joseph was lost for words, it felt as if he might have just awoken from a long nap, for he wasn't at all panicked. He risked a question: "Is this place . . . well . . . is this Heaven?"

Peter scratched the prominent mole on his left cheek. "Bwahaha. I'm afraid not." Hearing this, Joseph tensed. "But don't worry, it's not Hell either. Far from it. The afterlife in its entirety is a Tellurian farce. You're not even dead in the traditional sense. We resuscitated you in our dimension."

"Ah, that's weird," Joseph mumbled, taking this in. *Tellurian?*

Peter checked his quartz watch. "I only have a couple of hours, so we'd better get a move on. Today, I'm going to give you a tour of my homeland, as well as show you to your new home. Let's walk and talk."

If you say so. Joseph didn't take this as a question, so followed dutifully behind.

Peter leading the way, they proceeded away from the sundial and into the garden. Hundreds of strange, stunning perennials bloomed over the rolling hills that surrounded them, like something stolen from a beautiful dream. Besides the many butterflies fluttering about, bees swarmed around marigolds and ripe, juicy-looking fruit dangling from the branches of evergreens.

Joseph watched as Gabriel fidgeted on Peter's shoulder, limbs moving slowly, little fingers and toes tracing invisible lines in the air. *Why on Earth is his pet a sloth? More importantly, why am I even here?*

Throat dry, questioning if he might be dreaming this, he said, "So, tell me. If this isn't Heaven . . . or Hell . . . then what is it?"

Peter beamed. "And here is the big reveal: you have arrived at the Republic of Reality, Hyleberia. What you see around you is a real island on Earth in the Pacific Ocean. This is where you will spend the rest of your days, serving the needs of the planet. I am the Prime Minister of this island, and the world at that."

Joseph gasped, realising the implications of the madness he was hearing. "Wait a second! The Republic of Reality?"

Looking down, he noticed he was wearing brand new clothes—a blue Hawaiian shirt, beech chinos and moccasins. As they paced along, Joseph racked his mind about his past and life, finding it hard to remember.

"Yup, the one and only world republic," Peter said, and added, "By the way, Tellurian is our word for normal humans. You might also hear another word I and other Hylebarians often use, 'colt'. It means the youngest person on our island—as of now, that's you. Hyleberia, you see, is an administrative centre, a government for the Earth. We live here in paradise in the 5th dimension, hidden from Tellurian eyes. Oh, isn't it exciting? There is so much for you to learn."

The two of them strolled by a row of tropical palm trees and came to the centre of the garden. The colours of all the bright, exotic flowers on display made Joseph squint, like staring at the sun. Yet he felt even more dazzled by the incredibility of all that had just been said.

A million queries ran through his mind. "So, what do you mean by administrative centre?"

"Simply put, we administer the world here," Peter revealed, as his eyes wavered over Joseph. "We also call it a divine Parliament. If you were expecting to see angels or cherubs around the corner, I'm sorry to disappoint you. You see, as Prime Minister, I farm out the smaller tasks of the world to workers like you. That's how the Earth is run so efficiently. And you are one—"

"One of the workers?" Joseph blurted, before biting his lip.

"Yes, one of the souls chosen by the Animah Sweepstakes.

In general, the selection process is completely random, although some exceptional souls like Cleopatra are explicitly chosen by me to join our ranks, Honorary Hyleberians. Essentially, then, you have just won the biggest and best lottery in existence. In fact, honestly you've been sedated slightly so that you do not faint from the shock of it all."

Sedated!? Nothing is right about this, at all. Joseph found it hard to grasp that he was really dead, which alone would merit some time to process. But the revelations followed each other like dominoes falling, one after another, too quick to register. Peter went on to tell him that reincarnation was actually real, which made Joseph's jaw drop. He also said that due to the so-called Colt Accommodation Law, he had to move in with a roommate, someone called Mr Wagner, as he settled into Hyleberian life over the coming weeks.

Peter warned him he was not immortal and could still die from injury, and so not to jump off cliffs. However, the ageing process here was slowed so significantly that he essentially would never die of old age. It was at that moment Joseph realised his memory had mostly returned. Yet how far away his past life felt already. The Southend streets, all of his things, Mace, Thomas and Melanie. . . they were nowhere in sight in this new, extremely bizarre land.

The hedges narrowed as they went on, and Joseph spotted a silver gate on the horizon, decorated with diamonds on each of the curved bars. It seemed they were about to leave the park. As a light gust of wind blew over him and sent his unbrushed hair flying, he stared at an array of gushing sprinklers arranged in a perfect triangle, and noticed a squirrel with an acorn clasped tightly in its hands racing under overgrown ivy. Joseph became aware of a pounding pain in the recesses of his skull, a migraine, which he knew he had a history of experiencing as a man, or a Tellurian, as Peter called it. *Drat. This really isn't Heaven. Too bad I left my aspirin in*

Southend. Damn. I'll never get to go home again, will I? Thomas . . . Melanie . . . Mum. . . .

Hand on the gate, Peter queried, "Anyways, shall we carry on into the city centre? I do hope, incidentally, that you are enjoying your complimentary clothes. Moccasins are my favourite type of shoes. So comfy."

As Joseph nodded, Peter opened the gate and they walked towards the city centre. Distant sounds of the metropolis became audible, growing steadily louder while the buildings drew nearer. The roads had no traffic, the streets were well-maintained and the air free of pollution. There was an increasing sense of realisation in Joseph's mind that this might all be real, and not just a random dream. While his moccasins met the concrete and he breathed in the sweet-scented afternoon air, he reckoned he couldn't possibly be hallucinating. He had never dreamt anything remotely as vivid and random.

Hyleberians looked more or less like individuals you would find on 21st-century Earth, other than some eccentric fashion choices. He noticed a man with Rapunzel-length hair casually wearing a bubble suit, and a lady on a skateboard in a gamboge yellow ball gown, going down the street with no apparent thought to their conspicuous attire. A shirtless fellow ran along with a leashed puppy, with the peculiarity being the pug seemed to be green; and most eye-catching of all, a brunette woman strolled by whose shirt was almost entirely transparent. Joseph thought this was a bit strange, but then he saw a man wearing the same thing. Maybe it was a popular fashion trend around here.

"Good morning, Peter!", "How's things, Prime Minister?", "What's the news in Parliament?", the Hyleberians asked him as they walked by, and Peter would respond modestly, "Oh, nothing much. Things and stuff."

"How long will it take to get used to the fact that I died?" Joseph asked, as they passed an odd shop called Tony's Halo

17

Hats. It sold a variety of hats that hovered a few centimetres over your head, at least going by the guy who came out with a levitating baseball cap.

"A few weeks. Sometimes months . . . a couple years, at most. It depends. But most settle in quickly, much quicker than they expect," Peter said, as Gabriel squirmed on his shoulder, hugging his neck. "Look at it this way. You have been given the chance to start a whole new second life in Hyleberia, free of your past. Not everyone gets that!"

This sounded rather good to Joseph, apart from leaving his previous life behind so suddenly, although he had been planning on skipping town. He tried to recall how he lost his life, but it wouldn't come.

"It might help if I found out how I passed. Bring some closure," he uttered, as images of his own lifeless, decaying body accosted his mind.

"Are you sure you want to know? Might ruin your first day."

"I'm pretty sure."

"Oh, fine. Here you go. Toaster fire. To be precise, death by smoke inhalation in your sleep," Peter revealed.

"What!?" Joseph exclaimed, going pale. "Oh . . . the damn flea market, rusty toaster. I should have fixed my smoke alarm. I knew that damn thing was not working."

"You'll get over it in no time. Well, we're almost at your apartment. Later, there will be a second half of the tour, and tonight a special surprise," Peter said. "I'll be busy this afternoon with the Divine Council, debating a possible new element addition to the periodic table, *noumenium*. Therefore, one of my dear friends will give you the last part of it."

"That would be great," Joseph said, eager to have a drink of water. He wondered about the special surprise.

As they ambled down a suburban street called Plotinus Drive, he caught sight of luscious, fresh leaves and brightly painted mansions. All the buildings looked expensive, their mowed lawns guarded by newly painted picket fences. It was not until they got to the end of the cul-de-sac that Peter gestured him onwards to a sideroad. Before long, they came to the broken pavement that led to Miyagi Apartments, apparently denominated after the owner. Drainage pipes dangled out at odd angles and damp walls were visible with uncovered spackle. He spotted piles of rubbish, sweet wrappers and broken glass, littering what a sign revealed was called Sophist Street. From what he had seen elsewhere, it seemed many of the roads in this strange land were named after Tellurian figures and ideas, including Einstein Road and Destiny Way.

Peter handed Joseph a key and gestured him inside Miyagi Apartments, and then took him to the elevator. As they waited for the doors to open, he noticed it had been graffitied with the words: "The Prince of Darkness is near. He will ascend again". The writing was in pink spray paint, and it jarred with the dusty aluminium.

"Prince of Darkness, it says. Is that a real . . . I don't know . . .?" Joseph said.

"No, no. I will ask the management to look at who did that," Peter said with a note of disapproval. "Don't worry about it. A *funny* joke, I suppose. I, Peter, am the one and only authority of Hyleberia."

"That's a relief," Joseph said, only half convinced. "His name doesn't exactly make him sound like a barrel of laughs."

"Your apartment is C52," Peter continued quickly, as they exited the elevator and approached his new door. "I'll give you some time alone now before part two of the tour. If you need me, just drop by Town Hall and book an appointment with my secretary, Ms Beechum. Well, that's everything. Lovely meeting you! Bwahaha."

Not particularly ready for this goodbye, Joseph uttered, "You too."

It felt almost as if he was saying farewell to a new school chum, and so he was not expecting what came next. In the hallway outside C52, Peter embraced Joseph in a warm man hug.

"Wait!" Joseph exclaimed as Peter departed to the elevator, and the hallway's stench—stale nicotine and chlorine—invaded his nostrils. "Before you go, as the Prime Minister do you, er, know the meaning of life?"

He didn't even know why he was asking this, but it suddenly occurred to him that Peter might know.

Peter chuckled, stepping into the elevator as Gabriel sat smiling widely on his shoulder. "The meaning of life? Say, why don't you wait and see?" he said cryptically.

The Prime Minister looked pleased as the doors closed with a dull thud. Peter and Gabriel were gone. For the first time since his arrival in Hyleberia, Joseph was all alone.

The lightbulb flickered as he noticed a painting on the wall of an abandoned mansion on an eerie islet. He walked over and stared at it for a few seconds, just thinking. There was nothing else to do but accept this utterly bizarre situation. Gathering himself, he took a deep breath, raised his key and proceeded into his new home.

It was not exactly a warm welcome.

A scream escaped Joseph's lips as a strong tide dragged him away. The flood surged out of the door opening and caught him, an intense undertow pulling him to the opposite wall. It was like he had just opened a portal to the Pacific Ocean. Dazed, legs splayed and head smashed against a radiator, he laboriously got up. Joseph looked down at his moccasins and chinos, now soaked. The rest of the water drained slowly out into the hall.

Gazing through the doorway of the apartment, Joseph tried to work out what had just happened. Then, the fellow who must be his roommate, "Mr Wagner" stepped into view.

"Hey, you! Why the hell did you open the damn door?" yelped the man.

Joseph stared at him. His face was partly concealed by a shaggy mane of hair of a much darker shade than Joseph's own. He was wearing a tie-dye shirt, sunglasses, and swimming trunks. Mr Wagner seemed to be a few years older than him.

"Didn't you see the sign?" Mr Wagner asked angrily.

He gulped. "Sign?"

Joseph realised that maybe he should have knocked. There had been a strange smell of chlorine in the hallway, come to think of it, and very faint music too. He recognised the song on the record player visible playing in the corner of the hall: *A Whiter Shade of Pale*, by Procol Harum.

"Oh, it fell off," observed Mr Wagner, examining a piece of metal on the floor. "It said: 'NO ENTRY. WATER HAZARD', but the ink has faded and now it's gobbledygook. I guess I can't be *too* mad at you, then."

He strode down the hall and turned down the music, then returned with arms crossed.

After a few seconds, looking through the door, Joseph realised what had occurred. This insane fellow had refashioned the apartment into an indoor pool, and he had accidentally let the water all out! The pool, of course, was no more. Inflatable ducks and swimming floats were left sadly beached on the carpet floor.

"Sorry, but may I ask why you've made the apartment into a pool?" Joseph asked, bewildered.

"Why doesn't everyone?" Mr Wagner replied, still with a growl in his voice. "I've lived a hundred years on this damn planet and I'll relax how I want to relax. At any rate, I presume you're my new roommate. To be honest, it wasn't my choice to have a roommate, but I didn't have a choice because of the dumb Colt Assisted Accommodation policy. It seems it's my turn on the list, unluckily enough."

He nodded slowly. "Oh, that's nice of you. Well, my name is Joseph Shields."

"You have weird eyes, Shields. And I'm Raymond Wagner," he said.

"Uh, interesting."

Joseph extended his hand for a handshake, but Raymond didn't seem to care. He paced to the living room, and Joseph followed cluelessly.

"I'm from glorious Munich. Born 1902, died 1929," Raymond said, which explained his slight German accent. "Where are you from?"

"Essex, England. Southend-on-Sea," he said. "Born 1998."

"Oh my. Horrible country," criticised Raymond. "I visited that hellhole you call England back in 1927 for a work trip. Miserable experience. Rained cats and hogs, and the people were either posh or too *chavvy*, as you Brits would say. Ugh, I hated it."

Joseph shrugged. "Cats and dogs? Well, 1927 was a while ago . . . pre-Brexit and pre-World War Two."

If this was all true, he was talking to a crotchety young man who was actually over triple his age. In fact, this whole age thing greatly confused him. Shouldn't Hyleberians all be enlightened sages if they had truly been alive so long? Joseph certainly didn't think Raymond's attitude fit the bill of an elderly man.

"Whatever—I didn't fight in any stupid world wars. Well, I guess I'll show you around," Raymond said as he beckoned him out of the living room. He headed over to the mini-fridge on the counter, his unshod feet squelching on the carpet. "Oh, but before that . . . I'm thirsting for a Haoma."

"A what?"

"Oh, you should wanna know. A fantastic Hyleberian beer. You want one? Couldn't find these bad boys in Southend."

"Sure," he said, and Raymond handed him one.

Cracking it open and taking a sip, the drink proved utterly delicious, bubbly in Joseph's throat with a delectable lemon tang.

"Nice. That is really good," he said, thinking that this beverage may well be his favourite thing about Hyleberia so far.

Joseph slipped off his moccasins and saw that his soles, moist from the flood, were also slightly red. It seemed traipsing around the city in those flimsy shoes didn't agree with his feet.

"Now, for your tour," Raymond said, his finger fluttering like a wasp as he pointed around. "Right. There's the visualiser—television in Tellurian parlance, the fire alarm, the window." He then showed Joseph the storage closet, and the bathroom. "Keep your laundry to yourself, buy your own food, and make sure to take care of cleaning your bedroom and all that. Make sense?"

It was a small flat, the wallpaper faded, likely as a result of Raymond's pools. Strewn about the rooms were many peculiar things that Joseph wanted to inquire further about: a poster of a local band, *The Unangelic Angels*; a so-called *Earthglobe* that held a realistic miniature version of Earth inside, by the looks of it updated in real-time; and a large stack of hundreds of vinyls, many of which, from a cursory examination, were 60s' Tellurian rock. But Raymond seemed eager to get the tour over with. When they came to Joseph's bedroom, he noted the simplicity of its furnishings: a single bed; a brown cupboard; a desk and a wall-length mirror. Besides some mould and cracks on the wall from water damage, it was nothing to complain about.

"And that's everything. I'm fed up with swimming, so I'm going to play *Super Smash Bros* on my N64," Raymond remarked lazily, as his hairy knees carried him down the corridor towards the last remnants of his pool. "*Tschüss*. That's German for goodbye, genius."

"Really? You're going already?" Joseph asked.

"Why not?" Raymond responded, stopping and turning around.

"Dunno. Do you have a job around here?"

Raymond sneered, leaning on the wall of the hallway. "Of course, how else would I buy Haoma and everything? I work in the Water Department. But I'm pretty low down on the administrative ladder. I have a cushy position in precipitation; you may have heard of it."

Joseph clenched his fist, ignoring the suffocating stink of chlorine hanging about the apartment. It was starting to sink in just how much of a pain Raymond was going to be to live with. "Is that why you made the pool?"

Raymond immediately raised his hand and pointed it at him. Then, as though he had a hose hiding up his sleeve, water spurted out of his fingers. A gushing stream spilled onto the floor, forming an uneven puddle around Joseph's feet.

"Impressive!" Joseph gasped. "How did you do it?"

"*Proficiencies*, we call them. Everyone in Hyleberia is given powers depending on their job," he said with a shrug. "And so, duh, mine is water manipulation. Welp, catch you later."

Somehow, this was only the third or so most mind-bending thing Joseph had learnt so far today.

His roommate was gone. As a yawn travelled up Joseph's throat, he decided to worry about why Raymond was such a grump later. Apparently, he was dead, and so he felt he now deserved at least a short moment to deal with that. He found himself a piece of ciabatta bread from a cupboard in the kitchenette and traipsed into his new bedroom. Raymond hadn't given him permission to eat this, but Joseph did not want to bother him and didn't much care about his rules.

I needed this. Joseph finished the last sip of his refreshing Haoma, and placed the empty can on his desk. *Raymond, what a guy. I don't think I'm going to get along with that German man.*

Looking through a lower drawer, he found a slim laptop with "Hylebook" engraved on it, which had a note saying he could browse it, but participation on the Tellurian internet was strictly banned under penalty of "exile". He took it out and sat on the bed, resting it on his chest and creating an account. Having found the browser and connected it to the internet, he was on the edge of searching his name to find his obituary. Ultimately, he decided that there was no point, at least for now. What solace would seeing "Essex Man Killed Due to Fire Started by Malfunctioning Toaster" headlines really bring him? But then Joseph realised something absolutely joyous.

If he was dead, that meant he would never have to repay his debt or skip town! His earthly obligations were no longer valid! It was as Peter said: he had miraculously been given a second chance.

Ding, ding, ding!

The doorbell rang from down the waterlogged corridor.

"Hey, roomie, can you get that? I'm in the middle of a game!" Raymond shouted from the living room.

Joseph felt his stomach drop; presuming it was him, he hadn't expected his second tour guide to arrive so soon. He got to his feet and headed for the door. *No point keeping them waiting. Funny, being dead is much less restful than I expected.*

CHAPTER 3

CORRUPTION

JOSEPH FELT RATHER LIKE A MAN ADRIFT ON FOREIGN WATERS, floundering to keep his head above the waves of confusion and novelty that he had plunged into. Yes, it was all too weird to be believed . . . both incredibly lucky to be here and unlucky to have died. It was like he had been separated from his old "Tellurian", as they called it, life by a wall. There was no going back.

What did it matter now that he had been a convenience store clerk nobody? What did it matter that he had been contemplating running away before his death? What did it matter that loan sharks had been hounding him because he was a spendthrift and had a gambling addiction, and he'd felt like a failure every day because he couldn't go to university like his best friend? These things were all irrelevant now. Melanie and his mother must be preparing a funeral . . . how strange to think.

According to Peter, Joseph had been sedated, and he wondered if it was starting to wear off now due to his racing pulse. Someone was humming to themselves outside the front door. After putting back on his soggy moccasins that he had just taken off, he opened the front door to a man with tan skin, blonde hair and an oval face.

"My name is Thaddeus Deaus, your second tour guide. Sorry I'm so early. Good to meet you," the man greeted with a husky voice, his dark eyes fixed on Joseph's frame.

"Good to meet you too, Mr Deaus," Joseph mumbled. "I'm, er—Joseph Shields. They tell me I'm dead."

"Oh, call me Thaddeus. I know your name, J-man; I've read your file. Yes, I know all about your life, Joseph Santiago Shields." He chuckled as Joseph blushed. "Well, not *everything*. Peter asked me to help out this morning; I'm going to show you around the parts where he didn't get the chance. We've got no time to lose."

"I'd like to read this file. I highly doubt it's a thriller, knowing my life." Discomfited, he added, "I would grab my coat, but I don't have one. No clothes, actually. Could I, uh, go and get them?"

"Nope, you won't be going back to England any time soon, but no worries," affirmed Thaddeus. "We have a welcome package with some basic clothes to keep you going, including a coat. I'll get that for you later. You won't be pyjama-less come sundown, I promise."

As they exited, he observed Thaddeus' piercing navy eyes. He had a scar through his eyebrow, and his left eye kept twitching. His brawny arms were as wide as his forehead, and he was wearing a polo shirt and cargo trousers. Thaddeus led Joseph down the staircase, and before long, they were wandering back down the path that Peter had guided him up earlier. Joseph couldn't stop glancing at his bright hair, which seemed almost glistening, as if someone had covered it with bright yellow paint.

The instant they had left the gardens of Miyagi Apartments, a frightening figure jumped out at them from behind an ivy hedge. Joseph froze. His first thought was that it was a mugger, but he seemed to simply be a madman. His crusty beard fell down to knee height, and his plaid coat had many tennis ball-sized holes. He smelled as if he had just gone swimming in rotten eggs.

Standing in front of them, the hobo rambled deliriously, "The ascension! Descent is coming. Cone of golden death. Bah. He's visited me in my dreams! The hunger. Stolen, stolen, stolen! Follow the light of peril. The falsities! Sempiternal lie. Mathias. Watch the doorway of theoretical epiphenomenalism. Golden calf. Immanentise the eschaton! The lie, the lie, the lie!"

"Sorry?" Joseph asked, stepping back in terror. "The lie?"

"The lie of eternity. The ego of the flower. The hunger of the weak!" the man muttered with wild eyes, his arms flapping up and down as if he thought he had wings. "I am a golden goose."

The disturbed fellow kept on rambling. Joseph looked at Thaddeus as if to ask: *should we be running away from this insane man*? Yet Thaddeus wore a bemused, calm face, not even slightly unnerved.

"Just ignore Nigel," Thaddeus said, ushering him onwards with a pat on the shoulder. "He is always accosting passersby in this area of town. Frankly, he's become a public nuisance."

Joseph followed Thaddeus, turning to take another look at "Nigel". He did not seem to care that he was speaking now to nothing more than the void of air they left behind. The strange man's nonsense faded to silence as they turned the corner.

"What's his issue, then?" Joseph asked, thinking Nigel reminded him of his senile Grandma.

Thaddeus sighed as if he had just spotted a stain. "Nigel's not right in the head. He refuses to work or take medication, and so for the past few decades, he has simply wandered around speaking gibberish to whoever will listen. I'm sorry if he ambushes you like that. Just try to ignore him. In my view, he ought to have been kicked out of Hyleberia years ago. Maybe I'll say something about that to Peter."

Joseph scratched the crown of his head. "Oh, do you know Peter well?"

"Ah sure, we are good friends. He's always asking me to do odd jobs like this, the things he can't be bothered to do," Thaddeus divulged, sounding a tad bitter. "Anyhow, let's move on from that cuckoo. Do you have any questions about Hyleberia?"

Of course, he did, and Joseph asked a lot of questions over the next few minutes, still quite distracted by the upcoming "special surprise" that Peter had mentioned. It transpired that Thaddeus was a so-called Controller, which meant he intervened in Tellurians' lives to ensure fate was balanced, like some kind of karma police. Even crazier, Joseph was going to be studying at the local school, where he would get an education about the world and Hyleberia before finding a job here.

Suddenly, Thaddeus grasped Joseph's arm and brought him to a standstill. "You see that? Everyone calls it Shrivatsa, short for the Sacred Honoured Research International Varsity Administrative Theological Societal Academy. It's the home of the infinite knot of knowledge where you will be learning, also widely known as Hyleberia Academy. A beautiful building, huh?"

"Yeah. Wow," Joseph said in awe.

The large schoolhouse was peaked by a bell-tower cupola, and had a wide veranda overhung by a dun roof. The window casings were decorated with fancy multicoloured, moulded shapes: squares, triangles and circles.

Thaddeus let him in and guided Joseph through the halls. It had three floors with rooms of vastly different sizes, and voices were coming from most of them. There were books everywhere on display, such as *How to Modify a Fundamental Physical Constant Without Anyone Noticing* and *Gravity: the Pros and Cons*.

"I'll just see if Ms Sadeghi is available to say hello to you now," Thaddeus said, as he sidled up to a classroom door's window, fogging the pane with his breath. After a brief knock, Joseph heard muffled voices and a drumbeat of heels. A woman came out bearing a clipboard with cryptic scribbles, which from a side glance loosely resembled some kind of quantum mathematical equations.

Ms Sadeghi looked to be in her seventies and had pearl earrings, grey hair and several missing teeth, which she smiled without. In a mellifluous voice, she said, "*Salaam!* You must be Joseph Shields, the new colt. Oh, I *am* so looking forward to getting to know you. So, how are you? I do hope you're not too overwhelmed."

"I'm, uh, fine," said Joseph a little timidly. "Dead, apparently, but fine."

"You're from England, right? I'm from Persia, the Sasanian Empire. Have you heard of it?"

He nodded, and said, "Yeah, I think so. I'm thinking of Cyrus the Great?"

"Not quite, but close enough." Ms Sadeghi beamed. "I think you will find our classes a lot more difficult than on Earth. You don't get any official textbooks written by Peter there!"

"I'm so glad I never wasted my time studying in school, then," Joseph quipped, uncertain whether he should harass her with questions now or later. "Can I have a look at the syllabus?"

"Yes, I ought to show you your new SHOMAT textbook, *World 101,* which contains it," said Ms Sadeghi. She walked over to a filing cabinet in the corner of the hall and pulled out a textbook, as large as an encyclopaedia. She returned and placed it into his excited hands. "Now, it may look a bit difficult to you, but don't worry. We'll go over the whole syllabus on Monday morning. As they said in Persia, doubt is the key to knowledge!"

Holding the textbook felt like lifting a small child. Arms aching, Joseph turned the front page of the juggernaut. "I'll just have a skim through this key to knowledge, then."

In a bold font above a picture of Earth, the book read: *SHOMAT: Science, History, Ontology, Mereology, Axiology, and Teleology for Beginners, World 101* by Peter. Not knowing what they meant, Joseph asked Ms Sadeghi, and she said ontology was the study of being, mereology of parts, axiology of value, and teleology of purpose. Apparently, there was also going to be some logic and epistemology, the study of knowledge, which sounded quite hard but Ms Sadeghi assured him it would be "very basic." He turned to the syllabus, which had a list of the subjects and what they would involve. He was going to be learning about a billion things, and as his studies progressed, he would be funnelled into specialist studies. Most of the words in the book Joseph didn't understand, or had ever heard of.

"In a short time, you'll be taking a career profiler test, which will determine what studies you may pursue after you complete our introductory SHOMAT course," Ms Sadeghi revealed. "I'll be your only teacher for now, and you'll be studying along with the other beginner students. When you pass the SHOMAT test, there will be a wide selection of courses for you to pursue under specialist teachers, before you earn enough credits to graduate!"

"Cool," he said, clumsily handing the textbook back to Ms Sadeghi, which she said he would be able to pick up and take home on Monday after class.

Thaddeus chose this moment to interject. "In any case, we are sorry for interrupting you. Soon, I'm going to take Joseph to the *Pnyx*. He's got a treat ahead of him—a debate on the existence of disease, with Peter on stage, of course."

What? That must be the special surprise. "Disease, huh? So, not exactly a standard debate topic," Joseph said, confused.

"Oh, no problem, I was just marking papers. Joseph,

please remember that your classes start here on Monday, and they will be 8 am - 4 pm," she replied pleasantly. "Make sure to get an alarm clock!"

"Right. Are you going to come to the debate too, Ms Sadeghi?" Joseph asked.

"Maybe!" she squealed, rubbing her hands together excitedly.

After this, Joseph and Thaddeus began their tour of the Hyleberian markets. It had been over an hour since seeing Shrivatsa. Now the sky was darkening, a gentle breeze blowing through the coppiced boxwood bushes. Joseph was feeling overawed by everything, his insides pierced by a deep sense of shock. As he passed a French restaurant, Les Amis, Joseph gazed at the menu, and saw all the prices here were in drachma—the local currency. Thaddeus explained how they followed the Greek economic system here, Greek culture and thought much revered. They were just leaving the area in front of Les Amis when something peculiar happened. He noticed a group of four in their fifties, or at least their bodies were, eating outside the restaurant. Then, unprovoked, he overheard one of them, an older man with a mullet hairstyle and gigantic eyes, mutter under his breath, "Damn colt is staring. More like a dolt. Thinks he gets special treatment, eh?"

Joseph gulped. *Seems I'm not as popular as I'd have liked. . . .*

Soon it was night and getting rather frosty outside, as they began walking towards the Pnyx. On the way, Thaddeus led him by the Thermae, the public Hyleberian baths, which were modelled on the Roman bath system and were free for everyone. He also showed him the Heroon, a shrine dedicated to the ancient hero, Achilles, who Thaddeus revealed was not at all mythical and had actually once been a Hyleberian.

Ambling around all these new places, Joseph was starting to feel as if the Hyleberians might not like him, although he wasn't sure why. Several times he observed individuals glaring at him like a strange animal, or muttering to their friends as soon as he was out of sight. Of course, his attention kept getting directed elsewhere by the many astounding things to see. He stopped thinking entirely about his potential unpopularity in Hyleberia when Thaddeus showed him the incredibly lifelike wax model of Peter that was standing in a street lamp illuminated park, and beside it, a vending machine that held fresh caviar and crab.

Joseph wished he had a coat as he noticed his breath fogging. He and Thaddeus sauntered along a country street, not a soul in sight.

"This is the way to the debate?" he asked, starting to shiver.

"Yeah. The Pnyx is on the outskirts of town," said Thaddeus with a paling face, as he trudged alongside him, squinting through the dark air. "It's far away from town because the debates are considered sacred, separate from business matters."

After what felt like several hours had passed, the Pnyx emerged into sight. It was a large, flat stage, demarcated by diagonally curved stone and lit by torches. Joseph's breath laboured, as he felt more tense than excited about the event. He didn't fully understand what a *debate* even meant in the context of Hyleberian culture.

Peter stood on the stage along with another fellow, who had a large face with a double chin and an eye-catching nose ring. He chewed gum and was wearing baggy jeans.

It seemed like the benches were supposed to hold a hundred people, but there were at least two hundred here. Joseph nearly tripped over several attendees' feet as he ambled around. A whiff of what seemed like grilled red meat scratched at his hunger while he found his way among the crowd. The loud thrum of crowd chatter prevented clear thinking. He felt out of place, like a dog among cats, especially after Thaddeus disappeared, saying he was going to buy them holy dogs. This was nothing like his normal Saturday plans, watching TV most likely or playing video games.

There was a man there dressed very oddly in a black gown, which Joseph idly lingered near as he waited for Thaddeus. The man looked distinctive, like someone he had read an article about once, and Joseph supposed it would be logical for some "Honorary Hyleberians" to be at the debate.

Suddenly, the man turned. "*Bonjour*! Yes, you there. Staring at me, are you?"

"Sorry," Joseph said, forgetting himself. "Er—I think I know you. Uh . . . Napoleon?"

A French accent came out of the man's dry lips, brown pupils lingering over Joseph. "Napoleon? What an insult! I'm no idiotic, four-foot warmonger. Who else could I be? Think!"

Joseph's lips creased. *Not a clue. I'm so stupid.* The man's hair was long and somewhere between black and deep brown. He had an arched nose and leathery skin.

The Frenchman rolled his eyes. "I am the one and only René Descartes."

Joseph stared at Descartes. "Who?"

"The famous French philosopher of the Enlightenment!"

"Oh . . . Descartes, yeah," he said quickly.

"Don't pretend you know me if you don't," Descartes said sternly.

"I think I've heard of you," Joseph stammered, feeling short of breath. "Don't feel bad. I never even went to university. Couldn't afford it."

Descartes maintained a straight face, unamused, taking out a comb and brushing his hair. "And are you going to introduce yourself?"

"Oh, sorry. I'm Joseph Shields, the new colt around town," he said meekly. "I died yesterday from a toaster fire, so forgive me if I'm not thinking straight. I'm from England and I worked in retail. I guess you are really famous, then?"

"Yes, I am, and very important too," Descartes said, scoffing as if this was a highly idiotic comment. "But to be blunt, I lost my life aeons ago. Do you really think I still stand behind all the stuff I wrote as a Tellurian?"

Joseph shrugged. "Dunno."

"I won't deny, of course, that there was a great deal of genius in my old books. *A Discourse on Method*, in particular, stands up. Yet I am not who I was when I wrote those works, my lovely Queen Christina—long dead. I can see now there were simply not sufficient resources for a seventeenth-century Frenchman, surrounded by total ignorance, to come to solid conclusions about the nature of reality in the meagre timespan of life allotted to him," Descartes said.

He nodded leisurely, and said, "Oh, I see. Soooo, you've changed a lot?"

"More than a lot. I care little about fame and accolades now, at least not Tellurian ones." Descartes frowned, and said with a snide tone, "I care about truth. *Cogito ergo sum*, I think therefore I am, is what most people remember me for. Ah, the wasted potential! I'll have Sparknotes know my work contained a lot more depth than a stupid three-word phrase and a few paragraphs."

"I can see that you might find it repetitive, whatever it means. But it must have been incredibly influential on philosophy since you're so well-known," Joseph replied.

Descartes sighed pensively. "You know what, I'm not in the mood for talking about my legacy right now. I'm going to sit down for the debate—perhaps you could drop by the Philosophy Society sometime. It's one of our only worthwhile clubs on this island, among Knitting Society and Sheep Spinning Club," he invited.

"Oh, yes! I would like to, I think," Joseph said. "When is it?"

But Thaddeus reappeared at this moment, and Joseph's question never received an answer. "Good evening, Descartes. I see you've been introduced to the colt," he said, holding the food.

"Thaddeus, is it? Perhaps you ought to keep a closer eye on him. He was rather bothering me with his incessant questions," Descartes muttered, wandering off.

Thaddeus handed Joseph the holy dog, much like a hot dog, except that Thaddeus revealed the meat was from dodos, not in fact extinct in Hyleberia. Famished, he dug into it immediately.

"I don't know what Descartes' problem was. By the way, who's that next to Peter?" Joseph asked, staring at the man on the stage as he enjoyed the tasty dodo meat.

"Um, Colin Rodgers. . . . Canadian guy. I haven't spoken to him for decades, so I can't claim to know him well, but he seems a nice enough chap. He's the first opposition for the debate, I believe," revealed Thaddeus. There was bustling movement and a clearing of throats. "It's about to begin. Let's find a good seat before they're all gone."

Thaddeus brought Joseph towards the second row of benches, and they managed to squeeze into two seats to the left of an obese Asian woman in a strange glowing dress. Everyone was quieting down, but the atmosphere was still electric. The Hyleberians were all garbed in the most absurd range of garments one could possibly imagine, from sarongs to plastic jeans. Some of them were shooting him dirty looks. As Joseph craned his neck to get a good look at Peter, the crowd held their breaths and their leader promenaded to the stage's front.

Peter greeted, "Good evening, my sons and daughters. I hope you're all sitting comfortably tonight. I welcome you to the Saturday debate. As usual, tonight, five randomly selected Hyleberians will get thirty minutes each to spar with me about a certain issue. The issue of the present debate will be the ethics of the existence of disease. My debaters and I only found out the topic this morning, so we had the same very small amount of time to prepare. Let's see if we have any announcements . . . oh, yes! A very important one."

Joseph's face became hot as Peter's eyes locked onto him, heart accelerating. All of the townspeople's beady pupils were no doubt on him as well. *I'm sure they think I am a dolt too.*

Peter's voice was loud despite the lack of a microphone, as he pronounced, "Not to embarrass him, but I want to let everyone know that a new member of our noble society joins us today: Mr Shields, a young man from Essex, England. He's a retail worker, senior school graduate, and utterly charming. I'm sure he'll make a great addition to our community. Won't you give us a wave, Joseph?"

"Thanks," Joseph greeted, forcing his lips into an upwards curve. "Hi all. Be patient with me while I get settled into . . . uh . . . Hyleberia. I definitely don't think I deserve . . . uh . . . special treatment."

Peter stated, "We hope you feel at home soon enough, Joseph. It's great to see a new face in the crowd." He turned back to everyone else. "Let's get on with the debate, then! First of all, let me introduce you all to the moderator, our one and only, Ms . . ." And then, from the Pnyx proscenium, holding notes in her hands, came out, " . . . Maryam Sadeghi!"

"Greetings, all," Ms Sadeghi said mincingly, stepping into view with a staid smile. She had changed into a pantsuit, and wore a sophisticated sautoir necklace and charm bracelets.

The first round of applause was deafening. Ms Sadeghi proceeded to stand at the lectern between Peter and Colin, her lips turning parallel. The debate commenced, with the crowd rapt in silence.

"My first question is to Peter," stated Ms Sadeghi stiffly. "Tellurians have long expressed displeasure with the needless suffering of man and woman alike on account of disease. Complaints have been raised especially as to the necessity of diseases that seriously inhibit the life quality of innocent children, including the common cold, chickenpox, and many more. My question, then, is what is the divine justification for these? Would it not be advisable and possible to limit such harmful conditions to those more used to suffering, such as those closer to death, the elderly or the otherwise disabled?"

Joseph frowned. *What the hell does that mean?*

Peter stepped forward with a composed, unworried look on his face. "Firstly, thank you so much Ms Sadeghi for hosting the debate, and may I say your eyes look as arresting as the rings of Jupiter tonight," he said, Ms Sadeghi's cheeks turning an angry red. "Now, let me be clear, I hate to hear such complaints about the world because they are based solely on a misunderstanding of the purpose of divine law. My role as Peter is not to provide worldwide happiness, but to lead the government of Hyleberia and ensure the continuance of life itself. There is no feasible way to prohibit one type of suffering and preserve another without eradicating the very concept. If I were to impose rules that ban disease, the world would become, bluntly put, dull. The sense of adventure would vanish because Tellurians could easily live indefinitely. Without pain, as I always say, there is no life!"

At once, applause like a bomb going off spread among the crowd, along with many cheers and whistles. Thaddeus was clapping as well, and Joseph felt carried along with the excitement, although he was not sure if he was following Peter's logic. But surely, he had misunderstood.

"Colin, your response?" said Ms Sadeghi, tapping her question cards to her chest tensely.

"Uh, I have several responses, Ms Sadeghi," Colin slurred like he had drunk too much, as he scratched his armpit in a chimp-like manner, ogling the sky. A painfully slow 30 seconds passed before his next words came. "Uh, uh, uh . . . if not adults, why can't we have lives without babies getting, y'know, diseases et cetera? I mean, it'd be possible. Why can't you just, uh, do it? And, uh, another thing I would improve about babies is the amount of arms. Why can't they have more than two? Kinda like Doctor Octopus. That'd be fun. Didn't the, uh, Prince of Darkness support that?"

Joseph facepalmed. *The first opposition is not exactly making a strong case. I wonder if I ought to say something. Dad died of cancer. Does Peter think that was right? And what did that that guy say about the Prince of Darkness?*

Colin didn't last long. By the end of the hour, five debaters had tried to prove the immorality of disease, and all woefully failed. Still, Joseph remained entirely unconvinced.

Peter looked satisfied after being declared the winner by Ms Sadeghi, rubbing his hands together and clicking his tongue in his cheeks. Increasingly frustrated, Joseph had found the courage to put his hand up to volunteer himself, but he wasn't picked. He had found the debate very bizarre, and the time had crawled by.

Over an enthusiastic applause, Peter concluded, "So, I suppose I have won again! Thanks so much for attending, everyone! It is natural for me to be the wisest and the most intelligent, but some of you had some interesting points, nonetheless. And I do think it's paramount for me to hear your ideas and arguments in these debates, as it helps inform my Prime Ministerial decision making."

The crowd continued clapping, and cheers resounded loudly as they gave him a standing ovation.

"Thank you, thank you. I don't deserve it. By the way, I do have another announcement," Peter remarked, gesturing to the crowd to sit down. They slowly quieted. "Indeed, I need to speak about this matter before we close. Recently, the moon's perigee has been reducing at a rate that only happens about once every three or four decades. When it gets to 221,524 miles, which will be rather soon, we're due a lunar eclipse, and this has interesting cosmological implications. Most of you will know, but every time one of these occurs, the world goes through a *Pralaya,* a death and rebirth. This sounds dramatic, but remember that the only visible consequence will be the eclipse itself. My point is that in a few weeks I will depart on a short retreat for Recalibration. So, if you have anything urgent to tell me, book an appointment ASAP. And that's all. I hope you enjoyed the night!"

Joseph had little idea what this *Pralaya* thing meant, and was too tired to care. The crowd's thunderous, posturing applause made it hard to think, everyone getting to their feet for a second ovation. And that was still not enough. Somehow, the third standing ovation lasted for ten tedious minutes.

Fighting to keep his eyes open after a tired yawn, Joseph turned to Thaddeus. "I'm beat. I mean, I did just die. Shall we go?"

"Sure," Thaddeus said in mid-clap, and they both sidled out of the seating and away from the Pnyx.

Now that night had come, Hyleberia fell still. It was remarkably peaceful. But Joseph's headache and tiredness impinged on his enjoyment of the nocturnal atmosphere. Thaddeus and Joseph ambled home under the radiant glow of street lamps.

"Didn't you enjoy the debate?" Thaddeus questioned, perhaps sensing unease.

He was silent for a few seconds. "You call that a debate? Seemed more like a bloody joke to me," Joseph said pointedly.

Thaddeus stared at him and Joseph gulped. Teachers in Birchwood Senior School had always said that he had a tongue on him. It looked like that bad habit had not died when he'd died.

"Joking, joking. That's good ol' British sarcasm—people

can never tell," he said at once, as they passed by the Thermae they had visited earlier.

Thaddeus laughed in response. "You got me. I knew you must have liked it. Everyone, and I mean *everyone*, loves the debates. They take place every Saturday."

Change the subject, change the subject, change the subject. "Incidentally, do you know anything about the, er—Prince of Darkness? Could you tell me about him, maybe . . .?"

"Why do you want to know?" Thaddeus asked, furrowing his brow.

No clue. Joseph shrugged. "I heard about him this morning —curiosity is burning. Well, I mean, I just saw his name somewhere and then Colin mentioned him during the debate. Probably it's just graffiti, but I'd like to know if . . . uh . . . I dunno."

He didn't fully understand why the Prince of Darkness came to his mind just then. It was one of the infinite things in Hyleberia he wanted to know about. Most likely, as Peter had suggested, it was just the creation of someone graffiting on the elevator.

With a concerned frown, Thaddeus said, "I don't know if I should say anything now. You'll have to ask Ms Sadeghi. We learn about this in Shrivatsa, strictly according to the organisation of the syllabus."

"Why shouldn't you say?" Joseph asked, voice drawling from fatigue. "Come on, I wanna know."

Thaddeus' hackles seemed to rise as he processed this comment. He interlocked his fingers. After a pause, he gave in, "Okay, fine, I'll tell you. You'd learn eventually."

"Tell me what?"

Thaddeus swallowed. "This might come as a shock. Nowadays, most Hyleberians don't talk about him much because it's ancient, forgotten history. In fact, the real name of the Prince, as he is now called, has been banned from almost all records. But millennia ago, the structure of Hyleberia was quite different. In fact, Peter didn't keep all his power to himself, as he does now as the sole Prime Minister. Hyleberia and the world were divided between Peter and the Prince, in a joint constitution as co-Prime Ministers. This government didn't work out too great for anyone, not at all. The Prince became hungry for power and the Divine War broke out."

Astonished, Joseph asked, "The Divine War? What the hell happened?"

Thaddeus' eye was twitching a lot. "It was the only war, and we call it The Great Schism. Anyway, long story short, Peter won and the Prince was exiled. And that's about it."

"*About it?*" he gasped, mouth agape. So it was true . . . the Prince was real. But what did this mean, and why had Peter been so averse to talking about him?

"Pretty much, J-man," Thaddeus asserted. "But do not mistake what I have said. The Prince of Darkness is never, ever coming back. His government has been completely purged from the world for millennia and millennia. Nowadays, the biggest thing we have to worry about is taxes. The Prime Minister, or as we call him Peter, is the single divine authority."

Divine authority? Joseph swallowed, rubbing his eyes that had developed bags by this point. The author of that graffiti on the elevator would certainly have him believe otherwise about the Prince. "Well, I've never met him. Maybe the Prince of Darkness is misunderstood," he said.

"Aha, trust me, the most evil man to ever exist is certainly not *misunderstood*. It is said that a truthful word has never come out of the Prince's mouth. Some people say he can lie even in his sleep. But that's enough for now," Thaddeus asserted, left eye spasming as he scratched his scar and looked at the pavement. He sped up his pace, and Joseph had to hurry to keep up.

"Hmm, if you say so," Joseph muttered, still extremely

curious for more details. "I don't think I'll be able to sleep much after all this."

As Thaddeus guided him back to Miyagi Apartments, Joseph could not help thinking about the War. . . . How had Peter won in the first place? What exactly had incited the conflict? He was going to get to the bottom of this.

Traipsing home, their conversation came to a pause, and Joseph managed to lose himself in awe of the constellations, sparkling above. Joseph could not remember seeing the stars so clearly in Essex, likely due to light pollution. He had always been such a complete nobody back home, absolutely nothing special about him whatsoever, no job and no goal for his life. But now the issue of university fees had been solved, and his debts forgotten, so in Hyleberia Academy he had a blank slate to make something of himself that would have been impossible before.

Joseph decided there and then, he would prove Thomas wrong about him. He would become a somebody. He would make a life here as a Hyleberian, however strange it seemed.

WEEEEWOOOWWWOOOEEEEWWW.

Interrupting Joseph's train of thought, a very loud noise erupted out of nowhere. Sirens. Several of them had abruptly emerged from the ground. It took him seconds to react, as the floor trembled with the huge, shrieking sound. A few passersby in the vicinity looked shocked and started running away. Joseph wondered whether it was an earthquake alarm or something.

Thaddeus leaned over, his voice suddenly alarmed. "Get back to your apartment at once," he hissed to Joseph, looking flushed. "You remember the way?"

"Uh, I think so," Joseph said, gazing around as several frightened people appeared from the Pnyx and sprinted by. "What do the alarms mean?"

"I couldn't say," Thaddeus said, visibly disturbed. "I have to check what this is all about. You'll be OK, then?"

Joseph felt his palms sweat. "Probably."

"Good. See you later," said Thaddeus, and he dashed off.

In the distance, as Joseph watched Thaddeus disappear behind a wall, he spotted Descartes tripping over and slamming his face on the ground. Joseph gasped, but it appeared Descartes was not hurt, as moments later the French thinker got up and ran to a sideroad, long brown hair trailing behind him.

Heart racing, Joseph quickly continued down the street, feeling a bit lost. The sidewalks were either emptying or already deserted, all the Hyleberians fleeing and some even screaming. Plant pots smashed, food stalls turned over; the ruckus was causing more damage than whatever the supposed threat was. The sirens kept on blaring as Joseph spotted Miyagi Apartments faintly on the horizon. He hastened his stride and soon came to the pavilion, noticing people were gazing out at him from the windows, possibly thinking him stupid for still being outside.

Just as he was about to enter the front door to the apartment lobby, a familiar fishy scent and babbling voice approached.

"Flee the cone! The cursed cone! Kill the golden cone," Nigel repeated with a frazzled and angsty tone, his eyes bulging over his acne-ridden skin. It seemed he didn't know what was going on and was scared about the noise.

Looking at him, it occurred to Joseph that Nigel didn't have anywhere to go for cover. What if a bomb was about to go off? Joseph had no idea if the threat the sirens indicated had just started or was about to end.

Suddenly, a look of clarity came upon Nigel's face. "They made me like this! Don't believe them. Any of them. I'm the sane one," he yelled.

"What?" Joseph asked, astonished.

But then Nigel resumed his ramblings. "Hippo of misfortune, daughter of hyle, inkling of Sabbat. The cone!"

He gulped, replaying the words over in his mind. Exactly what was Nigel trying to say about a cone?

"Nigel, do you want to come inside Miyagi Apartments?" Joseph, out of breath, hissed through the icy dark. "It seems we're supposed to return to our homes."

"Kill the cone, the golden calf of misfortune, of loves, of lies," Nigel rambled on incoherently.

"I can't tell what you just said, but I'm going inside. Feel free to follow me," he mumbled, deciding to get the hell out of there.

As Joseph hurried in and up the staircase, he heard footsteps behind him and turned around to see that Nigel was coming hesitantly into the lobby. Joseph was not sure if Raymond would appreciate this impromptu invitation. So, he decided to leave Nigel downstairs and let him choose to follow him or not. He could always go check on him, and he was safer inside the complex, either way.

Joseph was annoyed, but not particularly surprised, to see new puddles sloshing along the floor of their apartment after he unlocked the door. He hurried towards the living room to find Raymond.

"Hey. Do you know what's going on?" Joseph asked, glad to see Raymond was safe on the sofa, even if they didn't get on so far.

"Nothing good," Raymond answered, his N64 Controller lying on the carpet. "I had to run back from the night's Tennis Club match when it started. It was havoc out there; everyone looked terrified."

"Yeah, and I just came from the debate. So, what do the sirens mean?"

Raymond twisted his lip in recollection. "No clue. People are freaking out, it seems, because the sirens are associated with . . . the War. They used to go off when the Prince of Darkness was making an attack on Hyleberia, millennia ago. The town is in quite a state of alarm." Then, Raymond paused, and his eyes drifted towards the visualiser screen. "Wait, look!"

He read aloud the teletext being displayed over the newscaster: "EMERGENCY BROADCAST FROM PARLIAMENT TO BEGIN IN FIVE MINUTES."

"Peter's making a broadcast, I guess," Joseph observed, startled.

"Yeah. The news guy doesn't know anything; I watched him stammering. An emergency speech from Peter has only happened once or twice since my arrival in Hyleberia, and they were always announced a few hours in advance," Raymond said breathlessly, as he strode over to the fridge and pulled out a couple of Haomas, the sirens still whining like an injured hound outside. He threw Joseph a cold one. "Haoma? Seems like your first day isn't going to be restful."

"God, yes," Joseph said, as he caught the beer.

Raymond and Joseph sat back down on the sofa, both cracking their Haomas open. The sirens had stopped sounding as much now, he realised. In fact, for a few seconds, he thought they had ceased completely, before . . .

WEEEEWOOOWWWOOOEEEEWWW.

The "visualiser" screen soon faded to an image of an empty office. Before long, Peter stepped to the front of the image, looking in a much less good mood than at the debate. He had an earnest expression, as he stared directly into the camera for a few seconds before soberly pronouncing:

"Greetings, sons and daughters of Hyleberia. This evening was supposed to be another beautiful one on our blessed island, indeed, a time for relaxation, socialisation and prayer before the busy week ahead. Unfortunately, that is clearly not how things have transpired. I am afraid I have to announce some disturbing news—minutes ago, confirmation came in that the evidence of corruption is undeniable."

Joseph's jaw dropped, and he was surprised to see that Raymond looked just as confused.

"Raymond, what does he mean by *corruption*?" he asked.

His roommate shouted curtly, "Shut up, Shields! He's about to say something."

"On account of the imperative to make sure nobody gets contaminated by the corruption, we'll need time to locate the source and cleanse it completely from the island. The Divine Council and I have decided that we must announce some restrictions over the next few days. First, from this message onwards, a Hyleberia-wide quarantine is to be put into place."

"We're sodding quarantined? What tripe!" Raymond cursed. "I've not been quarantined since the Spanish Flu, before I died. I was supposed to go to the Discus Club *and* Film Club tomorrow. Oh, and those were my last cans of Haoma—just my goddam luck! I could kill—"

He continued swearing, concluding the only positive was missing work.

But Joseph had good reasons to be annoyed, too. He wondered whether this meant his start at the Hyleberian Academy on Monday was going to be delayed, still trying to work out what exactly Peter meant by corruption. It seemed he was not using the term in the normal sense.

Peter went on about further restrictions, before he wrapped up his speech.

"Please take care, everyone, and of course, report any oddities or suspicious behaviour to the police. Additionally, the colt of Hyleberia must immediately report to the police station for questioning. This is an order. The authorities have already been dispatched to escort you," he stated.

Joseph's heart stopped. *But wait a minute. There's only one colt, isn't there?*

Seconds later, as if the authorities had been outside waiting for this very moment, there was a thump on the door and someone shouted, "POLICE. LET US IN, NOW. WE ARE NOT AFRAID TO USE FORCE!"

Joseph's blood ran cold. It seemed as if Southend had never been further away. In a few moments, he was put in handcuffs and escorted through the night to the local police station. Cuffs chafing against his wrists, Joseph cursed under his breath those damn toaster pedlars.

CHAPTER 4
THE ACADEMY

Hyleberia Police Station's holding cell was by far the worst place Joseph had been so far on this absurd island. There was a foul stink of urine that refused to go away, and a puddle in the corner that looked like faecal matter mixed with vomit. A rusty toilet was fixed on the wall in the corner, but Joseph had only used it briefly, as the mosquitos buzzing around the seat were not particularly inviting. Overall, it was no Ritz, and certainly not worthy of a divine world government.

Sighing, he rolled over on the holding cell bed, angling his back against the lopsided mattress in what must have been his tenth attempt to get comfortable. Joseph started to wonder if his attempt to make a life for himself in Hyleberia was going to end before he got his feet on the ground. He had not even started at school yet, and he had already been arrested, much like he surely would have been if he had not died. It had been two long nights of trying and failing to achieve anything resembling sleep.

Joseph had been kept in prison for all of Sunday too, it being Monday morning now. He was starving, having only been offered a small bowl of soup and bottled water. To make matters worse, a broken spring would not stop pushing into his spine. With a moan, Joseph leaned up, eyeing the aperture, a barred window through which the early morning light began to seep faintly through. It seemed to feed into the parking lot of a doughnut shop, judging from the fresh smell of sugar and what he could make out outside.

"Hello, is anyone there?" Joseph called in the direction of the bars, standing up and breaking the silence. "Sergeant Rufius? Can we talk for a moment?"

There was no reply for a few seconds, and then slowly the clack of heels against the laminate flooring began. Joseph stood up and walked over to the tarnished bars, where Sergeant Walter Rufius appeared with arms crossed, scratching his poorly cut moustache. From his limited experience with him, Joseph had acquired a poor impression of the Sergeant. Out of the five officers that had come and detained him the previous night for questioning and testing, he had been the least considerate.

"Yeah, Shields?" Sergeant Rufius said, scrunching his middle-aged, slightly wrinkled cheeks as if he was sucking a mint. He wore a police uniform much like those of Earth: an open-necked black tunic, and a dark blue shirt with badges and epaulettes. Rufius had a Texan, or at least a southern American accent.

"Can I speak to Peter?" Joseph asked, vowels prolonged due to lack of sleep. It still sounded stupid to speak of Peter like one were referring to a neighbour or regular fellow. "I really think this treatment must be some violation of Hyleberian rights. I have been kept here against my will, in this horrible holding cell that seems like it was last cleaned centuries ago."

Sergeant Rufius scoffed, a very supercilious look in his eyes. From his limited experience with Rufius, Joseph had acquired a poor impression of the Sergeant.

"I'm afraid, colt, there's nothin' I can do. You really think that Peter wouldn't already have come to speak to you if he wanted to?" he grumbled, crossing his arms. "I'm sure he's evaluatin' your case carefully at the moment with the Cabinet of Administrators and the Divine Council. The holdin' cell needs an update, maybe, but we don't exactly get a lot of opportunities to use it. This is the first time we've had a corruption for years."

"The Cabinet of Administrators? Divine Council?" Joseph repeated in confusion.

"Don't try my patience. If you don't like this island, you're free to return to Samsara. That's the cycle of life and death, if you hadn't heard. But I wouldn't fancy your chances in reincarnation if you get on karma's nerves. The last exile we got here stabbed a man and went back as a dung beetle, if rumours are to be believed," Sergeant Rufius groaned, leaving.

Alone again but even more fed up, he stomped over to the small barred aperture, standing up on his tiptoes and turning his neck so that he could get a little morning sunshine on his face. Joseph could see a park out there and even a few people walking by in the distance. If anyone noticed him and walked over, he could theoretically have a conversation with them. . .

.

Four boring hours passed before Joseph heard any news. He occupied himself by recalling all the faces he would never see anymore, now that he was dead. Suddenly, muffled voices became audible through the cement walls.

"So, is he holding up all right?" echoed the dampened, warm tone of a woman from the hall, as she spoke to Sergeant Rufius. "Joseph must think we are treating him like a thug."

"He's fine, Ms Sadeghi. Do you want me to get him?" Sergeant Rufius asked.

"Please do, at once," Ms Sadeghi affirmed, her words reverberating. "Now that they have found the corruption proper, I feel I have to apologise. He has every right to be angry."

Perhaps Joseph would have felt relief to be getting out if he were not so fatigued and annoyed. He refrained from smiling or frowning at Sergeant Rufius as he returned and let him out. For now, he resolved, he would do what Brits did best—complain without complaining. But the fact was he had never been good at this, and his true feelings tended to slip out.

"Joseph, how are you holding up?" Ms Sadeghi asked, silver hair curling as he came face to face with her beside the front desk. A glance at a clock on the wall revealed that it was approaching 7:30 am.

"Bit tired—didn't get a wink," he commented with a sarcastic undertone. He shot Sergeant Rufius a bitter look with bloodshot eyes. "I've been arrested, given no explanation why, and kept in a tomb of a holding cell for two nights. But that's death, I guess."

"Ah, now come on, what an exaggeration," Sergeant Rufius remarked, hand loosely resting on the pistol in his holster. "We've been treatin' you just fine. Gave you food and water and everything."

"Not really," Joseph said, scowling at him. He hadn't meant to be quite so rude, but every word he had said was completely true. *So much for complaining without complaining.*

As Sergeant Rufius handed him back his things, he told him that he was free to go. Joseph remembered that his first lessons were supposed to begin in a half-hour. He hadn't showered, eaten or brushed his teeth.

Ms Sadeghi was extremely apologetic. "Peter told me to say sorry on his behalf, Joseph. He promised it won't happen again. I'll tell you all about the corruption in a minute. Let's get you a doughnut or something, to cheer you up after that ordeal before your first classes. Nice day, Sergeant Rufius," she said, nodding goodbye to him.

Joseph followed, and despite his tiredness, felt a surge of gratitude to feel the fresh air on his face once again.

It couldn't have been a more beautiful Monday, the sky a radiant hydrangea blue. Hyleberia was chock-a-block. The Police Station that Joseph had been locked in was a two-story burnt clay brick building, tucked into an alley behind *Taste of Heaven Doughnuts*. The quarantine was obviously over, but did this mean the corruption had been found, and if so, who or what was it?

"First of all," Ms Sadeghi said. "Peter wants to assure you that he never thought you had anything to do with the corruption. However, given your recent arrival, the Divine Council insisted that you be arrested and tested. Thankfully, your tests came up negative. Unfortunately, he was too busy to come himself."

"Don't worry at all," Joseph replied, finding himself in a strangely forgiving mood, at least to Peter. "I would just consider some changes to the holding cell, and the staff. Anyway, why did they think it was related to me? And what even is a corruption?"

"That is something you'll learn in detail in class," Ms Sadeghi said and puckered her lip, eyes wavering over Joseph. "In short, the world as you know it is ruled by divine laws, which are kept in the Library of Divine Laws. Things or people that infringe these laws are what we formally call corruptions."

"So, er, if I'm not involved after all, what *was* the corruption?" he asked, as they ambled unhurriedly inside of Taste of Heaven Doughnuts.

"I think it was just a bureaucratic error of sorts," Ms Sadeghi said, but did not finish her answer until after she had bought Joseph a sugar-coated, caramelised doughnut. "The exact law that was broken and why, though, is not something that you should concern yourself with. In fact, I don't even know myself."

She's not telling the whole story. Joseph reflected it over some more, as they walked along and he tucked into his doughnut. *I arrive and one day later Hyleberia is in meltdown?* It didn't seem to him that one needed to be Sherlock Holmes, or more relevantly Descartes, to work out that there might be a connection there. But for the moment, he didn't protest.

Ms Sadeghi raised her hand as if beckoning forth a fresh topic. "Forgetting all of that, let's get you to your first day of classes. I'm sure you're eager to get started. I thought I would show you the outside of Hyleberia Parliament on the way."

Joseph nodded. "Sounds good. The only issue is I haven't washed."

At this point, Joseph realised his headache had returned, along with a general sense of dizziness and nausea.

"Oh, no problem. Body odour is a modern invention," Ms Sadeghi affirmed, leading him onwards.

Parliament was impressive in more ways than one. The sinuous eaves of the roof were mounted by ceramic chariots drawn by lifelike horses, and patterned with copper palmettes. A fountain with little cupids riding dolphins was sitting in the gardens leading up to the front doors.

Ms Sadeghi certainly had a way of speaking that entranced her listener, and he felt it would be rude to inter-rupt as she started to lecture about the history of Hyleberia. She revealed Parliament had been built in 340 A. D., and so it was the oldest building in Hyleberia still standing. Even crazier, it had apparently been designed by Vitruvius himself, a famous Tellurian architect.

"Could you explain the whole point of a Parliament in Hyleberia if Peter is the, uh, head honcho?" Joseph asked, as Ms Sadeghi led him by the Parliament marbled steps.

"Though Peter is Prime Minister and thus ultimately in charge, Parliament is the central forum for Administrators and Ministers. In these hallowed halls, all the laws of creation are debated and maintained. In addition, they broadcast Monday Question Time to ensure divine accountability. There will be one tonight, in fact," Ms Sadeghi explained. "Well, I suppose we better get to Shrivatsa if we don't want to be late. Why don't I meet you there in a few minutes?"

And so, Ms Sadeghi let Joseph wander around for a short time before school. This wasn't enough time to get anything done, yet he did manage to pop into one of Hyleberia's supermarkets, Zeus' Basket, where he put on some Ambrosia de Chanel cologne from a display and ate a tooth-paste-flavoured biscuit sample from their bakery. Subsequently, Joseph hurried into Hyleberia Academy, a bit nervous about making a decent impression. The classroom door hung open. He stepped inside to find three pupils, as well as Ms Sadeghi sitting at the front of the classroom sorting through a file of worksheets. It smelled of pencil rubbers and shredded paper.

"Joseph! Glad you made it. Welcome to your first day of class. I'm so glad the corruption was found and the lesson wasn't postponed," Ms Sadeghi greeted joyfully as if they hadn't just spoken, her hair falling like a waterfall around her neck. She must have just put on several rings and dangling earrings.

"So am I," he said, eyeing his fellow students. Their chairs faced the blackboard, but everyone's faces without exception were staring at him with slack-jawed expressions. The text-books were splayed open on their square desks, pencil cases next to them. "So, should I sit down, then? Nice to meet you guys. Sorry, I didn't even bring a pen."

"That's no problem at all. Make yourself comfortable," Ms Sadeghi told him. "It's always such a fun day when we first get a new student. Why don't you all introduce yourselves? Names, short summary of your Tellurian life, career goal, and manner of death if it doesn't reopen old wounds."

Joseph sat down and gave a short self-introduction, which felt very strange to recall in words after all that had happened. Mentioning the corruption debacle, they seemed to have already heard of his involvement and release. Out of the three students, an ageing Asian man was the first to speak when he had finished.

"Hey, why did Adam and Eve do maths every day?" the Asian man asked, grinning.

Joseph shrugged. "No clue. Tell me, please."

"They were told to be fruitful and multiply."

He burst out in laughter. "Good one."

"Anyway, sorry about my bad jokes. I'm Chen Huang," said Chen. A man in at least his early sixties, he had thick eyebrows and grooved skin like rutted dirt. He was bald and wore a red t-shirt and slim-fit trousers. "There is not much of interest to say about my Tellurian life. I was a peon in rural Guangdong Province, dirt poor. I died when some punks tried to rob my soybean harvest money. The reason it's taken me so long to pass SHOMAT is that I didn't get to go to school at all when I was a Tellurian. Now I'm studying to be an Administrator of Crops. I want to make the case for better yields and less insect pests."

"Oh, right. That's cool of you," Joseph said, scratching his chin.

"My turn! Death by smoke inhalation, you say? Ohhhh. That's, like, rough," a young woman opined, twirling the ends of her hair in her fingers. "I like your eyes. They're . . . different."

"A toaster caused it. Could be worse, I guess," he said. "No pain."

"I'm Emily Nadine," Emily revealed with a thick American accent, although not southern like Rufius. Wearing a light blue blouse, she looked like a perfectly nice teenage girl, her blonde hair hanging loosely over the back of the plastic chair. She had thick red lipstick on and high arched eyebrows. "Long story short, I was, like, a senior in Massachusetts about to graduate high school at last when a fucking balcony I was standing on at a party collapsed. It was April Fool's Day, some kind of divine practical joke on me. But it's not so bad.

Nowadays, I'm studying to be an Administrator of Food so that I will be able to, like, test candy for goddam drachma. I got it on my career profiler, and I, like, just knew it was meant for me!"

"Emily, watch your language with the colt!" Ms Sadeghi cut in at the end, baring her missing teeth.

"Oh, no worries," Joseph said, thinking Emily the most normal person he'd met so far. "And wow, sorry to hear that about your death. Nice to meet you and everything. So, did you live to see Obama become president?"

"Nah, I died with, like, Bush the second, sadly," Emily recalled. "But at least I got to leave before the recession."

Joseph nodded, a bit discomposed. *She seems to like the word like. Good thing I think I like her. She's beautiful.*

"*Hola.* I guess that leaves little ol' me. I'm Francis Rodrigo from Puebla, Mexico," said the last one, a man who was probably one or two years older than Joseph. He had an undercut hairstyle and a protruding jaw, as well as a painful-looking patch of burnt skin under his right eye. There was a snake tattoo on his wrist. "My manner of death was . . . let's just say, it's something I prefer not to talk about. Otherwise, my life was not exemplary, but it's no secret that I was a part-time crack dealer. I'm studying to become the first Hyleberian poetry and video game shop owner."

"Well, that sounds fun," Joseph said, trying to sound less exhausted than he was. "Poetry and video games: an odd combination. I like both, though. I'll have to visit your shop when you graduate."

"Not any time soon, then," he quipped. "I dropped out of Tellurian high school. But as my *abuela* used to say, *nunca es tarde para aprender*. It's never too late to learn."

"Francis has invented a whole new type of shop. Have you thought of a name for it, yet, Francis?" Emily inputted.

"Uh, nope. Maybe Rodrigos," Francis suggested, shrugging. "Although that sounds like a Mexican restaurant."

Class quickly began after the introductions. They had all been set their own classwork to do today, so Ms Sadeghi soon pulled Joseph aside so that she could give him *World 101*, this time to keep.

"You'd be wise to start studying this immediately. You'll have a comprehensive exam next year, in addition to the career profiler test in a short while," she warned him.

Ms Sadeghi seemed cognisant of Joseph's lack of third-level education, so they both acknowledged that for the SHOMAT test he would need some help.

On the cover of the SHOMAT textbook was printed an endless, tangled knot, seemingly the school's symbol. As he paged through the tome, Joseph realised his knowledge was more limited than he would have liked. His brain began to ache when he turned to the teleology chapter, and was greeted with a diagram displaying the different types of *ontos* and *teloi*: biopoietic, teleoqualic, ontopotent; and next to that pages and pages of all the different aspects of the world's manifestation: hydrophany, petrophany, aerophany, along with long lists of essences. This history chapter included a page of the timetable of the birth of the cosmos, including the date of the Big Bang and an account of world expansion. It was certainly rather strange having not long ago spoken to the author (and sort of the subject) of the textbook, Peter. As Ms Sadeghi continued informing him about the lessons he would be receiving, Joseph turned to the glossary and was confronted by even more esoteric terminology.

"The others have all already passed this?" he asked, as he glanced at them absent-mindedly. "How are you going to teach me with them in the same room, then?"

"No, the others have failed it multiple times and are retaking the test next year. Besides group sessions and tests every week, there will be a lot of self-study involved," Ms Sadeghi revealed, as she rapped her rings on the desk. "I will be spending time with everyone individually, though. We're more of a university than a school."

"Sounds different to my old school, for sure." Joseph rubbed his aching forehead. "Can we start with Hyleberian history? Maybe the Prince of Darkness? I'm really curious about him."

Perhaps due to reverse psychology, Joseph found the fact that everyone was disinclined to talk about this supposedly evil figure made him all the more interesting.

Ms Sadeghi looked slightly taken aback by his mention of the Prince of Darkness. "That wouldn't follow the syllabus, I'm afraid," she said, and flicked a few pages to the front of the teleology chapter, eyes goggling slightly out of their sockets like she was a marionette. "You will start on page one, and then slowly make your way through to the end."

"I hope I don't let you down. I had such a bad memory for historical figures and dates at school that my professor used to call me a drinker of the Lethe," Joseph stated. "Could never remember my pencil case either."

"Never fear," Ms Sadeghi affirmed. "You will get through Shrivatsa and graduate just as every Hyleberian in history has, even if it takes you decades, which is quite possible."

Francis had been listening in, and jokingly interrupted, "For me, make that centuries!"

Centuries? I hope not. Joseph paged through *World 101*, finding that Ms Sadeghi had both a motherly side and also a patronising, self-serious quality to her, which made her equally likeable and unlikeable.

Ms Sadeghi spent the whole morning with Joseph introducing him to the course, while the others busied themselves with their own work and exercises, often chatting among themselves to their teacher's chagrin. After some hours had passed, he jumped to his feet when she announced that it was time for lunch.

Joseph shuffled out of the classroom with the others, not

really knowing if he should attempt small talk. Before long, they dispersed and he was left with half an hour to do whatever he wanted in Hyleberia. Ms Sadeghi had given him his long-awaited welcome pack, yet there was still so much that he had planned to buy the day before, such as clothes, food and deodorant, that he did not know where to get started.

Disoriented, Joseph looked around the buzzing so-called Platonic Plaza. Palm and banyan trees with lush leaves were the only source of shade from the glorious weather. On the edges of the road were fancy restaurants, many of them full, and fresh smells of lunch drifted over such as chicken wings and spaghetti bolognaise. Having tried a couple of stores, most only accepted cards, while all he had was some drachma from the welcome pack. But he managed to buy a cup of delicious "salgam" juice from the local convenience store Ontomart, which had endless strange products, from chocopunch to cowboy boots and mock wings. He ambled to the club sign-up board as he sipped his tasty juice. There was an odd mix of normal and totally bizarre associations; from Synth Society to Murder Mystery Club, Hyleberia had quite the selection of things to join.

Now, Joseph just had to find some food. He looked around, thumbing his chin. While scanning the crowd, he froze suddenly, bringing him and the stream of pedestrians to a brief halt. "Wait a second," he muttered to himself.

Somewhere among the crowd, he had spotted a face he recognised. But the figure disappeared as soon as he had appeared, and Joseph realised he was seeing things.

He took a breath, flushed, reflecting on what had just happened. The truth was Joseph thought he'd seen his father. *Perhaps I'm going to be the next Nigel. They didn't even look that much alike.* Joseph contemplated how long it would take to get used to Hyleberia. He had to get it into his head: he was no longer in Essex, or even Europe, *or* even society! *I'm dead now, just like Dad. I have more in common with skeletons than anybody I used to know. And it couldn't be him, anyway. It would be too unlikely.*

As he walked past the shops, the eyes of curious passersby flitted over him, like news of his arrest had spread. Starving at this point, Joseph settled on a pizzeria called Nectar Pizza that advertised special divine toppings on a sign outside. He wandered inside. A flamenco song hummed above the murmur of the crowd, the restaurant itself rather nondescript. A server took Joseph's order of a Hawaiian slice with manna, and delivered it from the oven in about thirty seconds.

Sitting there, Joseph speculated what his family was thinking now, if they had moved on yet. Probably not, if they cared for him much, for it had only been a few days. Those at his senior school would probably be thinking about him too, that strange boy who had been too poor to go to university like them, and died tragically after his A-levels. Would Caroline, Joseph's mum find out all about his secret debts now that he was dead? Dad would be furious if he were still alive. Joseph became lost in thought, his right leg almost stimming, eating bite after bite of the pizza. The manna looked like gold dust and tasted succulent like nothing else, sweet like honey but savoury at the same time.

Diiiing.

Joseph heard the door chime as someone entered. It was the teenage girl from his class, Emily, her handbag straps slung over her shoulder. He said nothing but glanced at her curiously as she ordered a slice for herself. Then, turning around, he sensed her nonplussed, jade eyes fall on his back.

She made her way over and asked, "Can I eat here?"

"Feel free," Joseph said.

She sat down and took a languid bite out of her pepperoni slice. Joseph admired Emily's face; she had a healthy, youthful glow and was quite pretty.

"How did you find class?" she asked eventually. "Not too intimidating, I hope?"

Joseph felt anything he said would be simplistic. "Oh, very intimidating. You?"

"Not bad. Now you've arrived, for the first time since I arrived on this island I'm not the colt! If you need any help as you settle into your apartment and everything, feel free to call," Emily said.

Joseph thought back over the various miracles he had seen over the past few days. "Not sure how quickly I'll settle in. It's a bit nicer than England!" he said.

Emily laughed. "I bet. It is, like, kinda cool that we're both from modern history, isn't it?"

"Yeah, everyone else here is ancient," Joseph agreed.

As they chattered, he began to get a feel of Emily's character. She spoke with experience beyond a typical teenage girl but still somewhat youthful; Joseph supposed he was still just a teenager too, albeit barely. He was starting to get the hang of remembering that one's physical form didn't represent psychic age here.

"It will be fun to have somebody around who can understand my nineties references, for once!" Emily said, giggling. She nibbled the melted cheese off her crust. "The truth is that everybody comes from such different eras and cultures, but you soon forget that. The community is really kind and welcoming, like, mostly."

"Kind and welcoming? Not sure about that," Joseph said. "Actually, I got called a dolt on my first day."

"Oh, I'm not surprised," Emily remarked. "There are always loads of crazy stories going around about colts. People used to think I died by swordfish for some reason, and I heard one rumour about you that you were, well, a Satanist."

"A what!? Well, I feel worse than moronic so far," he lamented, finishing his pizza slice and wondering how much of a mess his hair looked right now, "but I guess I'll have centuries to become smarter."

"I flunked the SHOMAT exam on my first try, and my

second, and my third. It's really, really hard. But one day I'll pass. Ms Sadeghi is an amazing teacher; she can teach anything. She has read almost all the books in the public library, Bibliotheca, which is, like, basically the world inventory. Like every book ever written."

"Every book? That's a lot of porn," Joseph said, intrigued as a levitating man casually passed by the window. "Cool. Maybe I could get some beginner's books to help me get up to speed about everything."

"Why don't I show you it, as we go back to class? It's on the way to Shrivatsa," Emily said, and then licked the last bits of cheese from her fingers. "But we'll have to be quick."

They left the pizza place and strolled to Bibliotheca. Emily said that you could order any book from history, including from an extensive collection they maintained of supposedly lost literary works. He found his focus on her voice ebbing away as he determined what he should read first. As it turned out, Bibliotheca was not as impressive as it could have been, just a tiny office building. According to the librarian, the books were all stored in a multidimensional warehouse called the Akashic Records on a peninsula off Hyleberia. After his card was sorted out, he handed Joseph a form to fill out with his book requests. He could only take out three at a time. There was a small list of their most popular loans. On the spur of the moment, he jotted down *The History of Cardenio* by Shakespeare, the *Book of Giants* by Mani, and Homer's *Margites*, apparently all famous lost books.

"And do you have any books about the War?" Joseph questioned. *Why do I keep bringing that up?*

The librarian frowned, typing on the keyboard. "Only one or two. Most are banned, of course, as all copies were burned long ago. Or kept in the Library of Divine Laws. Only government books such as *A Hyleberia History* are allowed about that."

63

"Oh, can I add that to my loans?" Joseph asked, a bit disconcerted.

"We're going to be late for class!" Emily hissed from the doorway, her line of sight fluctuating between her watch's hands and Joseph.

Back outside, Emily and Joseph lost no time as they strode back to Hyleberia Academy, neither of them wanting to be late. The afternoon sky was strung with the contours of impressionist clouds, a slight whooshing breeze in the air sending Joseph's unwashed hair around like untrimmed weeds. It seemed that the high street had quietened down, and there was a calm ambience in the air. As a group of four on a quadricycle overtook them, Joseph said, "Things are peculiar around here, aren't they?"

Emily's crimson lipstick gleamed as she smiled. "Can't argue with you there. You ain't seen nothing yet. Just wait until you meet Alexander the Great. Yup, he's a Hyleberian. Works in accounting, I think."

"Wow. Can I say something?" Joseph said. He had been wanting to articulate some thoughts for days, and now it seemed they were finally coming out. "The debate about disease; Nigel, the homeless guy, and the fact that nobody cares to sort him out with a home and treatment; and the book banning thing—none of it makes any sense to me. Not to mention, the whole Divine War ... uh ... the Great Schism. I don't know, something smells fishy on this island. Have you ever seen *The Truman Show*?"

A pink flush was creeping slowly up her cheeks. She brushed her fringe back, hair twisting around her fingers. "If it's the Joseph Show, then they forget to let me in on the channel," Emily said and put her hand on his, concern mixed with annoyance dawning on her face. "Look, we don't have time to talk now. But it is not a good idea to be mouthing off about Hyleberia's flaws or whatever in public. Hyleberians worship Peter sometimes in a way just like a Tellurian divinity, and they don't, like, want things to change, or appreciate blasphemy."

"Is it blasphemy to criticise him? If so, call me a blasphemer. To be quite honest with you, Peter certainly does a good impression of a, well, a dictator," Joseph explained.

Brow furrowing, Emily didn't appreciate his comments. "A dictator? He's the Prime Minister of the World! If anyone heard you talking about Peter in this heathenous way, you'd get a black eye in no time. People see him as their father; they idolise him. And it is not surprising: he is the reason we're here! Look, let's talk about this in private. For now, we should both forget this pagan nonsense and get back to classes," she said.

"You should've seen how they treated me in prison," Joseph stated, a little shocked by his own words. He didn't even know why he was being so confrontational. "It seemed the government was ready to have me thrown out for nothing. I'm still not exactly sure what the corruption thing was all about. And I couldn't say yet, I mean, Peter was nice to me when we spoke, but I can't deny that he did seem a bit . . . fake."

"Yeah, well, the government was no doubt sceptical of a colt arriving right when a corruption occurred. It's quite reasonable." Emily's hair play had reached a new intensity, as she tugged on the ends like she was trying to tear them out. "Stop being so ridiculous. He's Peter, not Stalin. Maybe you were expecting this place to be some sort of heaven. If so, you're going to be sorely disappointed."

They were now standing right outside Hyleberia Academy. There was nobody much around, but Emily still looked nervous. "Would you rather I lie about what I think?" he asked.

"Maybe you're just a contrarian," Emily accused roughly, striding in front of him. "Why don't you live here for more than . . . what . . . three days before you act like you know everything? I think I'll walk ahead."

She went too quickly for him to catch up, her whole demeanour changed. Joseph followed slowly behind, deep in thought.

Overall, he was not sure if he had been right in sharing his thoughts with Emily after her admonishing remarks.

During the second period of the day's lessons, Ms Sadeghi gave him some reading to do about Duns Scotus and the meaning of the concept of a necessary being, which he was largely left to finish alone. The adjoining page concerned the relationship between *Purusha* and *Prakriti*, Hindu concepts about the difference between matter and spirit. He was going to be doing a test on the Greek Gods next week, like Poseidon and Artemis. All of this was a bit over Joseph's head, even if it sounded rather interesting. But the range of topics in the SHOMAT textbook was incredible, and a good percentage wasn't boring. Ms Sadeghi had said something earlier about how the course would "*make the ineffable effable*". Later in the day was his first group session, where they all sat in a circle and discussed Descartes' philosophy, and then went over in detail how he was entirely wrong. Then they were taught about the colours of the electromagnetic spectrum, and Ms Sadeghi let them try some special glasses which allowed them to see a strange shade not visible to the human eye without them, *ceran*.

It is scarcely an easy thing to make time fly by when studying, but that's exactly what seemed to have happened when the end of lessons arrived at 4 pm. Ms Sadeghi cleared her throat and wiped the chalkboard.

"That's all for today, everyone. First day, all right, Joseph?" she asked.

"I don't think I've ever learnt so much in a day," he said, figuring out how he was going to carry the encyclopaedic

SHOMAT textbook home. "Cheers, Ms Sagedhi. See you tomorrow."

"Yeah, *gracias* Ms Sadeghi," Francis said, making his leave. "I really think I'm getting the hang of ontology now. I just need to work on my teleology and hopefully I'll be graduating in the next few centuries."

"You'll get there, Francis!" Ms Sadeghi said supportively.

"Francis, you've got such bad self-esteem," Emily quipped. "You did miles better than me in the Pythagorean test last month."

"Meh, I got lucky," he said modestly.

Ms Sadeghi beamed, waving him off with cheery fingers. The only negative of the lesson was that Emily had been side-eyeing him for much of the second half. Joseph asked her, as they left the building, if she wanted to meet up later this week. She said sure, but seemed rather evasive, as if she was afraid of Joseph after his comments. The sky was a bluish orange, the bracing late afternoon air providing a slight chill. He hardly got a chance to talk to the other two students, Chen and Francis, as they headed home chatting.

Lessons at Hyleberia Academy were four days a week, Monday to Friday with Wednesdays off. He made the back-breaking journey home down Rhode Road, *World 101* like a dumbbell in his hands, in a pensive mood. *How quickly will I get used to this ridiculous school? Nothing like Birchwood Senior School. 30 pupils to a class there.*

When he arrived back at C52, after throwing the textbook on his bed and hearing the visualiser, he went into the living room. Raymond was sprawled on the sofa, eyes glued to the screen. Water pooled around his feet, hopefully not urine. It felt as if they had not seen each other in years.

"Whatcha up to, bud?" Joseph asked, trying to be friendly as he fetched some orange juice from the fridge. The "bud" comment was, of course, ironic. He couldn't think of anybody he viewed as less of a bud than Raymond after their introduction, at least not yet.

Turning around, he saw that Raymond's face appeared angry, and distinctly unamused.

"What am *I* doing?" he asked heatedly, as he threw a Haoma can on the floor. "You're the one who was behind bars this morning. Tell me! Are you on the limb? I won't rat you out . . . for now"

He levered his left eyebrow. *What the hell is he on about?* "On the lam? Don't be ridiculous. They let me out this morning. I'm as innocent as a lamb."

"How would I know?" Raymond hit back. "You could have given me a call. Not that I care that much, I mean, but still. You've just disappeared for two days. What am I to think?"

"Turns out, it was just an honest mistake. What are you watching?" Joseph asked. He spotted that there was an image of the inside of Parliament on the screen. "Cool. Ms Sadeghi took me there. That's where they debate all of the divine laws. Is it Question Time?"

Arms out with palms forward, Raymond explained, "They announced on HB1 that Peter is airing an exile of the corruption at 4:30 pm. I thought it was going to be you!"

Joseph rolled his eyes. "Sorry to disappoint. Bet you would have loved that, eh?"

He sat down next to Raymond and watched the live feed of the Hyleberian Parliament debating chamber. The benches were crammed with Administrators dressed in ceremonial silver robes. Peter sat on his throne at the front, wearing fancy laced, gold-inlaid velvet robes. Joseph snorted when he saw the glittering crown on Peter's head too. It was tessellated with high carat diamonds of various sizes, emitting a faint blue glow. This was the first time he had seen the Parliament in session, and he was surprised to observe that they wore such ostentatious uniforms. Gabriel was nowhere to be seen.

"Why don't people call him King Peter?" Joseph scoffed to his roommate.

He watched as Peter stepped forward from his throne and addressed the bowing Administrators. It was just like watching the emergency announcement on the night of the sirens, except that daylight streamed in through the window, and Joseph did not expect this time he was about to be arrested.

"This Sunday, my cabinet received a notice from the Office for the Detection of Corruption that they found a corruption in the fifth quadrant of Hyleberia," Peter pronounced, voice loud and stately. "This was the cause of the sirens, and I can now reveal that said cause was a certain Hyleberian who did not conform to the tenets of a newly passed law. He has now been found and is about to be exiled. I want to emphasise that the corruption has absolutely nothing to do with the long-vanquished Prince of Darkness, as some ridiculous rumours might have you believe."

"What does he mean?" Joseph asked.

"Someone contradicts the Library of Divine Laws, I guess," Raymond informed him, eyes not leaving the screen for even a millisecond. "And they've found who it is."

"How does he do it? I mean, how does Peter exile people?"

Raymond gulped. "I've never seen it. I've heard rumours, though, and. . . ."

He didn't finish.

Oh, screw this. Joseph's mind was racing, his hands restless. *This is getting too weird. Remember when my biggest concern was paying the bills and getting that new video game. . . . I miss the banality somehow.*

Hyleberia Parliament's debate chamber reminded Joseph of the House of Commons. The vast hall had a rectangular shape and felt imbued with a historical aura; the parallel benches were made of cushioned rosewood, and where the

Speaker's Chair of the U.K. Parliament would normally have stood was a golden throne. Speaking of the throne, it was by a long shot the most eye-catching element of the chamber. The chair back was studded with gemstones—sapphire, ruby and amethyst; the armrests were sculpted with shapes, while the legs were plated with dark obsidian. Slack-jawed, Joseph gaped around the chamber as Peter stood intimidatingly at his throne.

"I think they're bringing out the corruption now," Raymond observed.

From the back of the chamber, two police officers with their hands around someone's arms brought out the source of corruption. Joseph and Raymond shared horrified reactions. It was apparently one of the few people they both knew in Hyleberia.

"Nigel!" shouted Raymond, who leaned forward and pointed to the slovenly figure.

"What? How is he the corruption?" Joseph asked, astonished. "What law did he break?"

His filthy beard and neglected grey coat appeared at the centre of the screen, the high-definition cameras roaming over him like a reality show. Steered by Sergeant Rufius and a woman officer, Nigel did not look upset, just utterly confused. He likely didn't even know what was going on. He was limping, and kept waving his arms up and down like he was being attacked by bees.

"I heard him outside our apartment on Saturday, the night the police arrested you. I wonder what he did wrong."

"Didn't know you knew Nigel. I was the one who let him in. I thought he was in danger," Joseph said in incredulity. "This is such rubbish. He just has some mental illness or something. And now they're going to exile him? I hope exile means sending him on holiday."

The Administrators jeered in the course of Nigel's slow trot to the front. There were about two slow minutes of constant crowd ridicule before the homeless man reached the throne of Peter, and then everyone quieted down. It was much like the heckling of the House of Commons, but louder and more cacophonous. Though his words were barely audible on the visualiser, it was clear by his mouth that Nigel was speaking gibberish like usual. Perhaps he could be argued to be speaking in tongues, but if so, Peter didn't seem to find it charming. The Prime Minister's glare towards Nigel was one of haughty disdain.

Peter faced the Administrators, a dark expression on his face, as his crown's jewels glimmered on his head. "Exile is more than warranted for any corruption, and this Nigel nitwit is no exception," he explained. "The evidence of corruption has been traced with complete certainty to him—and so—there is no chance of a mistake. As such, there is no point in delaying. Truly, he does not seem to be of sound mind, so it is clear that he is not contributing to our community anyway. Are there any objections?"

There was none. "Wretched fool!", "lover of sin", "dirty pagan" and "exile him now!" were among the many caustic jeers supplied by the crowd.

As his robes rested loosely behind him on his throne, Peter beckoned forth Nigel's attendants. "Thy kingdom come, thy will be done."

The Administrators grew quiet as the two Sergeants forced Nigel down to his knees, and brought him right up to Peter's feet, like a slave about to be whipped. Joseph could only see Nigel's bowed head, but he was sure he heard a scream of pain among the crowd noise. Meanwhile, Peter pronounced strange imprecations as he placed his hand over Nigel's scalp. In a crawling position, Nigel appeared to be writhing as his face lay horizontally on the floor.

All of a sudden, Peter, whose face had been looking very intense, formed an almost pained expression.

"Let there be light!" he screamed.

A bright jolt of sapphire blue lightning burst out of Peter's hands, aimed directly at Nigel's scalp. The homeless man's neck hung limp, face immediately lifeless. His dead body fell to the floor. There was stunned silence in Parliament, and in C52.

What all of this meant had just become clear to Joseph. The exile was not only from this island, but also from his body. So it wasn't really exile, in fact, more like an execution. It was murder.

Emily's caution from lunchtime resounded loudly in his mind, "Maybe you were expecting this place to be some sort of heaven. If so, you're going to be sorely disappointed."

And it was all because of toast.

CHAPTER 5
DIVINE REPOSITORY

On the morning of his sixth day in Hyleberia, Joseph woke up to himself drowning.

"What the hell!" he yelled, as he gasped for air, leaned up and saw the frightening sight in his bedroom. The carpet was covered with a layer of rushing water, growing ever higher.

Joseph's pulse quickened as there was a knock on his bedroom door, with Raymond's rough voice calling, "What's up? Ignoring your alarm clock?"

Sighing, Joseph got to his feet and opened the door, letting the knee-height water flood out.

Tomorrow would be the one-week anniversary of his arrival in Hyleberia. Several nights had passed since Nigel's "exile"-cution, as Joseph had taken to calling it when he thought about what had happened. He had begun developing a bit of a routine, although that is not to say every day didn't throw a billion new peculiarities at him. Naturally, it had been an overwhelming start here, and now that he had got used to the idea of a second life in Hyleberia, Joseph was finding it increasingly hard to convince himself that he belonged on this divine island. He simply wasn't the right type of person to be a Hyleberian, both in personality and qualifications.

"Do you need anti-depressants or something?" Raymond called through the door. "You seem out of sorts."

"No, I need you to leave me alone," Joseph ordered, lying back down and pulling the bed sheets over his head. But Raymond still wasn't budging. "If you want to know the truth, last night I made the mistake of visiting Melanie, my sister's Facebook page. I saw images of my own funeral. It was weird."

"So what? Is there a better reason you're being so lazy?" Raymond asked.

"That's not enough?" He groaned, wondering whether to tell Raymond about something. "Well, kinda."

"What?"

"It's just . . . when I first arrived in Hyleberia, I thought that I might be able to see my father. He died when I was young. Cancer: smoked too many cigarettes. I know that it's ridiculous, but I even mistakenly saw him in the street once," Joseph said.

"Oh, right," Raymond muttered awkwardly to the covers. "How old were you when he died?"

I don't want to think about that. I can still see the funeral clearly. It all seemed to happen so quickly. He wished he hadn't brought this up, pulling the bed sheets off him. "Sixteen. Almost three years ago."

"Ah." Raymond bit his lip, looking deeply conflicted about showing empathy. "Well, I guess this is when a better friend would say something motivational."

"Don't even bother. I'll go now," Joseph said, getting up and smashing the off button on his alarm clock.

"At last! The pity party is over. Thank the holy Animah!" he rejoiced with hands in the air, and left shortly.

The holy enema? Joseph quickly threw on a flannel shirt, bootcut jeans and his moccasins. He had found some time over the past few days, although not nearly enough, to buy some new clothes. He had spent most of the drachma in his welcome pack, and it was said the rest of his money would be coming monthly through mail welfare. Joseph grabbed some bread, his keys and new wallet, as well as his blue rucksack containing his SHOMAT textbook, and rushed out the door.

Joseph had memorised the way to Hyleberia Academy by now, so he felt relatively at ease having breakfast as he walked. Shoving unbuttered flatbread into his mouth, he recalled the past week and how something had seemed *off* in Hyleberia ever since Nigel's exile. It might be morbid, but Joseph couldn't stop replaying the disturbing scene of the exile in his mind. Simply by touching him on his head, Peter had taken the life out of Nigel, and it made Joseph feel sick. Was that really all Peter thought of his citizens? Would he do that to Emily or Francis if they broke a law?

On the way, he passed a man in a suit with five arms and legs and a woman in a feathered headdress with skin that was literally sparkling like diamonds. Upon arrival at Shrivatsa, Joseph stepped by a few students who must have already passed SHOMAT, and out of curiosity found himself peeking inside their classroom door windows. It was a bit intimidating to think SHOMAT was only an introductory course; he couldn't make head nor tail of these peoples' lecture slides. Entering his class, he was surprised to find that Ms Sadeghi's perfumed aroma was absent.

"*Hola.* How's Hyleberian life, Joseph?" Francis asked as he unpacked, leaning over to him with a lowered voice so that Emily and Chen couldn't overhear. They were sitting in the corner, chatting about a proposal regarding whether or not Peter should add another planet to the solar system to replace Pluto, called Jubo.

Joseph knew it was rude to stare at Francis' skin, but he couldn't help himself. It looked like somebody had thrown scalding water at him, burning an entire part of his face.

"Seventh heaven," he replied, unpacking *World 101.* "No complaints at all."

Francis snorted, scratching the snake tattoo on his wrist. "You can be honest with me. When I first started, swear to Peter, I was convinced for the first two weeks this was an LSD trip. It took me ages to fully realise it was not some vivid hallucination."

"It's pretty weird, yeah. I've spent four days rereading the first chapter of this thing," Joseph said, tapping the textbook. "The teleonomics—whatever that means—section especially just doesn't stick."

Francis, who was wearing a polka dot shirt and a slap bracelet, fingered his chin. "If you're struggling, imagine how I felt. I was a high school dropout, wouldn't touch a book with a ten-foot pole. Guess how many times I've taken the SHOMAT exam, and, *mierda*, I still haven't passed."

Joseph chuckled. "It's not looking good for me, then. I had to retake my A-levels, English secondary school exams. By the way, I also speak Spanish. I mean, sort of. I never practice it so I've probably forgotten it all, but my dad is from Spain."

"*Guay*! I barely knew English when I first arrived here. Thank the Animah Ms Sadeghi is a polyglot and speaks every language in the world, or I would've been in trouble," Francis said cheerily. "Now I'm a regular anglophone."

At that very moment, Ms Sadeghi arrived. Smiling knowingly, she stood in the hallway, dressed in an odd combination of a tartan pleated skirt and gleaming green high heels.

"Good news, everyone," Ms Sadeghi told them enthusiastically. "I've arranged a special field trip to the Hyleberian Divine Repository." She turned to Joseph. "This is a museum of artefacts from Tellurian history and myth. It's a tradition that all colts visit within their first month here. I've just spoken with the Director, and she's agreed to clear it for an hour, so that we can have it all to ourselves. We're going to head there right now!"

Unsure whether this was a good omen, Joseph followed Ms Sadeghi and the others to the Divine Repository. He remembered its direction from his tour with Thaddeus. Speaking of whom, he realised he hadn't heard from Thaddeus since his first day in Hyleberia, but perhaps he was busy with his Controller work, choosing which Tellurians deserved rain clouds and who merited to fall down in ditches. . . .

Entering the Formica-topped glass doors, Joseph had a feeling this was going to be one of the most absurd hours of his second life. As might be expected from a Divine Repository, the plethora of impressive relics to see was extensive. Though it somehow managed to fit in the middle of town, the Divine Repository's ceiling scaled at least twenty feet above their heads, the walls decorated with impressive paintings of religious scenes.

The quintet's muffled steps over the applewood floors echoed as they entered the first exhibit. Each of the rooms was designated for artefacts and information about a specific genre of myth. So, the first room, Ancient Greece, was outfitted with priceless ancient Greek mythology-related objects, such as Hercules' sword. As Joseph admired the impressive sword, Emily stepped forward from out of nowhere and nudged him with her elbow.

"Pretty cool, huh?" she whispered from behind his shoulder. Her hair had been tied up neatly, lips smudged with rosy lipstick.

He shook his head, smiling slyly. "I've seen better."

She laughed, a teenage girl's giggle despite her real age. "I doubt that."

"So, this is supposed to be Hercules' real sword, huh? I thought he was just a myth?" he asked.

"Apparently, all the Greek myths are rooted in truth," Emily revealed nonchalantly. "Of course, Hercules would have returned to Samsara. Who knows what or who he is now."

Joseph nodded, a bit stunned. "I just hope all the monsters aren't real too."

With her jade pupils on Ms Sadeghi across the room, who was admiring Jason's golden fleece with Chen, Emily lowered her voice and leaned in to Joseph. "Look, the truth is, ever since the exile of that crazy man aired on Monday, I've been thinking about what you said, and. . . ."

"Yeah?" Joseph gulped, meeting Emily's dilated eyes. "And?"

He noticed she had a few tiny freckles on her nose that were especially visible in the museum's bright lighting. "Can we meet after class to talk about it? Somewhere private?" she asked cautiously.

"Of course," Joseph muttered, wondering what exactly she found problematic with the exile. Besides a few off-hand comments he'd overheard only accidentally, he had yet to hear anybody talk about the disturbing quality of Nigel's exile.

"No worries. How about on the beach at 4:15 pm?" Emily said.

"Sounds good," he affirmed. "Right after class?"

"Yup," she said, before absent-mindedly meandering away to have a chat with Francis.

Hmmm. What could be so secret that she needs to talk about it alone? Joseph kneaded his fingers, lost in thought as he walked over to have a look at Achilles' cradle.

Though he easily could have spent the full hour in just the Greek room of the Repository, Ms Sadeghi soon took them straight to a Zoroastrian area, apparently an ancient Persian religion. Upon setting foot in this exhibit, she waved Joseph over to come to look at an Achaemenid statue of a Faravahar. Given her Persian heritage, it seemed that Ms Sadeghi was keen to explain its origin.

"Have a look at this rare artefact, Joseph," Ms Sadeghi exclaimed. "This is a famous Zoroastrian symbol. You see, Peter is impartial towards all mythographic expressions of our government. In composing the SHOMAT syllabus, he collated the most cogent concepts of the myths, science and philosophies of the world into one work."

A bit confused, Joseph said, "Oh right. Why isn't there a section of the Divine Repository dedicated to the real, uh, Peter, and, uh, the Prince of Darkness?"

"There is! But the Prince of Darkness isn't part of it, of course. Peter would never permit any public display, even a historical one, about him," Ms Sadeghi informed Joseph, eyeing her watch. "Now, we'd better get a move on. We only have half an hour left till the public is allowed in."

There were some exhibits dedicated to faiths that Joseph had barely heard of during his Tellurian life, such as the Yoruba religion and Manichaeism. The Buddhism room had a rather disturbing Sokushinbutsu, a terrifying mummy of a monk called Maitreya that made Joseph jump when he first saw it. Another interesting room was the one devoted to Jainism, which had a series of impressive sculptures depicting Tirthankaras, or spiritual teachers of the Dharma. The most interesting things he saw were probably a golden plate said to be made by King Midas himself, and a rare Viking runestone. There was also a section on all of the Greek and Norse Gods. Joseph had got quite good at remembering the Greek deities by now, since he had to learn them for a test.

He was most eager to see the display about the true nature of Parliament, because he had yet to fully understand this. Instead of the name of a genre of myth titling the gallery, this exhibit of the Divine Repository was called "Peteric Hall". It was fronted by a painted portrait of Peter himself in his usual suit, with Gabriel on his shoulder, and a sign that pointed to "Peter's Divine Manifesto".

Joseph looked interestedly around and walked to the sides, where he noticed a display case with a strange golden object inside, and an obsidian plinth on top that read:

Before the world, the Animah existed completely apart from form. Although it was eternally content and perfect in its glory, it craved to give manifestation to the wonders of its powers, so it created space and time. Herewith the world was sublime beyond words, and thus the Animah thought it appropriate to create an audience for the world it had created. To wit, it created Earth, the planets and our Prime Minister, Peter.

"Why isn't the Prince of Darkness mentioned in this?" Joseph asked the person who was nearest, who happened to be Francis.

"I've seen this before. He is. Read the footnote," Francis advised, staring at his phone where he was playing Tetris, perhaps the least interested of the four students.

Joseph lowered his gaze to the bottom of the plinth, which in minuscule writing ran:

> This cosmogony, or account of the world's origins, has been abbreviated to exclude the role of the vanquished Prince of Darkness, although more about him can be found in *A Hyleberia History*.

"That sucks," Joseph remarked under his breath.

"The Prince is a controversial subject. You know what that is? I love this damn thing," asked Francis, chuckling. He had crept around Joseph's back, his eyes scanning an object under the same placard.

Joseph didn't know why, but lately, he preferred talking with Francis than most of his other classmates.

He followed Francis' eyeline. "Nope."

His friend was pointing over at the display behind the text. Joseph squinted at the mysterious item that the museum label hung over. It was a golden prism, a cone, but the text that Joseph had just read didn't seem to have anything to do with it.

"I learnt about this in Shrivatsa years ago. It's called the Golden Cone," Francis explained. "It's the device that was used to model the world, supposedly, and the most priceless item in all of Hyleberia, and the world."

Looking up at the walls, Joseph noticed a security camera pointing in their direction, as well as a turret next to it.

Haven't I heard about this from somewhere? Oh yeah, didn't Nigel used to say something about this? And somewhere else too.

"That's nuts," he exclaimed, staring at the cone. "It's like something from *Star Wars*."

"Totally. Apparently, it's the first thing created in space and time," Francis revealed, "sort of, to test the waters of divine creation, before the Animah created the world and everything else. They say the owner of it acquires divine powers. When you look into the night sky, you can sometimes see the traces of the cone, which Tellurians call background radiation."

The golden cone glimmered like the birth of a new dawn. It sat on a piece of tufted red velvet, but there was nothing about the object which revealed its supposedly divine qualities besides its generally enigmatic design.

"Weird," Joseph said, impressed.

"Yeah," Francis laughed. "Looks kind of like a vibrator, doesn't it?"

Joseph squinted at the cone. "A little."

At this point, Chen approached and joined them in examining the cone. "A fellow peasant in China during a drought season once told me cones are the future. I wasn't convinced, but he did have a point," he quipped, apparently a joke.

As interesting as the golden cone was, they soon moved on, with Joseph particularly enjoying the Sumerian and Scientology exhibits. But there was an exhibit for every type of myth, so far too much for a single visit. As they reached the last chambers of the Divine Repository, the Jewish, Islamic and Christian ones, his upcoming conversation with Emily remained at the forefront of his mind. Unfortunately, there appeared to be no souvenir shop when they came to the end, and Ms Sadeghi announced it was time to head back.

When they all got back to classes, Joseph was given a task on the history of the birth of stars and their evolution. He breathed a sigh of relief when the clock struck 4 pm. This was the end of his first week of lessons, and while he was glad that his knowledge of teleology had improved greatly, he badly needed some time off. Still, Ms Sadeghi gave him a few difficult exercises to complete over the weekend. After he had said goodbye to the others, he lingered outside Shrivatsa's doors, waiting for Emily.

"Had a nice day?" she asked, stepping outside, signalling for him to follow her.

There were many sailboats sailing around that afternoon; they pulled peacefully in and out of the pier, leaving rippled wakes in the cobalt ocean. The seaweed-strewn sand was dotted with boot-wearing ramblers, so Emily strode over to a section of the beach too soggy for anyone else to linger. Joseph wished that he had bought better shoes—his worn-out moccasins were soiled.

"Let's hear it, then," Joseph asked, realising a moment later he'd sounded a bit rude.

Colour surfaced on Emily's face, as if she was about to reveal something highly embarrassing. "I'll just spit it out, then. I know I acted outraged when we talked about Hyleberia the other day, but I've truthfully been thinking about . . . about running away from this island. If I did, would you want to come with me?"

"What?" Joseph exclaimed. "How come? You called me 'heathenous' the other day."

"Yes, it sounds stupid but what you said . . . awoke something in me." The breeze sending her hair flying, she said cautiously, "I don't know about you, but personally, I would like to see my mother and father once again in the flesh. Maybe it would be a bit easier if I could bring a pet here like my old Rottweiler, Barney. But I'm not allowed a pet permit."

He could hardly believe his ears, even with everything he had heard the past week. "Have you brought this up with Peter or Ms Sadeghi?" Joseph asked with a crinkled nose.

"Of course, not! As if they'd react well. Peter would say it's too dangerous, too reckless. But I disagree. I never got the chance to have a final hug with my parents, my boyfriend, my dog. Instead, I was kidnapped and forced to study at Shrivatsa. You see those interdimensional boats." She pointed to one of the incoming yachts. "They could take me back to America in a few days if Peter wanted."

Joseph did not speak immediately after she had finished her sentence. He looked down at the ground, and let her words like fertiliser slowly sink in.

Only when he had fully thought it through, hands placed in his pockets, did he respond, "My problem with Hyleberia is different than yours. Deep down, you probably understand that there's a rationale, however wrong it may be, that you are not allowed to see your family. I'm more concerned with the strange way things are run around here, and in particular, the exile of Nigel."

Emily crossed her arms. "Could you elaborate?"

"He was insane, yeah, but no good reason was given for why it had to happen. Seemed like murder to me," Joseph said suspiciously. "I don't understand why prison wasn't an option."

"Well, why don't you complain to Peter or Ms Sadeghi's face, if that's what you think I should do?" Emily hissed.

"I just arrived a week ago. It's not my responsibility. And what do I know? I was a cashier."

"Excuses, excuses. If that's your response, why care at all?"

Joseph's insides churned. If someone had told him ten days ago that he'd meet Peter, begin a course written by him, and develop profane thoughts about his secret government. . . .

"Anyway, I'm afraid the answer is no," he added, pushing back his messy fringe. "I can't run away with you."

"Come on," Emily said, lip curled. "We can just sneak out at night, hijack an interdimensional boat, and be back in the real world in no time."

"I've just arrived here and still have more to figure out. Maybe in a few months I'll change my mind, but for now, I'm staying put to get to know this place. Yes, I miss my old life. But I'm learning to move on, and frankly, I was in enough trouble as a Tellurian," Joseph explained.

It was at this point that Emily's hair-pulling had become so intense several strands fell out.

"Fine! If you're, like, not going to even consider it, what's the point of even talking?" Emily snapped, voice breaking as she stormed off. "I just wish Barney was here!"

"Emily, wait!" he called weakly, but she would not turn back, and he let her go.

She was gone, and it looked from behind like she had burst into tears.

Well, that was odd. Joseph stood there and gazed thoughtfully at the interdimensional boats sailing around Hyleberia. *I feel bad for her. But I don't regret anything I said, not really.*

It was certainly a shame if Emily had taken a dislike to him; as well as being the most relatable, Joseph thought she must be the most beautiful Hyleberian he'd met so far. He began the walk back to Miyagi Apartments, glad that he had nothing else to do for the rest of the day. It had been a particularly draining one.

"Hey, hey!"

All this wool-gathering was interrupted by a tapping on his shoulder, and a familiar voice. He looked back, noticing at once the navy eyes of a Hyleberian that he hadn't seen for a week.

"How's it going, mate?" asked Thaddeus brightly, glancing at Joseph's squelching moccasins, shoes which he was tiring of himself. "I saw you on the beach with a girl, and thought that I would catch you, see what's up. You got a girl-friend already?"

"Oh, no. That was just Emily, a girl from school," he said, with an unpleasant throb in his head. "I was just wondering where you'd disappeared to."

"Sorry about that. I've been busy with Controller work. I took a trip to Spain to decide the result of several people's karma," Thaddeus revealed. He looked in good spirits, and was slightly sunburnt. "In fact, I'm fresh off the interdimensional boat home, J-man."

An impulse of intrigue took hold of Joseph, as he watched a bead of sweat trickle down Thaddeus' forehead. He was wearing a sleeveless vest and jeans. "What kind of work do you usually do on these trips?" he asked.

"I am given files with an overview of Tellurian life details and satisfaction levels. It is my job to make sure that nobody is getting too big in their boots, or too down and out. But keep in mind, I'm only allowed to intervene in a way that appears natural," Thaddeus relayed.

"Don't you feel bad about giving people bad luck?"

Thaddeus chuckled, itching his thick arms. "When I do, they always deserve it, well mostly. This week, among others, I dealt with a gross, obnoxious manager of a jewellery shop in New York, who kept a slave in his basement. So, I arranged for him to get in trouble with the IRS by sending in some of his documents anonymously."

"Well done. And so, do you have Proficiencies?" Joseph asked.

"Yup, of course," Thaddeus confirmed as he suddenly vanished, eliciting a sharp gasp from Joseph. All remained silent for a confusing three-second interval, before he instantly appeared again. "Invisibility. Although, it's a bit different from, say, an invisibility cloak—I leave my body behind in the 8th dimension, and bring it back when I want to be visible."

Joseph gaped in a stupefied trance. "Oh, yeah? That's so cool."

"There's some much cooler Proficiencies: psychokinesis, reality-warping, astral projection," Thaddeus said. "Anyway, this is random, but how about coming with me for a trip on my boat? I can give you an ocean tour this time."

"OK, sure! I would love a break from all my teleology homework," Joseph agreed, thrilled.

"I've got to leave for another trip tonight, to Antarctica actually, so how about on Wednesday in a couple of weeks? There's a four day work week in Hyleberia, so you won't have school. We can meet at the harbour."

A good way to get away from Raymond, at least. "Sure. Looking forward to it; I haven't been on a boat trip for years. I need to do something, you know, relatively normal again," Joseph confirmed.

Thaddeus stepped away. "Great! I better get back to work. See you, J-man!" he said, turning invisible and leaving.

"*Adios.*"

Surprisingly, Joseph felt in a very good mood as he headed home.

It evaporated, however, when he arrived at the door of C52 and saw water seeping underneath. Unlocking the door, he found it was ankle-high throughout the apartment, seemingly leaking from Raymond's bedroom. *Why is Raymond so insistent on making this place into a pool? He's nuts.* Before heading to his room, Joseph slipped into the kitchenette to grab a Haoma from the fridge. There, he glimpsed a small pile of packages on their living room table. Leaning over them, he saw they were addressed to him, maybe his Bibliotheca books. He scooped them up into his arms quickly, but just as he stepped into the living room doorway, Raymond hung up the phone and called out his name.

"Joseph, my pal!" he greeted, standing up from the edge of the sofa.

Joseph turned around and squinted at him suspiciously. "Yes, buddy."

They had taken to calling each other affectionate terms like pal or buddy, although it was always sarcastic.

He peeked at the visualiser screen. *Super Mario 64* was on pause, and Raymond was on the underwater level, which seemed ironic to Joseph. The controller was still in his right hand.

"How was Shrivatsa?" he asked.

"Fine. We went to the Divine Repository," Joseph answered, taking a sip of the Haoma he had just picked up.

Raymond pointed at the screen. "Do you wanna play?"

"No, thanks. But I used to play that game all the time with my sister. Good times."

"It's amazing! I wish video games were around when I was a Tellurian. All we had was cards. Maybe we can play *Smash Bros* sometime," Raymond said, smiling.

He nodded, and was on his way out again when Raymond asked another question:

"So, what kinds of things are you learning about in school?"

Joseph shrugged. "Teleology, mostly. Y'know, the study of purpose. SHOMAT stuff. It's not exactly what I'm used to, but it's cool."

Raymond rolled his eyes. "I found that course deadly boring. The education system gets more interesting when you finish beginner stuff and get to specialise."

"Yeah, that will be nice," Joseph said abruptly. "Is this where you ask for a favour?"

He didn't think he had a particularly well-honed sense for

when people wanted something from him, but it was clear now; his roommate simply had no subtlety. Joseph believed he was a fairly tolerant person, but Raymond had been unbearable to live with over the past few days, constantly calling him names and shooting him with water when he wasn't drinking out of his hand.

Raymond coughed into his palm. "How astute of you. Well, it's not a favour *per se*. I was going to be playing doubles tennis with a couple of friends tonight, but my mate, Benny, can't come. I was wondering if you would take his place?" he asked.

Typical Raymond. "I thought you said I wasn't allowed in the Tennis Club," Joseph said.

"This isn't a club event, it's just among friends. Honestly, a girl I'm interested in is coming, and we are probably going to have drinks afterwards at the local tiki bar. I wouldn't ask you, but Benny is being forced by his boss to work all evening."

"Sorry, Raymond," Joseph said, turning around and having a closer look at his new books. "I'm not in the mood for your hijinks. My priceless Bibliotheca books have just come."

"Come on, then, what can I do so that you'll come?" Raymond called down the hall, somewhat desperately. "We need a fourth player. What if I did your laundry for a week?"

All of a sudden, Joseph had an idea, one so good it might well justify doing the favour for Raymond. He turned around, a mischievous grin forming on his face. "Fine, I'll come on your stupid date on one condition," he said, squaring his shoulders. "Stop making pools inside of the apartment. It's not the place for it: go to a real pool. You could have killed me this morning! And I can see the water is destroying the floor and walls."

Raymond groaned as if this was a terribly large compromise. "Deal. But you'd better be on your best behaviour. I'm really into this girl. Maybe one day she'll live here instead of you. I'm your senior as well, remember that. You should respect your elders," he grumbled.

"How kind of you, gramps," Joseph murmured, only saying the word "jackass" when he had left the room, eager to read his new books.

As he sat down at his desk and ripped open the packages of lost books, Joseph thought about just how incredibly odd this was. No Tellurian had read these compositions for centuries, and yet they were no doubt some of the most important works in the history of literature, sitting right in front of him.

"In 56 A. D., the Prince of Darkness, formerly known as Mathias, mounted an evil campaign in favour of universal suffering and pain. His manifesto promoted a -9.5 AHH, Average Human Happiness level," Joseph read the first page of *A Hyleberia History*. "Conversely, Peter argued for a 10.0 AHH, an intelligent and wise solution."

Mathias, who the hell is that? I have to read on.

Raymond knocked on the door again, demanding he get ready because they were about to leave. Joseph remained still for a moment, but as the knocks on the door crescendoed, he felt himself slowly adopting a stoic attitude. *I'll get this over with, read later.* With no time left to shower, he threw on some lighter clothes and trudged into the hallway.

"Finally, you're ready. Let's go, then," Raymond demanded, holding the front door open for him and eyeing his watch. "Hurry!"

With an occasional throb of pain in his occiput after the long, tiring week, he followed Raymond's whistle-stop foot-steps to the tennis court.

"So, give me some background on these girls," Joseph asked, as they paced down Sophist Street.

Raymond bounced the tennis ball up and down on his racket and started waffling. He was wearing tennis clothes, unlike Joseph. "Aislynn's the one who I'm interested in. Very attractive. I'd marry her tomorrow. An Irish lass, she works in the Water Department with me, but this is the first time we're meeting outside of work, a quasi-date. Good personality as well—that's what matters . . . apparently. The other one I don't know zilch about. She's her friend; I think her name is Jenny or something, and works in the government. Aislynn just said she would bring a friend."

Joseph braced himself to try to flirt. "OK, she sounds nice. But I'm warning you, I haven't played tennis in years. I'll be crap," he said.

"Just don't embarrass me," Raymond ordered, jaw tightening, hair shaking lightly on his shoulders. He had rather good-looking locks, much longer than Joseph's and better maintained.

Though it was 6:30 pm, the effulgent sun was still beating down on his skin like a never-ending blush, Joseph's face constantly hot. On the way to the tennis court, they passed by rows of dazzling shell-pink birds-of-paradise and fuchsia peonies, and Joseph noticed a large statue of Peter's throne, with the golden cone emblazoned on top. Below it was an inscription of the island's motto: "*Nec deus intersit, nisi dignus vindice nodus inciderit.*" Raymond translated it for Joseph: That a God not intervene, unless a knot show up that be worthy of such an untangler.

After waiting for ten minutes, Joseph turned to Raymond, absently swinging the tennis racket he'd rented from the local shop. "What was the point of rushing over here if they're late?"

Raymond gnashed his teeth. "Do you think I'm some sort of soothsayer, smart-arse?" he snarled.

Finally, after twenty minutes had gone by, Aislynn showed up. As he shook her hand, she peppered Joseph with friendly questions.

"Ah, so this was your first week! What's the craic? Are

you feeling at home yet? Week one only comes once. Did you enjoy it?" Joseph struggled to decipher her strong Irish accent. She was a gorgeous woman, her hair bright auburn and face covered with make-up. "In case you don't know, I'm Aislynn O'Connor from Galway, Ireland. I'm an Administrator working alongside Raymond in the Water Department, specifically, evaporation."

"The *craic* is good. So, you're also from the British Isles, if we include Ireland? I was born and raised in England," Joseph said, staring at her.

Aislynn's eyes flashed. "To be sure, yes—18th century British Isles. That was before Ireland was even an independent state, of course. Ah, how things have changed!"

The problem was Aislynn hadn't brought her friend because she'd got sick, meaning Joseph being here was completely pointless. After a little more chatting, he followed them onto the tennis court.

Unfortunately, Joseph's bad luck finally seemed to return during tennis. He lost Raymond almost every game even though they were playing two to one, to his roommate's chagrin and Aislynn's pleasure. When it was getting too dark to play, they all headed at once to Tithe Tiki Bar, which was a five-minute walk away. Joseph didn't feel in a particularly temperate mood, thinking about how much he should drink as he followed them there.

The three sat down on stools in the corner around a circular, candle-lit table. Joseph was reminded of his pre-death meal with Thomas where he had last eaten out, and it made his heart flutter to recall. Tithe Tiki Bar was pretty quiet, except for a few patrons hanging around the bar, toasting and singing drunken tunes. Pleasant, easily forgettable Polynesian dance music was playing on their speakers. As Joseph looked over the counter, he saw a range of fresh fruit and snacks.

After they had all ordered their cocktails and snacks,

Joseph asked curiously, "How do shops and restaurants like this get all the supplies they need?"

"It's not complicated, Joseph. I thought you had some A-levels, or whatever they're called," Raymond said patronisingly, inclining his head. "The factories of our heavenly island are on Afflatus Isle, not far from central Hyleberia."

Joseph scrunched up his face. "I had just completed my A-Levels, not that they pertained to world government supply lines. And who works there, then, on this isle you mentioned?" he asked.

"The archons," Aislynn informed him. Noticing his confused expression, she added, "They help out with manual labour. Apart from that, some luxury items such as Hyle-books are imported and modified from Tellurian factories. The government has planted a few extremely wealthy people across the globe, who have trade lines with the fifth dimension."

"Oh, archons. So what are they like?"

Aislynn explained, "They're work robots, only allowed in Hyleberia for emergencies."

As the evening wore on, Joseph increasingly felt both drunk with tiredness, and just normal drunk. The three Mai Tais he ordered didn't help. As he enjoyed sip after sip of the rum and orgeat syrup concoction, everything became blurry, especially his sense of self. The other two began talking about a debate in Parliament concerning a possible new state of water with the qualities of plasma and liquids combined. He wanted to contribute to the conversation, but in his inebriated state, his mind kept wandering off and it didn't want to concentrate. The encroaching darkness had long covered the horizon, a frigid chill causing him to gooseflesh.

Joseph was just about to call it a night when their conversation caught his interest.

" . . . Oh yeah, totally. . . . Did you know that I used to go to Hyleberia Academy with that guy who was exiled? It was absolutely ages ago, obviously. Centuries," Aislynn said to Raymond, her eyes glittering like tinsel under the moonlight. "Nigel. Good riddance, if you ask me. I don't know why it took so long."

Raymond's eyes bulged. "No way! Was he always that crazy, or is that a recent thing? It was really high time for them to bite the bulldog and get rid of him. Now I can commute to work without being harassed about the golden cone, or whatever nonsense."

Joseph took a large sip of his Mai Tai. *I wish you would bite the bullet sometimes too.*

"He was always deranged, but in a different way," recalled Aislynn. "He used to be able to speak more coherently, and he had all of these strange delusions that Hyleberia was a fraud, some blasphemous conspiracy. I heard that as a Tellurian, besides working in a car dealership, he used to write this blog on mysticism and the occult. When he started his studies for the Colour Department, he started rambling more about the lies everyone was telling him. Over the years, his grip on reality just . . . deteriorated, until he couldn't tell who anyone was. I'm pretty sure it wasn't long after his graduation that he, well, went off the deep end."

"Do you remember," Joseph began to ask Raymond, sensing a topic he knew something about, "what he used to say about the golden cone, then? I saw that thing today at the Divine Repository."

"Nothing bloody important," Raymond chuckled. "He was an utter nutcase, wasn't he?"

"You know, I think he was the one who made that elevator graffiti," Joseph said, before he realised that none of them knew what he was talking about. "There was this writing on the elevator about the Prince of Darkness. They cleared it up now, last Tuesday—I checked."

"Oh, I saw that, but I doubt he had anything to do with it!

He can scarcely string a sentence together," Raymond remarked.

"*He could*, you mean. He's gone now. So, what kind of life did he lead on Earth?" Joseph asked, recalling the two confrontations he had with the insane man.

"I think he sold cars or car insurance, but saw himself as a Cassandra figure, even then," Aislynn revealed, as she rubbed her chin, a crowd in the corner of the tiki bar drunkenly performing Happy Birthday. "He loved to go on and on about demons and the apocalypse. I saw him once last year when he was in Asclepius Hospital, the Hyleberian medical centre. Funnily, he was rambling about *something* golden then as well. But he mostly kept to himself, kind of a loner type, and we only had a few overlapping years in Shrivatsa."

"He seemed like an interesting character, even if he's mad as a hatter," Joseph replied.

"Exile was bound to happen. That loon doesn't belong in a zoo, let alone a world government," Aislynn barked, sounding increasingly blotto as her voice slurred. "And to be honest, the creep was always flirting with me. He can reincarnate as a mole for all I care."

As the conversation went on, he began to feel as if his weary eyelids were being slowly loaded with concrete, even as the tiki bar owners turned up the music and opened up the dance floor. Perhaps Joseph was being a killjoy, but he decided when midnight appeared that he would have to make his way home alone, or risk falling asleep on the table.

"I'm going to call it a night," he announced, yawning and standing up. "Take care, guys."

"*Slán*, Joseph!" Aislynn said, goodbye in Irish.

"Don't get hit by any cars on the way back!" Raymond ribbed, as they all waved him off.

As Joseph stumbled home, after recycling that strange conversation with them in his head for a while, his train of thought returned to Peter. Everyone else on the island except him seemed to adore him and his eternal rule. What made him so likeable? Was he really so great?

Joseph feared he was starting to get slightly lost. He seemed to be circling around the same part of Hyleberia for the last ten minutes, as he kept seeing the shops repeatedly. *I need to buy a new bike.*

"*Hola*, Joseph? Looks like you're going to have a hell of a hangover tomorrow," someone's familiar voice called. "You're walking like a blind man."

Joseph jumped and looked behind him. He had thought for a brief moment that it was Nigel, back from the dead. Thankfully, it was just Francis from school, who was grinning in the glow of the streetlights.

"*Buenas noches*, Francis," Joseph greeted, unable to discern Francis' eyes in the dark. "I only had a couple of cocktails, well, five or so. Could have done with a few litres of vodka also, to be honest, after the day I've had."

"Good thing there's no school tomorrow; you don't have to worry about a hangover. I was just out here stargazing. It's my third favourite hobby after video games, and poetry." Francis raised the binoculars he held in his hand to show them off. "So, what kind of drunk are you? The angry or rambly kind?"

"I'm not sure. The sleepy kind, if that counts," Joseph answered, as he felt a fresh urge for the warmth of his pillow and covers. "You wanna take me to Miyagi Apartments? Please. I'm lost."

They made a beeline for Mulla Sadra Road, a shortcut apparently, Joseph following closely behind. Francis started talking about some of his group memberships. Apparently, he was part of Driving Club, where you got to go racing on a nearby isthmus with vehicles from all over history. This sounded fun to Joseph. As they neared the apartments, frightening marble statues appeared in a green area on the edge of the street that he must have missed before.

"Scary," Joseph observed, watching them glisten.

Francis explained, "Oh, they're statues from the War. This place is called the Bellum Garden. It's on the way back to Miyagi Apartments, as the crow flies."

Joseph stared at them. "They're terrifying."

"Nah, they're not so bad. Let's have a closer look," Francis encouraged bravely.

They both inched inside the garden. The statues were of various peculiarly dressed figures, in odd poses and bearing tortured faces, ligaments contorted in unnatural positions. That said, Joseph couldn't see them particularly well in the night.

Francis smiled, unfazed. "Wanna hear what I learnt about these boys in class?"

Joseph let out a laugh, trying to sound unperturbed. "Sure."

"In the War, there were many dissenters who rose against the Prince of Darkness. If they crossed a certain line, he would petrify them into statues, and put them on display so that nobody else would get the same idea. They say that Peter has tried to remove them countless times, but the Prince of Darkness made it so they can't be moved due to his divine Proficiencies. So they remain, one of the few remnants of the War," he elucidated.

"C-creepy as hell," Joseph stuttered, palms sweating slightly. If this was true, it was adding very much to his impression that he ought to find out more about the troubled history of Hyleberia. "Can't deny I'm freaked out."

"The Great Schism was a long time ago. Think of the ancient Spartan Tellurian wars. Yes, they are tragic, but modern Tellurians don't view them as the mass deaths they were for better or for worse; there's a sort of detachment from it. It's the same here. There's no reason to care about them anymore. It's ancient history," Francis reassured, but somehow only made it worse.

"Yeah, that's r-right," Joseph stammered.

"Don't worry one bit," Francis continued. "The Prince of Darkness is long dead, and he wasn't that bad—a fan of practical jokes, or so I've heard. Rumours go that his ghost lives in this graveyard; others claim he never died. Heck, he could be watching us even now. And another thing I heard is that you can summon his very spirit if you—"

But Joseph didn't hear the end of this sentence. All of a sudden, an icy sensation swept over his body, and a rush of light-headedness that he could not fight off. He felt himself falling into an endless abyss.

⌐⌐

"JOSEPH, *amigo*! Are you all right? *Mierda*, I can't carry you all the way to Asclepius Hospital."

He slowly opened his eyes. Francis was crouching over him, shaking his shoulders. It took Joseph a few seconds to realise what had happened.

"Did I faint?" he said, ignoring the feeling of blood rushing to his head as he slowly stood up. He had landed in a flowerbed of ripe begonias. Struggling for balance, he leaned on Francis as he got up and gazed around. They were still at the statues in the garden in the middle of the night.

"Yeah! What the hell happened? You were out for like two minutes," Francis exclaimed, flushed.

Joseph felt a sinister presence around. One of the most frightening statues—a corpulent man wearing a cap and bells, and bearing a pained expression—looked at him through the dark fog like his living soul lingered, trapped forever inside. What's more, now that he was awake again, Joseph suddenly noticed graffiti on one of the statues saying, "the Prince of Darkness is near", much like had been written on the elevator. Sweat dripping from his forehead, he was very eager to leave at once.

Catching his breath, Joseph uttered, "I've no clue what happened; I was hoping you could tell me. I just felt this freezing sensation, a jolt of terrible pain coming over me, and all of a sudden I was out cold."

"*Ay, caramba*! I thought you had had a heart attack. One time I sold cocaine to this kid and he really did have one," Francis revealed, gaping. "Glad it didn't happen again. Do you want me to take you to an emergency doctor, or something?"

He shook his head, pointing forwards. "Thanks, but I am good now. It was surely just my drunkenness getting to me. Let's get out of here," he said.

Both a bit disturbed by this incident, Joseph and Francis speed-walked out of Bellum Garden and to Miyagi Apartments. Yet he couldn't stop thinking about what had just happened with Francis, replaying it in his mind, as he slumped into C52 and had a shower. Could it merely have been tiredness that had overwhelmed him? Or, was there something or someone else in Bellum Garden that night, hiding in the shadows?

That night, when Joseph had fallen asleep, he dreamt that a pitch-black, freezing cold fog was passing over all of Hyleberia, slowly poisoning everyone; and he was the only one on the whole island who could see it.

CHAPTER 6
AFFLATUS ISLE

FROM A DANCING CAT TO A WOMAN WHO COULD TURN WATER TO chocolate milk, Joseph saw a lot of strange things over the next couple of weeks. He was convinced that Hyleberia belonged in the realm of fantasy or myth, certainly not real life. But it was one event on Sunday that dealt perhaps the biggest shock since his arrival:

"Shields, my dear pal, Peter just rang. He left you a voice-mail," Raymond called from outside his room.

Joseph had just got dressed and was now back in bed, reading through the second chapter of *A Hyleberia History*. He knew he had to leave imminently for his boat trip with Thaddeus. What Raymond had just revealed made his jaw slide wide open. "You're joking?"

"No, no, come and listen," Raymond requested, appearing in the doorway. "Would I lie?"

He directed Joseph out of bed and to the living room, and then held out the phone. With a sinking sensation in his gut, Joseph leaned over and pressed play.

"Hope all is good with you, my dear son. I trust that you are well on your way to settling into the Hyleberian rhythm of life at this point," Peter said, his voice muffled and crackling with static on the phone's loudspeaker. He sounded much more casual than on the visualiser during Nigel's exile. "Long story short, I'm going out of town for a few days for my Recalibration. Before I leave, I need to ask a small favour of you. Could we meet at Tathagata monastery at, say, seven pm? Feel free to ring my secretary, Ms Beechum if you need directions or cannot make it. I'll explain everything then. Godspeed."

Joseph gasped and pondered what Peter could possibly want. His tasks for the day meant it would already be busy, but he could hardly say no to him. Ms Sadeghi had given him some exceptionally hard homework, including a puzzle about Aristotle's four causes. What's more, the career profiler test was coming up soon—and although he couldn't strictly speaking study for it, Ms Sadeghi had said that he might not be eligible for certain careers if he did badly, so he wanted to try to prepare. This test was his only chance to make something of himself in Hyleberia. It seemed Thomas had been quite right when he'd said Joseph wasn't fulfilling his potential, but now that he had a shot, the question that haunted him was did he have any potential to begin with?

Joseph knew he would be worrying about the purpose of this meeting all day, and wouldn't be able to focus on either his homework or the boat trip. Besides, he didn't know how to act with Peter after witnessing Nigel's exile. He sighed, getting a vodka soda out of the fridge.

"Bit early to be drinking, no? First it was the Mai Tais, and now this," Raymond asked nosily, reclining on the sofa and picking up his controller, *Goldeneye* N64 on the screen. An Eagles song, "Lying Eyes," was playing softly in the background. Raymond loved hard rock more than anyone Joseph had ever met.

"Who cares? You drink Haoma all the time. For all intents and purposes, despite what they might say about this whole resuscitation business, I'm dead," Joseph said with a sneer, taking a swig. "Can't I live a little now that I have, you know, bit the dust? Besides, what do you think that Peter wants to speak with me about?"

Raymond quipped, "Maybe he wants you to take his job."

Joseph rolled his eyes, noticing that the apartment looked particularly messy today. Raymond had brought a bunch of papers home from work and dumped them in the corner, and the lightbulb kept flickering. To his credit, he had kept his promise and not made any more pools. "No, that's not it. Peter must have finally realised that I'm not meant to be a Hyleberian, and that he has no choice but to exile me. If so, I hope I get reincarnated as a human, and as the heir of a billionaire with a heart condition," he said.

"Nonsense," Raymond hit back hastily, pressing play on his game as he spoke. "You belong here more than me—you actually care about the world, the fate of Tellurianity. Morals to me . . . like, what are they? I don't care, well, not much."

"I only care as much as is normal," Joseph denied, chomping on some truffles he had just pulled out of the fridge. He had got into the habit of grocery shopping on the way back from school, and was now a regular at the local Supernatural Foods. "I'm sure any reasonable person in my situation would be a little nervous, being called to speak to the Prime Minister of the World. I wish I could go back to Earth and ask my friend, Thomas, what to make of all this."

"Who's he again?" asked Raymond, the James Bond theme playing. "Not that I care."

Not someone I ought to still be thinking about, I guess. I'll never see him again. Joseph remembered his old friend's distinctive face and unique character. "My best Tellurian friend."

"What was he like? Real boring, I bet."

"Thomas . . . he was opinionated and pretentious, but he wasn't always. He changed a lot after school and lost his fun side. I feel kind of bad about how I left things with him. To be honest, that's one of the reasons I was out of sorts the other day."

Raymond didn't even look up from the screen for a second. "What happened?"

What did happen, Thomas? Joseph recalled the fight they had had shortly before his death. *Do you regret your final words to me? Do I regret mine? Would you be glad I'm finally making something of my life?*

"I suppose it doesn't matter now," Joseph opined, looking towards the door.

"You brought it up, Shields," Raymond replied.

Joseph creased his lip, as he realised if he didn't leave now he would be late for his outing with Thaddeus. "Yeah, and I shouldn't have. I'd better be off. See you."

Raymond shot someone on the screen. "Fine, then. *Auf Wiedersehen*. That means see you, moron."

Stop being so neurotic, Joseph told himself resolutely, as he left his apartment and began the walk to the harbour. *Peter just said he wants a favour. It must be something banal. And what does Raymond know about anything? He's a tool. Note to self: never share things with him again.*

Joseph speed-walked to the beach, enjoying the luxurious aroma of the many exotic flowers planted in the city centre's gardens, which were swarmed by clusters of Red Admiral and Painted Lady butterflies. When he passed Bellum Garden he recalled his fainting incident, which he had now attributed to an alcohol-induced blackout, for lack of a better explanation. Yet something still seemed very odd about it. Could it really have been the ghost of the Prince, as he had begun to hypothesise, or was that just pure nonsense? It certainly felt like something had been lurking among the statues. To make matters worse, over the nights after this incident, Joseph had been having strange dreams that a dark, poisonous fog was suffocating Hyleberia. The same dream had happened more than once, which was fairly unusual for him.

Reaching the harbour, Joseph spluttered as a handful of windswept sand and gravel blew into his face. The scent of the salty, foaming ocean greeted his nostrils as he walked onto the wooden dock, admiring the rugged outcrop of Hyleberia's limestone cliffs. Looking around the boats, he didn't see Thaddeus anywhere. He might have given a more precise meeting location. The many boats of the shipyard were made fast alongside the plywood dock, sails swayed by the gentle morning zephyr like a cradle. There was nothing particularly about this place that would make one think that it was different from a Tellurian marina, and as he waited, Joseph debated whether these normal-looking vessels were the "interdimensional boats".

"Joseph!"

He leapt in shock, volte-facing.

"Are you trying to give me a heart attack?" Joseph yelped. It was, of course, Thaddeus, wearing a sharp cap and rimless sunglasses. He had clearly been invisible and just crept up on him, shouting Joseph's name when he was inches away.

Thaddeus laughed cacophonously. "Sorry, but that was kind of funny. Anyway, my boat is this way. Follow me."

He resisted the temptation to ask whether Thaddeus played these "pranks" on Tellurians, as the wind blustered his hair about and made it look even more chaotic than usual.

Thaddeus revealed his sailboat, which was rather small but not unimpressive. There was a small sign on the front, which revealed it was called *Charon's Boat*. It was girded by dead brown fronds and coconuts that had fallen from the palm trees, now rocking back and forth on the whispering waves.

Joseph eyed the water, staying far from the edge of the dock.

"You can swim, can't you?" Thaddeus asked, as he jumped on *Charon's Boat* without a hint of hesitation. "Not that you'll need to, unless you're in the mood."

"Kinda, I can do doggy paddle," mumbled Joseph, looking down at his shoes. He had never been a very skilled swimmer as a child despite his parents' attempts to get him in lessons. He calculated how much gravitational thrust he would need to attempt a jump onto the boat, without embarrassing himself and plunging into the water. It was not a huge gap, but still.

Thaddeus gazed at him expectantly.

Finally, Joseph jumped, grabbing onto the taffrail for support as his feet landed on the deck. He steadied himself hastily.

"Good job," replied Thaddeus. "I'll get you a life jacket just in case. There are a couple inside."

The crimson sail of the boat contrasted sharply with the bright blue sky. Life jackets donned, Joseph and Thaddeus set off from the harbour, the engine thundering behind them. From the ocean view, Hyleberia was just like a Mediterranean island, scraggy peninsulas jutting out like toes in jackboots. He could not believe how beautiful it looked from here, and yet Thaddeus did not seem particularly impressed as he steered the boat. It appeared to Joseph that, if Hyleberia were open to Tellurians, it would quickly become the most popular holiday destination on Earth.

"Where on Earth is Hyleberia in the Pacific, then?" Joseph asked, admiring the island.

"Well, J-man, Hyleberia is at coordinates 48°52.6 south and 123°23.6 west, around Point Nemo," Thaddeus said, smiling so that his teeth glinted in the light. "The interdimensional boats could take us there through a hypostatic engine called a Diverter, although this boat is not fitted with one. I'm sure the physics would sound a little hard to understand to the colt."

"You think? It sounds like something out of campy '60s sci-fi," Joseph reflected. "What would happen if a Tellurian accidentally landed on Hyleberia?"

Steering the boat around a pod of whales, Thaddeus said, "Although it is on Earth, Hyleberia is on a completely separate dimension and plane to other lands. So they would just pass straight through, kind of like a light mist."

Joseph tried to understand how this would work, and it just ended up hurting his brain.

"Wow, an invisible magical island. . . . So, do you know where the Tathagata Monastery is?" he asked after they had been sailing for a while. "Peter rang me this morning asking to meet there tonight to talk."

Thaddeus seemed to lose control of the boat for a second; it lurched to the left, but he quickly got it back on track. "Sorry. About what?" he asked curiously.

Joseph shrugged. "No clue. It seemed random to me. But I guess I'll find out soon enough."

Thaddeus, fiddling with the sails and the helm, called back, "The monastery is right by Wittgenstein Grove on the south of Hyleberia. If you want, we can sail round there, and I'll show you what it looks like from the sea."

He nodded. "Sure, sounds good. I think the meeting might have something to do with Peter's, er, Recalibration. Any idea what that means?"

Thaddeus' scarred eye twitched. "Of course. You see, Peter is, as we interact with him, limited to a human body. But he has a larger side to him than his embodied form. Recalibration is an essential process every few years for Peter to reconnect and adjust his corporeal body with the Animah. This has been crucial for him ever since the defeat of the, uh, Prince of Darkness during the War, and what Peter wants, Peter gets . . . ."

What the hell is this Animah thing? "Right. And would it be possible for us to visit Afflatus Isle? I've been told that there are, uh, archons there; they sound really cool," Joseph said, not fully understanding.

"No problem," Thaddeus agreed happily. "I was going to suggest that myself."

Only fifteen minutes of sailing later, and they came to a

section of the ocean where Thaddeus paused the engine, and pointed out the distant Tathagata Monastery. Joseph could make out the faint outline of a cloister with multi-tiered roofs and sculpted spires. Guarded by horseshoe crab-infested igneous rocks, the monastery peeked out from a grove of cedars.

Something is off about Peter needing to meet here. It would be like Boris Johnson ringing you to ask for a packet of crisps from the local store, only much weirder.

And after that, they sailed to Afflatus Isle, the conversation flowing like fine wine. Thaddeus told him about the best jobs in Hyleberia, his Controller work, and the films on display at World Cinema. He was surprised to finally learn about Thaddeus' Tellurian life. Apparently, he had been a poor shoe-shiner in Athens, and died relatively young at 31 in 1789 of thyroid cancer. Joseph did not see much of a connection between his story of origin and his self-assured, manlike personality.

Before long, Thaddeus announced that they were approaching the port. Joseph felt a wave of excitement at the thought of seeing the archons. The animal life of Hyleberia was seriously lacking, he realised: the odd puffin, crow, or guillemot could be seen occasionally flitting along branches; there were a few squirrels and insects here and there as well; but he had only ever spotted two or three dogs and cats.

"Hyleberia is so barren of animals, besides Gabriel, y'know, the sloth and a few birds, isn't it?" Joseph observed, as the boat approached a rocky crag of the isle.

"Apart from some notable exceptions like pet permits, they're mostly kept on this island," said Thaddeus, concentrating on parking the boat. "It's to avoid interference with the Animal Department, who design animal minds and behaviour."

Afflatus Isle appeared as beautiful as Hyleberia. The shore was dotted with redwings and fieldfares, swooping among the branches of baobabs and Monkey puzzle trees. As they pulled up next to the dock, which juddered as they both jumped onto it from the boat, the clear corn-flower sky was mottling with cotton wool clouds.

Thaddeus guided him down the steps to the gravel roads that were apparently laid all throughout the isle. There was nobody to be seen, neither man nor robot. He was about to ask where the archons were hiding. But at that very moment, a lone archon came zooming down the road.

"*Teee-bbeee-pwwww,*" the archon beeped, halting in front of Joseph and turning around on its wheels.

Joseph stared at it in disbelief. "Does that mean hello?"

The archon was hard to describe, retro and futuristic at the same time, made of old rusted metal but by any judgement incredibly impressive. It was making cute beeping sounds, moving on wheels structured to its base like a moving dustbin. The archon had a panel on top with about fifty unlabelled buttons. Thaddeus was about six feet and looked to be the height of two of them stacked on top of each other.

There was not long to examine it though, for within a few moments, the archon made a different pitch of beep and hurried in the direction of a wooden shed.

"Dammit," exclaimed Joseph, watching it slide away. "Didn't it like me? Never been good at first impressions. . . ."

Thaddeus chuckled, and said, "Dunno. I've heard they are alive inside, but completely unable to communicate outside their beeps and prerecorded messages. Let's follow it and see."

That's disturbing. He and Thaddeus traced the path of the archon. The little thing hurtled into the shed's doors like a cat to catnip. They walked into the shed, and soon found the machine had begun milking cattle.

Indeed, there were dozens of enclosures inside where Angus and Galloway cattle munched on grass. They all were quite at ease with the archons, as there were several others in here also milking. He squinted as he watched the droid extend a mechanical arm to the cow's udder and attach a suction cup that fed into its body. As the cow's output began to dry, the archon swiftly removed the suction cup with a *plop* sound and moved on to the next cow.

After they left the shed, the archons were revealed to be used for many tasks: reaping crops, picking fruit, mining, fashioning household products, and producing basic food-stuffs. Some of these assignments were accomplished in factory-like buildings on Afflatus Isle, and there were a few workers monitoring them in the buildings. Joseph even said hello to some of the bots, who told him a little about their jobs in robotic voices. It was slightly worrying to think they were being kept here as slaves.

It was a virtual zoo on this island. Besides the cows, there were hundreds of pens where species were kept and attended to by the archons. The geese, donkeys, monkeys, kangaroos and so on were all kept in comfortable conditions, and he thought he could have spent a week here looking around. Joseph had not gone to a zoo in years, so this would've been worth the visit even without the archons. There were hundreds of extinct animals to look at too, including quaggas, woolly mammoths and sabre-toothed cats. The Tyran-nosaurus rex was much more friendly than Joseph had imag-ined, the huge dinosaur allowing him to pet him on the nose, after some coaxing from Thaddeus.

"Amazing," he exclaimed in awe as he looked at a pigsty, where the archons were feeding a group of blue pigs Berk-shire leaves. "I can't believe how clever those things are. Reminds me of R2-D2."

Thaddeus just shrugged. "Don't get too excited. They are terrible, terrible cooks. Can't even make toast."

Joseph wiped a bead of sweat off of his forehead as they reached the back of the isle. Here, tasty-looking, fragrant papayas grew next to bright, levitating and rotating geometric statues. Several plump hippos and terrifying, apparently trained lions were even allowed to wander freely around the water and oxygen factories. He and Thaddeus had been exploring for an hour. Towards the end, Thaddeus seemed to be getting a bit stressed, and eventually pulled out a pack of cigarettes.

"I haven't for a while," Thaddeus affirmed, as he lit a cigarette up and then let a puff of smoke float in the air. "The health effects still exist in the fifth dimension, don't be mistaken. But we all need relief once in a while."

"Yeah, I used to be sort of addicted too, not that my mum approved," revealed Joseph, half-tempted to request a cigarette for himself. He had become addicted to smoking for a brief time soon after his father's death, but managed to quit after his mother found out and forced him to. "But why are you stressed?"

Taking another drag, Thaddeus remarked, "It's not you. I just have some tasks I've got to do after this weighing on my mind. Nothing interesting, office work. I've been given a lot of extra tasks by our 'Lord and Savior', Peter. If only he weren't so lazy!"

Sounds like he's pissed off at Peter. I wonder why.

Even though it had been several hours, Joseph found himself disappointed when Thaddeus announced that it was time to head back. The boat drifting home, Joseph chuckled to himself about how his science teacher at school would react if he knew about all of these wonders. But he frowned at the thought of all the SHOMAT homework that awaited his return, and of course his meeting with Peter. It would come as a relief when the holidays arrived in due time. Ms Sadeghi had confirmed—thank the heavens, that they existed here too.

"Thanks so much for the trip," Joseph said, after the boat docked, and Thaddeus had parked *Charon's Boat*.

Thaddeus patted Joseph on the shoulder, fussing with the sails as his left eye twitched and he rubbed his scar. "Maybe next week, we could do something in town. Go to the World Cinema or something? You know, Orson Welles works there. I might bring some of my buddies as well," he suggested.

"I could bring one of mine as well," Joseph added, as he jumped off onto the dock, before doubting whether he truly had friends here yet. "Either way, nice afternoon!"

He hastily walked home, unable to stop thinking about the incredible things he had seen. Even if Raymond had to play second fiddle to Thaddeus in terms of quality of friend-hood, for some reason, he was eager to tell him all about the exciting events of the day. In fact, Joseph didn't fully under-stand if they were friends or enemies.

Nonetheless, as soon as he stepped foot in the door of C52, Joseph was once more not pleased with what he found. Raymond was in the kitchenette with a bunch of his friends drinking alcohol, a Lou Reed song, "Perfect Day" thundering in the background as a few of them played beer pong.

Joseph looked quickly between their grinning faces; was this a party that he hadn't been invited to? He did not mind that they were having a celebration, but he soon spotted a small pool in the corner of the room, walled in by two sofas, which made him clench his fist. He also saw Haoma cans littering dumped everywhere, and a box of pizza with slices left fallen on the floor. His hands forming fists, Joseph groaned with anger. *Raymond promised that he would stop making pools inside of the apartment, and now this? The jerk!*

"What's that, Raymond?" Joseph asked with an accusatory tone, forced to shout to be heard over the thrum-ming rock music as he pointed to the pool. "And don't say you forgot."

Raymond smirked from behind his friends. "Calm down, fun police. It's not going to leak. It's just a small one," he explained unconvincingly.

Joseph put his hands on his hips, and then pointed to the walls, which were once again washed out and shrivelled. He felt like his mother when she visited him at weekends and complained his apartment was unclean. "Look at that! You made a promise that if I came with you that night, you'd stop making the pools. Seriously, I'm not being a killjoy, but shouldn't you be acting your age?"

"Aha, I'm in cold water, now aren't I? Actually, because of my age, I'm so old that I have dementia, sorry," Raymond contended, chuckling. "What's your name, again? Josephine?"

His friends burst out in laughter. They were a ragtag bunch from his tennis club, which Joseph didn't think he would get on with at all.

"It's hot water. And I guess promises mean nothing to you," Joseph replied angrily.

Raymond's cronies jeered again like teenage bullies. Joseph, who had become used to his roommate's antics, felt at that moment that this behaviour was the last straw. He considered briefly as he stood there that he might have been placed with Hyleberia's worst roommate. But his annoyance at his pool would have to wait. Even if the anxiety about having to meet Peter had waned slightly due to the distraction of visiting Afflatus Isle, he still had to get ready, and he wanted to have a shower and get changed beforehand so that he would avoid looking as dishevelled as he had been at the police station.

After storming out and looking through his wardrobe, Joseph quickly showered, changed clothes and left for Tathagata Monastery. There was no point leaving it until the last moment if he could not do a single thing with the head-splitting music.

Thanks to Thaddeus, he was able to find Tathagata Monastery in a reasonably short time. Joseph remembered going into the exam hall to take his A-Levels, and a similar feeling of trepidation filled him now. He came to the entrance of the monastery, looking around for Peter.

The monks were largely dressed in orange kasayas, Buddhist robes. They were wandering about their business, some meditating, others carving marble statues of saints, casting their eyes towards Joseph like he was a stray tourist. As he walked under the shadow of a phallic stupa, Joseph asked himself whether they had to get a job as well. He was impressed by the ornate Oriental architecture, which was a sharp contrast to the cityscape of central Hyleberia. Golden pilastered columns supported the water reed thatched roofs, which looked very delicate, as if they might catch fire merely under the pressure of the sun's heat.

"Joseph, you made it. Isn't it a beautiful evening?"

He turned and saw Peter standing beside a copper sculpture of what must be the Buddha, looking particularly striking with his white suit glinting like it had been washed and dry-cleaned two minutes prior. What's more, he had brought his agreeable, zen companion, Gabriel. The peaceful sloth was cradled in Peter's arms, lovingly hugging him.

But Joseph wasn't all that pleased to see Peter, simply not trusting him. He had called him a dictator to Emily, and still felt that was fair. He had murdered Nigel in cold blood, and had a very fake air to him.

"The evening? Uh yeah, it's not bad," he muttered hesitantly, pacing over to Peter's side.

"Bwahaha." Peter beamed, laughing. "Of course, I can control the weather, but I tend to let the Animah take its course with the seasons. In any case, let's saunter."

Animah . . . that word again. But what does it mean? Can't ask now or I'd look stupid.

They talked as they walked down a path that led them around the edge of the monastery, but Joseph was not enjoying the conversation. He could not reconcile that cold, murderous figure on TV with the kind and charming Peter he was walking with now. He remembered that he had suggested to Emily that he might complain to Peter about his reservations concerning Hyleberia, but at present, Joseph wasn't sure he had the guts. *Was she right? Am I a coward?*

"Last time I saw you was the exile on HB1," Joseph divulged, when they were far enough from the main meditation hall to be alone. They were standing under some lush evergreens, the evening light spangling through the branches like falling coins. There was a wonderfully sweet smell in the air, lavender mixed with sawgrass.

"Ah yes," Peter mumbled, looking at the ground. "That was very difficult for me."

Difficult for you, eh? You killed him. You're a murderer.

Joseph coughed. "I felt kinda bad for Nigel, to be honest," he said.

Peter swallowed. "I realise the exile must have looked very dramatic on the visualiser, but I will tell you this: I have always hated the theatrics of Prime Minister-hood. I would've let Nigel stay, but my Divine Council was pressuring me to take action. Thus, I didn't have much of a choice."

You're Prime Minister. Of course, you did!

Joseph couldn't think what to say. "I see."

A monk came by at this juncture and started uttering a Tibetan prayer for both of them. This lasted for a slow five minutes, "May all suffering quickly cease, and all happiness and joy be fulfilled; and may the holy Animah flourish for evermore!"

"Anyway, please don't feel pressured to say yes about the favour," Peter stated, moving on to the matter at hand as the monk left. Joseph braced himself for the big reveal that he had been waiting for all day. "I was hoping you might be able to take care of Gabriel. You see, I'm going out of town for a while on my Recalibration, and while Ms Beechum usually takes care of him, she is moving houses in the next few weeks and told me she doesn't think she'll have time."

"Take care of Gabriel. . . . What?" Joseph muttered, at a loss.

Realising what Peter was saying, he stared at Gabriel's grey face and bright green eyes, more than puzzled by this request. It was by far the most peculiar favour anybody had ever asked of him, both as a Tellurian and a Hyleberian. He had a sudden vision of dropping Gabriel from the window by accident. With that thought, he realised he couldn't possibly handle the responsibility of looking after Peter's pet.

"I'm afraid I've never looked after anything living that's more exotic than a hamster. Also, I don't think my roommate would be OK with it," Joseph informed him.

"It's simple," explained Peter, as he pulled a small brush from his pocket and absent-mindedly started brushing Gabriel. "You just need to make sure he's fed and healthy for a few days. Obviously, there's not much chance of him running away. He's good company, and it's nice to have a little companionship, even for me." An unexpected look of melancholy appeared on his face. "In fact, that's why I have Gabriel. I essentially have billions of worshippers across the world, and thousands of workers here in Hyleberia—but still, it can on occasion get a little lonely. It's not like I can ever get anything off my chest; I'm simply too important to show any vulnerability whatsoever."

There was something thought-provoking about having just been told by the secret Prime Minister of the Earth that he was lonely, but Joseph would have time to dwell on that later. He was still far from saying yes.

"I'm sorry, but why me?" Joseph asked, flummoxed.

Peter patted Gabriel's back like a baby. "You and Gabriel both took such a liking to each other on your first day. Plus, I figured that you might like a comfort animal as you get used to your new divine home."

No, we didn't. We barely even interacted, Joseph thought as he felt a pang of indecision and worry. Although technically there was the option to say "screw that!", he seriously doubted that he could convince his lips to say those words, or even a euphemistic translation.

"It doesn't sound like a good idea," Joseph imparted, noticing how Peter had ignored the roommate issue; Raymond hadn't given permission for this. "I mean, what will I do with him during class? You should find someone who has more free time."

"Yes, I thought you might say that. Fair enough. Don't worry, I won't force you," Peter admitted, a crestfallen frown forming on his lips. "That would be wrong of me."

Joseph felt his stomach turn: Peter was guilting him. "Good. I just really have got a lot on my plate already," he said.

"But to be honest, the main reason I wanted you specifically to look after him is that, well, everyone so far has refused. I've asked several colleagues and friends. They're all worried about disappointing me. It's a disadvantage of being Peter—people always want to please you. Yet there is always a part of them that is slightly afraid to be themselves or do something wrong. I admit, I got the feeling when I met you that, unlike most, you do not and would not lionise me in this way. And. . . ."

Peter continued complaining, and it began to sound as if he was on the verge of tears.

As Peter went on . . . and on, Joseph couldn't withstand the emotional blackmail any longer. "Oh, OK! I'll do it," he groaned, sighing heavily. He would just have to grin and bear it, he supposed, and hope Raymond didn't make too much of a fuss. "But don't expect me to be an amazing sloth caregiver."

Peter grinned, the mole on his cheek looking particularly large as he clapped his hands together. "Thanks so much, my dear son! Bwahaha. I just hope I didn't pressure you into it. You're the best, Joseph."

"The best, am I? I thought that was you. Well, where are

you going?" he asked, as he fretted about how he was going to deal with this new burden. "Your holiday home?"

"Indeed," revealed Peter, as he straightened his tie and flashed his ivory-white teeth. "There is a place a few miles from Hyleberia called Sabbat Islet where I go around the lunar eclipse to take a few weeks off and rest. You see, I have a lovely mansion. I don't even lock the door when I go because only I know where it is. I need to Recalibrate as I don't sleep otherwise."

Peter went on. It was interesting to hear that there had never, ever been another Prime Minister. If he died, another would have to follow, but this apparently had not happened in Hyleberia's aeons-long history.

They had circled around the monastery by this point, and Joseph had almost forgotten his other issues. However, he suddenly thought of Emily's situation, and decided to bring something up.

"Uh, by the way, I was wondering if, w-well," Joseph stuttered.

Peter smiled calmly. "Go on."

Joseph put his hands in his pockets. "I know this is a strange question, but is it banned in every situation for Hyleberians to get in contact with, er, Tellurians?"

"Why? What is the issue?" Peter asked, suddenly sounding very concerned.

At this point, another half-naked monk approached and effusively asked for an autograph from Peter.

"There are a couple of reasons," he said, stomach whirling once the monk had finally gone. "Most of all, I feel really bad that they all think I'm dead when I'm not really. Also, shortly before I died, I had an argument with my best friend while we were meeting about a loan. I kind of have, uh, some regrets about that."

"Regret is as natural as dew on the grass in the morning sun. But contact with Tellurians is strictly off-limits, I'm sorry.

According to the Hyleberian Statute of Divine Secrecy, inter-action with them is prohibited to everyone except to Controllers, and only to them in disguise. The risks are far too great. They could find out the divine truth, and even if they seem to agree to keep us secret, it would still be too danger-ous," Peter stated, as if this were a serious issue. "Rules are rules, and this applies to everyone."

"Yeah, I get that," Joseph affirmed. He was not only asking this question for his sake, rather for Emily. "I some-times feel like I didn't get a chance to end things properly. I guess that's selfish of me. Oh well, it's over."

As they chatted on, Joseph found himself evaluating the chance that he would be leaving the meeting with a sloth in his arms. Then, Peter simply slung Gabriel over Joseph's shoulder. He said that he was going to forewarn Ms Sadeghi about the agreement so that she did not give him any trouble. Gabriel felt as warm as a hot water bottle on his shoulder, but Joseph was afraid he would drop him, unsure how to hold the creature.

"So, what do I feed him?" Joseph asked, stroking Gabriel timidly, wondering if there was still a chance he could take back the favour. Though soft, he found the sloth uncomfort-able to hold, and likewise, Gabriel did not appear fond of his new caregiver, as he began wriggling his arms.

"Bye bye, Gaby. I'll miss you!" Peter kissed Gabriel on the forehead as Joseph struggled to hold him. "Ms Beechum will bring his things and food this evening. But sloths are very sturdy creatures; he will be fine as long as you treat him decently and love him a lot. You will certainly be the centre of attention with him in your care, I can assure you!" He made his farewells by the entrance of the monastery. "I'll let you get back home now. Thanks a million for helping me out with this!"

As Gabriel whined, Joseph grumbled, "No problem, I hope you have a nice Recalibration."

Peter beamed, ambling away. "Have a divine life yourself! And see you very soon, Gabriel!" he said.

Joseph headed home, cradling Gabriel awkwardly, his heart racing as he prayed that Raymond's friends had gone. As much as he liked animals, taking care of this damn sloth was the cherry on top of the cake of problems he faced, and he felt completely manipulated into agreeing to do it.

Perhaps it was unavoidable, but he decided to make his way through the backstreets of town, where there would be fewer gawking passersby. No doubt, everyone would be wondering why he had Peter's pet. Gabriel squealed as Joseph walked on, gazing around sadly for Peter to come back.

What a pain. Joseph groaned as he held Gabriel tightly and passed by a man with his skin inside out, trying not to stare.

"I'm looking after you for the next few days. You'll get used to it—wasn't my first choice either, honestly," he informed Gabriel, as Joseph entered South Hyleberia and turned the corner to a secluded alley.

In the next minutes, however, he began to have reservations about coming through this seedy area of town, and if it was really worth the risk to avoid prying eyes. It appeared to be the back-side of the high street shops, where nobody went but to dump rubbish. The cracked pavement was strewn with broken glass, mossy walls laden with barely readable graffiti, much like Joseph had seen on the elevator and in the park. As he paced quickly along, he could only discern a few words because it was so faded and illegible. Nevertheless, he did manage to make out a few commonly repeated terms, "darkness", "of", and . . . "prince."

He heard muted voices crescendoing from around the corner. Somebody was approaching. Perhaps he should have just continued on his way, but Joseph was in a tense and jumpy mood. So, he stopped and ducked behind an adjoining wall. His first, perhaps irrational thought, had been that they might be some kind of thugs, and if so, that they could try to steal Gabriel. As he looked behind him, he realised he was in the alley behind Supernatural Foods. He bowed down, half-sitting in the rubbish bags, which had fallen out of the stuffed bins.

The two voices grew louder. One of them was brassy and husky; the other was more high-pitched and feminine, with an accent, but still male.

"It stinks of putrid bananas. Why the hell did you want to meet here of all places?"

"Nobody ever comes down this trashy alley. Still, I think we should be careful."

Joseph could not recognise to whom the two voices belonged, and he did not grasp every word they said. They were still too quiet and heavily drowned in reverb, and he feared he could not glimpse them without risking detection. He held Gabriel around his waist, and huddled down, hardly daring to breathe.

"Let's cut right to the chase. You-know-who leaves tomorrow on Recalibration. We need to make sure that all of the extraneous variables are considered. We only get one chance at this, and then it's game over."

"Don't worry. The hardest part of the plan is going to be securing the you-know-what. After that, I've planned for all possible interferences."

What does that mean? Joseph closed his eyes as he concentrated on being as silent as possible; he could feel his heart racing. It seemed as if they were conversing about something criminal.

"And what about if we don't? What if something we can't foresee, like you-know-who, ends up coming back early? Then it'll be too late."

"There's a chance, but an opportunity like this won't come again. This is the only chance we have. Even if you-know-who does, we will still have the you-know-what. We can always—"

"Jaieoeoeow!"

The man stopped in mid-sentence.

"What the hell?" he exclaimed.

He had paused no doubt due to the fact that, at this highly inconvenient moment, Gabriel had decided to squeal, a shrill mewling, screeching cry. Joseph buried his nails into his left palm and threw his right hand over Gabriel's mouth.

"Shh," he whispered to the oblivious sloth, wondering if he should risk coming out.

"Did you hear something too?" one of them asked warily.

Joseph did not move a muscle, his head burning. Besides the bile rising in his throat, pins and needles overwhelmed his legs, increasingly painful to ignore.

"Probably just a door squeaking, but let's move, for safety," he mumbled.

"OK, lead the way."

Luckily, they paced off down the alley from where they had come. When he could no longer hear their footsteps, Joseph waited a minute to be sure, gripped Gabriel like a barrel around the waist, and sprinted as fast as he could in the opposite direction.

CHAPTER 7
GUARDIAN ANGEL

"W<small>HY THE HELL DID YOU AGREE TO TAKE CARE OF</small> G<small>ABRIEL</small>?" demanded Raymond, utterly furious.

The sloth supplies had been delivered to Joseph the prior evening by Ms Beechum: leaves, twigs and buds. It was the following day, and he was fixing Gabriel something to eat before heading to school. Taking a rip-it-off-like-a-bandaid approach, he had informed Raymond about Gabriel's arrival the previous evening by arriving with him in his arms. Outside the living room window, storm clouds were gathering on the horizon.

"I'm just such an angel, I guess . . ." Joseph mumbled frustratedly, as he unpacked his laundry basket and got a breakfast bar out of the cupboard. The loathsome sloth squirmed in his arms, resisting tired strokes of his head, clearly longing to return to Peter's care.

"Why would you agree to that responsibility? Can you at least keep it in a cage?" Raymond requested, groaning. He was sitting at the visualiser and playing *Diddy Kong Racing*, an outraged look not leaving his face. "This apartment is not your personal zoo."

"Oh, stop making a mountain out of a molehill. This isn't ideal for me either," he exclaimed, highly irritated. And the next words came out of Joseph's mouth before he knew it. "Look, Raymond. To be honest, I've been thinking maybe I should move out of Miyagi Apartments."

Joseph scratched his head; it had been said that he legally needed a roommate while he settled into Hyleberia, but nobody mandated that the roommate had to be Raymond—or borderline psychopathic.

Raymond faked wiping his eyes, as if he was crying. "Are you really breaking up with me?"

"As much as I love being called names and nearly drowned, I think it's time for me to go," Joseph explained.

"You don't understand me at all," Raymond shouted, arms folded, "or you would know why I'm like this. Why I don't take things seriously."

Joseph stared at Raymond; he had never seen him so piqued. "Don't I?"

"Nope!"

"Then, tell me. Exactly what don't I understand, Mr Comedian?"

Raymond interlocked his fingers. "The truth is, well, my life on Earth was miserable. I never enjoyed myself. For Chrissake, I was too busy making ends meet to even think about playing games."

"How come?"

"Life in Germany in the early twentieth century wasn't exactly paradise," Raymond said heatedly, looking down at the ruined carpet. "I was homeless as a child and a junior tax consultant in adulthood. The economy was tough. My everyday life, especially during my youth, was aimed at getting food on the table, and not becoming a hobo. You don't appreciate how lucky you are, being born with the luxuries of the twenty-first century. I would have killed for the internet or video games when I was alive. Even so, a lot here had it even worse than me: medieval peasants, Roman slaves, Dalits. As for myself, I'm making the most of eternity to do the things I never got to do. To enjoy myself. To have a laugh. You got to do those things before; I didn't."

Wasn't expecting that. "That's all well and good, but I just think you could be a little bit less of a jerk," Joseph muttered, surprised by this speech, as he reflected on whether his roommate had a point, and also if moving was even worth the hassle. Noticing the wall clock, he realised he had to leave any moment for Shrivatsa. "I've got to dash now."

"OK, dick. You know what, I've had enough games for today," Raymond shouted, throwing his controller across the room and disappearing into his bedroom.

Maybe the stresses of Hyleberia are getting to me. Was I too hard on him? I don't know. Joseph turned off the visualiser, lost in thought. He hadn't slept well the previous night. His career profiler test, which was taking place this very day, had incited him to study till 3 am, despite the fact it was not designed to be prepared for. Still, he had paged through the SHOMAT textbook for far too long, imbibing everything from "thaumaturgy" to "sophiology", whatever they meant, barely remembering a word. The only reason he cared was that they had said this test would have consequences for what job he would be able to do forever. He refused to end up like Thomas had said he was . . . a nothing, and so wanted desperately to do well. Gabriel had mostly slept snoring on a rag on the bedroom carpet, albeit twice waking Joseph up when he finally did drop off by crawling over him.

As he'd expected, holding Gabriel slumped over his shoulder quickly drew everyone's attention. The whole town seemed to cast their eyes in their direction, though he wasn't going to look for backstreets after last time. Gabriel was light enough that he wasn't too much of a burden to carry, fluffy arms clinging around Joseph's shoulders much like a toddler's. Some of the frustration Joseph had felt this morning lessened slightly at the touch of his soft, grey fur, and the sight of his cute Cheshire cat smile. But not much.

As he ambled along, he thought of that conversation that he had accidentally overheard. This was another reason why Joseph hadn't slept soundly, on top of his continual strange dreams. It still seemed to him that they'd been planning something suspicious, but what could it be? He barely noticed when his feet entered the door to the academy, only registering his arrival when he was walking through the corridors. They were always bustling with gossiping students, which made Joseph look forward to passing SHOMAT, as it was a bit restricting only having one teacher and three classmates.

Even if Ms Sadeghi had been forewarned about Gabriel's presence, none of the others had been.

"Joseph, what do you call an intelligent sloth?" Chen asked, after Joseph sat next to Francis at a desk and explained briefly the petsitting situation. The class had about 9 desks, but only 4 were ever seated.

Joseph was not particularly in the mood for jokes, his sense of dread like a heavy weight in his gut. "Dunno."

Chen grinned, looking very amused with himself. "A slow-mo sapiens."

He unpacked *World 101* and his pens. "Ha. You have a joke for everything, huh?"

"Well, I can certainly do more than hair and dumpling jokes!" Chen quipped, lowering his cap. "By the way, I often go to the Hyleberian comedy club and even do stand-up when I'm feeling confident. You should swing by some time."

He was bald, often wearing a baseball cap out and about, which suggested perhaps he was insecure about it.

"Maybe I will," Joseph said absently, this not being high on his list of priorities.

"So, tell me, why did Peter choose you to look after Gabriel?" Chen questioned, throwing his head back in amusement as he tickled Gabriel's furry head. "Back in my farm in China, we could hardly afford to keep cattle, let alone pets! Boy, I won't lie, I would've eaten Gabriel during the famine."

"I guess he's going away for a few days, and his secretary wasn't able to. He thought I might be a good choice because, well, reasons."

"Ohhhh yes, I saw they reported the Recalibration on HB1 this morning. Gabriel's so cute, isn't he? Like a little teddy," Emily exclaimed, wearing a plaid coat and a dainty necklace, leaning in close to get a good look at the sloth. Evidently, she had been listening, and proceeded to stroke Gabriel's face as if he was a toy. "What chubby cheeks. I might have to apply for a pet permit. I really want a dog! I don't know if I mentioned it, but as a Tellurian, I used to have a Rottweiler, Barney. Oh, he was the best dog you have ever met! He was loyal, sweet, playful, obedient, everything. I miss him even after all this time!"

Yeah, you might have mentioned it . . . before bursting into tears.

"They're pretty hard to get," inputted Francis. "I'm more of a cat fan myself. Used to have an Iberian lynx in Mexico."

Over the past few days, Joseph had noticed Francis was slowly becoming one of his best Hyleberian pals. He might have thought they wouldn't have much in common, but it appeared that wasn't the case. They had spent lunch together on Monday, and really hit it off in the friend department, though Joseph still felt he knew close to nothing about him.

"What is hard to get?" Joseph asked.

"Animals. My *amigo* says there's a centuries-long waiting list, because if too many animals are allowed on the island, it messes with the Animal Department, which configures their intelligence and traits."

"Yes, I heard that's true. I'd love a pet permit too," said Joseph gladly.

"Well, you have Gabriel now! I'd get a dog just like Barney. . . ." Emily said wistfully.

"Oh, Emily, you mention Barney every week," Francis remarked, chuckling. "Move on."

"I loved him," she snapped defensively. "There's nothing wrong with being attached to a pet."

The only person in the classroom who did not seem particularly pleased to see Gabriel and discuss pet permits was Ms Sadeghi. She had just arrived, and unpacking her files, she opined, "If Peter requested you to take care of Gabriel, that is his prerogative; but I'm sure he wouldn't want him to distract you from your studies and, most importantly, your career profiler. Put him in the corner."

At the mention of the test, Joseph felt a horrible, cold rush of anxiety pulse down his neck. He had done his best to prepare for it, although as he watched Ms Sadeghi extract the exam paper, he couldn't help but feel as if he was far out of his depth. The paper said on the front in huge bold lettering: HYLEBERIAN CAREER PROFILER.

"I'm nervous," Joseph said quietly to Francis. The dread in his gut was only getting worse. "My first exam. I've always hated exams. My fingers sweat."

"Don't worry about that, Jojo," Francis whispered reassuringly, leaning over. At this point, Chen and Emily had taken out their pens and were doing some work on mirror neurons. "The career profiler's not difficult. It's just general knowledge. Sure, it'll determine which careers you're going to be trained for, but you can always be like me and go your own way, train to do something domestic like be a shop owner or a postman. Anybody can do that."

"What if I do crap and end up as a dustbin Administrator or something?" Joseph asked worriedly, as he tried to work out what career would be the best for him. "I'm too clumsy for manual labour. I can manage a cash register, if that counts as a skill."

Francis chuckled. "Funny that you should say that.

Garbage man is what I originally got. I was kinda glad I didn't get anything worse!"

Joseph looked at him with an expression of confusion. "There's worse?" he asked.

At this point, Emily seemed to have cottoned onto the conversation, as she inputted, "Oh, the test is complete rubbish. It said I should be a Dandelion Administrator. What the hell is that? I wasn't having it."

"That's amazing compared to me. You shouldn't complain," Francis said. "Dandelions smell great. Rubbish doesn't."

But at this moment, Ms Sadeghi's shadow fell over them.

"That's enough talk," she interrupted, clearly in a foul mood, as she deposited the paper on Joseph's desk. "Time to take the test. I wish you the very best of luck, Joseph."

He gulped, reminded of his GCSEs in that hellish Birchwood Senior School of Essex full of his childhood bullies, where he had failed his A-Levels the first time.

Overall, the career profiler proved to be a challenge. It took him until lunchtime to get to the last page, and there was the constant distraction of Gabriel, who just sat there staring at him for most of the time. There were a couple of tricky questions he couldn't even guess, such as the difference between agathokakological, dysteleological, malist and agathist universes, terms which he did not understand. Other questions were not about his knowledge and simply concerned his likes and dislikes. He made use of all the time allotted. His focus in the last few minutes was so intense that he hardly noticed that Ms Sadeghi was standing over him like a hawk, waiting to slip the paper out from beneath his fingers the moment the clock struck midday.

"I will mark that tonight, and let you know how you did on Monday. I suggest you take your mind off it during the weekend, go do something nice, perhaps World Cinema. I heard they have a new Kubrick film from an alternate dimension, starring Meryl Streep and Tom Hanks," Ms Sadeghi recommended, as she tucked the exam into a folder. "And apologies if I seemed grouchy about Gabriel. To be honest, I've never understood why Peter even keeps a pet, but I suppose he knows best, as our wonderful and glorious leader. Who am I to doubt his wisdom?"

"Er, he said he gets lonely. And yeah, maybe I'll go to the cinema, see what they have showing there," muttered Joseph, worrying about how badly he did.

Joseph was not exactly sure what to do on his lunch break —he didn't want to go out in public with Gabriel, but was desperate to get some fresh air. His classmates were no help. None of them agreed to look after him. Forced to carry Gabriel, Joseph set off onto the high street, finding himself completely unable to evaluate his own exam performance, but still not able to stop thinking about it. Wondering whether to eat lunch in the town square or near the beach, he was suddenly approached.

"Hey, Joseph, want to have lunch?" Emily asked, as the midday breeze battered her hair.

Joseph didn't hesitate. "Sure, lead the way."

There was not any hostility in the air between them as far as he knew. Yet they had not spoken much since their little tiff on the beach. While he hesitated to call anything about Hyleberia normal, it was a normally sunny summer day apart from the distant storm clouds, magpies cawing and chirping in the palm trees that lined the sidewalk. Emily and Joseph both bought gorgonzola sandwiches from a local deli and then meandered about, chomping on them as they walked.

"It seems like Peter has really taken to you," Emily commented as they went down the cobblestone road aimlessly, numerous people staring at him. "Trusting you with his sloth and all."

Joseph turned red as he stroked Gabriel, nibbling on his sandwich. "I guess I'm his new bestie." Emily looked puzzled. "Joking. Well, I wish he hadn't given me this damn creature. I've got enough on my plate. Anyway, I suppose we should address the elephant in the room: your crackpot scheme to escape Hyleberia."

Emily shrugged, twiddling her thumbs. "Ohhhh. Yeah, about that. . . . Not long after I said all that, I began to realise I was being ridiculous. I mean, if everyone else isn't allowed to go home, why should I be the only exception? I just miss my family a lot. But so much more important than me, I guess, is the divine secret of Hyleberia. Maybe one day I will be able to get a dog as good as Barney, but for now, I guess I'll have to survive."

Joseph stared at her. He hadn't at all been expecting such a change of heart. "I kinda feel the same way. It's understandable; I miss my family, and my best friend too. But running away seems to me to be an extreme move."

"It is, it is," she said. "The only thing I don't miss in the U.S. is the partisan politics. Still, everything is so nice in Hyleberia that it's sometimes too good, you know? I both love and hate this island at the same time."

Wrapped in thought, he said, "I suppose. Still, there's a lot of weird stuff going on around here: Nigel's exile, for instance. That still seems off to me. The fact is I don't trust Peter, and everyone is such yes-men to him. Not to mention, I overheard this strange conversation yesterday. . . ."

Pleased to finally get this off his chest, Joseph explained the small extract of a conversation he had heard, as he finished his sandwich and dumped the wrapper in a bin.

Emily seemed interested, jade eyes widening as she made him elaborate on every detail. She asked him what he thought they meant, and he said he had no clue, which was largely true.

"I wonder what it was. I believe Peter's gone now on his Recalibration. If they're planning something, I guess we'll find out soon enough!" she exclaimed, thumbing her chin.

"You're the first person I've told. I would've said some-thing to Raymond, my roommate, but our relationship has been on the rocks. Even told him I wanted to move out, but I dunno. Depends on if I can find anywhere nice, I guess," Joseph told her, recalling their earlier conversation.

"Oh, really?" Emily cried excitedly, wagging her finger. "I happen to have, like, a friend in the same apartment building as me who is looking for a roommate at the moment. He's from Afghanistan. Could be fate! We could go now."

Joseph gasped. "You do? Well, I did have a good time at the library."

Gabriel squeaked like he had been listening along, and was glad to come too. This could be—Joseph thought as he and Emily approached the entranceway of her apartment complex, Terribilità Terrace—just what the doctor ordered. It was only a 5 minute walk, which was by far a better commute to Shrivatsa than at the moment, about half an hour, uphill.

There was a lot of construction work going on outside of the apartment complex: bulky men in yellow vests, trestle scaffolding, and concrete mixers that Joseph now knew were using materials supplied by the archons. Much of what the builders were undertaking appeared somewhat dangerous. Joseph spotted a pallet of bricks above him resting on a plat-form that looked slanted, like it might collapse into pieces if a pigeon alighted on it or a strong gust of wind came at an unfortunate angle.

"I think they're adding an indoor surfing simulator. Oooh, I can't wait!" Emily exclaimed. "I'm a really good sailor, y'know."

They took the elevator to the fourth floor. The hallway was incredibly fancy: there were expensive-looking paintings by Picasso and Malevich on the walls, and tasty complimentary chocolate drops. *Who named this place? It's anything but terrible. Makes Miyagi Apartments look like the sewers.*

After a few minutes of tenacious thuds on the man's

apartment, a hermit-like, wearied figure emerged, looking like he had not gone outside or had a bath in weeks. He had a bedraggled head of hair, an unshaven beard and he was dressed in blue striped pyjamas, stained with vomit.

"Hi, Mohammed. Are you OK?" Emily said, a chipper tremor in her voice.

"*Salaam.* Not really, to be honest," Mohammed laugh-coughed, sipping from his herbal tea. He was a Middle Eastern fellow with a turban, face sallow and nose runny. "I have been sick with the Grix for a few days, eating a lot, staying in bed. I'm sure I'll be back to normal in no time. The physician heals, nature makes well."

"Oh no, how did you get it?" Emily asked, leaning on the door jamb.

Mohammed wrinkled his nose. He had very dark eyes, almost as black as the night, and the door plate said his last name was Bashir. "A trip to the Middle East, I'm sure," he croaked, voice faint and raspy. "I just got back from Petra working on electromagnetism, to be specific. Travel often brings unexpected developments."

"Sorry, the *Grix*?" Joseph asked, in his usual bewildered state.

Emily clarified patiently, "The Grix is an illness that results from being out of Hyleberia's 5th dimension, sometimes acquired when working in Tellurian conditions. Mohammed spends a lot of time abroad testing, as an Administrator of Electrons." She turned back to Mohammed. "This is my friend, Joseph . . . and Gabriel. You quite possibly have heard of him, the colt. He's looking for a roommate and was hoping to have a viewing during lunch break"

"Ah, nice to meet you. Sorry, come back in a couple of days," Mohammed said as he faced Joseph, black eyes piercing his soul. "You taking care of Peter's pet, or something?"

"Yeah, a favour." Joseph nodded, stepping away, as he

was not keen to try to explain the reasons why for the millionth time.

"That's great, helping others always makes me feel better," Mohammed mumbled, and then started choking. "Actually, I feel something rising in my throat. . . ."

Not much wanting to be thrown up on, Joseph and Emily left immediately. As they made their way down the stairs, he wondered if this could be considered some form of treason to Raymond. *Oh, who cares? He's an idiot.*

Joseph and Emily exited Terribilità Terrace's double doors and began the walk back to school, as she began to tell him about her favourite sushi restaurant. Around them, jackhammers droned and hammers chinked, and then. . . .

Sshhhhhhh.

There was a sound of something sliding above. A large, blurred object above had just fallen off a pallet, a block of bricks. A builder's scream resounded from on top of the scaffolding, followed by a yell of, "Watch out!"

Looking up, Gabriel yelped, and so did Emily and Joseph. In instinct, he raised his hands in the direction of the load of bricks headed their way.

That was when something utterly bizarre happened. The bricks shifted from their falling trajectory. Very suddenly, they moved aside and collided at arm's length from them, smashing into the cement, erupting into pieces. *Crrssshhh.* As they hit the ground, for a split second, they made a booming sound like a machine gun going off.

Joseph and Emily squinted at the fallen bricks, both terrified. *What the hell was that?* Buzzing with adrenaline, neither one of them said anything.

"Sorry! Are you OK?" called the feckless builder, face appearing over the ledge and breaking the silence.

Joseph didn't say a word. He just looked at the scattered bricks, which were now hundreds of pieces of burnt clay, lying a few feet from them. Gabriel on his shoulder didn't seem remotely bothered, but Joseph realised he had almost died for the second time. He had a very clear afterimage in his mind of the brick's abrupt change of momentum. It was as if the bricks had been attached to an invisible rope, or a divine power had interfered and saved them. He looked at Emily in shock, who was no longer standing stock-still.

"Watch where you step, moron!" Emily yelled up, shaking her fist. "You nearly sent us to meet Thanatos! Do you realise how close, like, that came to killing us? You're lucky we're not back in Samsara right now!"

"I'm really sorry!" the builder screamed down, tripping on his heel, hardly keeping his balance up there even now.

Two minutes later, she tired of berating the builder and they proceeded back to classes, surely late by now.

"What just happened? Did you see the bricks change direction too?" Joseph, utterly baffled, asked when they were out of earshot of the construction crew.

"That imbecile nearly murdered us, that's what happened," Emily fumed. "I can't believe they let morons like that work here. To be honest, public services in Hyleberia are always abysmal. You should see the electricians. One time they messed up the wiring in my apartment so badly that the light switch turned on my blender."

"No, that's not what I meant," said Joseph, crossing his arms, as they hurried to Hyleberia Academy. "Did you see when the pallet of bricks was a second away from us, it changed direction? Kind of like . . . a miracle. Maybe. . ." Joseph looked down at Gabriel, who appeared completely unperturbed, smiling peacefully, ". . . he's my guardian angel. Maybe he saved us."

With crossed arms, Emily raised her left eyebrow and scoffed. "With no disrespect to Peter and his pet, and as cute as he is, the only thing Gabriel can guard is his own faecal matter. You must have imagined it. Let's just hope Ms Sadeghi doesn't punish us for being late."

133

Nonetheless, Joseph couldn't stop thinking about the miraculous force that had saved their lives, even after classes resumed. He kept glancing with newfound awe at Gabriel the Guardian Angel, who was sleeping in the corner. Gabriel certainly seemed like much more than an average sloth now. This lesson would have normally absorbed all of his attention. It was an interesting topic, McTaggart's A and B-theory of time, in other words the philosophy of time, and there was also a group discussion about the elements Tellurians were yet to discover. Prior to today, Joseph had witnessed the miraculous, almost magical events of Hyleberia like an observer of a strange movie. But it was a very new feeling to have personally been involved in one of them.

As the lesson crawled to its end, Joseph tried to decide who the best person to ask about what he had witnessed was. Besides not being in a particularly good mood, Ms Sadeghi wasn't an option; she had already said she didn't approve of Gabriel, and so wouldn't like to hear this.

He inhaled a deep sigh of relief when Ms Sadeghi called it a day. Emily rushed out as if he was a serial killer, but he wasn't planning on speaking to her anyway. Picking up Gabriel from the corner, he walked out the doors with Francis in tow. Today he was wearing a sleeveless "Hyle is Smile" T-shirt, and had a handsome new fringe-up haircut.

"*Cómo estás?*" Francis asked, as they both headed down the staircase. "You seem kind of off since the exam. Do you think you did badly?" He chuckled. "If it makes you feel better, you won't do worse than me."

Closing and opening his eyes, Joseph pulled himself together. He just hoped Ms Sadeghi hadn't noticed his distracted mind during the second half of classes.

"I'm not *off*. Confused maybe, as usual," Joseph said, and then in the next moment, he realised that Francis was a suitable person to ask for advice about this . . . the miracle he had witnessed. "Listen to what happened at lunch."

Francis proved to be a good listener.

"When something like that happens, it can put things in perspective," he said thoughtfully. "I had a similar experience as a Tellurian, where I fell on train tracks when I was really drunk and only got off just in time before I would've been mincemeat. Are you super grateful to be alive now? Is there a spring in your step?"

"Not really. I keep thinking of myself as dead, even if I've been 'Revitalised'," Joseph said cynically, as he held Gabriel tightly against his chest, feeling the sloth's sluggish heartbeat. "I am starting to think that Gabriel must be some sort of divine sloth. Maybe Gabriel is called Gabriel, like the angel, for a reason. Why else would Peter look after him if he had no use, no powers? Do you know when the last time somebody died in Hyleberia was?"

Francis mused, "Let me think. . . . Of course, we have Asclepius Hospital on the island, which can cure most ailments and injuries, even if they're incurable to Tellurians. But I heard there was this Hungarian guy once a few years ago who got locked in the Helios Tanning Salon sunbed and burned to death. Sad story. But that's not including Hyleberians who voluntarily leave the island to be reincarnated because they're sick of this place, I guess."

"Nice image," he said, suddenly feeling a bit sick.

"Accidents happen, even in heaven. Anyhow, dwelling won't help. Maybe we should talk about something lighter," Francis said. "Do you like video games?"

"Totally. I was planning on buying *Star Battle 2* before I died," Joseph said. "The first game is my favourite of all time. Haven't had much time to play since I arrived here, though."

"No way!" Francis exclaimed, grinning. "I bought that game last week! You can come over and play it at my place."

And so they spoke for a little while about video games. It was nice to distract himself from his problems, but a few minutes later, he said *adios* to Francis, making a point of his fatigue after the exam and near-death experience.

Still and all, Joseph could simply not forget the brick episode. It was just the way they had shifted direction at the exact moment he had raised his hand towards them. He knew that *something* had happened, but he couldn't work out what. *And why didn't Emily see it, if a miracle truly occurred, then?*

Gabriel did not react much to anything, but increasing mewling suggested he was famished after they arrived home, so Joseph quickly fed him some leaves. Thankfully, Raymond was still at work, giving him plenty of space and time to investigate his guardian angel conspiracy theory. He put Gabriel down in his bedroom and ran into the kitchenette to get some supplies. He was eager to test if there really could be any possibility that he or the sloth had moved those bricks. He did not see how it was possible; but at the same time, Joseph wasn't familiar with how the supernatural worked here.

He retrieved a couple of tennis balls from Raymond's bedroom; he would never notice because he had dozens. Then, he got a bowl from the kitchenette and set it on the floor of his bedroom. He held the tennis ball and aimed it towards the bowl. Joseph threw it, and right as it hit the centre, aimed his hand at the ball and tried to swerve it. He was sure this would look ridiculous to an outside spectator, but he didn't care.

The first toss yielded no result. He decided to give it a few more throws before packing up and reading. But he felt increasingly embarrassed with himself as the ball continued to fall into the bowl, displaying no difference of movement. He had reached the 15th attempt when he decided that this was a waste of time.

But before he gave up, Joseph realised the problem might be that Gabriel was not on his shoulder like before, and the ball was not aimed directly at him. He stood and picked up the sloth. Then, he aimed the ball above him so that it would bounce off the ceiling and hit him on the head. This time, aiming at it with his hand, right as the ball was about to collide with Joseph's forehead, the same miracle happened again—with a barely audible *swoosh*, it flew out of the way and narrowly avoided him.

Joseph breathed hard in disbelief. So, Gabriel did have some sort of abilities, but how and more importantly, why? He repeated the exercise several times, and on all but two occasions, it worked. What did this all mean? Was Gabriel his guardian angel? Did he somehow give Joseph powers?

"Shields, someone in there?" Raymond asked, looking in without knocking.

He must have arrived back home and Joseph hadn't even noticed. Raymond's snide glare scrutinised Joseph's bedroom, as if he were doing an inspection.

"No," Joseph replied instinctively, dropping the tennis ball.

"I see you've been keeping your room tidy. Good." Raymond's lips tightened as he spotted the ball. "What are you doing with that?"

"Playing fetch with Gabriel," he said shortly, holding Gabriel like a teddy bear to his chest, embarrassed by the incredibility of his own lie.

Raymond scoffed, stepping away. "Keep it down, and return my ball! I just got home from a long day. Now I want to relax with some *Goldeneye*."

And he left. Joseph was pleased that somehow Raymond had bought the fib. In the meantime, he desperately wanted some answers about this situation, but finding somebody to ask might be difficult at this time of day.

"Hi again, Raymond," Joseph greeted, stepping into the kitchenette a minute later.

"*Was geht*?" he said, tone suspicious. He was taking out a

Haoma from the fridge, and had not yet started his game. Joseph assumed this meant "how are you?" in German.

He didn't know how to bring up the topic subtly, so didn't bother. "Question. How do Proficiencies work in this place? How are they conferred? How do you earn them?" he asked.

"Why do you care about that?" Raymond asked distrustfully, sitting down and picking up his Controller. "It'll be ages till you have to worry about getting your own. Focus on SHOMAT for now. Took me about six attempts to pass."

"How about because . . . because I want to know?"

"I'm not Ms Sadeghi. Ask her," Raymond said, showing him a highly annoyed scowl.

Gabriel began tugging on Joseph's earlobes in a particularly painful manner. "But has anybody ever spontaneously developed Proficiency abilities, Aquaman?" he asked.

Raymond snorted. "Uh, no! They are not like erections. It was a few years before I got fluent in—get it?—water."

"Right. Is there some sort of, um, Proficiencies office?"

"Yes, it's on Hypokeimenon Avenue, near the Supernatural Foods. Now, if you don't mind, would you cut it with these inane questions and let me play my game?" he answered crossly.

"I don't know how this kind of witchcraft is so normalised to you," Joseph observed, stepping out of the door. "Oh, and by the way, I'm going."

"Where? To the office? Why?"

But Joseph didn't answer. He did not particularly feel like revealing any details about Gabriel's or his own powers at this point, so he made his exit and returned to his room. It seemed to him after this that the logical next step was to go to the Proficiencies Office and get more information.

He slipped on his trusty moccasins and popped out the front door with Gabriel on his shoulder, using the staircase because he did not trust the Hyleberian infrastructure after the earlier brick fall.

When he finally got to the office, it didn't give an indication of being anything more interesting than a toner merchant. At first. Workers were dressed in suits, faffing about with files and typing on odd-looking computers. However, several things such as a man on a motorised office chair, and a woman who was typing with her toes, gave the indication that it was not as normal as it might seem. The secretary proved completely unhelpful about his questions:

"The office closes in about five minutes. What is your Proficiencies ID?" a squat, harried-looking man at the front desk asked.

"I don't have one, sorry. I'm the colt," Joseph imparted, rocking an agitated, no longer asleep Gabriel back and forth like a baby. "I was just curious, which jobs do you have to do to get to earn telekinesis?"

"That's OMP346251, or the Object Motion Proficiency. All of this information is listed in the Proficiencies Handbook. Should I send you a copy?" he said, as a man in the background signed a form with some form of telepathic ink.

Not a very cool name, is it? "Uh, OK. And another random question, can animals ever develop Proficiencies?" Joseph asked, staring at a woman at a desk whose hands seemed to have just become staplers. "Like a magic dog."

The man frowned, and rudely remarked, "You came to our office out of curiosity for such a nonsensical question? It's a preposterous notion. Proficiencies are Peter-endowed abilities to transgress the laws of reality. When you've graduated Shrivatsa, there's a ceremony that takes place in Parliament, where you officially become your job title and get your abilities. Then, there's a long training period. So, they are certainly not like magic powers, and frankly, your question is an insult to my profession."

"Uh, right," Joseph said, suddenly wishing he hadn't come. "And—"

WEOEOWOWOEOEOWOWOWOWO.

And then, out of nowhere, the sirens went off. Joseph gasped as he saw them rise from the ground, even inside the office. Did this mean another corruption had been detected? Perhaps Gabriel had broken some kind of law by saving his life. The secretary and other workers jumped to their feet and dashed through the front doors, and Joseph swiftly followed suit.

A sudden sense of panic in the air, Gabriel made a terrified noise like an angry hamster; he didn't appear to like the ringing one bit. Joseph dashed out and back to the apartment, holding the sloth tightly.

The deep sky was dark grey like a freshwater pearl, and faint claps of thunder pealed in the distance. As an Englishman, the tropical climate of Hyleberia was often a little too hot for Joseph's liking, so he was not entirely opposed to seeing a bit of rain on the horizon.

Arriving back at Miyagi Apartments, he went into the living room to check in with Raymond. He was sitting with his back straight on the sofa, an aberration from his usual posture of lying with his feet up and a half-finished Haoma in one of his hands. *Goldeneye* was no longer on the screen. Rather, HB1 was blaring, as he had expected.

"Hi again, again. What do you think the hubbub is about?" Joseph asked, as he retrieved a Haoma from the fridge. "Probably it's something stupid like last time . . . right?"

He realised at this moment that he was trying to persuade himself, not Raymond. Joseph really didn't want to be about to head to that horrible holding cell for the second time.

"Possibly," imparted Raymond, who did not seem that bothered despite his posture, "but the sirens only go off once in a while, so either way, it's a pretty big deal. The visualiser newscaster said that, as Peter is away, someone from the Divine Council is going to be running things. They say this has not happened for aeons. He's going to give an announcement in a few minutes."

Joseph suddenly wondered if Peter's absence during the possible quarantine might be a problem. He questioned if there were arrangements in place in case he needed to return.

Gabriel had now calmed down a bit. Joseph patted him on the head paternally, and exclaimed, "Now, that's interesting. So some Hyleberian is going to be running things? Any idea who it will be?"

"Could be any of the bigwigs in Hyleberian politics. Fred Smith, Oisin O'Hara, Dola Ibrahim, Bogdan Stan, Sofia Petrova . . . any of them," Raymond said. "Hyleberian politics is really weird."

Joseph sat down across from Raymond to await the announcement, Gabriel on his lap. The visualiser screen flashed to a video feed of a room with peach-coloured walls and wine-coloured carpets, and an empty podium in the middle with a sign that read: "Head of the Divine Council".

"Do you ever go to Parliament for your job?" Joseph asked, as he waited for something more to happen on the visualiser, trying to momentarily bury his hard feelings towards Raymond. "I mean, aren't you an Administrator and all?"

"You're asking a lot of questions today. Curiosity killed the cook, eh? Regardless, only on special occasions," said Raymond shortly. "I'm only a Level 3 Administrator—not even a little prestigious. Mainly Level 1s are given the honour of attending Parliament every week."

How exclusive. Joseph scratched Gabriel's back to stop him from crying, as he was starting to whine again.

At the bottom of the screen, the crawler text reported: "The Head of the Divine Council Is About to Arrive to Discuss the State of Emergency".

Joseph felt blood rush to his head as the Head of the Divine Council waddled into view. He was a walrus-moustached, dumpy man. It seemed he had dwarfism of some sort. He was dressed in a formal double-breasted suit. Climbing up the steps, he leaned over to the microphone and tapped it nervously, his humourless face lurking above the podium. After clearing his throat for what felt like minutes, a timid, mousy voice came out of his throat:

"Good evening, fellow Hyleberians. For the unaware, my name is Richard Hoskins, Senior Governor of the Divine Council. As reported last night, Peter has gone on Recalibration, and will be gone for an unknown period of time. Thus, I have been elected by the Divine Council to make this announcement and take executive decisions. The relevant emergency provision is stipulated in divine law, in short, that in the event of any executive action becoming required of an emergency nature during the absence of Peter, the Divine Council may choose democratically a Prime Minister in his stead. In the past fifteen minutes, I have been voted and conferred the duties of Acting Prime Minister. Now, as to why the sirens have been triggered. . . ."

"Is he well known around here, Raymond?" Joseph asked.

"Sort of," he replied over the speech. "He's often in the debates, arguing for something or another. He's been in politics for decades, and is a vocal conservative and separationist. That just means he thinks we shouldn't intervene in Tellurian affairs."

"Where's he from, then? Sounds English."

Raymond shrugged. "Wales, I think. Ah, I guess he's British like you. Now, be quiet."

Richard continued in an authoritative voice, "We have already found the cause of the sirens, and I regret to inform you that it is not a simple corruption like last time. There is no easy way to say this. A precious, priceless, greatly beloved artefact and treasure has been stolen from the Divine Repository: the golden cone. While we are still reviewing the security tapes, it appears that the cone was taken from the museum between 5 - 6 pm today, after it had closed. Nobody has been arrested so far, although a certain temporarily anonymous individual is being questioned and is under suspicion. Be that as it may, on account of the severity of this crime, everyone is to be quarantined to their lodgings until further notice."

"The *golden cone*. I just saw that last week!" Joseph exclaimed, stunned. "And I overheard this conversation with people talking about stealing something yesterday."

Raymond gasped, equally shocked. "You did? Why didn't you tell me before?"

Joseph shrugged. "It doesn't matter now, does it?"

As Joseph quickly explained the details, he was keeping an ear open for a knock on the door, and Sergeant Rufius' arrival with handcuffs. Thankfully, no such knock arrived. For now.

But the speech wasn't quite over. Richard was summing up.

" . . .Without wanting to incite alarm, an emergency as serious as this has not happened, if memory serves, ever, and especially not while Peter was in Recalibration. There are at present no intentions to summon the Prime Minister during this time—that would be a grave error. Recalibrations typically take a week to three at most, so we hope that quarantine will be able to end at worst, when he returns, but likely as soon as when the culprit is confirmed. The thief will, of course, be dealt with and punished to the full extent of the law. Thank you all for your time," Richard concluded.

The Acting Prime Minister stepped down from the podium, and HB1 switched feeds to a bewildered newscaster, whose subsequent speech Raymond muted. Joseph felt at sixes and sevens. It was difficult to know how to react to all this. The sirens were still wailing at an incredibly loud volume in the background, as if the world itself were screaming, only muffled by the walls.

"Crap, crap, crap. I guess we're going to be stuck here for a while," Raymond complained over the blaring noise, standing up and walking to the fridge to evaluate supplies. "Too bad—looks like you are almost out of food. You're going to starve at this rate."

By the tone of his voice, this possibility sounded rather good to Raymond, who was turning on the oven, getting out spaghetti sauce and mincemeat to cook up his dinner.

"So, any ideas who stole the cone?" Joseph asked, crossing his legs. He relayed some more about the conversation that he had eavesdropped. "I wonder if that had something to do with it. But what would be the purpose of taking the cone? I guess it has some kind of divine power."

"Does it, for realsies?" Raymond asked, washing the cutlery he had used last night. "I heard it was the thing by which the world was made. That's all I know, really. Everyone around here practically worships it."

Joseph groaned thickly. "You should know more than me!"

Raymond frowned at him. "What I'm most interested in is why these emergencies and things keep happening right after your arrival. Are you the spawn of Satan or something?"

"Of course," Joseph said uninterestedly, getting to his feet and walking down the hall to his bedroom.

"Is that why you have a tail? I always wondered," Raymond called back.

Fortunately, in a few minutes, the headache-aggravating sirens turned off. Even so, Joseph did not see how he could do anything productive that night, too unnerved by everything that had occurred to shut off his brain.

He spent the next few hours trying and failing to read. At around midnight, with Gabriel on his shoulder, he attempted the tennis ball trick once more. Gabriel seemed to be able to have some effect even when the ball was not falling down on his head this time. It appeared that his furry companion's presence gave him some form of ability. He had discovered it was impossible that the telekinetic powers were coming solely from him, as whenever he tried to move the tennis balls without Gabriel, he couldn't do a thing. But it did seem that Joseph was somehow involved, as objects only moved when he willed them to.

When he finally dropped off, on top of the fog dream, Joseph had a terrible nightmare about a merman uprising. In the background of it, a dull, thudding noise boomed that refused logical explanation. He could not tell what it was, but the roaring, rumbling crashing seemed to grow louder throughout the night.

Joseph awoke shaking from a nightmare, sweat dripping from his forehead. He got up and looked through his wardrobe to work out what to wear today. Then, he heard something odd: the thundering noise from his dream. It was still there. He realised quickly it must be a real thunderstorm.

"Do you know if we're allowed to go outside yet?" he asked drowsily, predicting that Raymond would be in his usual spot as he strolled into the living room.

But Raymond was hardly even paying attention, he realised, as Joseph glanced over. He was standing as if petrified, leaning with his eyes and nose inches from the laminated glass, steam building up from his breath on the glass.

"Haven't you looked *al fresco* this morning?" Raymond exclaimed, a note of astonishment in his voice as he pointed outside.

Still sleepy, Joseph mumbled, "*Al fresco?* What? That's just a storm. It'll clear up, right?"

But after approaching the window and seeing what was going on, Joseph knew at once his words had been very pre-emptive. A surging layer of water coated the grass and pavements of Miyagi Apartments, waves streaming over the courtyard like it was a pool. Flowerpots that had stood upright yesterday were now washed away, or smashed into shards. Rainfall continued to descend, thunder raging, and dark, silvery clouds were blocking the sun. This flood was not stopping any time soon, he realised, as fright surged through him.

Hyleberia was drowning.

CHAPTER 8

GOLDEN CONE

JOSEPH HAD NEVER BEEN SO SICK OF BEING INSIDE. IT WAS reaching mid-afternoon, and the rain continued to pour, the water level outside steadily rising like a guillotine's blade. He had not yet left the front door since his return from the Proficiencies Office. Joseph had received a mass email from Ms Miyagi, the owner of the apartment complex, reporting that there had already been damage to the apartments. Regrettably, things were not improving.

At this moment, Raymond lay sprawled on the sofa, clipping his nails and staring at the ceiling with his mouth wide open, while Joseph sat near him at the living room console table, trying to read but unable to concentrate. Raymond's record player was by his side, playing a 45 of the Beatles single "Rain" over and over again, either to annoy Joseph or just because he was bored out of his mind.

"If the rain comes, they run and hide their heads," Paul McCartney sang for the tenth time.

Joseph had spent much of the morning reading lost works of literature, watching the clueless newscasters on HB1, and staring out the windows with bleary eyes. Though he was struggling to focus, in his hands currently was *A Hyleberia History*. The book did not contain much information about the ancient history of the island such as the Great Schism or the Prince of Darkness, just one short deeply biased chapter. The most interesting titbit Joseph had found so far was some pictures of Hyleberia from the past, which appeared very different, with predictably less advanced technology and a bearded Peter. It seemed that Hyleberia in large followed Tellurian technological trends, with the exception of archons and some devices that were far beyond modern Tellurian capabilities. It was highly strange seeing Peter appear in the pictures with historical figures who lived too early to be photographed, such as Domitian and Pharaoh Akhenaten, and there was even one with his arm around Thaddeus.

"I'M SO BORED! I just want to go outside. Who would have thought water could become my arch-nemesis in a single night?" Raymond cried abruptly, at last raising the record player needle.

"Maybe it's karma," Joseph replied, turning a page. "For you or me. I used to be really unlucky, and then ever since I arrived in Hyleberia, it all sort of stopped. I have a feeling the unluckiness is coming back, with a vengeance."

Gabriel, expressionless and sleepy, was dangling from the table with a bored expression. Joseph had taken to letting him explore the apartment on his own. He found it was harder to maintain his attachment to the sloth when he kept urinating randomly on the carpet. Still, it was nice to have someone, or something else, to talk to.

"Why don't we see? Do you wanna play a board game, Josephine?" Raymond proposed, as he sat up. "I have Monopoly and Who's Who."

"No thanks," Joseph answered, listening to the rain patter outside. He was trying to understand a term in the book, *Ichor*, which kept coming up. "Unless it's the silence board game. I've got things to do."

Raymond had tied his long hair into a bun during quarantine, and today he was wearing a tracksuit for some reason.

"Come on, fun police! It's not like we're doing anything, just sitting here."

"Tell me, why is this even happening? Can't the weather department just turn off the rain? You're in the department, aren't you? Figure it out. Press the sun button," Joseph pointed out.

"You don't get it, smartarse. Just because I'm a Water Administrator doesn't mean I can stop this. Peter holds all power over Hyleberian meteorology. Otherwise, some newbie could set the wind to a thousand miles an hour, and blow us all away in a tornado. Peter is responsible, in fact, for all laws that govern Hyleberia."

"Look how well that turned out. So, why *did* you become a Water Administrator?" Joseph asked out of curiosity.

Raymond scratched his neck and blinked. "Oh, I just really like water."

Joseph made an unsatisfied grant. "You also like Haoma. Why not become a Haoma Administrator? Give me details."

"I suppose there is some more background, but it's kind of a sob story." Raymond put his nail clippers down and looked at Joseph with an aggrieved expression. "You see, when I was a baby my . . . Mum and Dad died from drowning on board the Titanic. They loved travelling. I got rescued, but after that, left as an orphan and struggling to survive on the streets on my own, I developed an aversion towards water, hydrophobia, I guess. I hated it, and never went swimming my entire life. When I arrived here—I actually died from lead poisoning from the apartment where I was living—and got Water Administrator on my career profiler, I decided that it was high time to face my fear," he explained. "And after a few decades, now I love the damn thing!"

Joseph stared at him. Raymond's tone had become a tad serious when he spoke about his parents.

"Wow, the Titanic. Sorry for your loss," murmured Joseph, not prepared for this reveal.

Raymond got to his feet, annoyed. "Yes, I know it's *so* tragic—look, I don't want your pity. What about you, then? Your origin story. Why didn't you, y'know, go to university like people of your age usually do?"

Joseph laughed. "That's easy. I couldn't afford it. But Thomas, my friend, kept trying to get me to go, saying I should take out a loan, how I was wasting my life by just working in retail."

Raymond avoided eye contact. "Why was he such an ass?"

Joseph pushed his fringe back, wondering when he was going to find time to get a haircut. "He was judgmental and idealistic about my potential, I guess. In hindsight, maybe he was right," he said. "Look, I have to get going and do some things in my room. Sorry about the game."

"Stupid me for thinking you would be able to have fun," Raymond shouted, sitting back down and putting Rain on his record player again. "Don't bother me for the rest of the day."

That's fine with me. Joseph picked up Gabriel, sloped off to his room, and relaxed on his bed with his Hylebook balanced on the sheets.

Yet after a few minutes of browsing, he was interrupted by an alarming noise. As someone knocked on the front door, Joseph's stomach clenched. *Oh no, the police are onto me. I'm in trouble. I don't even know what I did, though.*

He guessed that Sergeant Rufius had found some reason to arrest him, likely linked to his apparent sloth guardian angel, or something else incriminating. He got up and quietly walked to the bedroom door jamb, but when he heard Raymond's footsteps, he realised that his roommate was already at the front door. Feeling his hands tremble slightly, Joseph put his ear against his door.

"Can I help you?" Raymond asked.

"Yeah. I'm Thaddeus Deaus. We've met once before, at the Galactic Gala a few decades ago, I think."

Joseph felt his heart decelerate at once. But why was Thaddeus here? He swung open his door and strode down the hall. Thaddeus was, for the first time in his memory, looking rather tense and concerned. He was dressed in a wrinkled raincoat, eyes both red. Dark blue veins formed tree roots on his forehead. He had Wellington boots on which were, much like all of his figure, drenched.

"Looks like you have just been through a car wash," Joseph observed, as Thaddeus came into view.

Thaddeus, miserably grimacing, warmed his hands on the apartment radiator. "Yes, but I'm not the issue here. The police have asked me to come and get you." Joseph felt his every muscle become taut: so, his fears were well-founded. "Don't worry, you're not under suspicion. They just want to speak to you about someone else. We have to go right now."

He stared at Thaddeus, tapping his foot. "Details, please?" he asked, unintentionally sounding a bit rude.

Thaddeus' left eye looked particularly twitchy today, as if he had something very large stuck in it. "There's been an arrest regarding the theft of the golden cone," Thaddeus said gravely. "The police are questioning everybody who recently spoke to the suspect. Apparently, that includes you. Nonetheless, I don't think they will take much of your time. You'd better leave the sloth behind."

Raymond butted in. "Joseph has been fraternising with the thief?"

"No. . . ." Joseph wrinkled his nose. *At least, I don't think I have.*

"I should have known," Raymond continued, throwing his arms up. "A criminal under my own roof! This is how you repay me for letting you into my home!"

Joseph knew he was being sarcastic, but he still wasn't amused.

"Shut up. I'll get my shoes," he snorted, stepping back

towards his room. "But I have a feeling that I will need something stronger than moccasins."

Raymond groaned angrily, "You're not borrowing my clothes!"

As he hadn't had much time to shop since arrival in Hyleberia, his fashion options were extremely limited. In the end, Joseph managed to persuade Raymond to lend him some clothes by paying several drachmas for the loan of each item, not that his roommate was particularly pleased about it even then. He threw on his Baja hoodie and a heavy raincoat that Raymond had bought from a fashion shop called *Sthyle*. He also lent him a pair of shoes other than those worn-out moccasins, tennis trainers, although boots would have been preferable. Joseph picked up Gabriel from his bed and tried to hand him to Raymond.

"Thanks for the clothes. You have to look after him, too. I can't take a sloth out in this weather," he pointed out to a louring Raymond. "He'll freeze to death, won't he?"

"What! No way," Raymond shouted, pushing Gabriel away like the sloth was diseased. "The clothes are enough!"

Joseph rattled his brain for other solutions about what to do with Gabriel, but none came. Thankfully, after five minutes of persuasion and further pressure from Thaddeus, Raymond somehow agreed. Joseph could only hope that Gabriel's guardian angel abilities didn't manifest while he was away.

"Ugh, guess I don't have a choice, but you'll be paying me for this," Raymond said, reluctantly taking Gabriel in his arms like he was a poisonous snake. Gabriel looked between the German and the Englishman with a pained expression, as if Joseph were handing him to a sloth eater in disguise. "And I'm not playing with him. He'll have to entertain himself."

"I'm pretty sure he's easily entertained. Just don't let him out of your sight." Joseph scratched Gabriel on the ear with some fondness. He had to admit that he had got attached to the sloth, despite their rocky start. "Bye, Gabriel. Take care."

"So, any news when Peter will be back?" Raymond asked Thaddeus, as Gabriel crawled on his shoulder, making a frightened sound.

Thaddeus frowned grimly. "There's no precedent, sadly, so it's a matter of guesswork. Recalibrations take anywhere from a week to three months." And then he said slightly passive-aggressively, "If only Peter planned better. . . . He's always been a bit impulsive and very trusting, too. But don't tell him I said that."

"Excuse me, three months? That Richard Hoskins fellow seemed to estimate much less," replied Joseph.

Thaddeus shrugged. "He's trying not to alarm people. Everyone expects the eclipse is the awakening date, as is the general trend, but during past Recalibrations he has over-slept. To tell you the truth, it's suspected that the golden cone's absence has led to a corruption of weather processing, and so is the cause of the storm. Unfortunately, the Divine Council is estimating the weather might get even worse."

Joseph's heart dropped. *How could it get worse?* His mind flashed to images of disaster movies where New York and other cities get levelled by floods. *Why did I have to arrive just before all of this?*

Thaddeus stared at his boots in a hangdog way that didn't exactly reassure anyone, his wet scar glimmering under the lightbulb. "Let's go now before we tempt fate, J-man."

"Break a leg," Raymond said as they left and he slammed the door shut, but Joseph wasn't quite sure whether he meant it literally or not.

Everything seemed fine on the way down the staircase, but when he and Thaddeus reached the ground floor of Miyagi Apartments, the extent of the flooding became all too clear. The bottom two steps of the stairs were no longer visible, the water in the lobby reaching knee height. He could tell it was bad from the window, but up close the damage was much more visceral; he could practically smell the rotting wood of the mouldering walls. The Sputnik chandelier above the hallway was flickering on and off ominously; sprinkles of Pincushion moss from the garden had drifted into the hall, floating aimlessly; and perhaps most curiously, a single Canadian goose was swimming by the postbox, flapping its wings, helplessly honking.

Joseph gasped at the sight of the bird. "Poor goose! We'd better let her out."

"Yeah. Rain last night was insane," Thaddeus revealed, as he rubbed his hands together for warmth. "Pipes have burst and Tathagata monastery had to be evacuated. Hopefully, we don't get hypothermia. Right, I'll go ahead and open the door, then you follow me out. The current can be pretty strong, so try to keep both of your feet firmly planted on the ground."

Thaddeus forged ahead through the flooding to the front door. He shooed the goose down the hall in front of him. He heaved the door open, leaning against the wall for support as the water streamed in. The now hissing and clearly unhappy goose swam out, neck bent against the rain. Another wave of the flood surged into the hall, brimming over Thaddeus' lower legs.

"Come on!" Thaddeus barked, as he held the door open for Joseph.

Eyes flickering between Thaddeus' face and the over-spilled door, Joseph found it difficult to persuade his instincts that the eddying, dangerous-looking whirlpool of water that covered the floor was the right direction for his legs to go. Having finally managed to convince them, the water's temperature was utterly freezing; he hoped that he would get used to the cold in a few minutes, and not be dealing with this agony the whole journey to the Police Station.

Joseph's teeth chattered, an eruption of goosebumps spreading down his arms. *How could the weather have changed so quickly from sunny to this mid-winter climate?* Ten layers would hardly be enough for these conditions. Joseph supposed he had been stupid to think his poor fortune could be over for good. For perhaps the first time since his arrival and the start of his new existence, his Tellurian life seemed in some ways better.

"Lovely day," he commented, as he exited the complex, and accidentally stepped on a flowerpot shard. "Ouch!"

"Yeah." Thaddeus didn't smile, jaw clamped, stepping forward and beckoning him through the icy murk.

The streets were deserted. Covered by clouds, the sky was smeared with black and crumbly grey like a charcoal painting, the piercing air resembling conditions one might find back in Southend on a particularly harsh December day. As Joseph and Thaddeus stepped through the flood to the Police Station, the water swelling and rippling around his feet, Joseph looked through the circumambient windows and noticed that many of the shops had had their merchandise ruined, including Tony's Halo Hats where the hats were no longer floating.

After a period of silence between them, as they stepped past Ontomart Joseph decided to reveal to Thaddeus the conversation on which he had eavesdropped. It seemed that it was time to stop acting like this incident had never happened. "Can I tell you something?" Joseph asked Thaddeus. After Thaddeus nodded, he continued, "I must confess, the other day, I overheard a conversation about the golden cone theft, that is, before it happened."

"Really? What exactly did they say?" Thaddeus asked, staring at him as the water splashed over his heels.

"There were two guys; I didn't see who, but they must be the thieves," Joseph asserted, and then explained the scraps of conversation he had made out before they disappeared. " . . . Something about making the most of someone's absence to take something."

"Hmmm. It's interesting, don't get me wrong. But if they didn't mention the cone specifically, it's very likely unrelated," Thaddeus said sharply, as he turned away. "And besides, surely, you couldn't have heard well hidden in some bin bags."

"But it really sounded like they were planning on taking the cone," Joseph said, rubbing his head.

"I just think it's a bit far-fetched that they would gather to discuss such a top-secret criminal operation in broad daylight," Thaddeus opined, eye twitching wildly. "And also, the police already have a suspect, and they believe he was acting alone."

"Oh, right," he said distractedly, intrigued by Thaddeus' certainty but not exactly convinced by his logic. "Well, you're the expert, I guess. I'm just a blockish retail worker from Southend."

Why did he dismiss me so quickly? At this point, Joseph was getting slightly annoyed with Thaddeus. By the time they reached the police station, he felt he might be more ice sculpture than man. Sergeant Rufius was sitting at the front desk with a policewoman, a snide, unhappy moue on both of their impassive faces. Joseph's instinct when he spotted Rufius was to run, such was the bad impression the man had made during their previous encounters. They stood up and turned to Joseph as he came in, as if they had been expecting him.

Joseph muttered, "You wanted to see me?"

"Y-yes," stammered the woman with pigtails of thick ginger hair, and a surly face that had large lips and penetrating eyes. She had very acned skin, apparently a rather bad speech impediment and was shaking slightly. "I'm S-Sergeant Alice Whi-te-te, and I'm going to be a-asking you some q-questions t-today about our s-suspect."

He didn't know how to react. "Oh, OK. About what, who?"

"I'll take you into the questionin' room," Sergeant Rufius

stated, licking his lips like a bulldog offered meat. He seemed to be growing a mohawk these days, which somehow gave him an even more malicious presence. "You've said you wanted to handle the rest, then, White?"

"Ye-yes," Sergeant White said, cheeks red. "I d-did. I n-neverr q-question s-ssuspects. I n-need p-p-practice."

Joseph let himself be led away from Thaddeus, feeling like a sheep to the slaughter. The walk with Sergeant Rufius soon proved to be the epitome of awkwardness.

"So, how have you been, Shields?" Sergeant Rufius asked as he guided Joseph through the hall into the questioning room. His tone was uncaring, bitter.

Joseph stood as far away as possible from him. "Brilliant. Where are you from, by the way?"

"Tennessee. And I've been utterly sublime, busy with the Hunting Society," Sergeant Rufius revealed, cracking his knuckles. He had the air of someone who had been a proficient schoolyard bully.

"Oh, right." There was a revolver on Rufius' belt that suddenly looked rather threatening. "Nice gun."

"Thanks. You see, guns are prohibited on Hyleberia to everyone but the police. But there's an islet not far from the harbour called Mortem Islet where there's some game, and all sorts of guns otherwise banned can be loaned. Huntin' Society mostly hunts bison, but last week I got a giraffe! I had its head framed on my mantle as well, next to my elephant and anteater heads," Sergeant Rufius explained, as he imitated shooting a giraffe with a thumb gun.

Joseph remained silent; he wiped his forehead.

Sergeant Rufius added, "You're not vegetarian, are you? To be honest, I don't have much respect for 'em. From my perspective, all real men need at least five steaks a week to get protein. In truth, I only eat animals I've shot myself, and I 'specially love elephant meat."

Joseph coiled his fist. "Oh no, not vegetarian."

157

"Good," grumbled Sergeant Rufius ambiguously with a deep, low-pitched voice. "Can't stand 'em."

Thankfully, this was as far as that conversation went. The questioning room had two plastic chairs, one plain desk and an ancient-looking visualiser with a VHS player hooked onto the wall. Sergeant Rufius didn't overstay his welcome. A couple of minutes after he had gone, and after Joseph had made himself uncomfortable on perhaps the least comfortable chair (if it could even be called that) he had ever sat on, Sergeant White entered. She sat opposite to Joseph and offered him a half-full cup of dingy water.

"So, what's going on?" Joseph asked, playing with his fingers.

Sergeant White appeared extremely shy; she was practically unable to speak without holding her hand partly over her face. "An i-individuual that you m-may havve met d-uuring your s-hhort time in Hylebberia has b-been arrested un-dder suspicion of st-tealing the g-oldden co-ne."

He stared at her, mouth wide open. She was rather difficult to understand. "Who?"

Joseph waited with bated breath for the name to be revealed. It came torturously slowly out of Sergeant White's slim lips: "F-Francis Rodrig-go."

His Adam's apple jumped slightly. "Francis!?"

This news made as much sense to Joseph as the world Prime Minister being a middle-aged guy with a pet sloth. Why on Earth would *Francis*, a poetry and video game enthusiast, steal the golden cone? Francis was the last Hyleberian Joseph would have pegged as the thief. Of course, he didn't know the man particularly well, but his Tellurian criminal history was only drug-related as far as Joseph knew. Instantly, he remembered one of their most relevant conversations: it was *Francis* who had introduced him to the golden cone in the museum.

Sergeant White's voice seemed intended to be calm, but

there was a tension to the interaction that could not be covered by her cool demeanour. "Y-you know him, t-then?" she asked.

"Yeah. . . . I mean, we're in the same class, and we're friends," he said.

Sergeant White was about ten percent as intimidating as Sergeant Rufius, but Joseph did feel rightly or wrongly that Rufius was constantly plotting his own murder. The questions went on, covering every little detail of Joseph's impression of and interaction with Francis over the past weeks.

"Why is he your prime suspect?" he asked during one of the rare lulls in between questions. He had by now told her about the conversation he had overheard, only to receive a similar uninterested response to the one Thaddeus had given. "Surely, it's more likely to be one of those sketchy people in that alley than an innocent student!"

"Unf-ffortunately, h-h-alf heard whisperss don't amount t-o muc-c-h f-or our invest-t-t-igation. Besiddes Francis' c-crimin-aal ba-c-c-kground a-s a-a T-tellurian," Sergeant White said, without once saying a word correctly, "he w-was the only persson f-f-oundd on f-footage capptured of the c-crime itsself."

"What about witnesses? Surely, you need more evidence than a video," Joseph pointed out.

"W-would you l-likke to see the video f-footage youurself? It's vv-ery i-incrim-mminating."

"Sure," he said instantaneously, not sure what he was expecting,

She left and swiftly returned with a videotape, which she plopped into the VHS.

"Hh-old on, on-ee mom-m-ment," mumbled Sergeant White, as she fiddled with the rewind and forward buttons. The screen's image fuzzed as she very slowly found the time-stamp. "H-here. Your f-friend, R-Rodrigo, apppears in a f-few s-seconds."

Joseph stared at the screen as the Divine Repository came into focus. He recognised the place it showed, of course—the same location that he had seen the golden cone in the display not long ago. However, in this case, the museum was shuttered, with only a faint glow of remaining daylight. On the screen, a figure that was undeniably Francis entered the security camera's range of view. He was dressed in black, like a proper thief might be, except for the curious absence of the most important part of any disguise —a mask. Joseph felt like he was watching some sort of practical joke as he saw him, without even sneaking or feigning any caution, run up to the display cabinet. It quickly became evident that Francis had no criminal acumen. He pulled out a hammer, aimed it at the display, and *smash!*

Joseph looked back at Sergeant White in disbelief, speech-less, as she turned off the screen.

Sergeant White made a condescending facial expression. "He c-claims to have no r-r-recolllection of these e-events, and we havve not yet r-recovered the cone. The r-reposit-ttory was c-closed at the t-time. We have s-poken with all t-the p-people that he is knowwn to have i-interacted with that d-day. Now, d-do you have any c-comm-ments r-regarding the t-t-ttape?" she asked.

Speechless, he didn't. The questioning continued for half an hour after that, with Sergeant White cross-examining every aspect of Joseph's brief friendship with Francis. Most of the questions, he had to ask her to repeat several times.

"How was it?" Thaddeus asked, after Sergeant White directed him out of the questioning room to the Police Station hall, and returned to her office.

Joseph heard the rain hammering down outside, as he steeled himself for the journey home.

"It was fine," he muttered, still extremely confounded. But he wanted to get back as soon as possible so he could think about it all properly. "Shall we go, then? I just want to visit the grocery store on the way. I need some supplies. Also—"

A call of his name sounded from down the hall, resulting in this thought being cut off.

"Joseph? Is that you?"

He swivelled around. Joseph recognised the voice at once —Francis, he was there. It was even coming from the same holding cell he had occupied on his last visit to the police station.

Startled, Joseph called back, "Francis?"

"*Si*! Come over here," Francis called with a harrowed, exhausted tone.

Joseph glanced around for Sergeant Rufius and Sergeant White at their desk, but did not see either of them. They must be currently talking about the interview. He did not know for sure, but almost certainly they wouldn't allow him to converse with Francis. To Joseph, this seemed like even more reason to dash over there.

He was accosted with bad memories as he reached the holding cell. The terrible conditions hadn't improved at all since his short stay here. Behind bars, Francis looked bedraggled and unwashed as he stared at Joseph. This was no surprise: the holding cell shower's water pressure was a joke, and likely the pipes were frozen.

"Hey, *amigo*," Francis, unshaven, greeted him dejectedly. "I suppose they've shown you the tape at this point, convinced you I was the thief."

Joseph looked through the bars. "Yeah, they showed it to me. So, tell me then, did you do it?"

An outraged countenance on his face, Francis exclaimed, "No. It's complete *mierda*. That wasn't me! I have no idea how, but someone, somehow, is framing me."

"What do you mean?" Joseph asked, as his pulse raced.

Francis gripped the bars, lines forming under his alarmed eyes. "Look, I know we don't know each other that well, but I can assure you of this . . . the last thing I remember before all this happened is returning to my apartment after class, not long after our talk about Gabriel. I felt weirdly cold, there was a sudden pain, and then I must have lost consciousness. I have absolutely no recollection of anything in that video."

"J-man," Thaddeus warned from behind, putting a hand on his back. "You're not supposed to—"

"Just one moment!" he shouted back, swiping Thaddeus' hand away. He leaned in close to the bars, nose almost touching them, and before he even knew what he was saying, averred, "I don't believe it was you either. Honestly, I heard a couple of guys conspiring about the theft before any of this happened. They said something about their plans to take the cone. I told Sergeant White, but she just dismissed it."

"You have to find out who they are. I can assure you that whatever black magic someone is using, I did not steal a single thing," Francis said, a sudden look of realisation appearing on his face. "Oh, I should tell you . . . I have a theory about who the true culprit might be! Do you know—"

"WHO GAVE YOU BLASTED PERMISSION TO SPEAK TO THE SUSPECT? GET AWAY FROM HIM, SHIELDS, BEFORE I PUT YOU IN THERE TOO!" Sergeant Rufius yelled.

Joseph's heart froze as Sergeant Rufius stomped down the hall. He placed a strong, hairy hand on his shoulder and swung him around, practically punching him away from Francis.

"I didn't realise talking to suspects was banned. Don't bite my head off," he defended himself, wishing he had heard what Francis was about to say.

"SHUT IT, SHIELDS!" Sergeant Rufius screamed, unappeased. "IT'S OBVIOUS!"

"Joseph!" Francis called after him, as he was forced away.

He couldn't do anything for the short-term but let himself be dragged out of the station by Rufius' brawny arms, and then be thrown back into the thrashing rain. Joseph didn't want to become the next head on Sergeant Rufius' mantle. As his already soaked feet landed in the weltering floodwater, Sergeant Rufius screamed, "Go home now, Shields, unless you are longing to be behind bars again with Rodrigo. This time, you won't have Peter to save you!"

Sergeant Rufius strode inside without turning back, while Thaddeus helped Joseph to his feet and they both started walking through the misty rain.

As they stepped through the flood, Joseph remembered that he too had been the victim of a false accusation in Hyleberia. Moreover, he had a good reason to believe that Francis wasn't the thief, the overheard alley conversation, and was fond enough of his classmate to have a little faith that he was perhaps being framed.

The devastating, frosty gales raged worse than before as Joseph and Thaddeus waded back to Miyagi Apartments. Thaddeus reported that he had to go fetch someone else after this, as he was helping the short-staffed police with the questioning about the theft. On the way to the police station, it had seemed to Joseph everything was closed, but he now noticed a faint glow of light discernible from a convenience store. This was a prime opportunity to stock up on much-needed supplies—Raymond had banned him from borrowing food since the quarantine, and he was running low on just about everything.

"Look," Joseph yelled over the discordant rain, distracting himself for a moment from Francis as he felt the wind lashing his face. "Can we stop in there for a minute?"

"Sure," shouted Thaddeus, hood covering half of his face. "I'm hungry for some lunch."

Joseph and Thaddeus hurried into Supernatural Foods. There was not a soul to be seen in here today, aside from one earmuff-wearing checkout girl. Breathing a sigh of relief at the warmth of the store, Joseph picked up a basket and followed Thaddeus over to the produce section. Out of the cacophony of the rain, it seemed the pertinent moment to reveal his feelings about Francis.

"Something about this golden cone theft seems dubious to me," he confided in Thaddeus. "And I just don't buy that Francis was the thief. He denies it completely, and was very convincing."

Thaddeus picked up the last baguette and scoffed. "Haven't you seen the surveillance footage? Sergeant Rufius showed it to me earlier. It's hard to ignore."

"Yes, of course," said Joseph, selecting a broken apple strudel from one of the otherwise empty shelves. "I'm not saying that it didn't appear to be Francis in that clip, but something's off about it. Maybe he's being framed. There's no way that he would be stupid enough to smash the display, grab the golden cone and run without even putting on a mask. How did he even get in there in the first place?"

"They're still working that out," Thaddeus said, brow furrowing. "I'm sure there are ways."

"I've seen you turn invisible, people produce water from their hands, and things levitating. Unless this whole thing has been a bad dream, it's not beyond question that someone could find a way to alter the tape so that it appeared like it was Francis taking the cone. Perhaps there's even a Proficiency that allows you to take control of somebody's body," Joseph said, and suddenly recalled a relevant memory. "Oh yeah, I was actually with Francis the other day, and something similar to what he said happened. I lost consciousness, just like how Francis described it. I think it could be linked! And wait a minute, Francis said the Prince of Darkness' ghost lurks in Bellum Garden. . . ."

Thaddeus shrugged offhandedly, eye twitching. He didn't seem remotely interested in Joseph's view. "That's a bit of a jump. I mean, more than a bit. As for me, I trust the police's judgement; they have been trained to investigate this kind of thing."

Joseph frowned; he wasn't convinced in the slightest. Francis was a cool guy. To be sure, he looked a bit scary with the snake tattoo and the burnt skin, but he was not a thief.

"Forgive my language, but I think the Hyleberian police are a bunch of bastards. They treated me like hell when they arrested me, Sergeant Rufius especially, and did you see how he just yelled at me? I don't trust them one bit," Joseph asserted.

Thaddeus was hardly listening. "Maybe you just need to accept that your first impression of Francis was wrong. You've only known him . . . how long?"

Joseph had largely lost track of time. "Dunno, not long."

"See? A few seconds in Hyleberian time."

Feeling patronised, Joseph sighed in quiet disagreement as he picked up some gummy bears.

Thaddeus added, "Either way, I think Richard Hoskins is doing a bang-up job of running Hyleberia, especially considering that there has not been an Acting Prime Minister in, well, ever."

He's trying to change the subject. Why is Thaddeus so opposed to the possibility of Francis' innocence? "Hoskins? I couldn't really say, but he has only just been given power," Joseph dismissed, putting some challah bread in his basket. He had not particularly been following Hoskins' incumbency, but was getting slightly irritated with the condescension with which Thaddeus had been treating him. "I mean, what did the Divine Council think was going to happen while Peter was gone? My feeling is that they should retrieve Peter from Recalibration ASAP."

Thaddeus criss-crossed his eyebrows and frowned. "Peter's Recalibration is an important process, and to interrupt it would be extremely dangerous. Besides, we usually rely religiously on the Library of Divine Laws, so there would be no need for executive action." Joseph made a bewildered look as Thaddeus explained, "The Library of Divine Laws is a hall on the east of Parliament where all the divine laws are kept. You wouldn't be allowed inside; it's restricted to the political cream of the crop."

"Oh, right. I think Ms Sadeghi mentioned it," Joseph said vexedly, having landed in a rather bad mood.

As he filled his basket, Joseph debated whether his first impression of Thaddeus rather than Francis had been wrong. By the time he had reached the last aisle, the shelves barren, he could barely find any more food besides virgin boy eggs, balut and maggot cheese. *Yummy. I would rather eat my foot than this stuff, and I'm not picky.* All of the newspapers, such as the Divine Times, were days old. He passed a ragged poster on the noticeboard, which he absent-mindedly read:

The once-in-a-lifetime lunar eclipse and Pralaya is coming up soon. While Peter's on Recalibration, come to the Platonic Plaza for the special viewing event, have a few drinks and some fun with your friends! See venue and further event details below.

Joseph sighed. *I don't even like him, but now I wish it would hurry up so Peter can wake up.*

"Is there some sort of supply vault on Hyleberia? I barely found enough to last me two days. Food is clearly running out," Joseph asked, ready to go to the checkout.

"Don't worry about supplies. There are plenty on Afflatus Isle in case of emergency. A giant shipment comes twice a week from there," Thaddeus revealed unconcernedly. "The only problem will be if the water freezes. Then, I'm not sure what will happen."

But what if it does freeze? "Hopefully, we don't all starve to death. That would suck," Joseph commented. "I was not planning on dying so quickly after the first time."

During the checkout, Joseph asked the girl there if she had any cigarettes. Unfortunately, she said they were all out, but it was probably for the best that Joseph didn't give into cravings. After so long, he was also longing to do some gambling to destress, but was sure the local Tyche Casino would be closed.

After buying the food, plastic bags in hand, the hike back was just as awful as he had expected. It seemed Hyleberia was turning into Antarctica. As Thaddeus said goodbye to him at the door to C52, all Joseph wanted was warmth. It was kind of Thaddeus to take him back, yet Joseph didn't have a high view of him after how he acted today. In the living room, Raymond was languidly eating marshmallows, ogling the newscaster on HB1, a well-endowed blonde. Joseph heard her drone on about rain as he walked in, tiredly putting away the groceries:

"As the torrential rain and flooding continues, the Divine Council headed by Richard Hoskins and the Council of Administrators have been in crisis talks all day. Acting Prime Minister Hoskins is expected to give another speech this evening, and he is likely going to address the food shortages across Hyleberia, in addition to fears of upcoming electricity outages. He previously announced that progress has been made in returning Hyleberia to normal, but challenges remain due to the unceasing storm. It is predicted that tonight at least a Category five hurricane will make its way through Hyleberia, which could uproot some buildings and cause other structural damage. There have also been signs of potential earthquake activity. Let's all pray the Animah remains in good stead."

A Category 5 hurricane? And earthquakes? What if the flood's just the beginning?

Raymond turned an alarmed face to Joseph. The Beatles' "Yesterday" was playing quietly on his record player, apparently a small progression from Rain. "Things are going to hell, aren't they? So, how was the police station?" he asked with a slightly drowsy voice.

Joseph sighed, as he hoped that the heating wasn't going to go off before his bath. "It was not great," he said emptily. "Will tell you the specifics in a few, if you want. I need to warm up."

"Good idea, chum, have a toasty bath," Raymond agreed. "Why not have some nice, hot buttered toast to boot? I have a very good toaster. That'll make you feel good. But don't be long."

Joseph froze, mind flashing back to the day he died. Raymond had never asked how it had happened; he was so self-centered. It was impossible to be confident when he was being sarcastic. "No, thanks. I'm not a big fan of toast, for some reason."

Drawing a bath, he dug into his newly purchased challah bread and gummy bears, a strangely tasty combination. He stayed in the bath for longer than he ever had in his life. Joseph was so much in nirvana by the time he had finished washing, and got into his own clothes, that he scarcely noticed Raymond calling his name:

"I want to know who the culprit is now. Come, come, come! Joseph!"

Have I been living with a five-year-old in disguise? Joseph returned and, standing in the doorway, relented to explain all the strange aspects of what he had seen and heard at the police station. But he still had no idea how he could fulfil Francis' request to exonerate him, or if he even ought to try.

"It's obvious," voiced Raymond, who had been listening intently to the whole strange series of events. "You're just a fool who got tricked by that Mexican devil—a damn fool."

Joseph gasped. "I'm no fool; you are! Besides, what reason would Francis have to be acting innocent to me? I can't do anything for him. I don't have any proof of his innocence."

"You're in denial," Raymond replied dismissively. "Major

denial. By the way, I'm friends with the guy on Cosmobook, although we never talked. He always struck me as shady. He has this really lowbrow tattoo, and he looks like someone ripped half of his face off."

"What's Cosmobook?" Joseph asked.

"Only Hyleberia's most popular social media site," Raymond answered, as if this was highly obvious. "Of course, as a colt, you wouldn't be able to make an account. It's restricted to people who have been here five years."

Joseph had never heard of this website before, perhaps indicating how much he had left to learn about Hyleberia. Nevertheless, a rather good idea came to him. "Could I go on your Cosmobook account and have a look around, then?" he asked, hands in his pockets.

"For a reasonable price. . . . I hardly go on that crappy website, at any rate. It's a bunch of dullards showing off," Raymond replied, leaning up on his chair, an evil smile forming on his lips. "Also, put my clothes back in my room."

Damn, he's just like Thomas. Joseph went to his bedroom to fetch the drachma he stored in his drawer. *He wouldn't take me to the hospital if I were on death's door, at least not if it were going to slightly inconvenience him.*

After giving Raymond some drachma and returning his clothes, he took the password off him and went to his room. Lying on the bed with his Hylebook on his chest, Joseph logged in to Raymond's account. He could hear the storm raging on, but it felt cosy to be safely under his covers. Cosmobook seemed to be advertised as a big part of Hyleberian life as he logged in; Joseph was excited to get his first look at it. This was one aspect of the island's way of life he hadn't even touched yet.

On the site, he scrolled down people smiling over meals, discussing their newest opinions and sharing emojis. Raymond was not that popular, with only 56 "friends" in total. This was maybe not indicative of his popularity, as his last post was from several years ago, a picture of him in a suit next to the Water Department building with a huge smile on his face, above a caption: "4th day as a Level 3 Administrator. Loving my new job!"

Peter's profile was seemingly friends with everyone by obligation. His latest post read: "I want to let everybody know that I'll be offline for a while. Tomorrow, I'm leaving on Recalibration. If you need to contact me, please leave a message with my secretary, and I'll reply when I get back. Otherwise, the Divine Council and the Cabinet of Administrators will take care of everything while I'm gone. Have a divine life!" Joseph looked through the comments and cringed at the many fawning replies.

He looked up "Francis Rodrigo" next. His profile picture came up immediately—an image of him in a sports team-branded sweatshirt, standing with a brooding pose in front of the Pnyx. Joseph scrolled down. Francis had 154 friends, although he hadn't posted in the past few days. Joseph read a couple of his posts. Most of them were about his membership of the poetry club and his interests in games and astronomy, but one was more personal. Posted about three months ago, it read:

> Today is the anniversary of my arrival in Hyleberia. Cheers to all the folks that I have met over the past three decades. My life on Earth was messed up; I was not literate, sold drugs, and I . . . you get the picture. It's goddam amazing to have this opportunity to better myself, make *amigos*, and hopefully in a few years, own the poetry and video games shop of my wildest dreams.

Joseph had not seen a more wholesome post in his life. As he scrolled down the posts, his impression was strengthened that the chance that Francis was really some conniving dissident who had been plotting a golden cone-related divine *coup d'état* was slim. That said, Joseph supposed he couldn't come to any solid conclusions based on a social media page.

As he looked through a few other profiles, Joseph felt he was becoming a stalker, though it was interesting to see this virtual side of everyone he had met. Emily posted a lot of photos of recipes she had cooked; Chen shared a lot of Chinese memes and videos from his shows at the Hyleberia Comedy Club; while Ms Sadeghi and Thaddeus didn't seem to have a profile at all. Joseph was surprised to spot Winston Churchill's profile; he had no idea he was a Hyleberian, and was now a professional golfer.

Then, Joseph had a strange idea: could Nigel have a Cosmobook page? Joseph was astonished to find that he did indeed, although all of the posts were from several years ago, and it appeared they had been blocked by Cosmobook on account of "containing inappropriate content". Nevertheless, it said Nigel's full name was Nigel Bernard, and he was also from England. His profile pictures featured an image of a dapper man in a suit that looked nothing like what he had become. Joseph discovered there was a link to his blog that was still active, and he was able to read Nigel's posts. The blog was called *New Age Nigel*, and had a lot of essays about obscure topics like Gnosticism and the occult, subjects which Joseph barely understood.

It took him an hour to read every post, which were very confusing yet undoubtedly well-written. *How did Nigel end up so demented? Something is peculiar about it.*

After he had done all he could regarding investigating Nigel, Joseph suddenly leaned up in alarm.

A wave of panic swept over him like poison. Where was Gabriel? He had last seen the sloth hours ago, writhing in Raymond's arms as Joseph had left for the Police Station. But when Joseph had returned and taken the bath, he had somehow slipped his mind.

He sprinted into the living room; Raymond was still there, yet Gabriel was nowhere to be seen.

"Have you seen Gabriel?" Joseph asked, panic-stricken.

Raymond licked crisp dust from his fingers, staring at the newscaster's cleavage repulsively. He had a half-eaten packet of Seraphic Chips in his hand. "Who?" he asked, without a care in the world. "I thought you took him when you got back. I was watching the visualiser."

Joseph didn't respond. In disbelief, he walked to the window and, in the distance, spotted a gigantic spiralling tornado, tearing through the port and sucking up everything in its path.

CHAPTER 9
ACTING PRIME MINISTER

Mr Brown squinted at Joseph sceptically through the dark, and asked, "What's a sloth? An animal?"

Joseph sighed, pointing his torch at the old man's wrinkled face. He replied, "Yeah, a furry creature. A member of the Pilosa order, according to Wikipedia." *How doesn't he know? I just arrived here and I do.*

It had been more than one slow day since Gabriel had gone missing, and to make matters worse, after the hurricane Miyagi Apartments' power and hot water had gone completely. It was freezing even inside, and so Joseph had borrowed one of Raymond's thickest coats. As far he could see from the windows, the hurricane damage had been severe. The night when it had hit was terrifying; Joseph had never heard wind and rain be so loud, and he had thought Miyagi Apartments was going to collapse.

Overall, this had been the hardest week since his arrival in Hyleberia, and still, Peter was nowhere to be seen. Unwashed and malnourished, Joseph had been wandering alone through the dark corridors with only a dim torch, looking for clues about Gabriel's location. There was nothing else to do but pray that a neighbour had either found him or knew where Gabriel was.

At present, Joseph was talking with an ageing man with weathered skin, who had tiny, reddish ears. Mr Brown lived in apartment C59, only a short walk down the corridor from C52. He was at least the tenth resident he had spoken to so far today, all of them without a hint of luck.

"What do they look like? These so-called sloths?" Mr Brown questioned, staring at him.

Joseph frowned as he scratched his chin, thinking the man had dementia. He didn't want to tell him it *was* Gabriel; that would involve too much explanation. "Er—never mind. Forget it," he said, finding this pointless.

Seconds later came the predictable *slam.*

"I hate sloths," Joseph cursed to himself.

Miserable, he slumped to the next neighbour's apartment. The whole sloth escape seemed impossible. First of all, Gabriel was too slow to get very far. Secondly, the windows and doors of their apartment had all been closed. And thirdly, most importantly, why would he leave? *Should have said no in the first place to Peter. But he just had to give me that sob story.*

Joseph bit his tongue from uttering an expletive rhyming with clucking. He had already visited half of the apartments yesterday, so there were only a few neighbours left. Unsurprisingly, he didn't enjoy getting the door slammed on him by Hyleberians frustrated about the weather, eager to return to their normal lives. They often used him as a punching bag for their annoyance at being quarantined.

Realising that this was hopeless, he returned to the apartment. Closing the front door, he put the torch down on the hall cabinet. As he walked to the living room, he glanced out the corridor window, and squinted at the misty grey sky. By some miracle, the rain had largely stopped, but the hurricane had torn through Hyleberia and left a trail of wreckage behind. Thankfully, Miyagi Apartments was still standing, but it was not likely everyone else had been so fortunate.

Raymond was growing exceedingly less cheery. He had

grown so tired of being inside, waiting for the power to return, that he was no longer on the sofa where he usually sat but lounging on the table by the window without music. Even the Beatles no longer appealed to him, not that they had the power to play them. Of course, Joseph was getting fed up as well; he wasn't sure which of them was closer to cracking.

"Any luck?" Raymond asked when hearing him enter the living room, not bothering to look away from the fogged-up window view.

Joseph groaned, "What do you think?"

Raymond punched the wall, and yelled, "Damn you, Hyleberia!"

Joseph felt like punching something as well, but he managed to bottle up his anger, at least for now. "I share the sentiment. At least when Peter returns, I can always blame you."

Raymond continued to avoid eye contact. "That's fair, I guess."

While he still felt like telling off Raymond, a few days had passed, and he could no longer bring himself to be furious at him. To be sure, he had scolded him rather a lot, even shouted, when he had first lost Gabriel. Yet he could see Raymond seemed to feel guilty about it, and in the monotony of the past few days, their on-the-rocks relationship had improved ever so slightly. At least, Raymond's insults and pejorative comments had been issued at a lesser rate as of late.

Joseph walked over to the fridge and took out the Stag Semen Stout he had bought recently, and which he had been avoiding for a week. There was not much else to drink, pipes frozen.

"Here's an idea. Maybe the dumb sloth got kidnapped," Raymond speculated from out of nowhere, cracking his knuckles. "Someone from the inspection team crept into the apartment and stole him when I wasn't looking."

Joseph took a sip of the beer, and gagged almost immediately. Unsurprisingly, stag semen was absolutely disgusting, like drinking urine. He threw the bottle across the room, and muttered, "That's not very likely. I asked Ms Miyagi yesterday, and she said none of her staff even saw him. Hopefully, he didn't fall out the window. If only I had some distraction from all this, but there's nothing to do."

He had been filling his time not looking for Gabriel by reading the lost books that he had borrowed. As to Joseph's supposed telekinetic powers, they seemed to have vanished since Gabriel left. It was clear, then, that the sloth had been his guardian angel and the one who had endowed the protective force to him. Gabriel, as annoying as he had been, had become a part of the furniture while he had been here. Now it seemed like something was absent, and Joseph was worried the damn sloth was dead.

"I'm fed up," Joseph groaned, pent-up frustrations churning through every fibre of his being. He wanted to rip his hair out; kick down the rubbish bins; take every remaining can of Haoma, and shake them until they exploded. He had been caged in this apartment for far too long. "If Peter doesn't come back soon, Hyleberia is doomed. You know what, I can't just sit around for another day. What I need is to come up with a plan, if everyone's just going to fiddle around while Rome burns."

Raymond was unimpressed. "What can you do? Going out is banned."

I don't even care anymore. At this moment, out of nowhere, he had an unimpeachably good idea. "Oh, you know what? I'm going to head to Town Hall right now to speak to Richard Hoskins, Acting Prime Minister!" he said. "He can sort things out."

"You're an insane man," Raymond replied at once. "Do you realise how busy the Divine Council and Hoskins will be with the crisis? The Acting Prime Minister won't want to talk with an ignorant colt with a superiority complex. Besides, you barely even know the way there."

"That's no problem," denied Joseph, as he brushed his greasy hair forward, which he hadn't been able to wash since the pipes froze. "I'll just, uh, get Thaddeus to take me."

"How?"

He paused. Indeed, getting there would be a problem; Thaddeus would just say no to taking him, in all likelihood, and the landline phone wasn't working. Not to mention, Joseph wasn't even sure they were friends anymore.

"I'll go alone then. I can find it. If someone asks why, I'll just say I'm, uh, telling them to make an announcement Gabriel's missing," Joseph explained, as he strode towards the door. "Don't bother trying to dissuade me."

"It's better to be sorry than safe!" Raymond called after him, mangling yet another saying.

Despite Raymond's protests, a raging fire of determination burning inside, Joseph went back to his room to garb himself in Raymond's newly loaned warm clothes. As he threw them on, he found it excruciatingly difficult to organise his scatter-brained maze of a mind. Of course, Gabriel wasn't the only issue he was currently dealing with. How could he help poor Francis? Even avenge Nigel, if that was the right word? Joseph hoped very much that Richard was sympathetic; otherwise, he was not sure what he could possibly do.

On his way out, Joseph felt Raymond's disapproving glare on his back, as he stood with arms crossed in the hall. "I don't know why I'm even warning you, but you will regret this," his roommate warned. "It's a mistake. Just don't come crying to me when you get arrested."

"I'm a grown man, Raymond," Joseph remarked dismissively, and stepped out the front door. "I can make my own decisions, and my own mistakes. See you later."

At the bottom of the stairs, the water had risen several inches. Joseph splashed into the deluge and out of the complex. He was surprised to see that the clouds were chalky white, and the air felt quite bearable for the first time in what felt like years. A rainbow carved a line through the sky like an expensive, multi-coloured bracelet. *Does this mean the bad weather's almost over? The past few days have been particularly terrible.*

The streets were still deserted and half-flooded, and the tornado damage was conspicuous. Random objects had been scattered to places where they shouldn't be, mattresses and fridges lying in the middle of the road. Several buildings had had their roofs pulled off, including Ontomart. This was the first time that Joseph had gone out since his visit to the police station with Thaddeus, so he was refreshed to feel the breeze on his face, even though his feet were soaked.

He had never been inside Town Hall before, and it took Joseph about an hour to find the large building. It was on Telemachus Road, not far from Hyle Lounge Nightclub, the local disco. Outside of the building lay a dead beached dolphin, which was quite upsetting. The Town Hall had corbelled walls painted in honey gold and sonic silver, muntins lacquered with rare jewels sculpted into symmetrical geometric shapes. Castellated like a fort, the domed roof looked like it might have been designed by Michelangelo. He hadn't spotted any signs of life at all in Hyleberia until he walked through the giant whitewood front doors.

Ms Beechum did not look happy as she eyed Joseph approaching her desk. She was an elderly woman much like Mr Brown, except much more angry-looking. Her tortoise-shell glasses were several sizes too big on her long, pointy nose.

"Can I help you?" she asked proudly.

"Yup. I need . . ." Joseph broke off, gazing around Town Hall in awe.

Now inside, he could only stare at the stunning decorations: Dropa stones on plinths, and rare, priceless paintings by Renoir and Matisse. Even Buckingham Palace could not possibly hold a candle to this, in Joseph's opinion. Ms Sadeghi had mentioned something earlier about how Hyleberian architects were greatly inspired by Islamic architecture, including floral motifs, elaborate patterns and calligraphy.

"Were you given authorisation to come here?" Ms Beechum asked, scratching her nose.

"Not strictly speaking," he mumbled, bracing himself to explain the Gabriel issue. Unfortunately, there was no good way to put it, "but I needed to come—it is an emergency."

So, how to break the bad news?

"An emergency?" she asked sententiously.

Just get it over with. Joseph swallowed. "Yeah. I need you to make a Hyleberia-wide notice. You know Peter gave me his pet sloth to look after, Gabriel, and well, I'm afraid he has gone missing. I've been looking for him for two days now with no luck. And I would also like to speak with Richard Hoskins, if possible."

Joseph had expected her to explode when hearing this, even to jump across the desk and punch him, but instead, she just peered at him like he had a screw loose. Ms Beechum was the one who had dropped off the sloth supplies, but she had only stayed for 5 seconds and barely spoke a word to him.

"Ah, I see," she said, her hoarse voice cracking. She picked up her landline phone and pointed to the waiting area while glaring at him like an annoying spot. "Please sit while I make a call about this. The Acting Prime Minister is incredibly busy. He has been in consecutive meetings for days about the crisis response and hurricane repairs. I will see if he has time for you, though I very much doubt it."

Sucking his lip glumly, Joseph sat in the waiting area. To distract himself from his nerves and numerous concerns, he tried to decide what he would be doing right now if he had never died. *Probably sitting at home, watching Netflix. Unless I had gone through with my plan, and ran way. Essex seems like a universe away.*

Almost half an hour passed before Joseph heard footsteps approaching on the marble floor. Looking up, he gasped when he saw who it was. Richard Hoskins, Acting Prime Minister himself, had stepped through a door and was striding towards him. But this wasn't the most confusing part —Joseph thought he was dreaming when he saw the animal with him.

Richard was holding Gabriel in his arms.

It didn't seem even remotely feasible. *How* could Gabriel, an undeniably very idiotic sloth, have possibly escaped from their apartment and then found his way through the awful weather conditions to Town Hall?

"So, you're Shields, the colt?" greeted Richard, eyes on Joseph's baffled face.

"That's me," Joseph uttered, sounding very confused.

Richard was standing by Ms Beechum's desk. In person, he seemed somehow much shorter and more harried than the cameras had portrayed, eyes swollen and thick circles under them.

"Would you like to come into the Holy Office for a few minutes?" he asked. "I only have minutes before my next meeting."

"Sure, sure," Joseph said, getting to his feet and desperately wanting answers.

"Excellent." Richard turned to Ms Beechum and instructed her, "I'll have an espresso, if you don't mind. Camel milk. Two sugars, and a teaspoonful of honey."

"Yes, Mr Hoskins," Ms Beechum agreed, standing up and walking over to the coffee machine.

Joseph didn't restrain himself from shaking his head in bewildered disbelief as he followed Richard into his office. Town Hall was enormous; it was a five-minute walk to Peter's (or, for now, Acting Prime Minister's) Holy Office, and there were several security guards standing around it, reminding Joseph of the American Oval Office. They all had revolvers or shotguns, but Joseph deduced additional defences could be through Proficiencies, as he witnessed one security guard shooting lasers out of his sleeves. When Richard let him into the Holy Office, Joseph recognised the colour of the walls and the fancy podium—the visualiser announcements that Richard and Peter had done must have been recorded here.

The inside of the Holy Office had a large redwood desk, which held a photo of Peter smiling next to Gandhi and Boudica. There was a large red carpet across the floor embroidered with a painting of the golden cone, as well as the Hyleberian motto.

"How do you have Gabriel?" Joseph asked once they had arrived, tripping over his own words as he gazed at the sloth's calm, innocent face. He had been meaning to ask this on the walk here, but Richard received a phone call, and had rather rudely chosen to take it over speaking with Joseph. Gabriel's arms were clinging around Richard's neck, and Joseph did not think that the sloth had even noticed him since their reunion moments ago. "I was looking after him."

"Ah, it's a funny story, actually," Richard replied, without a hint of guilt in his flighty voice. "I didn't realise that Peter had given Gabriel to anyone. So, I assumed he was missing, and I summoned him with my apportation Proficiencies. Even though I am only Acting Prime Minister, of course, I have been given the whole gamut of Proficiencies to match as far as possible Peter's natural abilities."

"What's apportation?"

"In short, it's the ability to teleport objects . . . or animals."

Apportation? Joseph shook his head. *What a bizarre explanation.*

"Oh, I see. But hold on a minute," muttered Joseph, only half-understanding this and deeply annoyed. "If you can teleport anything you want, why don't you just summon the golden cone here?"

Richard sounded deeply uninterested as he explained, "One endowed with apportation can only summon things that have previously been held. I carried Gabriel momentarily ages ago, as do all government ministers during the swearing-in ceremony. Thus, I was able to summon him." He casually teleported a pen across the room into his hand. "See how it works. But I wouldn't feel comfortable summoning anything so important as the golden cone, even if I had held it."

Joseph wasn't convinced. "You could still try. . . ."

Richard walked around the desk, so that only his head was visible. "Word to the wise: don't talk about things of which you know little. Either way, if I had known you were minding Gabriel, I still would have simply sent someone to get him. I do feel that it is important now that I am in power for me to be seen in public with Gabriel."

"How come?" he asked, feeling more than ever that the Acting Prime Minister wasn't going to be of any help.

Richard twirled the pen in his fingers. "Over the years, Gabriel has become a strange but crucial symbol of Hyleberian strength and prosperity. In these dark hours, retaining a sense of Hyleberian solidarity, identity and purpose is crucial. Well, I say 'dark hours', but now that the storm has stopped, things should rapidly start getting back to relative normalcy."

Gabriel squeaked as if he agreed.

"I spent two days looking for Gabriel, worrying about if he had been kidnapped," Joseph said reproachfully, thinking Raymond would laugh out loud when he found out what had happened.

Despite his better judgement, Joseph couldn't shake the feeling of responsibility for the small creature. He was strangely affronted about what he could only consider the theft of the sloth. *So now that Gabriel is kidnapped, I guess I never will be able to move things again? That animal was my guardian angel. . . .*

Richard glanced at his glossy stainless-steel watch. "All's well that ends well. Is there anything else you would like to speak with me about? I've got three minutes before my next meeting, so I can't dilly-dally, colt."

Joseph was starting to wonder why Richard's voice sounded a shade familiar. Maybe it was something about his Welsh accent.

"I've got about a hundred things, now that you mention it," Joseph said.

"Such as?" Richard said.

He couldn't think of even one, now that he was being put on the spot. "Such as, uh, is the quarantine going to end any time soon?"

"I have good news on that front." Richard beamed. "We are going to be importing some vacuum archons from Afflatus Isle to clear up the water ASAP. The hurricane damage will be less easy to remedy, but we'll get there. I hope, then, that the quarantine will be able to be called off by Friday."

"Right," said Joseph. "And, uh, Francis. Is he—"

Richard pressed his lips with a slight frown. "Francis Rodrigo, the golden cone thief?" At this moment, Gabriel began crawling over Richard's face, which he didn't seem to like. "Oh, you stupid sloth! Get off me, pest."

"Uh—not quite, I mean—"

Pulling Gabriel off his countenance, Richard interrupted, "Please don't worry about that Mexican heathen anymore. He will be taken care of, in fact, I haven't announced it yet but I can reveal he will be exiled in short order," he stated with a self-satisfied expression.

Joseph squinted at Richard. "In short order?"

"Yes." Richard stepped back in front of his desk and

strode back and forth, a grave look on his face. "Mr Rodrigo is clearly beyond reform. I can assure you that in the next few weeks you will be able to go back to Shrivatsa like normal, and forget that that malevolent lawbreaker ever troubled you."

Joseph felt his jaw tighten. He looked down at the carpet in thought, although he always had to look down to some degree when talking to Richard.

"Wait. You mean . . . you're going to exile him before Peter even returns? Is that even allowed?" Joseph asked, hands fidgeting in his pockets.

Richard nodded swiftly. "I'm *Acting Prime Minister*—of course, it is. If Peter doesn't return in the next week or so, I have little choice. I'm sorry to have to break this to you, but Francis is too dangerous to risk keeping him."

He gaped. "Why not just wait till Peter gets back? Isn't there a word for that, uh, murder?"

Richard smirked; his was a snide, uncaring smile. "There are many reasons, colt. Most obviously, we have no means of confirming at what date Peter will be back from Recalibration. It is asking for trouble to keep a corrupted criminal here for an extended period of time, waiting for him to escape and use the golden cone for malevolent ends. Besides, the video evidence is overwhelming."

"What about a trial?"

Richard shrugged. "Unnecessary and impossible. He is clearly guilty."

"Maybe *you* are guilty. You haven't even recovered the cone yet. How can you be sure that he wasn't framed? And even if he were guilty, wouldn't you need him alive to find the cone?"

Joseph got the feeling that he was starting to get on Richard's nerves.

Indeed, Richard's face had become stiff, and his already cold tone seemed to be getting frigid. "No offence, but this isn't a matter that should concern you, colt. Mr Rodrigo is a heathen—there is no doubt about that. Not in the slightest. Why are you asking? It almost makes me think you might be involved."

Joseph hated the gruff way he called him *colt*; it sounded like a swear word.

"I just think he is innocent. And please don't patronise me. Whether he did it or not," Joseph began, as Richard ushered him out with his eyes, "at the very least, Francis has the right to be tried in a fair court."

Richard groaned, as he wrestled to keep Gabriel from agitating. "Ah, but that's where you're wrong. Your way of thinking is still moulded by Tellurian legal norms. You don't understand that running Hyleberia as if it were a democracy would be a fool's errand."

"I'm just saying—"

Richard raised his voice and held his arms out with palms forward, "Can you imagine if we voted on divine laws? The rules of gravity and chemical reactions would change every few years—it would engender a universe of complete chaos. Joseph, you'll think me Machiavellian for saying this, but people are stupid. What a strong government needs, first and foremost, is a strong Prime Minister. The important thing for Hyleberia, and the world, is stability. Exiling a proven culprit will surely reinforce that."

"That's apples and oranges; I'm just talking about a trial, not voting," Joseph said, before he could be interrupted. "Look, here's the deal: I overheard a conversation of these men saying something about stealing the cone, and I think they might be the real criminals. Only, I didn't see their faces."

Richard started, looking a bit jumped. "Did they mention the cone specifically?"

Joseph scratched his neck, as he felt Gabriel's glare on him. "Er, they used a code, but—"

"And did you see who these alleged 'real criminals' were?"

Joseph pursed his lips, and explained, "Well . . . strictly speaking, no. But I really think—"

At this moment, the Acting Prime Minister's mind seemed to break. "SHUT YOUR MOUTH WITH THIS NONSENSE! HOW DARE YOU DISRESPECT YOUR ACTING PRIME MINISTER! YOU ARE THE RUDEST COLT I'VE EVER MET IN THE PAST MILLENNIUM. PETER IS GONE NOW, AND SO FOR ALL INTENTS AND PURPOSES, I AM YOUR PRIME MINISTER. YOU OUGHT TO BE GLAD I'M NOT EXILING YOU RIGHT NOW!"

Joseph stood there goggle-eyed, astonished. Gabriel seemed to be afraid of the shouting, as he flapped his arms and legs about slowly in terror. "Calm down, Richard. I'm just—"

"I DON'T GIVE A DAMN WHAT YOU HAVE TO SAY, COLT. GET OUT OF MY OFFICE, NOW!"

"You don't need to yell," Joseph replied, stepping towards the door. It was as if he had been teleported back to Birchwood Junior School, when a teacher had furiously scolded him for talking in class with Thomas.

Acting Prime Minister Hoskins grimaced, giving up holding Gabriel and placing him on his desk. "Get out of my office, now," he said quietly, turning away. "Or I'll call my guards."

Not keen to be thrown out physically, Joseph had little choice but to depart at once, disappointed to not even be allowed to say goodbye to Gabriel. *What a grouch.*

Stunned by Richard's outburst, Joseph wondered on the way home if Peter would agree that Francis needed to be exiled. There was a good chance, he considered, that Peter would concur with Richard; after all, Peter was the one that had exiled Nigel without a trial. One way or the other, it was certainly clear that Richard Hoskins had a major temper.

Trudging up the apartment complex stairs, frustration about the situation racked Joseph's mind. *Why am I even so sure he's not guilty?* he asked himself. *I just am.*

"So, what happened?" Raymond asked, the second Joseph returned home and set foot in the living room, clothes soggy. His roommate was predictably waiting on the sofa, slack-jawed and impatient for news, paging through an old copy of *Universe Today* magazine.

"It wasn't terrible," Joseph affirmed optimistically, and then explained some details of the meeting, omitting the tiff of his difference of opinion with Richard.

Raymond gaped. "That sounds worse than terrible to me. Abysmal, even. Brilliant news regarding Gabriel, though. I can't believe I was letting you guilt me for that!"

Joseph had to admit to himself "abysmal" was putting it nicely, and he hadn't even told Raymond the whole story. He didn't think the populace of Hyleberia would be so glad to have Richard as their Prime Minister if they had seen his anger issues.

"It's done now. I just don't know what I should do next," Joseph lamented, his hands forming fists, as Francis' words replayed in his mind from that short visit to the holding cell.

"How about some porn?" Raymond said.

Joseph was thinking more about mounting a rebellion against Richard. "I'm not in the mood. All the evidence points to Francis as the culprit, and they're going to exile him before Peter can return to give his opinion. If I don't do anything, they'll kill him. And I don't even—"

Raymond cut him off, "You just have to accept, Shields, that this isn't your moral responsibility. Not at all. In fact, nothing is. Haven't philosophers got a word for this? Nolism?"

Nihilism? But what if it is my responsibility? Joseph scratched his chin.

"Thomas once called me a nihilist. I don't know if I am though. What are you trying to say?" he asked.

Raymond put his magazine down and shrugged. "Things here in Hyleberia are and have always been done a certain way. You think that people in the U. K. are patriotic? Well, how long ago was that country founded? Hyleberia has been around since the origin of Earth itself, and so, Hyleberians are passionate about maintaining the way the place is run."

He sounds just like Emily. "I don't even care about tradition," Joseph said fiercely. "Francis is my friend, even if we barely know each other, and I don't think it's right to exile him just because of a videotape."

"He's really convinced you, huh? Are you trying to say someone is framing him, then?"

Joseph paced back and forth, trying to think coherently. "Possibly. Superpowers exist here, and yet nobody has heard of disguises? What I really need to do is talk to Francis, and hear his side of the story. Right when our conversation was interrupted by Rufius at the holding cell, he seemed about to tell me who he thought was the real culprit."

"It's not like the police are going to allow that," Raymond barked in a low voice. "Anyway, let's just thank God—or maybe not *God*—about Gabriel. And you're lucky you didn't get in trouble for breaking quarantine. I guess they're getting lax now."

Joseph kicked the sofa in frustration. He wasn't particularly pleased about Gabriel's kidnapping, despite it being good the sloth had been found. Then, all at once, his second great idea of the day came to him. He stood bolt upright as his mind worked, deciding its feasibility.

"I've just figured out how I can talk to Francis," he exclaimed.

"Yeah? Is this your saviour complex acting up?"

Joseph explained eagerly, "I remembered that there's a barred aperture in the holding cell that feeds right onto the lot behind Taste of Heaven Doughnuts. What I'll do is sneak down there at the dead of night tonight, find Francis, and then see what he says really happened."

"This is not an action movie, bro," said Raymond grimly, as he stood up. "You are worse than an insane man, y'know— that is downright suicidal. Risking your behind just so you can have a chinwag with Hyleberia's most wanted. You are the limit, Shields."

While it was true that he was a bit worked up after that disaster of a meeting with Richard, Joseph felt that his desire to talk to Francis was perfectly reasonable. "I'll tell you this," he affirmed, wagging his finger. "I'm not going to let Richard exile Francis like they did with Nigel. If having a saviour complex is wanting to stop a corrupt government from murdering someone, then I admit I have one."

Joseph stormed out after this, a groove of determination on his brow. *I'm going to do it,* he told himself. *I will. Don't let Raymond get in your head. He doesn't know anything. And screw Richard.*

While Joseph did not lose his sense of resolve by evening, he did change his plan somewhat. In the end, he decided that it would be best to sneak out the following night, when he had more time to plan his route to the police station, and more of the flooding had evaporated.

Joseph didn't sleep well that night. He would dare say that he had scarcely had a night with more to worry about than this one. 2 am came and Joseph's heart was still beating like he had run a marathon. *Are you really going to do this? And what good will it do? Even if you speak to Francis, you're not going to know whether he's telling the truth.* Nonetheless, even with all these doubts, he couldn't think of a better course of action. The full existential aspects of the insane situation that Joseph was in only became fully apparent to him in the middle of the night, when the outside world was so still that you could hear a pin drop.

No hour, minute, or second passed at what Joseph would consider a normal rate the next day. He stayed in his room constantly in an anxious state; he couldn't possibly face Raymond's ribaldry and nosy questions about his plans. If he let him get in his head, Joseph knew that he might start doubting his reasons, and he wanted to prevent the possibility of this.

To keep himself as occupied as possible during the long day, Joseph attempted telekinesis multiple times. The trouble was, he had no idea on how to provoke any effect without Gabriel, or if it was even possible. He thought at first that simply concentrating on producing movement would produce better results, but this wasn't the case. No matter how many times he stared at a tennis ball and willed for it to move, stomach clenched, the results remained imperceptible. Even when he threw it at the ceiling and let it fall on his head, nothing happened, except he got a rather sore cranium. It was remarkable to think that Gabriel had changed the direction of all those bricks. Joseph was glad that he hadn't told anybody anything more than vague suspicions about this. He didn't want to cause any more chaos in Hyleberia. *Oh well, it was nice while it lasted. No more sloth powers for me.*

When the time to leave finally came, 1 am, Joseph didn't want to bump into Raymond on the way out. On tiptoes, he crept outside his room as quietly as possible.

"Are you doing your little prison break tonight?" Raymond scoffed, standing in the middle of the hall.

Joseph jumped and turned towards him; he had thought his roommate was asleep, and was only hoping to grab a snack before sneaking down Miyagi Apartments' staircase to the holding cell. He chose not to respond, walking past him like a ghost, getting some of the last mouldy tofu from the fridge.

"You are, aren't you?" Raymond continued, following him

into the kitchen. "What an utter maniac. And what if I get accused of aiding and abetting a—"

"Oh, shut up. It's not a bloody prison break. Don't be a tattletale," Joseph shot back, as he poured himself a shot of malt whisky. "It's simply a midnight stroll. Not a big deal at all. And if I happen to end up at the holding cell and speak to Francis . . . it is what it is. I didn't get in trouble last time, anyway."

Raymond rolled his eyes. "But you'll get lost in the dark, and last time you weren't sneaking around the damn police station! You've the orientation skills of a broken compass."

"Maybe I will. It's a risk I'll have to take," Joseph affirmed, either bravely or recklessly. "I found Town Hall without too much difficulty."

"In daylight." Appalled, Raymond sighed. "Look, there's no other choice for it. I'll have to come too."

Joseph's mouth fell open. "Huh?"

He explained, "It'll be far safer for you and for me if there are two of us. This way, there will be someone to keep a lookout while you have a confab with Francis."

Perplexed, Joseph replied, "Very bad idea. You don't even care about Francis!"

"Well, if you don't bring me along, I'll . . . report you," Raymond said snidely.

"Report me? You wouldn't dare."

"I would."

Joseph tried to argue, but Raymond would not budge. *Hmmm. Raymond might say that he's worried about getting in trouble himself, but is that really the sole reason he's doing this?*

Joseph said nothing as he thought for a moment. Raymond was like a carthorse when determined, and by the rabid look in his eye, he was not going to be changing his mind before sunrise.

"Fine," snapped Joseph. "Let's go then. Right now."

Raymond pointed at his figure with an expression of disgust. "Wearing that?"

Joseph looked down at his sweatshirt and jeans. "What's wrong with this?"

"You should change into some darker clothes to lower the chance we get spotted," advised Raymond, who was himself already wearing an almost vanta black tracksuit bottoms and a grey duffle coat, seemingly pre-prepared. "Wait a second, you can borrow something of mine. I think they'll fit. We must be similar sizes."

He came back a minute later, and threw Joseph a dark hoodie, black khakis and trainers.

"Let me guess, for a price," he grumbled, examining them.

"Oh, of course," Raymond said maliciously. "But we'll worry about that later. Change."

Joseph took them back to his room, wondering how Raymond was so knowledgeable about the correct way of sneaking out at night. It wasn't until he had changed that the train of fear he had seen on the horizon fully struck him, knocking all of his daring into pieces. *Should I really be doing this? Rufius would love to catch me.* It felt far more nerve-wracking to sneak out at night than the day. In this case, Joseph and Raymond had no reasonable excuse if they were caught, besides that they had forgotten about the quarantine and were out for a night walk. But that was not even remotely believable. Overall, they would have to be very careful.

Joseph and Raymond slinked down Miyagi Apartment's staircase, struggling to keep their footsteps quiet. The flooding was thankfully only a few inches high at this point. The electricity was still out though, and the complex was dark and creepy, like a haunted house.

The strange duumvirate raced down the empty streets of Hyleberia like two thieves in the night. Fortunately, the journey into town in large part was much easier than it had been only two days earlier, yet the raw breeze was not to either of their likings. Every random sound Joseph heard—a perched crow spreading its wings, a gust of wind rattling a dark street lamp—felt like the footsteps of Sergeant Rufius about to bust them. Thankfully, this didn't transpire. But Joseph glanced behind him and was sure several times he could see another's footprints rippling in the water.

Raymond hastened Joseph onward at a breakneck pace, and before long, he stopped paying as much attention to the eerie sounds. Neither of them said a single word during the whole journey. In hindsight, he was glad to have brought Raymond. His roommate seemed to have an intuition for the shortcuts and concealed darker areas of Hyleberia's geography, which any make-do route conceived by Joseph couldn't have matched.

By the time they reached the police station, Joseph was trying to think of what to say to Francis. Raymond guided them along the opposite side of the high street so that there was a reduced chance they would be spotted. Upon the instruction of his pointed index finger, they dashed around the back of Taste of Heaven Doughnuts until the spackled, hawthorn-overgrown wall that belonged to the police station appeared in sight.

They had arrived. Joseph felt like a child who had run away from his parents, not where he should be and half-tempted to go home. As he slowed his pace and got to his knees, he crawled to the wall and scanned the penetrating night air for the barred window. Shaking like a tube man, he whispered through the gelid dusk behind him, where Raymond was on his hands and feet, "You wait here! I'll go speak to Francis. Hopefully, he is still awake. And alive."

He heard only a husky grunt in reply from Raymond, who was shrouded in darkness.

Joseph blinked uncomfortably as he wormed along the wall, fingers tracing the rugged bricks, hoping against hope that at some point in the next few seconds he would be able to detect the gaps in the aperture. It was desperately tense, and Joseph worried for a few moments that he might have misremembered the location of the holding cell.

It took him ten minutes before he sensed a hole, although it felt more like ten hours. When he finally found the steel of the aperture bars, he lowered his face to the ground and stared inside, looking for a trace of Francis. He gasped: Francis was there. Joseph could see him. The police station had lost power, so he had to squint to make out his figure through the dingy gloom, but it was definitely him. The holding cell looked half-flooded.

"Rodrigo, Francis Rodrigo," Joseph hissed through the bars, his voice quieting on the last syllable as he remembered that Sergeant Rufius was likely sitting just down the hall. He felt his heart race at the thought of him creeping up on him from behind, and double-checked there was nobody there. "Francis!"

Movement. There was a rustling.

As his eyes adjusted, Joseph could suddenly discern Francis slumped against the wall, half-standing. Looking around for the source of the noise, Francis stood up fully and cast nonplussed glances towards him. Finally spotting Joseph's head in the aperture, he slowly came over.

"*Hola!* Who's there?" Francis asked, trepidation in his voice.

"Joseph. You know, Shields."

"What the hell! Jojo, what are you doing here?" he exclaimed loudly.

Joseph warned in a half-whisper, "Keep your voice down. I'm not supposed to be here. I've come to talk about the theft, to hear your side of the story."

"You've not come to break me out?" he asked disappointedly.

Joseph felt suddenly like a failure. "Um, I don't know how. Did you want me to?"

Francis' haunting, moonlit teal eyes peeked out of the bars, as he mumbled, "I kinda hoped you had. Maybe that was a bit unrealistic."

"Sorry, Francis, but I want to hear your side of the story about the golden cone theft," Joseph said, rattling the bars in the small chance they were broken or loose.

"Don't bother, I tried that," Francis sighed, his face quite blank.

There was a silence of several seconds.

"So, how are you holding up in there? Joseph asked.

"Nobody here believes me; they are treating me like I am some evil, conniving criminal. I've no idea who fabricated the damn tape, but someone must have it out for me," Francis remarked. "I feel like bloody Che Guevara."

"I believe you. I tried telling Richard Hoskins, but he wouldn't listen. Who do you suspect really did it? You were about to tell me when you got cut off," Joseph asked impatiently.

"Oh, that. I was going to say Chen. I never really trusted him," Francis disclosed with an unpleasant tone. "He always seemed really phoney with his jokes, and generally like he was scheming something to me."

"Chen Huang?" Joseph gasped. "Any other reasons why it might be him?"

"No, not really. Sorry, it's the best I've got," Francis said darkly. "I'm so much help, aren't I?"

Joseph thought it through, and wasn't immediately convinced. Chen certainly didn't seem like a criminal mastermind, at least no more than Francis.

"Well, I'll investigate that tomorrow," Joseph whispered, as he tried to ignore his shivering fingers. "I believe you're innocent. Something smells fishy to me. There's no reason why you would take the golden cone, and they seem really reluctant to give you a fair trial."

Francis nodded. "Exactly. I hate asking for help, but you

have to find out who really did it. At least, I'd really appreciate that. I don't want to force you to get involved."

"I have been trying. Sort of. I haven't made much progress so far," Joseph said, squinting through the musty air.

"Thanks, *amigo*," Francis said thoughtfully. "You're a true friend. Perhaps my only one, and we have just met."

Joseph didn't reply at first, lost in thought about how he could possibly help. He asked Francis to recapitulate his version of the events during the time when the golden cone had been stolen. But Francis reported absolutely no memories during the period of the crime. He claimed that when he had come to, he was simply in his bedroom, asleep on the bed. This was, apparently, just moments before the police busted down the door and arrested him. The last thing Francis remembered before that was walking home from Shrivatsa, listening to Spanish folk music on his Hylepod. Joseph felt blood surge to his head as his idea about what could have happened came to him.

"Do you remember blacking out at all?" he asked.

"Kind of," Francis recalled. "I was walking down the street when a bitterly cold force seemed to accost me, and then a sudden moment of agonising pain. A bit like a heroin overdose. That's the last thing I remember."

Thinking his speculation over, Joseph asked edgily, "Now, this might sound dumb, but do you think that someone or something might have possessed your body?"

"What do you mean?" Francis replied, bewildered.

"Took control of you, made you take the cone," Joseph explained. "You remember that night when I blacked out, in Bellum Garden? It felt like something was watching us. Maybe . . . that is linked. How you described passing out sounds exactly like what happened to me. It could be the same thing as was attempting to possess me then, but failed. You might say this is far-fetched, but you said the ghost lurks there. Maybe, just maybe, it was the ghost of the Prince."

He could practically feel Francis' mind working. "Oh, yeah. I had forgotten about that. It may just be the ghost! It did feel like I'd been possessed, at least, like something had taken over me when I woke up. Maybe you could try to find out if anyone in Hyleberia could do that, possess people, I mean. If you can figure out who or what has the ability, you could nab the perpetrator."

"Joseph, hurry up! I think I just heard someone," Raymond hissed through the dark.

Swallowing, Joseph tried to recall if he knew anyone who did, but the problem was he only knew about fifteen people on the island, and none of them particularly well. "Did you perhaps see anything suspicious that night when I fainted in the garden?" he asked, feeling like he was grasping at straws. "Any clue may help. I'm no Sherlock Holmes, but I'll do my best."

"Not really. Let me think . . ." Francis hemmed and hawed. "Oh, there's one thing, but it's probably nothing. While you were out, I did see somebody in the area. I didn't mention it at the time because it was just that Controller guy. I've seen him around town lots of times. He passed by, saw you and left like it was nothing."

Joseph had a distinct impression that this was going to be a very helpful clue. "Who?"

"Er—T-Thaddeus D-deaus is his name, I think," Francis said.

He felt his mind freeze. "Thaddeus!?" Joseph exclaimed. "What the hell was he doing there?"

CHAPTER 10
THE EVIL DEMON

It seemed very much to Joseph that Hyleberia had turned from Heaven into Hell. Reclined on the armchair in the living room, it had just reached 9:55 am on Sunday and his pyjamas were still on. He spooned Frosted Amrita into his mouth, a sugary divine cereal that wasn't particularly healthy, and stared at the visualiser in a bad mood.

Thanks largely to Raymond, he and Joseph had made it home that night at the police station without being spotted. Joseph didn't like to think what would have occurred if Sergeant Rufius had found him by the window. And yet, Thaddeus and Chen—who now seemed to be the prime suspects, or at least persons of interest—had been nowhere in sight ever since the next morning had arrived, despite Joseph combing much of Hylenet for their details. This was still the best lead he had, and it wasn't much. It seemed his quest to start a life in Hyleberia had now been superseded by the much more pressing need to save Francis.

Due to the quarantine being lifted, for the first time in a while Raymond was nowhere in sight too, busy hanging out with his tennis friends and making the most of the restoration of freedom. Although the flooding had improved over the days after the night expedition thanks to the vacuum archons, a variety of archons with suction nozzles that had been unleashed all over the island sucking it up, the tornado damage was still a problem and the weather remained dreary.

Joseph clutched his head, sighing at his never-ending headache and nausea as he watched HB1, electricity now fully restored. The news anchor, a round-faced woman in a red frock, droned on about the flood clear-up.

Yet he couldn't stop thinking about Thaddeus, and the strange, far-fetched, and unshakeable idea that he was framing Francis. What his motive might be remained unclear, but Joseph couldn't deny the evidence. Both the revelation that Thaddeus had been seen on the night of his collapse, and the fact that his voice was, in retrospect, oddly similar to one Joseph had overheard in the alley, combined to suggest he was up to something.

"It's now time for the weather at 10 am," the weather woman announced.

Drat, Joseph realised upon hearing the time. *Better leave now or I'll be late.* He had a coffee engagement planned this morning at Emily's apartment. They'd arranged to meet the prior night, after he sent her an email asking if she had any spare headache painkillers. All of the pharmacies were still closed.

Feeling very much like a detective conducting an investigation, Joseph got up and dressed in slacks and a polo shirt, listening to music on his laptop as he thought about what his next moves should be. Having left Miyagi Apartments, the skies were misty grey, although a large improvement in contrast with before. He even noticed a celebratory mood in the air. A lot of folks were out and about today, either catching up with friends or just sitting on the Bermuda grass, chatting and eating picnics. Joseph doubled back when he spotted a buffalo grazing in Bellum Garden that must have been transported from Afflatus Isle, a piano sitting in the middle of the road and a vacuum archon that had got stuck and kept banging against a wall. But it seemed most were not displeased by the moody weather, and were simply happy to be out and about again.

When Joseph arrived at Terribilità Terrace, even though the building work had been put on pause, he was careful to avoid the area with the scaffolding where he and Emily had nearly died. The complex had minimal damage from the hurricane, although several windows were smashed, and by the looks of it, much of the scaffolding had collapsed. In a short time, he made it to Emily's apartment.

"Good afternoon," Emily greeted in the doorway. "How's the afterlife? Come in, come in."

As she beckoned Joseph into her sitting room, letting him try her freshly baked red velvet cupcakes, he explained where Gabriel was and looked around at the many fancy decorations. There was a Persian rug; an incandescent lava lamp; Flock wallpapered walls; and multicoloured pouffes in the corner, counterpoised by nail-hung paintings. Emily herself was dressed in a scalloped yellow blouse and jeans.

"Didn't know you were such an interior designer," Joseph said pleasantly, tilting his head around. "I wish I could be roommates with you. Maybe if Mohammed doesn't work out. . . ."

He noticed a picture on the wall of a happy Rottweiler; Joseph supposed it must be Barney.

"Oh, I'm not at all. This stuff is mostly my roommate's, apart from the kitchen supplies. He's kind of uptight, but he was actually quite a famous Dutch artist, Rembrandt. Maybe you know him?" Emily revealed casually, lips creased, gesturing to Joseph to sit down in a comfy armchair. "Would you like tea or coffee?"

"Tea, please. And he rings a bell," Joseph stated, quite intrigued.

As Emily got the kettle going, Joseph noticed she had a wide variety of ingredients on the shelf like edible gold and foie gras. On the sideboard, which could belong to Rembrandt, was a collection of Hyleberian books, *Tellurian Psychology: A Beginner's Guide*, *The Controller of Zhuangzi Castle* and *Andy Pandy and His Apotheosis*. There was also a huge encyclopaedia called *A to Z of Phenomena: From Air Shower to Zeeman Energy*.

After Emily poured them both hot drinks and Joseph had sat down, she said, "Obviously, it's been pandemonium in Hyleberia recently. I'm just glad the quarantine is over; I was drinking a lot of whisky to get through it. And the hurricane was awful. There is a lot to talk about, but firstly let's discuss—"

Joseph preempted her. "Francis."

Emily reddened slightly as she sat on the sofa, opposite him. "Ohhhhh. Yes, exactly."

There was an awkward pause. Joseph leaned back on the armchair and tapped his foot on the carpet. "So, the million-drachma question. Do you think he did it?"

She interlocked her fingers and glared downwards. "Well, like, yeah."

This was not the response Joseph had been hoping for.

He crinkled his nose and glared at her. "How come? I don't," he said.

Emily went pale. "I saw the tape, didn't you?" she asked.

Not this again. Joseph's stomach fluttered, getting frustrated.

He flinched. "Hasn't anyone in Hyleberia ever heard of video editing software? Or disguises? Even if he is guilty, he deserves a fair trial. When I went to speak to Richard to find Gabriel, he told me that Francis is going to be exiled before Peter even gets back!"

"What!? Ohhh, that's awful!" After processing this, Emily's doubtful jade eyes moved as she played with her hair. "Still, as to the evidence, you can't really video edit a person into a clip, can you?"

"I think so, why not? With modern technology and everything. I think it's called deepfakes." Joseph lifted his chin. "And have you forgotten the conversation I overheard?"

"You didn't hear anything about the cone, did you? And look, either way, maybe one of those guys you eavesdropped on was Francis. About the tape. . . . there is no denying that it would be hard to fabricate, even with the most advanced software."

"There are always ways. But I don't even think I believe that is what happened. I *know* it sounds stupid, but I believe Francis was, uh, possessed," he said, feeling her look of confusion and scepticism burn into him.

Imbibing her coffee, Emily looked at him like he had a screw loose. Her lower lip hung open above her mug, steam billowing into her nostrils. "Huh? Possessed?" she said in confusion.

After Joseph explained his theory about possession, he told her his idea to go find Peter, "He's the only one who has the authority to fix this, and I think he might be sympathetic to Francis. I happen to know he is on Sabbat Islet, Recalibrating."

At this, Emily laughed condescendingly. "'You happen to know?' It's common knowledge that Peter goes to Sabbat Islet to Recalibrate. But nobody knows exactly where the island is; it's a well-kept secret. And if we did manage to find out, are you really suggesting that we just hop on a boat and make off to Sabbat Islet? You're joking! Even if we could locate Peter, we don't know if he would agree with you about Francis," she said heatedly.

"You're the one who wanted to escape last time, hypocrite!" he said.

Emily crossed her arms. "But that was different—we wouldn't necessarily have come back, would we? And, I changed my mind. At least, I kind of did . . . don't judge me for this and don't tell anyone, but I found a way around the whole *no-contact* thing."

"What's that supposed to mean?"

She shrugged. "There's no law against *catfishing*. I set up, like, a profile as a 'distant relative' and I've been getting back in touch with my family over Facebook. It's harmless. I managed to get them to send me some new pics of Barney. He's really old now. That was partly why I wanted to go back to America, to see Barney one more time before he passed."

"What?" Joseph gasped, sounding scandalised. "What if they found out about Hyleberia? Wouldn't you be exiled?"

Hands on hips, Emily shouted defensively, "So, you want to run away from Hyleberia to fetch Peter, and now you're acting sanctimonious? Let's get back on topic. Do you really think Peter, you know, would be thrilled to be awakened from his slumber? More to the point, why are you acting like Peter's not cut from the same cloth as Richard?"

He wanted to say, *"Peter will be less harsh. Remember, he didn't exile Nigel out of malice, but because he contradicted divine law. I believe that he will see reason,"* but Joseph wasn't even sure of his faith in Peter himself. As he went silent, Emily made a convincing diatribe about the stupidity of his plan. Nonetheless, Joseph felt he had to do *something* to help Francis.

" . . . So, you really just need to accept your idea is, like, idiotic, Joseph."

Increasingly, Joseph thought that this dialogue wasn't helping in the slightest. "Maybe my plan was dumb. But the fact remains, that these next few days are probably the last chance we have to save Francis. It sounded like Richard is keen to get rid of him as soon as possible," he told her, and the argument came to a close.

"I can see you're determined, despite reason." Emily sighed, putting her mug aside. "Shrivatsa resumes tomorrow, so if you're sure, you'd better figure out a good plan soon. I do hope that Francis is innocent; I just don't know if I fully believe he is."

Shrivatsa. Oh crap. I'm not much in the mood for studying. Standing up, Joseph resolved to cross-examine Chen the following day, although he still doubted that he was the true culprit.

Deflated, he said, "I'll figure out something else, I guess. And I'm confident he is not guilty. I spoke to him shortly before the theft, and he was acting completely normally."

But in truth, Joseph was completely out of ideas much like his empty teacup, and a sudden throb of pain in his head aggravated an unignorable feeling of being stuck.

"I just hope that you're right," Emily mumbled, a glint of worry in her eyes. "Francis and I were never best friends or anything, but I always got on with him, and certainly don't want him gone forever. And I'm sorry if I, like, seemed uncaring today."

"I hope so too," Joseph affirmed. "I really do."

The conversation carried on for several minutes, and it soon became clear that even if Emily was not being particularly helpful, she was at least sympathetic to the cause.

As Joseph stepped towards the front door to leave, handing her his mug, Emily muttered, "As for now, Mohammed is recovered, and can give you a viewing. He told me to tell you that. Do you remember the way to his apartment?"

"Oh, really?" responded Joseph rather gloomily. "I guess I'll drop by now. Have a divine life, as they say. . . ."

"Sure. Oh, and wait. I almost forgot, the painkillers you asked for," Emily recalled, walking into her kitchen and then handing him a white pill bottle.

"Emily, that's a contraceptive," Joseph said, examining the label.

"Oh, sorry," she squealed, getting the right bottle. "My eyesight is getting terrible lately. Might need to get glasses."

Maybe the reason why you didn't see the bloody bricks!

"Thanks," said Joseph, taking one immediately. "My headache is like perdition today, and I constantly feel like throwing up."

Would Peter even care about Francis, if I went to get him? Joseph ruminatively made his way down the hall to Mohammed's place, waiting for the pill to kick in. *He allows millions of needless false convictions every day. Why would this be any different?*

Joseph rapped on Mohammed's apartment. As his potential new roommate opened the door, his skin radiated a much healthier glow than the last time Joseph had stopped by, when he had looked near-death.

"Thanks for dropping by, Joseph. Come on in," Mohammed greeted, his deep, baritone voice quite pleasant as opposed to the hoarseness during his Grix.

"Cheers, mate."

Mohammed had waist-length dark hair like a monk, which fell out of his turban. Joseph hadn't noticed before because they were covered, but his arms were laden with Arabic bracelets. He wore a short-sleeved, round collar Middle Eastern robe.

He apologised profusely, "Sorry about turning you away last time. It took me a week and a half to recover from the Grix. Now, I'm right as rain, even if rain doesn't have a very good reputation around here lately. So, tell me, what's the issue with your current place?"

Joseph shrugged, and said, "The commute, poor living conditions, but mostly my current roommate is driving me up the wall. His name is Raymond Wagner, and he may be Satan incarnate."

"Think I've heard of him," Mohammed said, visibly intrigued. "What's his problem?"

Joseph complained about the pools, the loud music and the constant insults Raymond came up with. That said, as the complaints went on, he questioned whether Raymond really had been that bad the past few weeks. In fact, he had behaved rather decently with the whole Francis affair, especially by helping out during the police station trip, and they seemed to have moved on from their prior tiff. Of course, being a decent roommate was still far from being a good one.

Mohammed laughed. "Sounds like a real character! Well, the best way to get rid of an enemy is to make him into a friend."

"Yeah, so I'm really looking for someone . . . easier to live with," Joseph said.

"I can assure you that if you moved here, I would mostly stay out of your way. I am always busy with the Electrons Department—phonon drag and Ectons are my specialties, to be precise, and I also teach Proficiencies sometimes. You see, I am a Level 2 Administrator, and so I spend much of the day making sure that the Tellurian electrons are working as planned. It involves in-person tests around the globe. Not to mention, I'm often at my ex-wife's place for various reasons."

"Oh, you are divorced?" Joseph asked, stunned. It was perhaps the first divorced person that he had met so far on the island, or married. "You can marry in Hyleberia?"

"Yup. Marriage here can be eternal, so divorce rates are rather high. Love wilts if not watered. Yasmin and I don't live together anymore, but I spend a lot of time over at her place when our son is around."

"You have a son too?" Joseph asked, astonished.

"Yeah," Mohammed said. "Most of the year he's busy at Mooncalf School on Paideia Island, but parents are always allowed to visit. That's where all the Hyleberia-born kids go to study before they are integrated into the community."

Joseph had not heard about this segregated schooling system, and he didn't quite understand it. He hadn't even realised children existed on Hyleberia. "How come the kids can't just learn on this island?"

"It's suggested they would distract from our work, so they go study about a mile away on this island," Mohammed explained. "When they reach eighteen, the new recruits move here and slowly stop ageing. It's a good system, though I admit, it was rather sad to have to say goodbye to my baby when he was born. To a parent, a child is everything."

He nodded, unsure what to say. "I'd love to meet them. And your Proficiencies?"

"Oh, that. I can control electric currents with my mind. Turn on and off lights and electrify people," he said dignifiedly, turning on a light down the hall by pointing to it. "In any case, shall we begin the tour?"

Joseph resisted the temptation to ask him to showcase his Proficiencies further, as he nodded and they began walking around. Mohammed's place struck him as the paragon of clean and tidy. All of the rooms were bigger than in Miyagi Apartments. There was a large kitchen (not kitchenette); a comfy living room; two tastefully decorated bedrooms and bathrooms with bidets. There were quite a few expensive-looking framed pictures of saints and spiritual iconography, and tables with well kept bonsais. A copy of the SHOMAT textbook was sitting by the ice machine for casual browsing. The apartment's jalousie windows gave an excellent view of central Hyleberia, the Les Amis restaurant and the Hyle Lounge Nightclub.

When the tour was nearing its end, Joseph asked, "So, how much is the rent?"

"Around ten thousand drachma a month," Mohammed explained, his dark eyes piercing him.

Joseph gasped; paying for this place on his welfare would not be easy. He was reminded about how terrible he was with money. Since arriving in Hyleberia, he'd been trying to be more savings-conscious, buying the cheaper options at the supermarket and so on. But he still didn't feel very good at this.

"Wow, that's a lot. So, where's your current roommate going?"

"Money is a motivator. He is leaving to move downtown," Mohammed disclosed. "He's snagged a fancy new job in the Mineralogy Department, building diamonds and gold on a molecular level, and the commute is too far."

"That's, uh, convenient for me, I guess," Joseph mused, finding himself frustratingly unable to focus, his mind still fixed on Francis' upcoming exile. "Well, this place looks excellent to me."

As the tour came to a close, Joseph was edging towards the door to head home when the subject of Francis, in a rather unexpected way, came up.

"Forgive my curiosity, but were you called to the police station to testify over the past week? I heard that Emily was a few days ago," Mohammed asked abruptly by the door frame, standing in front of a painting of the golden cone.

"Yeah, I was," Joseph answered, caressing the stile of the door as he prepared to go. "A bootless errand, honestly. The police didn't listen to a word I said."

"Did you perchance know I was friends with Francis too?" Mohammed revealed.

Joseph stared at him, taken aback. They didn't exactly seem like they would be best friends. "No! I didn't know that at all."

"A friend is a present you give yourself, so I use the word *friend* loosely. When you spend as long as I have in Hyleberia —I arrived in 1253 C.E., so it's been almost a millennium— you generally meet everyone once or twice, if briefly. As for Francis, I encountered him a few years ago at a debate at the Pnyx about the abolition of congenital deformities. He seemed to me a down to earth, affable fellow."

Joseph nodded. "Ah, to be sure. So, do you think he stole the cone?"

"I couldn't say for certain," Mohammed remarked,

stroking his beard, "but . . . I truly doubt it. Personally, I feel they really should not judge him prematurely without examining all possibilities. Tellurians always say innocent until proven guilty."

He couldn't believe it—at last, at long last, someone actually agreed with him about Francis' innocence. But at this moment, Joseph didn't have it in him to tell Mohammed that power-mad Hoskins was perfectly fine with exiling Francis without Peter's permission.

He nodded. "I feel the same way. Somebody could easily be framing him. Francis claims to have no memory of the theft, that the last thing he recalls was returning to his apartment after Shrivatsa. After that, it's all black to him."

"Hmm," mulled Mohammed, squinting like he was concentrating. "And yet I'm told they have strong video evidence?"

Joseph bit his lip, rolling his eyes. "Kinda, it shows him taking the cone."

"Hold on a moment. This sounds to me almost like it could be . . . a Body Manipulation Proficiency."

He nodded instinctively like a bobblehead, but then caught himself. This was brand new, perhaps useful information. Stunned, Joseph asked, "Wait, what's that?"

Mohammed explained, "Body manipulation is a genre of abilities that endow one with the power to control, or possess bodies. I wonder if somebody could have used such a Proficiency to frame him."

Joseph choked. "But Emily suggested there's no such thing."

"No doubt, she's right. Body Manipulation Proficiencies were banned after the War, because they were argued in Parliament to be too liable to abuse and misuse. But perhaps somebody could have found a way to get around that. It's at least theoretically possible. Mind control is especially dangerous. Using it, you can literally make someone think they want something they don't. That was also banned after some murder or something, as it was ruled to be too dangerous. Additionally, telepathy, super speed . . . actually, a lot was banned."

This was huge news. Joseph was thinking so fast that he almost forgot where he was.

"That must be it!" he exclaimed, rubbing his hands together. "The day that the cone disappeared, somebody . . . or maybe even the Prince's ghost . . . possessed Francis that night using that Proficiency, and framed him."

"What, you really think so?" asked Mohammed, bewildered. "I was just speculating."

"Do you know how somebody would be able to obtain a Proficiency illicitly?"

"I'm not quite sure," uttered Mohammed, looking at the wall clock, "but nothing is impossible."

Joseph's train of thought returned to Thaddeus. Could he really have bribed someone? He asked as many follow-up questions as he could think of, before Mohammed insisted he needed to get back to a work project on electron-fermion interactions.

"Thanks so much for everything you've told me," he said, realising he had exhausted Mohammed of all helpful information. "And the tour, of course. I'll let you know about the apartment."

"I hope you figure it out soon, and Francis makes it out OK, of course," Mohammed wished him luck, closing the door behind him. "If anything, always remember: despair is criminal."

As he left the apartment and the complex, Joseph's mind felt encumbered by all the clues, as if he were trying to solve a crossword puzzle with no pencil. *So, what do I do now?* He scratched his arm, desperate to find some way to help. *I have to do something. There isn't much time left. If only Sherlock Holmes were a Hyleberian.*

Joseph decided to extend his walk home so that he would have time to think. He paced down Hawking Street until he ended up coming to the garden in which he had arrived in Hyleberia. There was a sign there, which revealed its name, Agape Green. It was strange, not much time had passed since his arrival, and yet Joseph didn't relate much to the person he had been on that very first day. Dew glimmering on leaves, he ambled through the silver gate and then along heliconias and blue passion flowers. Maybe doing nothing for five minutes would give him the clarity of mind he needed to find answers.

There were remnants of the tornado in the garden, oaks uprooted, dead birds, and many of the perennials looked to be on their last legs. The stream lapping gently against the sand, and the warm, tepid atmosphere of this lunchtime hour, made Joseph lust to simply recline under a tree by the sundial where he had awoken, have a snooze and forget his troubles. As he passed by a statue of the glimmering golden cone that was rotating in midair, he wondered where on Earth it could be.

But after five minutes of aimless traipsing, his worries remained largely unassuaged. *It all seemed so simple when I got here. I would have never anticipated all of this.* Bristling, Joseph was about to return home when he caught the eye of someone. It was a certain philosopher he had met a few weeks earlier. He was in a state of shock as he stared at the long-haired man.

Wearing a blue ascot cap and corduroys, there was Descartes himself, pottering down the garden path like he had not a care in the world. The internal debate in Joseph's mind about whether to say hello was quickly solved when Descartes strolled over and broke the ice.

"Well, I never! Joseph Shields, *ça va*? I thought I recognised you, but wasn't sure," Descartes greeted him, his grizzled brown hair shaking on his shoulders as he spoke. "Do you speak French, incidentally?"

"Hey, Descartes. Nope. Spanish and English. And I'm not bad, how are you?" asked Joseph, noticing his headache had improved somewhere along the way.

"Comme d'habitude," Descartes informed him, smiling widely. "It's great to be out and about, not that I haven't been putting the quarantine to good use."

Joseph felt strangely like he had forgotten how to speak now Descartes was near. He had googled him a few weeks ago, and countless books had been written about the man. "Ah, I see. You've been productive?" he asked.

"Oui. It's no secret that I have been penning my newest philosophical masterpiece, entitled *A Refutation of Phenomenological Nomadism, a Deleuzian, Benjaminian and Lacanian Prolegomenal Proema.* You haven't had a chance to read any of my new works, *peut-être*?" he said.

"That sounds like an easy read. And no, but it's on my to-do list. I've been kinda overwhelmed with everything," Joseph admitted, itching his neck as he caught sight of a lady who had liquorice hair extensions.

He immediately agreed when Descartes asked if he wanted to walk around the garden.

"I sometimes forget you are only a colt. Is there anything I can do to help you settle in?" Descartes asked, as they began ambling together. "Some advice about Hyleberia, or an *éclaircissement* of a difficult philosophical topic?"

On the spur of the moment, Joseph decided to bring up a topic that was perhaps unwise. He was going to tell Descartes about the terrible situation he was in. Maybe this sage, world-renowned Frenchman could advise him what to do.

"Can I get your advice about something? I need to get it off my chest," Joseph revealed, burying his hands in his pockets. "I just think I need someone else's opinion."

"Of course, go on," Descartes encouraged him, smiling warmly. "*Pourquoi pas?*"

And so, Joseph told him everything; like water from a bursting dam, the truth came out. Surely Descartes, who many held was the most important philosopher of the 17th century, would be able to offer some wisdom regarding this imbroglio.

"Enough," Descartes remarked, a sympathetic look on his face as he interrupted Joseph. "I'm afraid this is a very difficult personal problem, and I cannot solve it for you. I do not have any political expertise regarding Hyleberian affairs. It's between you, your friend, Francis, and the Hyleberian government."

"Oh, I'm sorry for burdening you," Joseph apologised, wishing he had kept it all in as they passed by a peculiar flower that was sparkling like diamonds.

"Don't feel sorry. Though I can't help, I would be glad to point you in the right direction. You've read *Meditations on First Philosophy*, I presume? As I have said, I disagree with ninety-nine percent of that ancient work, especially the ontological arguments. Nevertheless, the thought experiments have value. I anticipate you are familiar with the Evil Demon argument?"

"No, I haven't read it, I'm afraid," said Joseph, who hadn't read many philosophy books at all, if any.

"One of the thought experiments, as expressed in *Meditations*, was about an evil demon who intends to deceive the perceiver of the external world. Thus, the perceiver wouldn't have any way of telling whether what he experienced was real," Descartes informed him, as he pulled a joint out of his pocket and impassively lit it.

Is that even legal here? "Yes . . . so what are you saying?" Joseph asked, his brain cogs grinding.

Descartes smoked a puff. "You think someone is framing Francis, right?"

"Uh, yeah. I think someone, or something, possessed him to get his paws on the cone."

"Quite possible. What if an extremely powerful figure was in league with the Prince and had acquired these powers, which would allow them to frame Francis in a manner so convincing that nobody would ever suspect? And further, what if this individual were a master manipulator, right beneath your nose this entire time? Then that figure could be considered the Evil Demon to you and Francis, in an allegorical sense, deceiving you about something so basic you haven't even doubted it."

"Do you think it could be Richard Hoskins, then?" Joseph asked at once, mind flashing back to the time that Richard had had a fit when he was in the Holy Office. "I don't like him at all, to be honest. He's very grumpy."

Descartes stroked his chin. "It could well be. But please keep in mind, I've nothing against Hoskins myself."

"Hmmm. At the moment, I'm suspicious of several people, but not certain about any of them," Joseph admitted.

As they came to a bed of purple daisies, Descartes took another smoke. "Well, is there one you are most suspicious of?" Descartes asked.

Thaddeus. Joseph didn't even need to think. "Yeah. This Controller guy I know."

"Perhaps I shouldn't be acting like the Oracle of Delphi. My genius may be unparalleled, but even I once thought that the soul is in the pineal gland!" Descartes joked, as his maroon eyes danced. "In regard to your 'controller guy', you need to be thinking about getting hard evidence. Presuming he were the 'Evil Demon', if you were to confront him point-blank, most likely all he'd do is deny it. Be very careful, Joseph."

"That's a good point. And *au contraire*, Descartes, you're a very wise man," Joseph praised, realising his first impression of Descartes had been rather premature. "But Francis will be exiled in mere weeks, if not days, so I don't have long to figure it out. I confess I don't have much faith in the political system here. Ever since Nigel's exile, what with the bureaucracy and all, sometimes I feel Hyleberia is, uh, dystopian."

"Hyleberia is certainly not Arcadia, but is anywhere perfect? Do you not think I was suspicious when I first arrived?" Descartes asked him, and then chuckled as they stopped by a statue of a smiling Gabriel. "I'm known as *the* arch-sceptic! It took me about five decades before I started to accept this place as my new home. You've got to have faith in the Animah. It will lead you to where you need to be, what you should do, who you should become."

"The *Animah*?" Joseph repeated, baffled. "I've heard that word so many times before. What does it mean?"

"There are many words for it in ancient languages, although none in modern ones," Descartes revealed. "The Tao, Logos, Dharma . . . the animating force behind the flow of the universe's appearances, or, the structure of structure and the cause of causes. Some call it the only true God. In Hyleberia, we call it the Animah. Even Peter holds no sway over it and its plans."

"Hmmm. That makes sense," Joseph affirmed, still unsure of what to do, but regardless, appreciating the advice. "*Merci beaucoup,* Descartes! I'll try my best. For the Animah."

"That's the attitude," Descartes remarked, patting him on the back. "Make me proud."

If it were true that there was an "Evil Demon" framing Francis, Joseph resolved at that moment he wasn't going to let them get away with it. *The devil is, as always,* he thought, taking a deep breath, *in the details.*

CHAPTER 11
RESCUE MISSION

JOSEPH HAD A HORRIBLE FEELING IN HIS GUTS THAT THE CURRENT situation was delicately balanced on the edge of disaster, about to collapse. It was a seemingly run-of-the-mill Monday morning in Hyleberia. He had just washed, dressed, and he was now looking for something to eat and drink for breakfast. On the way to the kitchenette, he found Raymond in his usual relaxed position with his malodorous feet up on the sofa, staring vacantly at HB1.

"Did you hear the speech last night?" Raymond asked, as Joseph poured himself a glass of Haoma.

"Speech? No. I've been a bit occupied with saving an innocent man's life," Joseph grumbled, rummaging in the fridge for *Hylesticks* to snack on, a local brand of breadsticks.

Joseph had not been avidly following the recent political developments. He had spent the prior night in his bedroom, considering what to do and studying when he managed to concentrate. Joseph loathed that classes were restarting today, as they were going to interfere with his efforts to exonerate Francis. But he knew he couldn't bunk off as he used to do on occasion in Birchwood Senior School. For one thing, he had to go to interrogate Chen; for another, he was due his career profiler results.

Raymond pointed to the visualiser screen, where they were seconds away from replaying the latest Richard Hoskins speech. "Come watch this then," he said, suspiciously helpful.

Joseph sat down with fists clenched to watch the broadcast, sipping his Haoma and not expecting to enjoy what he was about to see.

There it was again, Richard's self-satisfied and self-important expression, along with his general air of being very in love with himself. He stood at the lectern, a punchable look on his face as he began to speak, even his Welsh accent causing Joseph's blood to boil. Somehow, his calm, poised demeanour on the screen gave no hint as to his irascible tendencies.

"I am glad to say that Hyleberia is quickly being restored to its former glory. Ninety-nine percent of the flooding and thirty-three percent of the hurricane damage is now cleared. The worst is over. Many of you will know that not long ago we arrested a suspect, Mr Francis Rodrigo, a student of Shrivatsa. It has become increasingly clear, and indeed, undeniable that he was the heinous criminal behind the cone theft. The Hyleberia Police Department has recovered unimpeachable footage revealing his culpability, and it seems he acted alone. Mr Rodrigo crept into the sewer system at approximately 5:15 pm and snuck up the sewer pipe into the Divine Repository. Then, conspiring to obtain the golden cone's divine powers, he disabled the turret, took the cone and hid it somewhere still unknown, engendering disruptions to normal Hyleberian weather. While we have yet to find the cone itself, on my authority I have personally ruled that Mr Rodrigo is too much of a danger to the community to justify keeping him on our precious island any longer. The decision has thus been made to exile him this week, on Wednesday."

"What crap!" Joseph gasped, skin prickling with anxiety. "That's *no* time."

"Actually, it's *some* time. About two days," Raymond replied, his voice sharp.

Joseph wasn't amused. "What am I going to do?" he asked, exasperated. "It's like *The Shawshank Redemption* or something."

"That a film? I don't get all your weird references," Raymond shrugged, and asked, "What were you *planning* on doing?"

Joseph peered downwards. "I don't know—kinda needed more time to figure that out," he replied.

"It's announced to the public now." Raymond looked unsure whether to pretend to care. "You might have to just accept it: your friend is a goner. Sadly, that's the squircle of life."

He glared at Raymond, furious at his callousness. "What if you were on trial? Would you want me to just shrug, and say, 'Oh, well. I hope he's reincarnated into something good.'"

"*Touché*. I just don't want you to get your hopes up if things don't work out. And to be honest, I don't know why you care. You just met the guy!" There was a pause, and then Raymond said something very out of the blue, "Is it something to do with your father?"

"What could it possibly have to do with him? Lung cancer got him," Joseph replied baffledly.

"I know. That's what I'm saying. Maybe you're projecting him onto Francis. Like . . . if you can save Francis, it might . . . I dunno . . . feel like you are saving the spirit of your father. It's like transference. Isn't that what psychologists call it?"

The spirit of my father? Huh? Joseph replayed the words in his mind, inflamed. *What bollocks!*

"That's the biggest load of nonsense I ever heard, discount Freud," Joseph snapped. "You know, I don't need someone as mentally ill as Raymond Wagner to diagnose me, thanks. This apartment is permanently damaged thanks to your psychotic recklessness."

"I'm just saying, maybe you feel like by saving him, you'll be saving your father. I've lost parents too, y'know. I know what it feels like to want them to come back," Raymond said. "Sucks, man."

"No, it's not at all related," Joseph said, glancing at the wall clock and doubting very much if there was any purpose to continuing this conversation. "Well, I better be off to Shrivatsa."

He stood up to leave, but stopped suddenly, as Joseph realised he should decide whether to bring up to Raymond his recent opportunity to move. Standing there, on the spur of the moment, he looked around and took in the apartment— the peeling walls, sagging carpet, mouldy ceiling and the furniture on which was scattered Raymond's records and pool toys. It wasn't as if this place was any comparison with Terribilità Terrace, with its spa and stunning views.

Yet for some reason, at this instant Joseph's tongue was hanging limp. *It just isn't the right time to bring up that I likely won't be living here soon. I'll wait till after Wednesday.*

Turning on his N64, Raymond groused, "Are you just standing there for a reason, Josephine?"

"Never mind, see you later," Joseph said, resolving that he would address this later, and as for now centre his attention on the more pressing issue of Francis' imminent exile.

He quickly grabbed a pear for breakfast, threw on his backpack and hurried to the Academy. As Joseph strolled along the streets, it seemed for the first time that the flood might have never even happened. While there was still a lot of damage from the hurricane, construction workers and builder archons had been brought to the island to work on the repairs. Like vacuum archons, builder archons were seemingly like normal archons, except for several construction-related abilities like being able to lift bricks and mix cement. The bright sky was such that he even spotted some Hyleberians sunbathing by Agape Green, wearing old-fashioned sunbonnets and bathing suits, drinking lemonade or reading novels.

But Joseph did not enjoy the weather; he couldn't stop thinking about what Raymond had just said about his father. He still believed the notion was ridiculous, and yet if it wasn't true, how could he explain why he was so sure about Francis' innocence?

When Joseph arrived at the classroom, everyone was already there chatting except Ms Sadeghi, which now meant only Chen and Emily. Joseph froze in the doorway as he saw Chen sitting inside; he had been thinking over what to say to him, but it had just slipped his mind. As he came into the room, Emily and Chen's conversation suddenly quietened. Sitting down and taking out his pen, Joseph felt their stares lingering on him like fireflies to a porch light.

"So, Joseph," Chen began to ask, lurching forward on his seat, "after the flood, do you need an ark? Because I Noah a guy."

With only slightly amused eyes, Joseph burst out in hollow laughter and uttered, "Good one. You are sooooo funny."

"For once, that is funny," Emily said, chuckling more authentically.

Chen smiled nonchalantly. "So, tell us. How did you pass the rainy days? Is it too early for hurricane jokes? Maybe I should wait for things to blow over. Y'know, in China when it flooded, we would be eating grass for a year! Fun times."

"Doing nothing much, to be honest," he said dryly with a shrug, seemingly unable to be a social butterfly at this moment. He glanced at Emily, who was looking at both of them. "You?"

Joseph felt his muscles tense as he tried to keep his cool. He planned to hear Chen's alibi before he accused him of anything, remembering what Descartes had advised him.

"Even at the comedy club, I've hardly been able to get my

mind off of Francis," Chen revealed, looking meaningfully at Emily. "The classroom is going to feel much emptier without him. But soon a new Tellurian will take his place, I guess. I hope they're nice."

"Is that true?" he queried, twirling his pencil in his hand.

"Of course," muttered Chen, biting his lip. "Hyleberia will need someone to replace Francis now that he's gone. The Academy gets new colts every few years. Somebody will take Nigel's place too, now that I think of it. So, I guess in no time we will have two new people in class. You won't be the colt for much longer!"

Now that he's gone? He's not gone yet. This was news to Joseph. He thought it would be very early to consider himself a naturalised Hyleberian. *Funny how quickly I've stopped caring about Tellurian affairs.*

"What do you think about Francis' upcoming exile, then?" Joseph asked, a sudden pain in his stomach. "Hoskins just announced it."

Eyes trained on him, Joseph was analysing Chen's expressions very intently, although trying his best to act casual.

"I heard. It's so sad, isn't it?" opined Chen emotionlessly. "But, I'm sure the exile is ultimately justified. Who does not punish evil, invites it."

Judging from his demeanour, Chen didn't feel even an iota of sadness. They all fell silent for a few seconds. "What do you mean by justified?" Joseph questioned, beginning to feel rather like a gadfly.

Chen said quietly, "Well, to think of what he was doing behind our backs. I mean, he must have already been planning his evil scheme when we all went to the Divine Repository. Perhaps he's been machinating for years."

"You and Francis," Joseph stated, raising his eyebrows at Chen and glancing down at his desk. "I thought you were at least slightly friends. Don't you think there is something preemptive about it? I mean, that they are going to exile him without Peter even being here?"

"Not really 'friends'. I mean, we had nothing in common. I acted nice enough with him, and I never let on about anything, but I dunno, honestly I was always hesitant about befriending a former drug dealer. Furthermore, the video that they captured," mumbled Chen curtly, "it was very . . ."

Joseph had had enough. Frowning, he slammed his desk and raised his voice. "Convincing?"

Chen snorted, fiddling with his bald-covering cap, looking highly embarrassed. "Uh. . . ."

Furious, Joseph eyeballed him and shouted, "Maybe you shouldn't be acting so holier-than-thou. Have you never heard of a wrongful conviction?"

Emily had been staring at them both and tugging at her pretty hair like it had ants in it. She interrupted, "Ohhhhh, don't get into an argument. Maybe Francis would want us just to trust the Animah. We don't have any say about what happens anyway."

"I doubt it," Joseph yelled with an eye roll. "He's not going on a sabbatical; they're going to kill him, just like they did with Nigel. And nobody even goddam cares!"

Joseph couldn't believe he just said this. Emily looked mortified.

"How over-the-top," she replied pointedly, arms crossed. "I'm not sure if Francis truly stole the cone either, so stop acting like Chen and I are gullible idiots. I'm just, like, not convinced we can do anything. It's not like you have any evidence to persuade us of his innocence. And—"

"Hold on, Emily, let me state my opinion, because Joseph interrupted," Chen interjected, standing and clenching his jaw. "Joseph, I know you are new, but you can stop acting so high and mighty yourself. We cannot lie to ourselves that Francis didn't take the cone, even if we don't want to believe it. We all saw him do it, and Francis was a criminal on Earth. You don't even know a thing about him, like how he died."

"What? Then, tell me!" Joseph yelled, tapping his foot agitatedly.

Chen narrowed his eyes. "You wanna know? Because you won't like what you hear."

Joseph scoffed. "How Francis died? Sure. Why not? Something bad, I bet!"

"Fine then," Chen screamed, seething mad. "Electric chair. He moved from Mexico to America and ended up killing four people, two parents and two children. They say he was trying to rob their house when the poor family returned home. His real name is Francisco, but he changed it."

Joseph slumped his shoulders; he couldn't believe his ears. He stood there rooted to the spot, as if paralysed. *So, that is why everyone has been so positive of his guilt.*

Slack-jawed, he turned to Emily. "Is that true?"

Emily didn't meet his incredulous stare. Her eyes were no longer visible, face cradled in her hands. "Probably, I heard rumours too," she mumbled.

Joseph didn't know what to say. Words came out of his mouth before he could think, "Well, maybe that was a false conviction too! And it's different." *What a weak comeback. But I need time to rethink this now.*

Chen sighed, lowering his voice, sitting down again. "You're grasping at straws, man. Maybe you think you figured him out better than us over, what, weeks?"

"No, I d-don't. It's just. . . ." Joseph stuttered, feeling abruptly out of his depth.

Chen continued, "Trust me, and I'm not saying it's a competition, but Francis' actions have affected me and will continue to more than it does you. He died a criminal, and never changed. *I* cried when I heard Acting Prime Minister Hoskins' speech. *You* barely even knew Francis."

"Maybe I didn't know him, but I know a *kangaroo court.*

That video doesn't prove anything," Joseph burst out. "It could easily have been doctored or faked. What I want to know is why this supposed world government is run like damn North Korea. I—"

But he never finished this sentence, for at that very moment, Ms Sadeghi strode through the classroom door. "Good morning," she greeted, gloomier sounding than he had ever heard her.

The room fell silent. Joseph sat down at once, acting like nothing had occurred. *How much has she overheard? She must have heard something. We were shouting.*

"Let's begin class by addressing the elephant in the room," Ms Sadeghi pronounced gravely, setting her books down on the front desk and bridging her fingers. "Certainly, it's every teacher's worst nightmare to learn that one of her students has been involved in criminal activities. And yet, that is my fate now, after two millennia of pristine tenure at Hyleberia Academy. Mr Francis Rodrigo—even saying the name makes my eyes water—has misled everyone in this room about his character, putting on a front of innocence while cooking up loathsome, blasphemous schemes of theft and divine sedition."

She started tearing up, monobrow dancing, and grabbed a tissue from her quilted handbag.

Joseph stared at her, not daring to speak. Despite ardently disagreeing, he could tell by her tone that she meant every word she said. Tears fell out of her sorrowful eyes.

Nose sniffing, she blinked back tears and tried to speak, "I k-know I can act like a t-taskmaster sometimes, but it's only b-because I care so much a-about my students." Ms Sadeghi's crying fit was at this point escalating into full-on sobbing, as she started to sound a tad like Sergeant White. "I'm so s-sorry that you three had to be q-questioned, but the p-police assured me it was n-necessary. Still, I'm a-aware that some of you might harbour f-feelings of betrayal, guilt and . . . denial after having b-been deceived by F-Francis. I have been t-alking with Acting Prime Minister H-Hoskins, and we a-agree that it is only right to offer everybody here a m-month of free grief therapy over the n-next few weeks at the Counselling Centre, over on Rousseau R-Road. To a-anybody who would like to take up this o-offer, come speak to me after c-class."

That's just perfect. Joseph rested his chin on his knuckle, and felt apprehension surge through him. *Francis will be dead in two days, but who cares, free therapy! Already got quite enough of that from Raymond this morning.*

After Ms Sadeghi had calmed down, class began. Joseph didn't utter a word during the lesson except when absolutely necessary. This became increasingly evident during the group session, where they were supposed to be discussing the mathematical universe hypothesis, but he basically refused to participate. Sitting there and stewing, he grew increasingly convinced that all of Hyleberia was against him—of course, with the possible exception of Mohammed and Descartes, although he didn't know them that well.

Yet Joseph had to admit, hearing Francis' Tellurian charge, his real name and his death by capital punishment had lowered his conviction slightly. It meant that Francis had been deliberately not sharing his whole life truth, and it suggested that Joseph did not know him as well as he had hoped.

When their lunch break arrived, as the others disappeared in haste for a bite to eat (no doubt eager to avoid more conflict with Joseph), Ms Sadeghi announced, "Wait a minute before leaving, Joseph. I still have to give you back your profiler test results."

"Oh, right," Joseph said, trying to read her voice. "Did I do well?"

With a neutral tone, she avoided eye contact and said, "Wait and see. It'll only be a minute."

As he got his official career profiler and paged through it, he was slightly disappointed. Among other errors, he had messed up the difference between Aristotle's *efficient* and *material causes*. He had also been marked down for saying his favourite food was pizza, which was apparently a bad thing, and that his least favourite insect was tarantulas. But Ms Sadeghi said even with that he did decently, and passed (65%) . . . so there was that.

"Ms Sadeghi, I can see the result, but what career does this test mark me out for?" he asked, confused.

"That's on the last page," she informed him, as she organised some files. "The exam is run through a state of the art computer system which analyses the results and determines your skill set, and then compares that to which jobs are available, or will be opening soon. Now, you will not necessarily be forced to take its suggestion, but you will be strongly encouraged to do so, as there are not always viable alternatives."

Joseph felt his stomach drop as he turned to the last page, and read the red felt tip out loud:

"Career Profiler Result: Level 3 Administrator of Dust. Huh?" He reread it three times. "What kind of job is that?" he asked, bewildered.

"Well, Mr Shields," Ms Sadeghi uttered, looking bemused as she prepared her papers for the group session after the break. "It's an important one. Think about all the dust in the world. Somebody needs to make sure it's working right."

Literal dust? He sat there, flabbergasted with his mouth agape. *This has to be a joke.*

Joseph shrugged. "I would've thought that was subsumed under some rubbish job, or something. Can't the Tellurians just, well, clean it up?"

"But what about the design of the dust? Not everything in the world is able to be automated. Apparently, dust is a bit more complicated than you presumed," Ms Sadeghi remarked, crinkling her nose.

He had to stop himself from scoffing, as Ms Sadeghi's tone

sounded rather fragile, and he didn't want to cause her to burst into tears.

"Aren't there any jobs available related to something practical . . . or something that's more . . . not dust?" Joseph asked, crossing his arms.

Ms Sadeghi pushed back her fringe as if Joseph's line of questioning was starting to nettle her. "Don't look down on dust. Every phenomenon is as important as the next. Maybe you should talk to one of the faecal matter, B. O. or halitosis Administrators if you think dust is bad."

"Right, so my life's purpose is managing something that nobody even likes. Makes complete sense," Joseph grumbled under his breath. *Maybe Thomas was right after all. I'm a nobody and will always be one.*

Stewing, Joseph was still rather displeased with this result as he packed up for lunch break. Some of his anger towards Chen he realised he might now be projecting onto that "taskmaster", Ms Sadeghi. But he had to admit to himself that he was on a warpath with everyone now, frustration surging through him. He was not normally a temperamental person; Thomas had once called him "mellow". *I need to calm down and think carefully*, he told himself firmly. *There's barely any time left until the exile, and I've got no plan at all.*

It was a sunny midday, which somehow made Joseph more depressed given his current problems. He found himself mooning about outside Hyleberia Academy, as if there were going to be clues hiding around the corner. Then, he ambled past Patroclus Street in the direction of the Divine Repository, looking around hopelessly. *Maybe the thief dropped his wallet. Not impossible.*

"Hi, J-man. How's the divine life? Whatcha been up to?"

Joseph stopped in his tracks and turned. It was him. Thaddeus was back.

Thaddeus' voice was carefree as usual, but it sounded much more sinister and conniving on Joseph's ears now. He was wearing a ragged plaid shirt and torn jeans. Of course, Joseph's perception of Thaddeus had radically shifted over the past few days. He tried to hide his surprise as his eyes locked on him; he did not want to give away his suspicions.

"Nothing much, T-man. Things and stuff," he greeted with a mask of carelessness, slipping his hands into his pockets. "Where have you been the last few days? I tried finding your number."

"Oh? Soon after I took you to the prison, I had an assignment come up in Malta, Controller work—only returned yesterday. Glad the flooding has cleared, and the hurricane damage has started being repaired. So quickly at that, too." Thaddeus smiled tautly, eyes sunken and shadowed, and asked, "What about you? Not skiving off classes, I hope?"

How convenient that you returned as soon as the flood was over. Feels like you've been hiding. Joseph hid his inner turmoil as best he could, faking a smile. "It's lunch break. I just thought I would go for a relaxing walk around town," he said, glancing sideways.

"Nice! Anyhow, honestly, I'm glad to have run into you, although I haven't even had time to change. Can we talk somewhere a bit private? The beach, perhaps?" Thaddeus looked down at the concrete pavement. "I need to speak to you about something. It's sort of sensitive."

"Er—sensitive? Of course," he affirmed, fingertips beginning to perspire.

"Thanks, J-man," Thaddeus said ambiguously, his face very hard to read.

Keep your cards close to your chest, Joseph reminded himself firmly, letting himself be led away. *Don't do what you did with Emily. At least for now.*

As the pair paced to the beach, Joseph tried to work out what the hell Thaddeus would want to talk with him about. His face felt hot as he thought about the possibilities. Either way, from the sullen countenance of Thaddeus' face and the strained silence that accompanied their walk, it couldn't be anything good. He hoped he wasn't about to be possessed, but it was too late to decline the walk to the beach.

They came to a shingly section of the shore divided by empty deckchairs, not far from where he had been with Emily during their private talk. Thaddeus brought them to a sudden halt. The midday wind sent drafts of sand around their feet, splotches of Hickory brown algae and Pacific razor clams circling them.

"So, what's up, mate?" Joseph asked, trying his best to sound indifferent.

"Um, this is awkward," Thaddeus muttered, covering half of his face with his hand. "The truth is, I've been thinking about the stuff you said about Francis—and—er, you might have a point."

Joseph avoided looking at Thaddeus' navy eyes, feeling as if his face was on fire. "Sorry, what?"

Thaddeus mumbled, "I also think that there is something weird about his . . . conviction."

"How come?" Joseph asked, heart hammering against his chest.

Thaddeus scratched his lip. "This might come as a shock, but yesterday when I got back, I had another look at the tape that the police are using as the main evidence, and there were a few aberrant things about it. So, I'm starting to think that, well, someone could indeed be framing Francis."

"Wow, really!" Joseph had a sudden coughing fit. Catching his breath, he demanded, "What aberrant things?"

Thaddeus explained that he had spotted that there was a mysterious jump in the tape when Francis appears in the video to steal the cone, and he believed that he was the first to notice. He had informed Sergeant Rufius and White about this, and even Hoskins in an emergency appointment, but none of them cared.

Hoskins is truly the worst man to be in charge of Hyleberia.

He's a total egomaniac. "What are you suggesting we do about it?" Joseph asked, perplexed by this sudden paradigm shift from Thaddeus.

Moreover, this new evidence completely contradicted his prior theory about possession by the Prince or an "Evil Demon". Or, did it? Why would Thaddeus be saying this if he truly had framed Francis?

"The only option," started Thaddeus, pausing dramatically, "is what you said that day at Supernatural Foods, to go and find Peter, to bring him back to set things straight. A rescue mission."

"You said it was too dangerous!" Joseph fired back, indignant.

Thaddeus breathed heavily, lowering his eyes. "It is, it was, and still is . . . but there is no alternative . . . We *have* to do it, awaken Peter, that is, if you want Francis to have a chance of surviving this." He crinkled his nose, deep in thought, and added, "Peter has always been a mixed bag, but he's fundamentally a . . . good person."

Joseph, bewildered, did not dare tell him that Francis had seen him the night of his collapse. *I can't tell if he's bluffing. What if he's just saying this because he knows I know? But what do I know?*

"So, will you come?" Thaddeus asked suddenly.

Joseph gaped. "I dunno. Are you sure it's the right move?"

"It's the best option we have. I find it very unlikely that Acting Prime Minister Hoskins could be persuaded, and the police department isn't budging either."

Joseph hardly even knew what he was being asked to do. He bought time by requesting more details. Thaddeus went on to explain that he wanted Joseph specifically to come and profess his belief in Francis' innocence to Peter at his mansion on Sabbat Islet, because Thaddeus himself had never met Francis, or only very briefly.

"Fine, I'll come," Joseph mumbled eventually, after

thinking for a few tense moments. *Saying I'll go doesn't necessarily mean I will. I can still back out.*

Thaddeus looked relieved. In a loud voice, he said, "I'm very glad to hear it. How about we meet at my boat tomorrow at 5 pm? That'll give me time to chart our course overnight."

Joseph nodded hesitantly. "Sounds good, I can come after Shrivatsa."

"Oh, and J-man—it might be obvious, but don't tell a soul about this. I can't emphasise enough, we need to keep our excursion capital-P Private," Thaddeus warned, a single finger raised to his lips.

Joseph quipped, "Never fear, I'm as trustworthy as they come." *At least, try to act natural. Thaddeus may not be your friend, but you have to pretend that he is for now.*

"I know. And sorry that I have surely distracted you from class," Thaddeus said and smiled weakly, eye twitching. "Well, hurry back to Ms Sadeghi, then. See you tomorrow."

Joseph felt as though he was carrying a newly blown lead balloon in his chest as the conversation came to an end, and he traipsed back to school. He was finding it impossible to get rid of the dread that churned throughout every inch of body, like a cancer that he had contracted. Despite having said so, Joseph hadn't decided yet if he really was going to go with Thaddeus, extremely curious about what the supposedly doctored tape implied.

The rest of the school day passed sluggishly. Joseph considered confronting Chen after class once again, but when the session finally ended, Chen managed to worm out before he got the chance to accost him. Emily and Ms Sadeghi were strangely quiet throughout the rest of the lesson as well. Joseph headed home that evening with a very unusual and perhaps foolish intent: to ask a certain German for his advice.

He found Raymond in the lounge playing a freshly acquired Nintendo game, *Kirby 64: The Crystal Shards*. Before he had even pressed pause, Joseph had begun telling him every word that Thaddeus had said. It seemed somehow that all of his annoyance at Raymond barely mattered anymore. The only things he didn't mention were the other worst aspects of what he had learnt today, such as Francis' purported mass murder, which made Joseph's throat become dry. *But does it even matter? That was decades ago, and even if he had been guilty then, he still deserves a fair trial now.*

"So, why did you say yes if you think Thaddeus is a big liar, liar, pants on fire?" Raymond asked, on the edge of his seat.

"Because I had no other choice. And Descartes told me I should be cautious about pointing the finger at people carelessly. If I am to do so, I need to be in a position to get proof," he said.

"What do you mean?"

"Haven't you ever seen a detective show? If I accuse him without any means to record a confession, it'd be pointless," Joseph explained.

From the sofa, Raymond looked vacantly at Joseph, who was pacing back and forth in an agitated mood. "OK. Are you going to go on the trip to Sabbat Islet, or not?"

"Dunno," he said under his breath, mind racing. "The fact that Thaddeus wants to retrieve Peter suggests I'm off-base regarding my suspicions. But if I do go, I need to bring some kind of hidden recorder in case it turns out I am right, so that I could acquire proof. Oh, hell, this is a right quandary."

Raymond scratched his head. "It's a toffee. Francis saw Thaddeus spying on you, then? I suppose that means he's up to something."

"A toughie?" Joseph nodded impatiently. "Well, it seems to, but perhaps it was just a strange coincidence. What if Chen's the real thief? I would be wasting my only and last chance to expose him. For tomorrow is basically the last day to free Francis, and if I go and am not successful, he'll likely be exiled by the time I get back. Also, Thaddeus might try to drown me for all I know, so I would need something for self-defence too. This is terrible; I just can't decide what to do."

"You need to stop stressing, bud. *Que sera sera*: isn't that what you Spaniards say? *Hakuna matata* is in the Lion King." Whether Raymond cared as little as these words suggested was difficult to tell; he had sunglasses on despite being indoors, so his eyes were not visible. "And I can't tell you what to do, bro. As you said at least once before, you're a grown man."

Joseph paced to the kitchenette island and back to the sofa. "Thanks so much for your wise words, mate," he said.

"To be honest, Shields, I often suspect you secretly harbour a death wish," Raymond commented through gritted teeth. "Ever since you arrived in Hyleberia, you've been making life as difficult for yourself as possible. It was never like this for me. My first few months were heaven."

"A death wish? I already died," Joseph replied, on the edge of storming out. "And I've simply been acting in the way I felt was right."

"Don't be rude to me, as I'm about to offer you a favour. You said you needed a way to record Thaddeus' potential confession. If you are going after all, you could always take my old Hylephone, in the hall wardrobe, and hide it. I won't even ask for payment. How nice is that? It has a voice memo app; I used to practise my whistling with it," Raymond said, picking up his game controller as if he wanted to return to Kirby and then whistling a Bon Jovi song. "See? I'm a really good whistler, didn't you know? I've just got out of the habit lately."

"A voice recorder on your phone? That's interesting. Well, I need to think about this alone," Joseph replied, leaving abruptly after realising this repartee was starting to aggravate his headache.

That night, unable to sleep and not having come to any

conclusions during the day, Joseph pondered at length what he should do. After weighing the possible choices for hours, every single one, he determined that he would go. If he didn't, he had no other course of action besides something absurd like a prison break. Hoskins and his cronies would kill Francis, and he would never be able to say he tried to save him. So, he was going to accompany Thaddeus to attempt to awaken Peter. *Easy as cake,* Joseph reflected sarcastically, as he felt his legs go numb under the bed sheets.

When dawn came, Joseph had barely slept a wink; it had been one of those uncomfortable, insomniac sort of nights where all he managed to do was twist and turn. At one point, staring at the ceiling, he asked himself whether his life had really changed that much since he had died, and Joseph found himself reflecting on the past. His father and he had a decent relationship, even if each of them had acute differences. Joseph and Dario had always found ways to bond, such as their shared enthusiasm for games and camping. Dario was also a keen gambler and the one who had owned the Mace, which his family had acquired when they moved abroad from Spain when Joseph was a baby. Caroline, who was from Southend, had met his father on an Erasmus year in Madrid, where Melanie was conceived. When Dario died, it had been very difficult for Joseph's mother to manage it alone.

Then, lying there and trying to motivate himself to get up, Joseph started thinking of the grief-ridden period of his life after his father's passing. It had seemed during those rebellious, angsty teenage years that life on Earth was fundamentally unfair, to give birth to conscious beings and then so quickly demand them to leave. Joseph supposed growing up means developing a begrudging acceptance of the mortal coil and life's various ills.

He made sure to get up early and pack his bag with supplies for the boat trip: bottles of water, snacks, and painkillers, for Joseph wasn't exactly sure how long it was going to take to get to Sabbat Islet. Locating the Hylephone in the wardrobe, and figuring out how to use it without Raymond's help, he decided that he would leave the Hyle- phone recording inside his rucksack for the entire trip. Perhaps the microphone would be muffled, but it would still be able to record anything said nearby. In addition, Joseph packed a kitchen knife in the bag in case things turned ugly. *Well, I hope not. But it's a last resort. Better to be safe than sorry.*

Joseph had breakfast at first light, largely so that he wouldn't have to bump into Raymond. He planned to leave before his roommate woke up. He saw on the visualiser while eating that the hyped eclipse was due the following after- noon. The news anchors on HB1 were chattering about it excitedly, with but a brief mention of Francis' exile, which was scheduled to take place in the morning so it did not inter- vene with the Pralaya. The co-occurrence of the two events was no coincidence, as it was suggested that letting a criminal remain in Hyleberia during the Pralaya would not bode well for the Animah. *Ain't got a lick of sense to me. They said that Peter is likely to come back soon after the eclipse. All they bloody need to do is wait a little while longer and he would return anyway.*

The next hour, Joseph tried to finish his SHOMAT home- work. It was a series of multiple-choice questions about first- order logic. He had largely moved on from teleology over the past few weeks to formal logic and quantum mechanics, both very difficult as he had never even properly studied informal logic or Newtonian mechanics in school. Before the trip to Sabbat Islet, unfortunately, he still had to go to classes, and this particular assignment was due today. Joseph could hardly read the words as he was too distracted. In the end, he just scribbled random ticks in the boxes, hoping luck, for once, was on his side.

Joseph felt he had done quite well preparing for whatever happened on the rescue mission, but it meant he had not left as early as was wise. As he was on his way out at 7:30 am, Raymond appeared out of nowhere and crossed him, half-dressed.

He sighed internally, simmering. *Just great. I never manage to avoid you.*

"You've been awfully quiet ever since our little chinwag yesterday," Raymond said with a furrowed brow, tangling his salmon-coloured tie. "What's going on?"

"None of your business," Joseph muttered, trying and failing to walk around him like a traffic pylon. "Can't talk right now. Will be late for school."

"Hold on a minute, Shields," Raymond said, giving up on his tie, blocking Joseph's momentum with his right arm. "Tell me what you're up to. Don't I deserve that, at least? I risked my behind that night at the police station. Do you think I did that just for my own fun?"

"Maybe, you like stealth video games, don't you?" Joseph shrugged, raising his eyebrows. "I never asked you to come."

Raymond replied, "The fact is that I did, and now I'm involved. I didn't care at the start, and maybe I still don't, but a part of me is at least a tiny bit invested in this whole saga. Are you going with Thaddeus tonight, or not?"

Their eyes met, and Joseph sighed. "Fine. Yes, I'm going. I'm just not in the mood to discuss it. If I disappear, I guess . . . tell the police Thaddeus murdered me," he disclosed.

"Wow, what a renegade!" exclaimed Raymond abruptly, putting on a scandalised tone. "I'm not going to try to discourage you. I guess I'll be worrying about what is going on tonight, then. Won't I, you lawbreaker?"

Joseph groaned. "I think you can manage. Pretty sure you care about your toothbrush more than me. Just cross your fingers we succeed."

"Hold on. Tell me more about your plan. Did you take my old Hylephone, or what?" Raymond called, but Joseph ignored him, somehow managing to slip past this time.

He raced down the staircase, thinking seriously. *It is actually good that Raymond knows, since he will be able to report Thaddeus if something bad does happen. Not that the authorities would believe him.*

The walk to school was filled with more dread, and his guesses about what was going to happen tonight varied wildly. Most of all, he hoped Thaddeus wasn't planning on abandoning him in the middle of the ocean, so he would have to fight sharks or jellyfish for survival like in a horror movie. Joseph was sure as he passed by Iscariot Avenue that the possibilities for disaster were endless, and yet he still found himself determined to go.

After arriving at Shrivatsa, handing in his homework and being given some extremely abstruse readings by Ms Sadeghi on the logic of quantum chaos, Joseph struggled to pay attention during the lesson so much that he feared Ms Sadeghi had noticed something was up. Likely, she was already suspicious after his behaviour yesterday. They had a group session about Tellurian rights that day, which was very awkward as Joseph yet again didn't say a word.

He spent his lunch break alone in the doughnut shop, thoughts spooling and unspooling through his mind. Emily had attempted to converse with Joseph when he was on his way there, but he had told her he didn't want to talk and strode the opposite way, quite annoyed at her after her behaviour over the past few days. Though his name hung in everyone's minds, there was no explicit mention of Francis during class.

When class finally ended, walking to the harbour and relishing a few brief moments of solitude, Joseph let out a quiet groan of trepidation when he spotted Thaddeus' boat bobbing up and down on the neap tide. He quickly pulled down his rucksack and set the Hylephone to record inside of it.

A moment later, like a seal, Thaddeus' head popped into

view over the gunwale. Joseph thought of the last time he had been on this boat with Thaddeus, and how much he had enjoyed himself. He didn't expect this outing to be quite as fun, to say the least.

"Are you ready?" Thaddeus yelled from the ocean, steering the boat over to the dock.

I died ready. Legs quivering slightly, uncertainty roiled in Joseph's mind. "Dunno," he said tremulously.

Thaddeus' voice sounded optimistic, but cautious. "Peter will be fast asleep, so he might be a bit peeved to be woken up. I just thought I'd warn you about that. Nevertheless, I anticipate that we have about a ninety-nine percent of success once he's up," he said.

"It's like Goldilocks and the divine Prime Minister. Fair enough," Joseph said, far from assured.

"Joseph! Whatcha doin'?"

Joseph turned around in shock, only to see Emily's buoyant face. She was wearing a tie-dye short-sleeved shirt, and had a deeply inquisitive look on her face.

"Uh, nothing much. What are you doing here?" Joseph asked, unnerved.

"I was just taking a walk and spotted you and, uh, sort of followed you. I wanted to talk." She peered over at Thaddeus' boat. "Thaddeus, right? I won't delay you. I'm just going to have a quick word with Joseph, if that's fine?"

"OK. Well, don't be too long," Thaddeus hesitantly called from his boat, sailing it over.

Emily and Joseph walked over to a quieter area of the dock beside two bollards, the calm wave noise belying the very real, worrying situation that they were both in.

"Joseph, I bet I know what you're up to. You're going with him to wake up Peter, aren't you?"

"Uh, kinda," Joseph said, scratching his neck. He did not see the point of denying it. "And I suppose you're going to go tell on us now?"

"No, not at all. Actually, I want to come too!" Emily demanded, her hair getting battered by the wind.

Joseph felt this had to be a joke. "What?"

"I've changed my mind. You're right; I lost my faith in Francis too quickly," she explained, a serious glint in her jade eyes. "The only proof is that dumb video. Ohhh, I know I change my mind constantly, but I really want to do what I can to help!"

Joseph stopped to consider the possibility of her coming. It was going to be very dangerous . . . he wasn't sure if it would be foolish letting Emily attend; but at the same time, she seemed adamant.

"I told Thaddeus that I wouldn't tell anyone about this," Joseph muttered. "It's probably not a good idea. If he finds out that you know, he won't be pleased."

"But I can help! I am a strong sailor; my dad taught me. I will steer the boat while you guys go wake him. I've even been doing some research over the past few days. You know your theory that Francis was possessed?"

"Yeah," he mumbled. "What about it?"

"I read in *A Beginner's Guide to Proficiencies*, possession is real, and there's a way to resist it if someone attempts it on you. What you need to do to stay conscious is to self-harm, to inflict pain on yourself and draw blood in whatever way. That way, the pain allows you to stay focused. I just thought that might come in handy."

Joseph nodded, only half-following. "That's interesting, but I'm not sure how helpful it will be. Let's see what Thaddeus says," he said, as he felt disposed to letting Emily join their group. "I'll tell him you figured it out on your own, and we can just hope he's not too angry."

"Great! Thanks so much," Emily said, grinning.

Charon's Boat was now docked, and Thaddeus was busy preparing the engine.

"Thaddeus, Emily wants to come on the trip, too," Joseph explained, as Thaddeus looked up at them annoyedly.

"Yeah, give me a chance. I can assist you two," Emily added with a pleading voice. "Promise!"

"What!?" Thaddeus asked, an irate furrow on his brow. "She knows?"

Joseph and Emily went on to try to explain the situation, but Thaddeus wasn't having it.

"Joseph, what did I tell you about involving others? Nobody else can come. It's too risky; who knows what could happen?" he said with a bitter tone. "Frankly, Emily, you do not know what you're trying to get yourself into."

"Ohhhh, come on!" Emily appealed.

And despite Emily's continued protests, it seemed Thaddeus wasn't budging. "No, the answer is no!" he repeated for the fifth time.

"Well, I guess I can't persuade him. Joseph, just remember what I said, OK?" she said, stepping over and hugging him. "And be on your guard. Anything could happen."

"Thanks, Emily. I really appreciate you trying to help, but you can assist much more by making sure Francis doesn't get killed before we get back. How does that sound?" Joseph said, hugging back.

"I'll try . . . ." Emily said, stepping away and playing with her hair. "Good luck."

It was time to go.

CHAPTER 12
MATHIAS' PLOT

JOSEPH BOARDED *CHARON'S BOAT* IN SILENCE, TRIPPING OVER A hammer lying on the deck before he sat down. As Thaddeus sailed them out of the harbour, Joseph watched Emily wave them away. It was now too late for them to go back, although he couldn't help but feel serenely calm about what was happening, rushing wind on his face.

Of course, the crucial question remained—was he sailing out here with a friend, or a foe? There was something slightly unusual about Thaddeus' voice today; he kept making a silvery laugh when Joseph asked about the cone, but he hoped that it was just because he was nervous. They had been sailing for about an hour without talking much, if at all. Indeed, besides his odd chuckle, Thaddeus seemed reticent. That was when Joseph started to ask the inevitable childish question: "Are we there yet?"

Thaddeus was wearing smarter clothes than yesterday, a blue flannel shirt and chinos, while Joseph was garbed in a plain beige chambray shirt, one of Raymond's jumpers and jeans.

"No, not yet," replied Thaddeus shortly, as he steered the boat over a particularly rocky wave. Then, he pulled out his cigarettes and lit one, taking long drags as if he was very stressed.

Having spent an hour soaking in the beauty of the waves, the crests and their undulating curves, Joseph was starting to get sick of all the blue. Bored, he took to staring at their fore-sail instead. Nevertheless, as the trip went on, Thaddeus' silence grew more suspicious to him.

"It's getting darker," Joseph pointed out, starting to get seriously ticked off as he watched the moon slowly begin to rise on the horizon.

"Yes," responded Thaddeus briefly, at this point on his fifth cigarette.

Yes? He tapped his foot against the boat's sole, frowning. *Say something, dammit.* Joseph's impression had always been as a Tellurian that when people reply with one word, that generally strongly indicates that they are not fond of you (or your question).

"How far are we?" Joseph asked, feeling increasingly doomed.

Thaddeus scratched his scar, thick arms on display as he steered the boat sideways. "Not far."

Subsequent questions didn't reveal anything more. Strangely, Thaddeus seemed to be slowing down the boat over the next few minutes. Still, there was no land in sight.

"So, do you prefer dogs or cats?" Joseph asked dully, at his wit's end.

This was a test question to see if Thaddeus was listening. It appeared not, because he did not say anything or react at all to the query. *Unless he prefers hamsters. Well, I doubt it.* It was as though Thaddeus had developed a sudden case of mutism.

By this point, Joseph had become convinced that some-thing was up. Of course, he didn't expect Thaddeus to simply smash his head with the hammer lying on the deck and throw him overboard; but since he was acting so strangely, Joseph was starting to think that it was in the realm of imminent possibility.

Suddenly, Thaddeus brought the boat to a halt in the middle of the ocean, throwing the anchor. Joseph was getting more than concerned, staring incredulously at him. He was glad that he had pressed record on Raymond's Hylephone before he had left the apartment. Hopefully, and he had tested it briefly, the microphone was good enough to detect whatever happened through the fabric.

"Is this when you reveal you're an Evil Demon?" Joseph asked in a disconcerted voice, still sitting on the deck. *Why did I say that? He won't get the reference.*

"Something in that realm," murmured Thaddeus, turning to face Joseph for the first time since they had stopped, his expression distinctly unamused. "We are a thousand feet from Sabbat Islet. Far enough away from Hyleberia's prying ears, and that Emily girl, that I can finally be honest with you, J-man."

"Honest? About . . .?" Joseph stuttered, gobsmacked.

"This is going to come as a shock," Thaddeus revealed, as he strode away from the steering wheel to stare into Joseph's soul, "but everything you have been told about Hyleberia is a lie. It is time for you to find out the reality."

He had no clue what Thaddeus was talking about. "OK."

"Did you not guess that something was off about Hyleberia as you settled in?" Thaddeus asked, laughing in a cold, callous way. "That it was a bit too *picture-perfect* to be the truth?"

"I suppose I did," Joseph said curiously. "But what do you mean?"

Thaddeus went on, "Yes, what do I mean. . . . I'm afraid you're in for a surprise. In short, the history that Peter has been teaching you, and indeed the rest of the Hyleberian populace, is a big fat lie. There are two divine Prime Ministers, still. And guess who the other one is?"

"Who?" Joseph said, gulping in shock.

"Yours truly," revealed Thaddeus, pointing to himself. "For the truth is I am not Thaddeus at all, and I'm not Greek either. I am Mathias, the second Prime Minister of Hyleberia."

Joseph gasped for words, thinking what Thaddeus had just said was somehow comical in its insanity.

"M-Mathias?"

"Yes," Thaddeus stated confidently, nodding. "The very same."

Joseph felt faint. "But the Prince of Darkness . . . people say he's dead?" he asked.

"The Prince of Darkness is not dead, yet he's not me. I'm the good Prime Minister. Peter has been impersonating me all this time. It's sort of like identity theft, except I allowed it to happen. And so you see, Thaddeus was a character I invented to try to befriend you. Peter is the true Prince."

"What?" Joseph questioned, frozen in fear. "It can't be."

"I'm sorry to break it to you. We are brothers of the same divine family, and Peter is in on the lie. The Animah co-created us. We might be called the original Cain and Abel, the two eternal divine Prime Ministers. From time immemorial we have had different views on the way that the world should be structured and governed," he went on.

"So, why the need for secrecy?" Joseph asked, peering anxiously at his rucksack.

"Let me begin with the true world cosmogony, not known to anyone bar Peter, me, and the Divine Council. At the beginning of the Earth, millennia ago, we naively thought that Hyleberia could be run with us as peaceful rivals, much like two opposing political parties. After decades of mounting tensions a Divine War was sparked, the Great Schism, which lasted for three grievous centuries. What you do not know, though, is that the Great Schism in fact ended in a stalemate rather than anyone's loss. Of course, we told the Hyleberian populace otherwise, and we faked my death so that this would never be discovered. For you see, we came to an agreement," Mathias revealed in a low voice, "that the world would exist with bliss and agony, and life would be equally terrible and beautiful. Thus, Peter became the known Prime Minister of Hyleberia, while I governed secretly behind the scenes, unknown to all except in myth, rumour and memory."

Even if he still didn't understand this much, Joseph felt at that moment he had never been more betrayed. It was clear Thaddeus had been nothing but an act. "Then you should have told me the truth about this twisted situation earlier! And everyone else, too," he exclaimed, getting to his feet with his mind racing. "But I don't get it: why bring me all the way to the middle of nowhere to tell me this? Couldn't you have just sent an email?"

Mathias explained, "I brought you out here because I couldn't tell you the truth about Hyleberia with idle ears listening. Yet there was an ulterior motive, I admit. Time has come for us to finally uproot the root of all evils. I need you to go to Sabbat Islet to assassinate my brother, Peter, for good."

Joseph fought for breath, utterly wordless. *This must all be a big joke. You've Been Framed or Candid Camera or something.*

Mathias paced back and forth, as he attempted to clarify, "Before you say no, please hear me out, J-man. You should know that Peter and his rule has incited endless, needless suffering on Earth, and he needs to be put to an end. That excuse of a Prime Minister has the delusion that existential absurdity is humorous, that it is worth a world of pain. You saw all this first-hand at the debate, of course."

"Stop calling me J-man. So, why the hell *me*?" he asked, befuddled and enraged. "I'm just a colt!"

"It has to be you, Joseph. I have been waiting for an opportunity to kill him, my brother, with no luck. It is the price I have to pay to save the world. Every other Hyleberian, essentially, is brainwashed. Before you arrived, I researched your file and I thought—yes!—a kindred spirit. And as I got to know you, my suspicions were confirmed that I had a colt who would agree with me. I saw the way your father died, how unlucky you were in life, and I read how you came to the realisation that life, as it is, was wrong. That there can be a better way."

"I wouldn't say that," Joseph said. "A bit of a pain in the arse, sometimes, yeah."

Joseph rested his weight on the gunwale, feeling bile rise in his throat. He had to stop himself from slapping "Mathias", utterly outraged. *He thinks he has me figured out. Doesn't have a bloody clue. I can't believe it . . . he's been lying to me and everyone else.*

"I anticipated that, if told the truth, you would agree with me that there has to be a change. Nonetheless, I had to deceive you until now for safety. I'm sorry about that, but it was far too dangerous to tell you the truth. As for the golden cone, I was forced to steal it. I knew that it was the only thing that could possibly end him," Mathias said.

"And what about Francis? I guess you are the one who incriminated him?" Joseph said.

Mathias looked at Joseph sympathetically. "Yes. And I'm sorry about framing that man, but it was the price I had to pay. However, I didn't know then that it would incite weather problems. As co-Prime Minister, I have unlimited Proficiencies and even of banned ones, so I was able to possess him. I took his body; turned invisible when necessary; climbed up the sewer; disabled the turrets; took the cone; hid it where only I knew, and left Francis in his apartment for the police. Of course, I plan to free him as soon as this is all over."

"Did you possess me as well, that night in Bellum Garden?" Joseph asked. "And follow me using your invisibility?"

Mathias nodded. "Well observed. I'm sorry about that again, but I'm afraid I had to. From what I could hear, I feared

Francis was inadvertently giving you information that might raise your suspicions, so tried to get you to change the subject and go home. I didn't want you to know anything that could lead you to me until strictly necessary, for it would be too risky."

Like I'm going to trust anything he says after all this. Mathias has some gall asking a favour. Joseph scoffed, "So, you were stalking me, in other words! Why don't you just possess me now to kill him then? Wouldn't that be easier?"

"It has to be your choice; Peter will be able to tell if I'm near. Besides, if you hadn't noticed, you showed resistance to my powers of possession, and so I remain uncertain whether taking control of your body would even be possible. It's supposed to be so seamless that you barely notice anything happened, but recently I seem to be out of practice with it," Mathias said, frowning.

There was strained silence for several seconds. "And Nigel?" Joseph questioned eventually.

"A long story. After he had obtained a job as an Administrator of Colours, decades ago, that conspiratorial man somehow became savvy to the divine secret, and threatened to divulge it. Thus, Peter decided to aggravate Nigel's schizophrenia through an illicit deal with the Psychosis Department," Mathias informed him. "With you around Hyleberia taking him seriously, and his ridiculous graffiti that suggested he was regaining self-control, Nigel was too much of a risk. And so a fictional law was added to the Library of Divine Laws, which triggered the corruption sensors. Your arrest was a short-term by-product."

"You're evil. . . . You killed him just because he found out the truth," Joseph retorted, feeling his hackles rise.

Mathias denied this, saying it was Peter's fault, and went on to profess that he had been lying to his brother about his subversive intentions for centuries. The agreement they had made to run the world together was known formally between them as the *Great Compromise*. As he claimed, they had become friends of convenience, and when Peter sent him under the moniker of Thaddeus to do various tasks, he always agreed under a fake front of guilelessness. Yet Joseph kept pointing out he couldn't trust Mathias after how skillfully he had lied about being Thaddeus, which he now said had been a character, or believe his suggestion that Hyleberians would blindly accept him as their new leader.

Eventually, Mathias paced to the boat's hold. He swiftly pulled out a kayak and a paddle. Then, he extricated a flat, copper compass that he deposited in Joseph's hand.

Placing the kayak down on the boat's sole, he informed him, "You will be able to row this kayak to Sabbat Islet in less than half an hour. It is not even a half-mile northeast. You may just about be able to see it from here if you squint." Mathias pointed in its direction. There was, indeed, a faint glint in the dark like a lighthouse, barely perceptible to the unaware observer. "I will wait here for you in my boat until it's over. If you agree, you will be remembered as doing the greatest deed in the history of—"

"Yeah, yeah. So this is my role in your little plot?" Joseph muttered, feeling empty inside.

Mathias explained the details, while Joseph placed his clammy palms together, feeling rather sick. He'd had two years to study for his A-Levels, but it seemed now that he had one night only to decide the future of the world. Apparently, this mission (if successful) would result in the liberation of mankind from suffering, which intuitively seemed like a good thing to him. The possibilities for error, however, were many: the chance that Mathias was lying; that Joseph might get caught by Peter, and if so he would be exiled for sure; and that he could not be certain that the utopia that Mathias promised would be as good in practice as it sounded in his speech. *Why couldn't Mathias have picked someone more intelligent? I have no clue. Did he really think I would just say, oh sure, let's kill Peter . . . why not? Because my father died. . . . People suffer. That's just life. It happens to everyone. And I've moved on, haven't I?* Joseph had asked for time to think again, but was soon interrupted.

"Have you made up your mind?" Mathias demanded, staring at his watch and tapping his foot. "I don't mean to rush you, but it's nearing 10:30 pm. In my view, you should probably leave before midnight in case something goes wrong, and you need to paddle back."

"Um," Joseph mumbled, panting. "I need more time."

Mathias continued to try to persuade him, "Just think of all the gratuitous despair, pain and horror in the world . . . cancer, hunger, terrorism—human history. It can all be cured tonight. If you," he went on.

Joseph thought for a moment, and then all at once, an epiphany-esque flood of clarity surged through his mind.

"Yes," Joseph affirmed, as he turned away and gazed vacantly at the serenely radiant, crescent moon above, illuminating the chalkboard-black sky. "I'll do it. I'll kill the Prime Minister."

"Excellent," exclaimed Mathias, smiling in relief. "It's the right choice."

The next hour passed like a shot, as Mathias gave Joseph further detailed instructions about how to kill Peter. It was not long before he was in the kayak, a knapsack with the cone on his back, paddling over the unsteady waves towards Sabbat Islet.

Shivering as flecks of the ocean fell on his arms, Joseph slowed down the boat, trying to recall why he had agreed to commit murder. Maybe he didn't even fully know himself. Simply put, Joseph had been overwhelmed with an indescribable, overpowering conviction that this was his destiny. It just seemed obvious at the time.

Now, however, the decision did not seem quite so straightforward. While Joseph began to see Sabbat Islet in greater clarity through the misty night, irksome doubts pestered him like flies on a sandwich. Nevertheless, from somewhere unknown to him, a brassbound will urged him on: *do it, do it, do it. You must go through with this*.

Panting, sweat running down his forehead, he rowed to the shore of the islet. Paddle meeting the beach's seaborne cowries and limpets, Joseph inhaled and exhaled deeply, already exhausted. The dark sea susurrated around him like a pit of snakes, as he beached the kayak.

Taking his first step onto the shore, Joseph felt an acute throb of pain in his head. With the smell of the briny atmosphere around him, he pulled the kayak up to a dry area of the coast, then began making his way down the cobbled path. It seemed to feed through a labyrinth hedge maze. The light that he had spotted very faintly from *Charon's Boat*, flickering bright orange like a candle, was now distinctly visible over the labyrinth's hedges, coming from a large mansion's window.

Squelching as he walked in drenched clothes, Joseph came to a sign which read:

> Welcome to Sabbat Islet. If you are reading this, you should probably not be here.

This inflamed Joseph's fears like a bad wen, but he tried to quell his worries as best he could.

Enervated and soaked, he forced his legs onward, reminding himself of all that Peter was responsible for. *This is justified*, Joseph tried to convince himself. The things Mathias had informed him about "Peter" one hour or so ago had changed his view of him completely. Now, everything Peter said had been proven to be a deceitful facade. To Joseph, then, in a sense the Peter he knew was already dead. There was no need to think anymore: he simply had to get it over with.

It soon became evident that there was no way through but

the shoulder-height hedge maze, a sign designating it the Maze of Athens. Recovering his composure, he stepped inside.

The maze proved to be full of twists, turns and dead ends. There were endless topiary sculptures inside shaped like odd-looking figures, and creepy faces he didn't recognise. One of the sculptures, a hedge woman, had a placard beneath that read "Aphrodite", Greek God of love and another ran "Ganesha", Indian God of luck. Joseph gradually realised the sculptures were of different mythical Gods, but what was their purpose?

After passing Enki and Loki's sculptures, Joseph was feeling increasingly weirded out and hopeless, as he realised he might end up trapped here all night. *Oh, this is just peachy keen. How am I gonna explain myself to Peter when he finds me tomorrow morning?* Several minutes later, out of nowhere, he realised the trick of the maze.

Joseph had learnt about the Greek Gods in Shrivatsa, and he found that if he followed them, Athena and Dionysus and so on, he seemed to be getting closer to the exit. Using this trick, it ended up taking fifteen minutes or so to solve the maze, Poseidon, Demeter and lastly Hera guiding him to the exit, although it felt more like hours.

When Joseph finally emerged, covered in hedge leaves, he was greeted with the front of the mansion.

His first impression was that it was one of the biggest buildings he had ever seen. The mansion looked like a combination of a fancy old hotel and the White House. There was a flag on top of the golden cone, seemingly the Hyleberian one. Almost all the walls were painted platinum white, and there were many uncurtained cylindrical windows, revealing that all the lights were on. It appeared Peter didn't need to Recalibrate in the dark. There was a sign by the front door that read "Domus Dei".

Joseph wrapped his fingers around the doorknob, noticing

crickets clicking, distant fireflies, and squalls of angry wind whistling in his ears.

Turning the knob, he found the door was unlocked. He breathed a sigh of relief, not particularly wanting to have to break a window.

Slowly, Joseph tiptoed into the mansion's main hall. After being in the dark for so long, his eyes had to adjust to the brightness inside. The mansion was silent, the hall heavily yet somewhat garishly decorated. Joseph gaped as he looked around, feeling that Peter was not a particularly good interior designer; there were all sorts of tchotchkes on stands, tables and the walls. He spotted a cuckoo clock, with a tiny model kakapo sitting inside, waiting to pop out of its hole. Paintings from various time periods and schools of art hung on the walls without any discernible order, a Van Gogh next to a Raphael. The furniture looked like it had been stolen indiscriminately from across the world, a Japanese zaisu positioned next to a Moroccan coffee table.

Cuckoo, cuckoo, cuckoo, resounded the clock suddenly, the little plastic bird popping out, almost giving Joseph a heart attack. It had just reached midnight.

The mansion was like a second maze, long corridors leading to vast passages, doors opening to wardrobes, rooms to more rooms. Joseph ambled through carefully and soundlessly, wondering where the hell Peter carried out his Recalibration in this huge building. *What's gonna happen if I don't manage to find him in this place, then?*

After ten minutes of hopeless searching, he came to a room with endless strange books, such as *How to Destroy a Universe In Three Easy Steps*, *The Highs and Lows of World Prime Ministerhood* and *The Ontogeny of the Omphalos: A Divine Novel.* Tempted to stop and examine these, he forced himself onwards; it would not be wise to take his time and look around. A contender for the oddest room featured nothing but a small, red table with a limited edition set of *The Golden*

*Girl*s action figures on top of it. Perhaps even stranger was the one with a large collection of waffles, colonoscopes and gerbils in cages.

Finally, he opened a door and heard snoring. Joseph could scarcely believe his own luck. Sure enough, poking his head into the room, he spotted the one and only Peter's black hair. The sleeping Prime Minister was tucked tightly in bed sheets, stirring slightly in his sleep, dressed in white pyjamas.

There was a painful throb in Joseph's chest, and he feared he was having some form of stress-induced stroke. He closed the door quickly to try to pacify and steady himself.

Five minutes or so passed of just standing there silently, as Joseph stared at an abstract Pollockian painting on the wall, trying not to hyperventilate. The colours having placated him, he felt self-possessed enough to at least try this. Bent double, hands shaking, he opened the knapsack.

There it was, the golden cone, glimmering like a shiny party hat at the bottom of the bag. Desperately nervous, he could not bring himself to touch it. Joseph stood there for several minutes, wondering how on Earth he was going to wield the cone to kill Peter. In a state, he remembered all that he had been told about the cone, and how it could endow one with great powers.

Slowly, very cumbersomely, he wrapped his fingers around the cone and picked it up with some effort. It was heavy like a small dumbbell, but not so hefty that one couldn't lift it up. *It's now or never*, he told himself, fighting off waves of fatigue. *You've just got to do it.* Gripping the golden cone tightly in both his hands, ignoring the feeling of its sharp edges against his skin, he reopened the door to Peter's bedroom an inch.

Heart thumping, Joseph looked around the Prime Minister's boudoir. It was entirely bare, basically nothing to comment on, the walls as colourless as milk. A giant, crystal chandelier dangled above the area beside Peter's bed, studded with hundreds of priceless-looking, kaleidoscopic sculpted gems.

He approached Peter's prone body, holding the cone out in front of him like a delicate plate. As Mathias had predicted, Peter was in a deep sleep, and he wasn't reacting at all to Joseph's quiet paces forward.

After a few hesitant steps towards the bed, he caught sight of Peter's sleeping face, deep in the arms of Morpheus. He looked as innocent as a child. *Is this really the monster that Mathias portrayed? Is it too late to back out of this? Amazing that Peter doesn't even have a guard. He is too trusting.* And then, Joseph recalled what Descartes had said to him the other day:

"*One of the thought experiments, as expressed in Meditations, was about an evil demon who intends to deceive the perceiver of the external world. Thus, the perceiver wouldn't have any way of telling whether what he experienced was real.*"

Thinking over whether the Evil Demon was really Peter, Joseph froze as he heard a mumbling voice. Whipping around to look for the source, mystified, after several tense seconds he realised it was Peter talking in his sleep.

Joseph stood speechless, staring at Peter's drooling face, trying to understand his strange words. Peter's voice was muted and most of the sleep-talking he didn't quite understand, but the language sounded like something out of Nigel's blog. As he twisted and turned, his somniloquy was getting increasingly agitated.

Another memory was triggered in Joseph's mind. This time it was a quote from Mohammed, which he had said after the apartment tour:

"*Mind control is especially dangerous. Using it, you can literally make someone think they want something they don't.*"

Joseph lowered the cone. Several sudden disturbing thoughts came to him in a single moment.

What if . . . he wasn't even making the choice to kill Peter? What if . . . rather than possessing him, Mathias had been mind controlling him all along, making him do this? And what if, even if Peter was evil, there was some way to reform him? *This doesn't feel right. Why would I make the decision to do this? It doesn't sound like me.*

Joseph was brought back to the memories of his first moments in Hyleberia . . . the day he arrived in the garden, met Peter, Raymond and Thaddeus (now Mathias), and that time in the corridor of Miyagi Apartments when he had said goodbye to his old Tellurian life. Shortly after Peter had hugged him and told him to wait and see the meaning of life, he realised that he had spotted a painting of Sabbat Islet, of course then unknown to him.

"Jaiowaoaoao!"

Joseph froze, as he heard a squealing behind him. Panicked, he rushed out of Peter's bedroom, closed it and stared at who had just appeared. It was Gabriel. He was sitting under the painting, looking at Joseph curiously.

How the hell did he get here!? Joseph paced over to Gabriel, got to his knees to pick him up and caught a glimpse of his green eyes. They were so pure and sweet, and they reminded him of seeing Peter's fondness for his pet, his love. Would an evil man truly care for a pet sloth so affectionately?

He couldn't do this. He couldn't kill Peter, not now, not ever. He'd believed that he would be able to murder him a few minutes ago, but now the assurance that he had built up had melted like ice. Peter was not beyond forgiveness, and Joseph was not a murderer.

Joseph put Gabriel on his shoulder, packed the golden cone into the knapsack, and made a run for it. Breathlessly, he sprinted down the staircase and the corridor. As he exited the door of Domus Dei, he feared that there was nowhere for him to escape to. *I'm sure Mathias will be chuffed with me, thrilled to bits.* Yet having no alternatives, he realised he had little choice but to row back to Mathias and to try to reason with him, or simply explain his actions. Hyleberia was just too far.

He ran back through the labyrinth, which only took him a fraction of the time, Gabriel squealing and holding onto his neck. Joseph re-found the kayak and pushed it into the frigid water. He jumped in, taking out the compass from his pocket to confirm the direction of Thaddeus' boat.

The stars, like punctured holes in the night sky, shined down on Joseph judgmentally. He felt a strange urge to head back and finish what he had started, but he was reminded why he couldn't murder him. Then, Joseph would become just as bad as Peter. Gabriel didn't seem to like the water, shaking like a leaf against his ear.

As Joseph rowed closer to *Charon's Boat*, he spotted Mathias' dark figure growing larger. Somehow, he reached the vessel without tipping the kayak. Frozen to the bone, after climbing up the boat's ladder and dragging himself across the linoleum barrier, Joseph collapsed with Gabriel beside him. As he lay there, he felt Mathias' cold glare roving over him. He was standing above his wet form, hands on hips, an incensed look on his face.

"Why the hell is he here?" Mathias asked, pointing to Gabriel, who looked positively delighted to be on board.

"I was hoping you would answer that," Joseph stated. "He just appeared in the corridor, out of nowhere."

"How annoying," Mathias snapped. "Anyway, what happened!?"

An excuse, an excuse. . . . Quick. I got a terrible case of diarrhoea. "Yeah, er—about that. I'd-developed a—" he stammered.

"You were a coward, weren't you?" Mathias snapped.

"Uh, yes and no. But I'm not sorry," Joseph stated. There was no point in lying. He decided to be honest as he took deep breaths and lay down supine. "I decided not to do it. I couldn't."

Mathias jutted his chin out and spat down on Joseph. "Pathetic! I thought you were the one who would finally end this. Do you realise what you've done?" he yelled. "All of the world will suffer now because of your cowardice!"

"The world as it is is not so terrible. There are good aspects of it, I guess," Joseph said, stumbling over his words. "Friends, food, entertainment, love or what have you. I mean, it's not perfect, but still."

"Easy for you to say!" Mathias remarked, pacing back and forth as Gabriel mewled on the tarp.

"At least, I don't think this is the answer. Also, honestly, when I got to Peter's room . . . this might sound weird, but. . . I developed a suspicion that you were, uh, mind controlling me," he explained.

"I suppose I will have to kill him myself then, even if that is accompanied by some risks," vociferated Mathias furiously, kneeling and staring at Joseph. "But you're quite right about one thing, I *was* mind controlling you."

Joseph stared up at him, bewildered. "You were!?"

Thaddeus' eye was twitching more than ever, and his scar looked somehow much scarier now that he was angry. "I was willing for you to do it of your own accord, but after all that tiresome prevarication, I realised that I had to put in your mind the idea that you wanted to kill Peter. Clearly, not deeply enough, for you demonstrated resilience, just as you did that night in the garden when that idiot, Francis was telling my secret," he shouted.

Joseph gasped at Mathias' navy eyes, blown away. *I didn't agree to murder Peter, after all. It was so odd—I was convinced I had chosen.*

"So, you lied?" he asked, stupefied.

At this, Mathias started laughing dementedly. He cackled, "Yes, I lied, fool. I lie all the time! I am the Prince of Darkness, the rightful Prime Minister of the World. Although, that's just a stupid name to refer to me, because my real name was forgotten."

Meanwhile, Gabriel stared at them both happily, utterly

oblivious to what was happening. Joseph had no words; this was terrible news, yet in a way, it was just as he had feared. He had been foolish to allow himself to be lied to and mind controlled by Mathias, but at least he had realised it before he did his evil bidding. *He has been manipulating me, all along. The tour, the boat trip . . . our friendship . . . and even an hour ago. Descartes was right about the Evil Demon, more than he knew. I've had enough of being a pawn. I've got to escape.*

Joseph got to his feet and shouted, "Buzz off, Mathias. You are a liar through and through. Well, your tricks didn't work on me, sorry to say," he snapped.

Terrified, Joseph eyed the kayak that Mathias had just pulled up and put in the corner, debating if he could use it to escape. But he kind of needed the Hylephone, which unless Mathias had found it, was still recording. He had left the rucksack lying on the deck when he had embarked on the kayak, but it appeared that Mathias had moved it.

"Lying is nothing to me. I've lived with your nonsense for weeks, even pretended to be your *friend*," Mathias chuckled. "Frankly, J-man, I was sick of you the moment I laid eyes on your weak, ignorant form. I am murdering Peter tonight, and when I'm finished with him, Gabriel will be next, and then you. I suppose I'll have to bring the idiotic sloth along with me. If I kill him first, Peter might awaken. If I leave him on the boat, he might escape."

"How?" Joseph exclaimed, equally baffled and irate. "You said Peter can detect you."

"Yes, he can detect me with our *beautiful* fraternal bond," Mathias explained sarcastically, as he walked to the other side of the boat and knelt down to pick up something, "but not if I take your body."

He stared at Mathias, too dumbfounded to formulate a plan. "You said I am resistant."

Mathias stood back up, holding something behind his back. "Yes, you are. However, I haven't tried possessing you when your lights are out. That should make things much easier," he revealed, a manic, psychotic grin on his face.

Joseph didn't know how to respond. "Lights? What do you—"

But he didn't get an answer. All of a sudden, Mathias stepped forward with a hammer and slammed Joseph with it square on the forehead. The pain was excruciating.

He fell to the ground, head on fire, losing consciousness for a few seconds.

Vision blurred, wrestling with the agonising ache in his occiput, Joseph shifted his weight on the deck and spotted Mathias put the handcuffs around his own hands, and then lock them around one of the masts of the ship. This seemed very strange to him; why would Mathias lock up his own body? The boat rocked, sending Joseph's prone form like a bucket to the other side of the ship. *The knife must still be in my bag; I have to get it, and now.*

Every inch of his body erupted in great agony. Joseph knew he didn't have time to deal with the pain. He frantically struggled to his feet, looking for his rucksack. He touched his forehead, chilly as the frosty night and a lump already forming on it.

Abruptly, he remembered what Emily had told him . . . the only way to resist possession was to inflict pain on yourself, to bleed. What if the pain he was already in wasn't enough? But the problem was Joseph was too weak to crawl to his bag for the kitchen knife, wherever it was.

He looked frantically for something sharp, and found a nail lying on the floor of the boat. With his shaky hands, he picked it up in his forefinger and thumb and stabbed his wrist with it, making a trickle of blood.

Then, before he knew it, Mathias had noticed he was still conscious and unlocked the handcuffs, stepping towards him once more. His figure contrasted with the moonlight, sharp facial features sneering at him like he was a bug to crush. He raised his hand, and with huge force smashed Joseph's face with the hammer again.

DARKNESS. Joseph had no clue how long he had been out before he finally came to, but realised within seconds that he had lost control of his body. It was as if he were paralysed, and to make matters worse, he couldn't see or hear anything. Joseph was horrified as he felt Mathias' spirit take dominion over him, a poison spreading through his body. *I should never have listened to him. Hold on to yourself.*

Then, very slowly, Joseph became able to see and hear. His body was in the kayak once more, paddling. But it was the most bizarre feeling—he was relegated to being an observer of his own body. Mathias had possessed him, so Joseph didn't quite understand how he was observing this. Hadn't Mathias made sure he was unconscious? Perhaps he didn't realise that Joseph was still awake inside.

In the next moments, Joseph realised in horror the significance of the fact that he was watching Mathias sail through the ocean with *his* body. Joseph, who could not control a limb, writhed in his tomb-like flesh, desperate to escape. Mathias was in possession of his limbs, organs, and was now paddling steadily towards the shore, using muscle memory that did not belong to Joseph.

Stop this! Joseph thought, in his first attempt to address Mathias. It was entirely in vain, or at least Mathias paid no heed. The waves around the kayak raged tempestuously, as if they were alive and trying to sweep them away from the islet. In spite of that, Mathias was rowing with much greater dexterity than Joseph had been.

Gabriel was dangling around Mathias' shoulder, Joseph realised. The poor sloth seemed disturbed by the ocean, and was making crying, squeaking sounds.

Joseph went on fighting for self-control of his body, the islet drawing nearer. No ligament of his body responded. It was like watching a bad horror movie where he could predict the terrible ending, but could do nothing to stop it.

Yet he was conscious . . . it must be the pain in his wrist.

Joseph remembered something perhaps important—his supposed telekinetic abilities, which were triggered by Gabriel's presence. *Could it still work? Maybe that's why Gabriel came. My guardian angel knew I was in trouble.* It was not likely, but he realised at this moment that this was the best chance he had.

Though it was hard to know how he was doing it, Joseph aimed his mind intently at the paddle in his body's hands, which Mathias was swinging through the sea. Nothing happened at first. Concentrating harder, and after a moment of intense focus, finally, Joseph managed to incite the paddle to jolt out of his grasp and fall into the sub-zero ocean.

"What the hell? Are you awake in there, J-man?!" Mathias yelled, bewildered by what had just happened. "Or am I just getting clumsy?"

Groaning, Mathias shook his head, picked up the paddle and continued to the beach. Joseph, on the other hand, might have exclaimed "*yes!*" if he still had a voice. By some miracle, thanks to Gabriel's miraculous arrival, he retained his ability to move things. But would it be enough to save Peter?

Joseph came up with a makeshift plan. With his telekinesis, he would make as much noise as possible in the house, and try to wake up Peter before Mathias got to him.

Having pulled up to the shore, Mathias' path through Sabbat Islet to Domus Dei only took a few minutes; he clearly knew the labyrinth well already, as he navigated through it in a very short time. Gabriel was no longer as happy as Larry, as he had seemed before. The sloth was crying, and was quivering like he was covered in ants, so Mathias struggled to keep hold of him. As Mathias stepped foot into the mansion, his pace slowed.

Joseph noticed the cuckoo clock again on the wall of the hall. Consequently, he focused all his energy on it, until something incredible occurred again; the clock flipped, fell and crashed on the floor. Mathias looked across at the shattered kakapo in a flummoxed state.

"Cut it out, J-man!" Mathias shouted to himself, like a frustrated child. He trudged over to the broken clock, looking down and scratching his head. "How are you awake? Did you do that?"

Of course, Joseph wasn't going to obey. Over the next few rooms, he focused on causing as much damage as he could. Paintings, vases, chairs, trophies; all of these and more, he threw, smashed and dropped. Some of the objects he even aimed at his own body, shooting them in his direction, which hurt like hell—his feeling of pain still intact—yet he had no choice but to indulge in this masochism. If he got his body back, he was going to have more than a few bruises. After observing all of this, Mathias was getting incandescent with rage as they came to the second flight of stairs, where Peter was lying fast asleep.

"Stop!" Mathias whispered to himself furiously, as he traipsed down the hall.

They were feet away from Peter's bedroom, Joseph realised, as fear pierced his very being. Joseph racked his mind for large items that he had seen on his own way here that he could break. Finally, he recalled: there was the chandelier hanging in Peter's room, which would surely wake anybody up if dropped. But he would have to be very quick and concentrate all his focus on it.

As Mathias approached Peter's room, seemingly knowing which one was his, Joseph spotted the Pollock painting hanging on the wall. Focusing his mind on it, he aimed and swiftly brought it crashing down on his own skull.

"ARGHHHHH!" Mathias let out a thunderous scream, and so did Joseph, at least internally. Hopefully, the shout had awoken Peter.

As Joseph felt pain erupt in his brain, praying that Peter had awoken, Mathias dropped Gabriel on the floor. Much quicker than Joseph had been, he pulled down the knapsack and retrieved the lustrous golden cone.

Muffled noises were coming from the bedroom. Feeling Gabriel's confused glare on him from down on the red carpet, Joseph listened intently for a second, and realised that the sounds were just snores and sleep-talking. *After all of that, Peter still hasn't noticed a thing! What else can I do?* Joseph knew he had to drop the chandelier, and as soon as Mathias opened the door; it was the only thing loud enough.

With his hand, Mathias felt the blood dripping off Joseph's forehead, his skull having quite possibly been cracked by the painting as well as the hammer now. Vision spinning, Mathias let out a second cry of pain, unable to restrain himself. He swung Peter's door open, and giving up stealth, rushed towards his brother, cone raised and apex pointed downwards.

There was a huge whoosh, a terrible crash, followed by a deafening crunch of glass. At a loss, Joseph felt the room tremble around him. *Have I done it? Drop the chandelier?* But he was consumed in a blur of confused delirium, as his body crumpled to the ground in harrowing agony. The last thing that Joseph heard before his vision faded again and he lost consciousness completely was a panicked, deafening scream.

CHAPTER 13

THE LIBRARY OF DIVINE LAWS

"C-c-omplete c-raziness . . . can't b-believe it . . . strains th-he im-magination . . . earth-q-quake . . . Never s-sseen a-a-nything l-l-ike . . . s-uuch insurre-e-e-ection in Hyle-b-beria . . . A t-t-traitor. . . ."

Joseph lay half-asleep with his eyes closed tight. He had just woken up, and he could hardly tell what the muffled voices around him were saying, their discussion dull and echoing somewhere in the corner of his mind. Gradually, their words, and eventually whole sentences became slightly clearer and louder.

"Yeah, it's wild. Security will have to be tightened after this incident. What I want to know is if it is such a good idea for Peter to be so trustin' of the colt, though? He could well have been in cahoots with that Thaddeus fella' all along."

"Shields? He s-seems g-guileless enough t-to me. A-apart from those w-weird eyes of h-his; they g-give me the c-creeps."

"Hmmm . . . I still don't trust him. Something about that man is screwy."

"I'm s-sure he's f-fine. Engl-lishmen a-rre al-w-ways du-lll in m-my experience. So, d-did you happen to s-ssee the e-clipse?"

"'Course. It was awesome. I went to see it with a bunch of my hunting buddies, before shooting a huge elephant. Great news the Pralaya went well and the new world cycle has begun!"

An urgent thought entered Joseph's brain—Francis and Peter, were they all right? Were they even still alive? He had to find out. Startled, his heart beating fast, he opened his eyes and sat up.

Looking around, he quickly observed that he was in a hospital room bed and dressed in a hospital gown. An empty catheter hung on the wall, a muted visualiser too, and there was a faint odour of iodine in the air. *Oh I know. This must be Asclepius Hospital, the Hyleberian medical centre.* That was a place Joseph had heard of once or twice, but never seen in person. He spotted that the two people who had been talking nearby were not exactly his favourites.

"Ah, he's finally awake—I mean, you're awake," observed Sergeant Rufius, looking down at him from the other side of the room. He was standing beside Sergeant White, both of them wearing nonplussed, po-faced expressions. Neither of them looked particularly pleased to see he was no longer sleeping. "You've been asleep for a while, colt."

"I have?" Joseph mumbled faintly.

Sergeant White's hand was covering her face behind her hands, while Sergeant Rufius' was resting on his holster like he needed to be ready to use it at any moment.

Annoyedly, Rufius grumbled, "He still seems pretty out of it. Shall we get the nurse?"

Sergeant White frowned. "No, d-didn't you hh-hear? Get P-Peter. He made it c-clear we sshould f-fetch him the m-moment that the colt w-woke up, bb-before ann-ybody a-and a-anything else."

Mohawk looking particularly sharp today, Sergeant Rufius frowned and nodded. "Right, I'll go give him a buzz. Don't let the colt out of your sight, White."

As Sergeant Rufius left, Joseph raised his hand to his bandaged forehead, which stung with a throbbing ache like that time he was hit by a car. He squinted as he recalled the blinding pain he felt after the hammer blow and the falling painting, all of which had now transmuted into a bland soreness.

After an infinite wait of non-stop thinking, Joseph finally heard Peter's knock and his dampened voice talking to the nurses.

The door opened and Peter stepped inside, but he looked nothing like he had the night at Domus Dei. Rather than pyjamas, he wore the very same dashing, bright white suit that he had on the day of Joseph's arrival. His smile was wide, and there was not a single sign of injury on his person. Gabriel, however, was nowhere to be seen.

"Thanks for getting me so quickly, Sergeant White," said Peter warmly, grinning. "I'll just need about five minutes with Joseph, and then you're free to question him as usual."

Sergeant White was blushing like a tomato, seemingly very terrified to speak to Peter. "No p-problem. He seems p-pretty d-dazed."

"No, I'm not," Joseph interrupted.

"Bwahaha. He'll do fine."

Joseph was surprised to hear Peter's laugh again; he certainly did not think there was anything remotely funny about the situation. Nodding at Peter, Sergeant White timidly took her leave. Joseph stared at his face and wondered if he truly understood the gravity of what had happened the previous night. He had very nearly been killed by his own brother, and indeed, Joseph himself.

"Forgive me for the mundane question, but how are you?" Peter asked, sitting on the edge of the bed.

He had great difficulty reading the expression on Peter's face.

"Well, my head hurts like someone poured hot coffee on

it," said Joseph impatiently, leaning up. "I want to know what happened Tuesday night!"

"What happened on that night," Peter said slowly, as he turned away, "is very painful. For me and for you too, I'm sure."

"Trust me, my head is a constant reminder of that," Joseph said, rolling his eyes.

"Well, let me explain . . ." the Prime Minister said.

Peter informed him that he was well aware that his brother, the real Prince of Darkness, had staged a coup. He had been woken up by the fallen chandelier, where he had found Joseph's injured body, and swiftly worked out what had happened. After waking, Peter had boated over to Hyleberia with Joseph's body and freed Francis.

Joseph gasped, solace and confusion washing over him in equal measure. Still, all was not well, he slowly realised, as an acute pang of anxiety appeared in his gut. "Wait, so where is Mathias? And what happened to the cone?" he asked.

"I'm afraid," said Peter slowly, bridging his fingers and dramatically pausing, "that Mathias is gone. He escaped, and he will almost certainly return. The cone, though, has fortunately been returned to the Divine Repository and is safe and sound. Thus, Hyleberia's weather issues have been solved. Its sudden removal caused the disturbance."

"Oh no," Joseph cursed, looking down at his bed sheets. *Good and bad news. Mostly bad, though. Mathias will surely want revenge.* "Is Mathias like Darth Vadar evil, or what?"

"I'm not sure who that is," Peter said, avoiding eye contact. "But I hold myself to blame. Even if both of us were complicit in the Great Compromise, I have been lying to Hyleberia for far too long. We acted like the only way to govern was to be duplicitous with you all. Mathias must have been plotting for a long time to usurp me. I can see now that I ignored many signs. I surely should have been preparing for this."

I need a Haoma. Joseph gulped, stunned by the absurdity of what he was hearing. He asked heavily, "Have you spoken to Richard Hoskins? He was Acting Prime Minister, and tried to exile Francis when you were away. My feeling is that he may be collaborating with Mathias."

Peter nodded sourly. "It's already been decided: there is going to be a hearing in Town Hall in a few weeks about the government's actions during my absence. It is possible that Hoskins will be removed from the council after the past week. I haven't heard good things from most people."

A hearing? I don't think that's really enough. He tried to kill an innocent man. "I think he ought to be expelled immediately. He's nuts," Joseph declared.

"It doesn't seem like—Mr Hoskins is—I'm sure—" Peter stammered.

At this moment, Peter broke off, erupting in tears and burying his face in his cupped hands. Joseph couldn't believe this. Peter was sobbing.

"Aww, don't cry," Joseph said, leaning forward and awkwardly patting him on the back. He felt like he was comforting a five-year-old. "Everything will be OK. Probably."

"A Divine War is almost inevitable now!" Peter revealed, as floods of tears ran down his cheeks. "Do you realise what that means? Divine Wars are nothing like Tellurian wars; they're a battle for control of the world itself. Worse, I am hardly less to blame than Mathias. It is just as much my idiotic mistake for trusting my brother's lies as his malevolent scheming. What's more, I've been complicit in lying to everyone about everything for aeons. I don't believe in disease! What nonsense."

"Why can't you start a new world?" Joseph asked, swallowing. "A better one. With infinite happiness and bliss, or something. You could easily do it . . . make the clouds candy floss, the rain chocolate milk."

Wiping the tears away, Peter muttered with a lachrymose voice, "There can only be one world, and sadly, Mathias' claim to it is just as valid as mine. It's obvious negotiations will be impossible after this. The Divine War will in all likelihood be bloody and long. The Great Schism, it seems, never truly ended."

"Oh," Joseph said, increasingly lost for words. "I don't know what to say."

Peter shrugged. "There is nothing to say. As we speak, without a body, Mathias is no doubt out in some far-off galaxy, roaming past planets, star systems, meteors, plotting his first attack." Sensing alarm on Joseph's face, he added, "That said, don't worry about him coming back for revenge; he is not so petty. All he wants is power, and I will be able to detect when he is near."

"In any case, it doesn't really matter now, does it?" Joseph muttered. "What's done is done. We know there will probably be a war, so you can prepare for it, right?"

Peter did not seem as confident as Joseph would have liked. "I suspect Mathias won't give us a choice. But yes, I'm sure, we'll have to. Either way, Joseph, I need you to promise not to tell *anyone* about this, not now. You must act like you have memory loss. I'm afraid Hyleberia isn't ready for the truth," he stated.

Oh crap. Here is why he really came to see me. Joseph gulped, and snapped, "You want me to lie, then? I thought you were done with that."

"What if I gave an ultimatum? For example, if I were to say that I would reveal the divine secret by the end of the year, confess everything to the Hyleberian people. Then, would you be quiet? You see, the truth is very delicate. And if divine protests were incited, strikes and so forth, this wouldn't just impact Hyleberia, but the whole world. In the meantime, I've made up an explanation for the press."

"Hmm, I don't feel right about it. The end of the year . . . ."

269

Joseph stroked his chin, his first instinct that he didn't want any involvement in keeping the so-called *divine secret*. "And if Mathias attacks before they find out?"

"Don't worry, he won't," Peter said assuredly. "Less than the end of the year. It will take me only a month or two to work out how to announce it, I imagine. Not a divine war, you'll be saving the island from a *civil* war."

"Well, I guess if it's just a month, but it seems wrong to me," Joseph said reluctantly, watching Peter stand. He was not expecting him to go so soon. "Leaving already?"

Peter glanced at him with downturned lips, tears no longer visible on his face but voice still a bit weak. "I've got much to catch up on . . . flood repair, a million emails, meetings. Yet mostly, I don't want to hinder your recovery. For now, sleep. We'll talk more later. Thanks for promising."

Despite the glut of questions that remained in his aching mind, Joseph sighed, reclined in the bed and did not object as Peter left. *Well, I didn't actually promise. . . . I'm still not persuaded that I can trust Peter.*

Joseph shook his head as he reflected on all that was said. Whenever he spoke with Peter, it was like he couldn't decide whether to be furious or effusive. He was so effortlessly likeable, but not necessarily for the right reasons. Nobody in Hyleberia had a clue about what had happened on Tuesday night, Joseph realised, and how close they had all come to having their whole island in the paws of an evil Prime Minister. Yet, even with Mathias at large, Joseph was too exhausted to fully appreciate the significance of everything that had happened himself. The insanity of what had occurred would take weeks or months to process.

Joseph did not have much time to think about this, for minutes later, Dr Adebe arrived. He revealed his main injury: a linear skull fracture. The good news was that he had suffered no brain damage and would not need surgery. The bad news was that the healing process would take at least a few weeks.

After Dr Adebe had gone, the Sergeants swiftly returned and began hammering him with questions. Even when Joseph recalled how he had almost killed Peter, which was a very intense memory, he forced himself to keep a straight face and deny any recollection whatsoever. It was a great benefit that he had a head injury, because this made the memory loss much more convincing. Sergeant White was rather understanding of this, but it frustrated Sergeant Rufius to no end that he could not get a single coherent answer.

"How fortunate that you can't recall a thing!" Sergeant Rufius shouted, crossing his arms and spitting in Joseph's face. "Come on, 'fess up, Essex boy. You were working with Thaddeus, weren't you? This whole business about memory loss is a big lie, admit it. I can always tell when people are lyin'."

"No, really," Joseph denied, rather intimidated, trying to sound as genuine as possible. "That's not true at all. I simply have memory loss. Have you ever seen the film, *The Bourne Identity*? It's sorta like in that."

With a large groan, it seemed that Sergeant Rufius had had enough. "You keep gettin' away with crimes, *colt*. It won't last for much longer. But I can see this is goin' nowhere so I give up, for now," he yelped, scoffing and storming out.

Apologising for Sergeant Rufius, Sergeant White quickly left as well, ginger hair trailing behind.

Joseph felt his body temperature cool instantly as he was finally let alone. But he was conflicted about why he was going along with Peter's lie. He didn't harbour any loyalty to him after his cooperation with Mathias, so why was Joseph helping him?

Changing the channel to HB1 briefly, Joseph found himself watching the replay of Peter's speech, which he had ostensibly given the previous morning upon their return while

Joseph had still been unconscious. The story he spun was mostly true apart from the fact that Joseph had gone voluntarily: in his version of events, Thaddeus had stolen the cone and kidnapped Joseph with the intent of forcing him to kill Peter, meanwhile waking him from his Recalibration. Apparently, Joseph had managed to fight Thaddeus off and save Peter, but unfortunately, Thaddeus had managed to escape. Feeling a surge of guilt, Joseph turned off the visualiser.

After the speech, when they began showing footage of the eclipse that Joseph had missed, he turned it off. He didn't really care that much, but it was a shame that he didn't get to see the rare spectacle. He decided to go to sleep shortly after.

"Joseph, what's up? *Cómo estás?*"

Joseph awoke with a start, certain he was about to find Mathias' twisted caricature of evil at his bedside. There was a hand on his shoulder; thankfully, it was just Francis.

Taking a deep yawn, Joseph took a sip of water and then faced Francis.

"I was having a nightmare," he gasped, wiping his forehead sweat away with his gown sleeve.

Wearing a flat cap with a "Sthyle" logo, Francis said, "Yeah, you were sweating. Are you sure you're alright? Nice bandages."

"I'll be fine. I can cope with bad dreams," he said, chuckling. "I'm tough, sort of."

As Joseph's eyes unblurred from sleep, he saw Francis looked in excellent spirits, a free man now, of course.

Francis smiled at him, and exclaimed, "I'm glad you're doing OK! Dr Adebe said you were not feeling well enough for visitors, but I felt I had to thank you, so I snuck in." He looked around for prying eyes and ears. "We should probably not be too loud; don't want to attract any unwanted attention."

"There's nothing to thank me for," Joseph said tiredly.

Great, so now I have to lie to Francis? Remind me why am I doing this?

"I think there is," Francis opined forcefully. "You saved my life and Peter. You're like a superhero! Anyway, I won't harp on about it. I brought you a couple of gifts to thank you for everything. Not much, but a little token of my gratitude. Most of the shops are still closed after the earthquake. . . ."

"Earthquake?" Joseph repeated, bewildered.

"Yeah, didn't you hear? While you were away Tuesday night, there was a magnitude seven earthquake on the island. Some buildings collapsed, and there is more damage," Francis stated. "It was like an apocalypse, man."

Crap. Must have been me. That golden cone is a bomb waiting to go off.

"Oh, wow. I had no idea. Somehow I missed it. Maybe they were trying not to worry me," Joseph remarked. "Is everyone OK?"

"I think so. Don't stress about it. Repairs have started already. Just focus on getting some bed rest. You did *asombroso*, Joe. More than great. Can I call you Joe?" Francis eulogised. "To be honest, I owe you a debt that I can never repay you. That holding cell was like Alcatraz and Guantanamo Bay put together."

Joseph cringed and dug his nails into his palm under the bed sheets; he couldn't deal with these unmerited plaudits much longer. "It reminds me of my pre-death friend Thomas. He used to call me Joe."

"Actually . . . speaking of death, to tell you the truth I, uh, never told you my manner of death for a reason," Francis mumbled. "I died by electric chair—another false conviction. That's the reason why the authorities here were so convinced of my guilt."

"Yeah, I'd actually heard that from Chen," Joseph revealed, acting unfazed, but glad to hear it was a false conviction as he had suspected.

Francis went pale. "Really? And do you care?"

He shook his head, not caring in the slightest. "Not really. As long as you say you didn't do it. And I mean, even if you did, that's ancient history."

"Oh, that's awesome, man. I would've told you before, but I am so used to people giving me the cold shoulder as soon as they find out: it's like I'm a leper!" Francis stated, twisting his mouth. There was the sound of muffled footsteps outside. "I better get going before the doctor gets back. Sorry if I woke you."

"It's cool that you came," Joseph affirmed, ignoring the dull pain in his forehead. "Made me forget my blinding headache for a while. And, er, maybe you can bring me some books and games to keep myself occupied over the next couple of weeks?"

"*Guay*!" said Francis warmly, as he opened the door an inch. "I've got this game system that can play everything from NES to the Nintendo Switch. I'll get it to you tomorrow. *Adios*, Joe."

Glad that Francis' crimes were now cleared up, Joseph waved him away.

The next few days passed in a blur of faces and horrible hospital food. More people came and visited Joseph after Francis, and although he was interested in getting back to his SHOMAT studies, as confusing as most of it was (and as dull as a small portion of it might be), he didn't mind reading whatever book he could find and waiting to see who would visit next. One day, Ms Sadeghi brought the student body of Hyleberia Academy for a sort of field trip—Chen, Emily and Francis again.

"I do hope you recover soon. We all are missing your presence in class," Ms Sadeghi greeted, her monobrow warping as they all entered the hospital room.

"Yeah, totally," Emily said, beaming. "We saved Francis, Joseph. I delayed the exile while you were gone. They were trying to have it done early in the morning in Parliament, so I triggered the fire alarm just in time. Luckily, that's when Peter arrived."

"It's true. In a way, it is just as much thanks to Emily that I'm not pushing up daisies!" Francis acknowledged gratefully.

"Wow! Well done. Thanks for coming," he said appreciatively, looking around at all of their faces.

"I'm sorry, Joseph," Emily whispered in Joseph's ear at one point, while Ms Sadeghi droned on behind her about his study deadlines getting pushed back. "I know I did eventually, but I should have supported you about Francis sooner."

"Don't worry," Joseph firmly told her, wondering what Emily's interpretation of Peter's speech was, since she must know it was partly fake. "Francis made it through in the end. And how are you doing, Emily?"

"Oh, me? I'm fine," she said quietly, looking sideways. "Shrivatsa is going well. I still, like, miss Barney and everything, but I'm getting by."

Joseph wanted to ask if she was still catfishing her family, but he couldn't in front of everyone. Chen also stepped forward to express his regrets, which he appreciated.

"I like your bandages, Joseph. What do you call an apology in dots and dashes?" Chen asked.

"Dunno," Joseph muttered, as he stared at him from the bed.

Chen adjusted his cap and displayed a lopsided grin, like food was in his mouth. "A remorse code! But really, apologies for how I acted. Of all people, I should have given Francis the benefit of the doubt."

Joseph laughed half-sincerely. "So humorous. It's no big deal, Chen."

"Oh, Chen. Let Joseph rest from your crappy jokes," Emily interjected, rolling her eyes.

Raymond stopped by once or twice along with Aislynn,

both of them giving him their "get well" messages. Joseph suspected that he had brought her along because he was physically incapable of a genuine expression of concern, and this provided him with a way of avoiding that. In his laconic way, he reported that Hyleberia was getting back to its normal "boring" self. But Raymond seemed suspicious of the version of the events that Peter had given on the visualiser, and quite rightly, of course. After this, Raymond seemed to forget the contradiction, or perhaps he just didn't want to look obsessive in front of Aislynn, who told him *"sláinte chugat"*, apparently good health to you in Irish. Joseph was not sure if he could go on with this lie, and still did not understand why he was being so helpful to Peter, who had acted incredibly foolishly and he didn't even fully trust.

There were more pleasant visitors than Raymond in the days that followed. Mohammed came by and congratulated him on saving Francis. He asked Joseph if he still planned on taking his room at Terribilità Terrace.

"I dunno," Joseph reported, as he played with his fingers under the bedcovers. "I need to check with Raymond and see what he thinks."

"No problem," Mohammed affirmed, biting his lip in an Arabic robe, his many bracelets visible and several of them glowing from his electron Proficiencies. "But I thought he was a terrible roommate? Why, then, would you need his permission?"

"He, er—is and isn't terrible," Joseph mused, deep in thought. *Not sure I could afford rent, unless I win big at the Tyche Casino.* "He's complex, like Marmite."

"Well, when one door closes, another opens," Mohammed quipped.

Shortly after this, citing the need to conduct a prayer, Mohammed tightened his turban and left. Luckily, Mohammed did not seem to be too cross about him being indecisive. Rationally, Joseph knew he probably should just go ahead and move away from Miyagi Apartments, but a part of him remained cautious.

Two weeks passed until, finally, Dr Adebe announced that the following day he could leave the hospital. It seemed like a year had gone by, even if he had kept busy as much as he could. Besides playing Hyleberian video games, like *Administrator Punch*, he did a lot of thinking during his stay . . . about what he wanted to do in Hyleberia as a job, his friends, his past and the future. Of course, the main thing that played on his mind was *that* night.

The day prior to his departure, Joseph received an opaline white envelope. He knew at once it was from Peter. He opened it like a shot. The letter was an invitation to meet him at Parliament tomorrow. Overall, this seemed to be the perfect opportunity to speak to Peter about his questions, which had been bugging him for weeks.

Joseph woke before dawn, and was disappointed to find that he wasn't allowed to depart before midday. As he had been asked to have a friend take him home, Raymond was to meet him and help carry his stuff to Miyagi Apartments, before Joseph left for his ominous meeting with Peter. The skull fracture had healed thanks to Dr Adebe's medicine, even if his headaches continued.

Soon enough, he was schlepping his things with Raymond down Anaximander Avenue, a side street in East Hyleberia. It was a summery day that Wednesday, even if a little cloudy. All the damage from the flood, hurricane and apparently earthquake had been cleared by now, and the city looked good as new. Joseph was not sure if appreciating the weather would be inappropriate given the grim state of things. The world was most likely about to be at war, which must be a terrible thing—nevertheless, he was still, against all odds, alive. Joseph felt a couple of eyes on him from passersby; perhaps they had heard that he had saved Peter, and were impressed to see him.

Eventually, Raymond asked, "So, pleased to be out and about?"

"Well, let's just say hospital food isn't my cup of tea," Joseph answered, rucksack feeling very heavy on his back, getting reacquainted with the feeling of sunlight on his face.

They passed a newly opened shop, Icarus Ice Cream. Although he was in a bit of a rush for the meeting with Peter after Raymond's lateness, Joseph had quite a sweet tooth subsequent to enjoying a chocolate box Francis had gifted him, and so he accepted Raymond's offer to go in. He opted for a Columbus Choc, while Raymond had a Sparta Supreme.

Joseph and Raymond licked their ice creams like little children, ambling along the street under the incandescent sun. The former spotted a husky dash by, white coat glistening as it panted. The dog's owner soon followed, a lean, out-of-breath Turkish man in a frilled shirt and men's culottes, taking a morning run.

"Wow, a dog!" Joseph exclaimed, as he watched the husky disappear into the crowd. "I've only seen them once or twice. Pet licenses must be rare, indeed."

"I've been on the waiting list forever to get a Tabby, and apparently I have ages to go before I even have a shot. I hate dogs, or Hund as we Germans call them, FYI," Raymond remarked.

After a silence, Joseph knew that this was the moment to bring up moving out. *I can't make Mohammed wait forever. Need to figure this out now.*

"In any case, there's something I wanted to ask," he said cautiously.

Raymond looked at Joseph expectantly. "Yes? Go on, call a spoon a spoon!"

"A spade a spade?" Taking a deep breath, Joseph did not see the point of delaying. "Do . . . do you want me to move out?"

Raymond laughed loudly, a wide grin on his face. "A ridiculous question," he said.

"Why is it ridiculous? I'm serious, Raymond," Joseph asserted, thinking of the grottiness of Miyagi Apartments. "I just want to know. I have an offer for a place that I've been considering taking. It seems to me that you're constantly complaining about me, the way I live, my personality —everything."

Raymond goggled at Joseph as if he was a Martian. "Do I really need to spell this out for you?"

"Spell out what?"

"Well, if you really need to have an oral confirmation, amoeba, here you are—no, I want you to stay. I'm used to living with you now. I . . . don't mind it."

It's a miracle. He said something nice about me. Kind of. Maybe it would have been wise for Joseph to consider this a bit, but for whatever reason, he didn't feel he needed to.

"Good to know," Joseph agreed, stunned, thinking this perhaps the highest compliment he had ever received from Raymond. "I won't move out, then. I'll continue to stomach you for a bit longer."

"Oh, joy to the world!" Raymond remarked sarcastically.

Surely Raymond was not a perfect friend, and Mohammed's place was nicer and closer to Hyleberia Academy, but Joseph felt that Miyagi Apartments had become his home and moving would be a chore. Besides, he was trying to be better with money, and he couldn't really afford the rent. He resolved that he would ring up Mohammed that night to let him know of his decision. Yet Joseph gulped as he questioned what and why he was keeping Peter's lie to him.

It was odd being in Hyleberia while knowing that he was the only one who knew the true state of the government, the divine secret. Joseph was starting to realise that he had to tell at least one person, and the desire to be free of this secret was building up in him like a bubbling volcano.

"But Raymond, there's something I need to admit," Joseph muttered, and went on to briefly explain the truth, as they stood outside Miyagi Apartments. "The story Peter gave about what happened on Sabbat Islet didn't really occur. Thaddeus is actually the second divine Prime Minister, and he was manipulating me to help with his coup."

"What!?" Raymond asked, astonished. "Is this your weird idea of a joke, Shields?"

"You think I'd joke? That's you!" he replied. "I've been keeping it in all this time."

Joseph went on to explain further, but there was no time to go into great detail.

"I'm just gonna hope you're high off your pain meds and play some Mario Kart," Raymond snapped, as they entered the door to the apartment, and he trotted off to his N64. "But if it's somehow true, and I don't fully believe it, I want to hear every detail of what happened that night."

"When I get back from my meeting with Peter," Joseph said, sighing. "I'm not even supposed to tell anyone, but I needed to get it out."

He threw his stuff in his bedroom, taking the rucksack from that night and hiding it under his bed. *I don't know what to do with the Hylephone recording. I suppose I'll have to check it out when I get home. Don't have time now.* Then, wishing a decent afternoon to Raymond even if he didn't believe him, Joseph set off for Parliament. He passed a bald stylite sitting peacefully on a pillar by Parliament, who nodded at him as he felt a sudden surge of guilt. *Am I just as bad as Peter to lie to everyone, when I know the truth? Besides Raymond. What a pickle.*

As Joseph arrived, he found Peter waiting by the Parliamentary gates. This time, Gabriel was sitting on his shoulder, not reacting as he approached. Joseph was deeply conflicted about how to behave, feelings more than mixed towards the Prime Minister.

"Look who it is," Joseph greeted, with a very neutral tone.

"Ah, here you are. Good day! Follow me if that's OK, I want to walk and talk," instructed Peter. "I'm going to show you something special today."

He followed Peter, stomach turning over. They walked in the direction of Parliament's front steps.

"Actually, there is this thing that's been on my mind," Joseph informed him. "But aren't you afraid people are eavesdropping around here?"

"Ah? Do start," Peter encouraged. "And no, I'm not worried; I have activated a Privacy Proficiency that means nobody in the vicinity can hear us."

"Oh, right. Where do I begin?" he exclaimed.

Peter smiled as if he hadn't a care in the world. "Bwahaha. Anywhere. I've seen *everything*, believe me."

Joseph had trouble maintaining eye contact, as he glanced at Gabriel's blissful expression. And so, the time had come to explain his guardian angel situation to Peter, and yet he suddenly felt rather aphasic and unsure how to put it into words.

"Recently, I can seem to, well, move things with my mind when Gabriel is near. In fact, he's the one that came to save me on Sabbat Islet that night," Joseph muttered quietly, feeling that he sounded like a mad man. "Is that, um, normal?"

He proceeded to explain further the bizarre details of what had happened, but surprisingly, Peter did not appear overly shocked.

"I'm amazed but not surprised. To be honest, I was already aware that something like this had occurred. How else would you have caused all that damage in my house while possessed?" Peter grinned knowingly, as Joseph's account came to a close.

"What do you mean?"

"You see, Gabriel is no ordinary sloth. As well as being the only animal capable of Proficiencies, he is in touch with the

Animah, and so he and I have a way of communicating that would be far beyond the abilities of an ordinary animal. Shortly before my departure, he became very agitated about your safety. For that reason as well as Ms Beechum's busyness, I decided to leave him with you. It wasn't my intention, though, for Hoskins to take Gabriel from you at the crucial moment. Thankfully, I believe Gabriel teleported himself to you that night on Sabbat Islet to save you."

"Wow," Joseph said, rubbing his head as they passed by the Bedbug Department. "So, he really was a guardian angel after all, in a sense?"

"Kind of. The divine field formed around Gabriel's body can greatly boost Proficiencies in strength. Of course, he's not limited to this; Gabriel simply has a way of helping anyone in a moment of need. What a clever boy!" Peter exclaimed.

Joseph froze, his eyes wide. So, the force on the bricks and the balls *was* really him. "Um, OK. But I don't have superpowers . . . I mean, Proficiencies?"

"And this brings me to the next topic, why Mathias chose you to be the man to murder me," revealed Peter, petting Gabriel. "The reason, in short, is that you are an Ichorian."

"A what?" Joseph exclaimed, baffled.

"In other words, you are descended from a prophet figure, such as Jesus, Mohammed, Buddha, Comte and their family trees. You see, you have Ichor, divine blood, a feature that is carried throughout the family trees of prophets. This is why you've always suffered from headaches and nausea, common for Ichorians who have not yet been tutored. In fact, they are the result of unchanneled Ichoric energies. You will be free of them soon."

"A prophet?" he muttered, thinking about his relatives. "What the hell! I'm not related to one."

"I think you'll find you are. Ichoric blood would have given you the suitable divine constitution to murder a divine Prime Minister as powerful as myself. And it may also be an explanation as to why you took so easily to using Proficiencies. It comes naturally and instinctually to you, particularly in moments of danger, and Gabriel simply strengthens your innate abilities. To others, his effect would have been uncontrollable, and so it is not usually something that is beneficial."

"I don't think that's right. I've never, uh, walked on water or brought anyone back from the dead."

"Bwahaha. I didn't say you were a prophet, just that you had one's blood."

"So, what does this mean?" Joseph uttered, even more confused than usual, as he spotted a sign to the Peanut Butter and Jelly Sandwich Department.

Peter rubbed his hands together. "There are many implications. Perhaps most relevantly, having Ichor means you possess the potential to use all sorts of Proficiencies without official endowment, following thorough training, of course. Non-Ichorians, however, can only access Proficiencies after they've been explicitly granted them by me."

They spoke for ten more minutes about Ichorians after this, winding through the many halls and passageways of Parliament that Joseph hadn't been shown before. Slowly, it started to sink in.

"Right," he affirmed, taking a deep breath. "An Ichorian . . . I just thought I was half-Spanish, is all. It's a lot to learn in one afternoon."

"Take your time," Peter said, beaming as if his crying fit were a distant memory. "I should also say, please don't hesitate to let me know if you need any favours. You saved me; it's the least I can do."

He was silent for a few moments as he thought through all of this. As interested as he was by the Ichorian revelation, Joseph felt a bit swept off his feet, and so resolved to put this to the back of his mind for now. "Actually, I do have a small favour to ask of you," he mumbled.

"Fair enough. What have I agreed to?" Peter asked, grinning boyishly.

Joseph gulped. "Actually, to be precise, two favours."

"Two? Don't push your luck." Peter nodded, laughing. "Go on. Tell me, then."

Joseph hesitated. What he was going to say next would sound incredibly stupid. He couldn't believe it at first, but during the hospital visit, he had started to miss Gabriel. And yet the first request wasn't even going to be for him.

"The first is easy and a bit silly: I want you to give Emily Nadine a pet permit," he said, feeling ridiculous.

Giving Gabriel a little hug, Peter chuckled, and said, "Bwahaha. That's a bit random."

"She has really been missing home and her Rottweiler, Barney. She told me that she might feel a bit better if she had a similar dog here." Joseph blushed slightly.

Highly amused, Peter laughed. "Easy. Consider it done. And the next favour?"

Joseph breathed a sigh of relief. "This is the serious favour: I want you to train me to use Proficiencies. The ones you say I am naturally capable of on account of being an, er, Ichorian. To be honest, I need to be able to defend myself when Mathias returns. It seems to me that after keeping the divine secret for you, I deserve this at the least."

Peter thought this over for a tense couple of minutes.

Eventually, seemingly quite reluctantly, he grunted, "Very well. But, Joseph, my condition is that we only begin after you have finished your SHOMAT. Does that sound fair? This is a large favour you are asking of me, as it breaks protocol to teach Shrivatsa undergraduates Proficiencies."

"Hmmm . . . I guess," Joseph said, recognising begrudgingly that this compromise was perhaps at least somewhat justified, as they came to a giant walled painting of Peter with Queen Elizabeth I.

"Good. It's decided, then," revealed Peter apprehensively.

"We're almost there now, at the place I wanted to show you. But first, I want you to see this, which is just as important in a way."

Peter pulled Joseph into an empty adjoining office, which smelled of toner and freshly printed paper. In the middle of the room, he was deeply surprised when he saw there stood a marble statue of a familiar figure, Nigel. It was incredibly life-like, with his familiar wrinkled, bearded countenance and dumpy hobo clothing.

"Sadly, I can't take back what I let happen to Nigel," Peter asserted with a regretful undertone. "However, I can still change how we think of him in the future. I'm going to have the local gardener set this statue up in Agape Green so that he is never forgotten, and issue a formal pardon for his crimes. I have also facilitated it that he gets reincarnated into a kind, financially comfortable family."

"It looks very realistic," Joseph avowed. *Not sure Nigel would want to be recalled as a hobo. But it's a nice gesture.*

Peter looked proud. "Indeed. Michelangelo himself made it, the Greek sculptor, who now lives in East Hyleberia."

They came out of the office, and were traipsing through the twists and turns of Hyleberia Parliament when they arrived at a huge, titanium door with a sign that read "Library of Divine Laws". There were turrets on the walls, guards and security cameras combing every inch of the area, not unlike the golden cone. Joseph gaped as Peter withdrew a large, rusted key from his pocket and slotted it into the keyhole. Gabriel too seemed anxious to see what was behind the door, judging by his dilated bright green eyes and shaking body. As much as he had complained, Joseph felt rather like kissing the sloth after all they had been through together, even if Gabriel seemed to barely know who he was after all this time.

"What lies behind here is the one and only Library of Divine Laws. All of the laws passed in Parliament are kept in this room," Peter informed Joseph. "This means that the whole of the world is dictated by this one library. It is the most heavily protected place on the whole island. As you might have gathered, it is off-limits to the vast majority of Hyleberians."

A few seconds later, they were standing in a gigantic room with hundreds of rows of stacked documents, shelves stretching ten feet high. It was nothing like Bibliotheca. As Peter showed him around, he saw that the laws were organised on stands with small silver signs that described their contents, such as "Electrochemical", "Nutritional", "Musicological", "Noological", and so on. Joseph gazed around, impressed. *If you set a fire, what on Earth would happen? Could've brought a lighter.*

"Can I look around?" he said, rubbing his eyes.

Perhaps Hyleberia was about to go to hell, Joseph shouldn't trust Peter, and he should share the "divine secret" with his friends right now, but now he didn't care, simply amazed.

"Absolutely," agreed Peter, with Gabriel smiling happily on his shoulder. "Feel free to have a gander at any of the books as well. They were reorganised a bit after the earthquake shook them up, but their wisdom never ages. They contain the rules of the whole world, from the rotations of the planets to the structure of the body."

"So, a bit different from my hometown library in Southend. . . ." Joseph said, as he picked up a random shelved papyrus scroll out of the hundreds, sat down and began to read.

CHAPTER 14
VENUS' MOON

OVER THE DAYS AFTER THE LIBRARY TOUR TIME SEEMED TO accelerate, and Joseph's life as a Tellurian was becoming more of a memory. Weeks, and then a month passed since Mathias' attempted coup. Joseph had managed to deflect suspicions about the true events of that night with everyone except Raymond, Francis and Emily. Indeed, after a couple of days, Joseph hadn't been able to stop himself from telling his friends the reality of what had happened. With the audio recording as proof, not one of them hadn't been shocked and appalled. Well, Raymond had been a bit more sceptical, "I mean, if the Prince of Darkness is still alive and you've not just gone loony, Peter's sure taking his time to announce it!"

But deciding to give Peter the benefit of the doubt, at least for the short term, Joseph had made them all promise to keep silent until his big reveal, whenever that would be. So far, they seemed to have managed it.

The first hints of winter arrived, and Joseph had finally found time to do the things that had been on his to-do list since day one in Hyleberia: buying a phone and better shoes, going to World Cinema (which played films from alternative dimensions) to see Citizen Kane 2; and trying some Hyle-berian delicacies, such as a Tree of Life Soup, a Japanese food called Shirako and chicken lollipops. That said, Joseph was still trying to reform his old money-careless ways, such as by buying a cheaper Hylephone Lite. In Shrivatsa, the topic of the past month being largely the astrobiology of the Milky Way, he had mostly restored his relationship with his fellow students. Still not pleased with being an Administrator of Dust, he had managed to persuade Ms Sadeghi to let him take the career profiler again next year. Nonetheless, his SHOMAT test remained on the horizon next year.

Chen was back in his usual comedic spirits with the bad jokes; Francis had quickly recovered from his arrest, and was apparently playing new video games; and Emily had taken Joseph out to lunch at several of the nicest restaurants in Hyleberia, keen to share with him her favourite eateries. Emily had also stopped getting in contact with her family, which Joseph felt was ultimately for the best. She had got her pet permit last week, and was delighted to receive days later an adorable Rottweiler puppy.

As for Peter, it had seemed lately that he was ignoring Joseph, sending apologetic emails that he was too busy to talk. They'd barely conversed since his tour of the Library of Divine Laws. And yet finally this very morning, Peter had sent him a short, to-the-point email saying he was going to reveal the truth the following day on HB1, and he'd even publicly scheduled an announcement. Everything was about to come out, and Joseph had no idea how bad the public's reaction was going to be, but it certainly wouldn't be good.

It was early evening on Sunday, December 4. Joseph had just been at his first Philosophy Society debate at the Town Hall, where he had watched Descartes spar with Heraclitus, an ancient Greek philosopher, about the nature of time. Emily had said she would be attending, and he'd seen her in the crowd but not yet caught her. This was also the day, Joseph realised randomly as he exited the building, of Melanie's wedding. He wondered if his now-married sister and Thomas

THE REPUBLIC OF REALITY

were still thinking about him, but either way, he hadn't forgotten them. Despite what Thomas might have said, Joseph didn't care anymore about making something of his life. After the events on Sabbat Islet, he had decided that he was perfectly fine with remaining a complete nobody.

Emily ran over after the event alongside Miffy, her cute but rapidly growing long-fanged Rottweiler puppy. He was just as adorable as Thomas' dog, Daisy, but in a slightly less obvious way.

"Ohhh, Joseph! Did you enjoy the debate?" she asked, a carefree mien on her heavily made-up face, as they stood in the porch outside the front doors.

"Wasn't bad," Joseph said casually. "I think Descartes looked a bit dejected to lose at the end; I saw him trying to hide his tears. Heraclitus pounded him."

"Yeah, seems so. Well, Miffy is such a good dog, I can already tell. I'm so grateful you managed to get me one, although it does make me feel a bit bad that it was, like, essentially a bribe from Peter!" she said, as Miffy barked happily at her.

"Hmmm. I guess it kind of was," Joseph muttered, half-smiling as he looked down at the hound and recalled that memorable meeting when he was told that he was an Ichorian.

"Anyway, how's it going?" she asked, stroking Miffy's adorably large ears. "You look a bit drunk. I am too, honestly!"

There had been zinfandel and brie at the society debate, Joseph and apparently Emily also had made the most of.

"I'm decent, thanks. Glad that holidays are starting next week," he said. "So, you're into philosophy?"

"Kinda. I like the big questions, the meaning of love, and so on," she said, winking with the smell of alcohol on her breath.

"It's interesting, for sure." Joseph stared at her, clueless as to what the winking meant. "Actually, I'm about to meet with Francis. He texted me this morning; we often meet up these days to play games and drink beers."

"Ohhhh, can I come too? I've been studying most of the day for my string theory test," Emily said pleasantly, buttoning up her fleece jacket. "It's getting so cold; I saw a Christmas tree up in the town centre today."

"I don't see why not," Joseph said, glancing at his Hylephone clock. "Let's go, then."

As Joseph, Emily and Miffy headed to Agape Green, passing by a woman with wheels for feet, he wondered about asking Emily on a date sometime. He liked her a lot and resolved that perhaps he would sometime, if he could build up the courage. She was undeniably very pretty. In any case, they soon spotted Francis by the park sundial, where they had arranged to meet.

Joseph grinned as soon as he saw Francis. "Hey, *amigo*. Good day? I bumped into Emily."

"Not bad. How's things, Emily?" Francis asked, nodding to both of them. "And Miffy?"

"Divine," she said cheerily. "Miffy's good too."

"Did you see the news today about the announcement? Peter emailed me to say he's gonna reveal the truth," Joseph said, who was now sure that it was Richard and Mathias that he had overheard in the alley.

"Of course. Well, I can only predict complete and utter indignation, and protests all over town," said Francis, chortling. "Millennia of deception is not going to go down well, to say the least."

"I bet. I've been struggling to keep it in ever since you made me promise to, Joseph. Still can't fully wrap my head around it," Emily agreed, looking towards the park as Miffy tugged her forcefully in that direction. "So, do you guys want to, like, have a late-night walk together?"

"Why not?" Francis said at once. "Enjoy the peace and quiet before chaos erupts tomorrow, I guess."

The sky was turning orange as night came, and Joseph was freezing. Tucking his hands into his pockets didn't do much to help, as the air had a nasty chill. He and Emily and Francis made their way through the park.

"My hands are numb. I'll get frostbite at this rate," Joseph complained, as he stretched his fingers in his pocket.

"Ohhhhh. Mine too," Emily said, rubbing hers on Miffy as she was caught in shivers. "It's almost as bad as the storm."

"So, besides the announcement, did you see the news on Friday about Richard? That he's been banned from Parliament for the rest of his life, and arrested to boot?" Francis asked.

"Of course. I just hope that Richard is chilly in the holding cell. Imagine his reaction to being put in that dump," Joseph said sadistically.

Francis burst out in laughter, his hands perfectly warm in the gloves he had just donned. "That's too funny, Jojo."

"Same. Deserves worse than, like, exile for what he was trying to do," Emily agreed.

Francis fiddled in his coat pocket to retrieve something, his binoculars it seemed, and meanwhile, a note fell out and drifted down on the pavement. He picked it up hastily, and stuffed it into his pocket.

"Oh cool, can I try those? Maybe I can see aliens," Joseph asked, looking at the binoculars. "I once went stargazing with my dad as a child, actually, when we went camping. We were always really into E.T., and would play a game: who can spot the spaceship first. I don't think either of us ever won."

"Sure. But I won't let you see this," Francis agreed, handing them and making sure the note was tucked in.

"Let me guess, a love letter to your secret affair," Joseph said, as he took the binoculars and placed them on the bridge of his nose, attempting to locate the moon.

"I wish. A rough draft of a poem. I barely ever share them with anyone," Francis uttered, laughing.

Joseph peered at Francis as his friend cringed. "Don't be shy, mate. I've never heard one of your poems," he encouraged.

Blushing, Francis chuckled and said, "Nope. I couldn't possibly embarrass myself more, unless I stripped naked or something."

"Go on! If you think it's crap, I can recall some of the lines of verse I wrote as an aspiring teenage poet to make you feel better. They're abysmal, but of course, I thought them bloody Shakespearean at the time."

Francis gave a sniff and stared at the ground, indecisive. "Uh . . . well . . . OK. If you insist, I'll read it, but let's find a good place to sit first. It's kinda long."

"I've heard one of his before; they're, like, pretty good," Emily said, as she took the binoculars from Joseph and tried them. Miffy was sniffing the pavement beside her, and kept aggressively barking at birds, scaring them away.

They soon found some dry grass in a park by a strange tree with fruit made of stained glass, and another elm tree sheltering them with its shadowed branches.

"Well, here goes," Francis said, after they had laid down on the ground, and got comfortable under the elm. "It's a free-verse work about the stars, my love for astronomy, funnily enough, and it's called *Venus' Moon*. I wrote it shortly after my release. Hope it's not too awful."

Joseph lowered the binoculars, put them aside, and stared intently at Francis' lips moving as he began reading. Pronouncing each word very slowly, it took his friend several minutes to get to the final stanza. Nonetheless, Joseph found himself enthralled from the first word to the last by the beautiful use of language; he had never seen this side of Francis before, the part capable of such lyrical insights.

" . . . and our dreams, rejoicing, reclaim Venus' long-forgotten, harvest moon."

As the last line was read, Joseph felt his skin tingling, and couldn't tell if it was from the cold grass on his neck or the poetry itself. Maybe an evening out with his friends was just what he had needed to forget the announcement tomorrow and the looming spectre of Mathias, no matter how frightening the possibility of a Divine War sounded. Joseph had taken to staring at the darkening sky without the binoculars towards the end of the poem. Far above, bright gold sparks flared in the dark, a shower of shooting stars. Looking up at them, he felt further from his dad than ever, and yet somehow, finally at peace with his absence.

"That was awesome, Francis," Joseph praised. "You're really quite talented."

Emily muttered, "Yeah, the only thing I'm not sure is, well, I don't think Venus has any moons, does it?"

"*Gracias*, you guys," he said. "And yup, that's the point. I was trying and failing to be poetic about dreams and stuff."

"Oh right," Joseph said, squinting heavenward. "I think I get it. You know, maybe Hyleberia is a dream."

"Yeah, I wouldn't be surprised either, Joe. Life is a dream," Francis agreed.

"Or one of us is hallucinating this all in some insane asylum!" Emily quipped, as she stroked Miffy.

"That's more likely," Joseph said, chuckling. *You know what, I suddenly crave some delicious toast.*

Lying for a few minutes longer, they soon got up and chatted for hours, before Joseph headed home at midnight. After he had said goodbye to Francis and Emily, he went straight into the kitchenette and made himself the first piece of toast he'd had in months. The first bite was the most delicious he had ever eaten. As Joseph lathered jam on the hot bread, he thought that maybe the pedlars' rusty toaster hadn't been such a bad purchase, after all.

ABOUT THE AUTHOR

Adam Rowan is an emerging Anglo-Irish writer of YA fantasy. He recently went on a trip around Europe and has a black lab called Mabel. *The Republic of Reality* is Adam's debut novel.

instagram.com/enstasy999
goodreads.com/22691906.Adam_Rowan

IF YOU ENJOYED THIS BOOK ...

Please consider leaving a review online.

Goodreads.com

Amazon

Google Play

Barnes & Noble

Kobo

Apple

Thanks for your support!

Printed in Great Britain
by Amazon